Blue
COMPANY

w l jennings

ISBN 978-1-64300-227-9 (Paperback)
ISBN 978-1-64300-228-6 (Digital)

Covenant Books, Inc.
11661 Hwy 707
Murrells Inlet, SC 29576
www.covenantbooks.com

First, a salute to Sir Arthur Conan Doyle.

I have enjoyed his *Sherlock Holmes* stories all my life, but it was his 1891 adventure tale, *The White Company*, that I used with students in Sydney, Australia, in the late 1960s. That book's tale of eye-opening adventures of national discovery by three young travelers—along with a bit of their nature—helped me shape *Blue Company*.

This book is dedicated to my own daughters and nieces and to the youth of today.

> *The world must remain an oyster for the youth to open.*
> *If not, youth will cease to be young.* (John Buchan)

I'm sorry that the older generations pried open your oyster and corrupted it. But all is not lost if you can find it in your hearts to step forward now both to forgive us and to help undo that wrong … to help us get our foot back on to the uphill road toward *E pluribus unum*.

If you can do that, the future will be brighter not only for us, but also for oppressed people everywhere. As our heroes frequently call out in the book, *We Will Win*!

CHAPTER ONE

Praise PAC for Lifting You and Me

*I*t was Thursday, August 14, 2036, and the bells of Dorn Tower were ringing out in a discordant and feeble summons, calling the tenured student-guardians and faculty of Arbor University to assemble in all due haste at the *Great Dome of the People*. Some of the very few non-guardian students who were awake that early, briefly shifted questioning eyes towards the sound, and even many of the townspeople, bustling through their early morning business, turned from their routines to look first in that direction and then very quizzically at one another. Those bells were seldom heard and never in the summer when there were few classes and most of the students were gone. Of course, all but the two now ringing had been destroyed twelve years before, in 2024, during the celebration of the *Formal Assumption* of exclusive control of all national power by the glorious Peace, Accommodation, and Culture Party (PAC), and these were supposed to be rung only for the most urgent PAC-approved reasons. That they rang now meant "come"—at once!

Yet, even the most casual observers could not have failed to notice that something was quite literally afoot long before they heard those bells. Most of the elect had begun their trudge well before those first weak bongs, having received orders on their short-range wrist Tracys, named after a hundred-year-old cartoon character's 'wrist radio.'

PAC had banned all electronic communications devices in the late twenties as detrimental to the good order of society, but the short-ranged Tracys were not only allowed, they were required for all student-guardians and faculty, leading some cynics to suggest that the devices should be called *tracers,* not *Tracys,* because they allowed PAC to know their wearers' location. But given the degraded state of technology, all such tracking was impossible—not that most in this era of *oneness celebrated* would think that to be bad. Those who mattered revered both PAC-the-dream and PAC-the-controller.

And the gathering student-guardians certainly mattered, all wearing the same vests, radiant in the amazing and glorious black, brown, and yellow of the PAC rainbow. Their red caps, symbolizing PAC's long struggle for ascendancy, and green armbands, declaring a holy oneness with the earth—*and with PAC,* proclaimed a unity that was further displayed by the look of sheer bliss on their faces as they moved in lockstep to answer the call. "PAC's call is our own true call," being the universal guardian saying.

Each and every one of these marching guardians had been selected according to fair and honest PAC Oneness procedures. Early in September, every year, the students of Arbor University were required to voluntarily vote for new guardians from a ballot of PAC-approved candidates, listed not only under the existing quota-categories but also from observer categories not yet officially quotaed. This year, four language groups (two dialects, two sign languages), the left-handers' group, and the shy people's group had been added. PAC officials then selected the winners from a scientific sampling of all student ballots, and the voters whose choices were selected were given the high honor of signing cards certifying that their candidates had been fairly chosen. The new guardians were then publicly proclaimed, and all of the paperwork was immediately destroyed. This last sad step was necessary to thwart any attempt by troublemakers to challenge the integrity of the system, all agreeing that PAC required no oversight because PAC is the fair and ultimate overseer.

And like the freely selected student guardians, the tenured faculty members who marched with them also mattered, so much so that they were not merely selected, they were chosen, even blessed, by the PAC-Fac-Select arm of justice that monitored not only their fair selection but also their continued right thinking. These tenured loyalists joined the procession wearing the same raggedy jeans style as the students but sporting PAC-correct colored capes instead of vests with their red caps and green armbands. And as they merged with the students into a single loyal line, all of their eyes misted because here they were, flowing as one into the Great Dome under the official *Peace Before Pride—PAC Before All* banner. Oh, how they could feel it! The air was heavy with the glory of it all. This coming event was going to be a unique opportunity to serve PAC.

The Great Dome of the people, a large glassed-over space covering an area still called the *quad* by some, connected the two main libraries to several other buildings, including a classic centerpiece once called Angell Hall but now right-named Egalitarian (Egg) Hall. This change had followed a protest in 2025 by the Quotaed-Atheist Rights group, claiming that the old name sounded too close to a religious word. As this was clearly a violation of their rights, the name was changed at once because nothing in this new era was to be left undone to avoid offending any PAC-approved and certified group.

"Such is the key to community peace, such is the mission of us all" ruled PAC.

Outside the dome, the townspeople of Arbortown remained focused on their own business. Arbor U affairs were seldom their concern and when they were, a *News and Views* broadsheet would be posted on the plywood news boards scattered around town at the federal feedlots, where the weekly food allotments were handed out—when there was food. These postings provided not only the PAC-approved news but also the only acceptable response to it. However, the officials were so busy they seldom got around to doing such postings; there had been none for months. No one knew why, nor did anyone bother to inquire, the virtue of quiet acceptance being well learned in this new day.

Acceptance, although seldom quiet, was also the mode of another motley group in town—the United States Support Reserve. Called the *federal forces*, they had replaced the old military branches after the great change of 2029, but they paid no more heed to what was happening on campus than the civilians did. Nor did they pay much attention to their main duty, which was to monitor this border point between the areas still under federal jurisdiction and the adjoining Detroit Manufacturing Zone (DMZ), now under the control of a very welcome Chinese division of the international *People's Provisional Forces*—all rightfully called the *Friendly Forces* or simply *the friendlies* by all who loved PAC.

Under current rules, the federals had little to do, and they did it in a manner and style never before witnessed in the American military. They slept in any of the many vacated private homes they wished, partied day and night, and in general blended in so well that it was difficult to tell them apart in dress, manner, or bearing from the equally idle students or even the idle portion of the more industrious townspeople. Of course, the officers were all female and the enlisted ranks male, with whites and Asians restricted to the lowest grades. And as little was expected of any of these men, they provided just that.

In the interest of peace, they were all unarmed, weapons being forbidden by the Windsor Protocol of 2032 because of concerns that careless federals might accidentally discharge one of the pellet guns they were then allowed to carry and thus force the very heavily armed Friendly Forces to respond, as would have been their duty, with rockets, missiles, and bombs. It was feared that such an event would cause an unacceptable loss-of-face to the friendlies, sent to support our troubled nation as we completed our now almost three decades long transition to a new era of negotiated dependency which, thanks to PAC, was to bring with it the much-longed-for dream of peace in our time.

Inside the Great Dome itself, rumors were now flying about concerning the nature of the event that was soon to take place. It all seemed so incredible to everyone; nothing like it had been witnessed at Arbor U since the reforms brought in by the PAC Formal Assumption. A student was to face the assembly, was to be judged, and as impossible as that seemed, he was to be cast out and forced to leave school without the automatic degree that had become every student's right. Such things were unheard of, but it was going to happen here today at Arbor University. Of course, it would happen only after a fair trial—because, deserving or not, that student would receive justice.

....

One person who would soon make his way through that crowd not only knew what was going to happen, but would sit on the stage and participate in the ceremony. He was Franklin W. Benjamin, professor of antiquated-core studies, who with his rumpled sports-coated short, heavy body and wisp-of-white-hair, polished head looked the part of a professor from a long gone era. In fact, he had taught in what once had been called the Department of English before it and all others of what PAC considered to be the spawn of the old western-privileged enlightenment had been consolidated into one small program. Barred now from teaching and research in his own field, he supervised the few graduate students monitoring the fewer undergraduates attending the new department's noncredit lectures, and he did a lot of reading. Of course, he read alone. None of the current students themselves could have read the literature of his department even if they had wanted to do so. It had been withdrawn years ago and was being held in a lingering long-term quarantine pending a somewhat overdue PAC quota-friendly fairness review.

"Glenn, this business won't take long," Benjamin said, speaking to the young man seated across from him in his study as he pulled on his professor cape and plopped a red cap on his head. "I'll be ready to celebrate launch day with you in about four hours."

"Yes, sir, I'll be here and waiting," the young man replied, smiling with affection as he watched Benjamin finish getting ready. Despite his outdated appearance, Glenn knew that his mentor still had his head and his hand in the games of *this current carnival culture* as the good professor called it and that he'd easily manage the new foolishness about to unfold at the dome. Still, he couldn't help marveling at the older man's obvious willingness to go along with his part in the upcoming sham even as he reminded himself that suffering such nonsense was only business as usual—and necessary for their cause.

On the other hand, and the young man smiled as he thought about it, today's farce was only a trivial, soon to be forgotten, PAC sideshow to an event both he and his mentor had looked forward to for years. As the professor had said, this was his launch day!

But that would come later, and in the meantime, despite his excitement about his own adventure, he couldn't help thinking about that poor helpless wretch who was soon to be tried. How ludicrous it was; the whole game was all on autopilot. He would be forced to face a sham show-trial and then be booted, degreeless, out of Arbor University. Glenn frowned as he thought about the kind of ex parte justice that, sadly, had become the accepted norm in this new era of PAC's faux fairness to all.

But sham show-trial or not, there was a real buzz about it around the world, a buzz that had attracted enough attention to fill the Great Dome today, drawing honored guests from as far away as New York, Chicago, and even China—via Detroit. Of course, Glenn knew that the Chinese observer was coming both for the trial and because of his long-term personal relationship with Professor Benjamin.

....

Indeed, the commander of the Friendly Forces, Colonel Fu Yujian, was the first notable ushered onstage in the dome, and it was the Michigan governor who escorted him to his place of honor before she joined the audience, sitting beside the department heads in the far back row. Then came the Arbor U president, escorting the noble PAC ombudstera who, as always, was there to see that the event was freely PAC and only PAC. Seated last on the stage was the most senior professor on staff, Dr. Benjamin, and on the president's cue, he stood and walked slowly to the podium to open the trial.

"Is the gathering gathered?" He called out the required question and those assembled responded to him, as always, with boos and catcalls that continued until a slightly built, quoted female, Middle-East-origin, pushed past him to take his place.

"I challenge your right as a member of an over-privileged group to address this assembly." She chanted her lines in a dull monotone without bothering to look at the professor, and following custom, he then bowed his head in silent submission, keeping it down as he backed his way to his seat amidst a thunderous applause. Seated to his right was the Chinese commander, who smiled and nodded as he seated himself, and to his left was the PAC ombudstera, who scowled at him as he settled into his chair. He smiled back and nodded, but she quickly looked away, busying herself with her notepad.

The new speaker watched until the professor was fully seated, and then turning back to face the front, she peered triumphantly out over that vast assembly, swallowing and clearing her throat several times before continuing with the required canned opening in a well-rehearsed voice, "Is the gathering, gathered?"

"We are comeback," came the answer, but not in unison. Instead, "the answer ebbed and flowed about the dome with voices lifting high and then low, far and wide, flitting verbal affirmations, coming it seemed from this place and then that place like PAC butterflies on the wing in the bright sunshine of our wonderful day," as one reporter later put it in her online piece, available in the library to PAC-approved staff, faculty and guardians only, the Internet-relic being forbidden to others. The answer she referred to came in different languages, dialects, and signs, and one noble observer-representative replied in dance, her answer requiring four minutes.

The speaker, waiting through it all, seemed to find the dance to be such a moving experience that she watched it with moist eyes and trembling hands until it came at last to a "marvelous and glorious conclusion," as that same reporter wrote. The room then fell very silent, and everyone watched expectantly as the now choked-up speaker, stepping up on her tiptoes, leaned toward the microphone to continue.

"It is now my great honor and high privilege to formally introduce the first and only president of Arbor University since the great and glorious PAC assumption," she announced. "Fellow guardians of PAC truth, please stand to welcome our perfect mentor extraordinaire, our own PAC inspired leader, Doctor Nancy Prudhomme."

The assembled guests applauded politely but without any real enthusiasm, that having been expended on their previous answer. Besides, all of their attention now was on the commander of the Friendly Forces, on the three chairs that sat empty on the other side of the stage, and on the closed door between them. Although thrilled at the prospect of being part of this history-making trial, they now tried to stifle their growing impatience by reading and rereading the words emblazoned on the PAC-affirming banner that hung over the stage: "Praise PAC for the gift of discipline, order, and uniformity!"

Ah yes, it was a new true era of uniformity. Even a visitor from afar, perhaps the Russo-European Union or the Federation of Cooperative African States, knowing nothing of Arbor U, would recognize the student and faculty outfits and of course the colonel's uniform. Indeed, such was the glory of this new age that these same clothes were worn by students and faculty around the world, and the military uniforms in many places were rightly patterned after those of the Tripartite Powers who had brought peace to the world.

But it wasn't the uniforms or world politics that now tugged at the minds of this audience, it was that closed door. They wanted to see it open. Their enthusiasm had been ignited and rekindled over and over again for all the honored guests. Each and every time one came in, they had dutifully pelosied up and back down again, beaming and spanking their hands in seeming ecstasy. But that was over and done with now, and they were eager to get to it, to finally feast their eyes on the dishonorable subject of this trial.

The president, however, had other things she had to do first. Now in her eighties, she moved slowly and stiffly to the podium, and after raising a hand to acknowledge the feeble applause, she turned to smile and nod towards the colonel before opening the trial. But that unsmiling officer's expression did not change, even after she proclaimed, "It is a great honor to have the commander of the Friendly Forces with us on this day, and I'm sure that I'm speaking not only for myself when I confess that his presence and that of his loyal command mark the realization of a long held personal dream, the end of that long night of the old American hegemony and the beginning of Our New Era, of our being *ONE with the world*!" And with those words, she held up her index finger in the sacred ONE sign, first introduced during the troubles of 2018.

The audience responded by erupting in the expected cheers, all springing to their feet, not in a merely exuberant cheerleading pelosi, but with a loyal oneness. And as they cheered, all of these jubilant faculty and students held up their own ONE finger, showing any watchful others that they each agreed with both those words and that dream. Then, as if switched off on some hidden cue, they all settled back into their seats to wait for what was to come next, and President Prudhomme, now beaming down at her beloved loyalists, called out the next set of ritual words, "Will the *Holder* come forth?"

In response, a short, slender, quotaed Hispanic female rose to walk down the aisle and up onto the stage. Stopping where directed, she stood just behind the president, but with her head down and without the usual triumphant face of a *Holder*. What was up?

The president stole another glance, smiling again, toward the colonel, who now seemed to be studying his fingernails, and then after turning to gaze solemnly around the hall, she called out, "In our continuing pursuit of truth, justice, and fairness to all, even we here sometimes become over-zealous. This spring was one of those times, and so now in the interest of true justice and fairness, we have freely decided—completely on our own—that we will spin the wonderful Wheel of Privilege an unprecedented second time to determine the coming school year's new *Holder*. But first, before we spin, our present, temporary *Standing Holder*, who was anointed only two months ago, will speak."

"Praise be to PAC and to the Friendly Forces who have brought peace to our land," recited the temporary Standing Holder, and clutching the podium with both hands, she sighed deeply, taking a moment to calm down before forcing herself to turn to face the colonel. And then, with her eyes down and in a voice that was barely audible despite the sound system, she read from the small card in her shaking hand, "Last May I was given the honor to be named the symbolic *Holder of Privilege* for my quota group." She paused to give in to a dry cough and then nervously took another long deep breath before going on. "But my own selection came only because of a sad injustice to a worthy individual and to his oh-so-very-worthy group that I now deeply regret with all my heart."

The colonel, shifting easily in his seat, looked up briefly, and as a confident smile slipped across his face, he offered the struggling young woman a brief nod. Her own face then brightened with relief, and as he turned his attention back to his nails, she continued to read from her card but now with a bit stronger and more confident voice.

"Last May, the *Holder-Wheel* was spun, and a nominee was identified, but it was not from this unworthy person's quota group. No, not at first. Instead, although the wheel stopped at the quotaed-Asian male slot, the individual selected to represent that category was not named because of foolish rules about what we at that time regretfully called *over-privilege*. I apologize now to all here and to any who have been offended around the world at peace because that good individual, worthy as he was, had to step aside. I was then selected and have since had the honor of symbolizing PAC fairness and justice with my own quota group as we prepared to enjoy the fruits of the Fountain of Privilege in the coming school year. However, we have seen the light and now know that we are unfair Holders of the Possession Arrow prize. Thus, I stand before you today to proclaim that, with PAC's guidance, we of Arbor University do now and will always act as one to denounce discrimination of all kinds and to undo all thought error."

With those words, she pointed a remote at the large round *Wheel of Privilege* mounted on the wall behind the stage, and it began spinning. It spun faster and faster, and then slowed and slowed until it settled click by click by click, edging to a stop on the very smallest sliver of a slot on that wheel, the slot marked, "white male." The audience gasped and all eyes turned first to the colonel, who didn't bother looking up, and then to the current *Holder,* who now stood holding her breath, as if waiting for something.

Behind her, Professor Benjamin dutifully stood and remaining next to his chair, he nodded politely toward the president and the colonel before turning to the audience to recite his own required lines from long experience in a loud unwavering voice. "By no right can we, an over-privileged group, accept the honor so offered."

The assembly pelosied briefly, and a new candidate, quotaed Asian male from China was quickly chosen, there being no protest from the Korean male previously selected. The colonel glanced up and just before turning his attention back to his nails, offered a quick smile and a nod to the professor who, now back in his chair, smiled and nodded back. Everyone in the assembly then stood as one or indeed as ONE and all together broke out into the soothing song they all loved as surely as they loved PAC:

> *Praise PAC from which all blessings flow*
> *Praise PAC for all it does bestow.*
> *Praise PAC from sea to shining sea*
> *Praise PAC for lifting you and me.*

. . . .

Outside, near the entrance, a solitary bearded figure wearing sandals and a dusty long white robe stood alone with his head bowed, mumbling as if in prayer. He was known around Arbor town as *the Marvelous Monk,* and the students and townspeople all treated him as a religious figure of sorts … or, more accurately, as a kind of good luck charm. They liked to touch his head or his tattered robes before tests or important life events, and many had done just that while walking by him on their way into the dome.

The story was that he had long been near-blind but could speak even though when he did it tended to be in meaningless phrases, outdated chants, or occasional emotional outbursts that were difficult to understand. Most took all of that to be a sign of his very old age—he was said to be over eighty, which they thought also accounted for his poor health. He always seemed to have a dripping nose and was constantly coughing and wheezing as he slowly moved about from place to place on his mysterious rounds.

Some said that he had been a priest at the large, long abandoned Christian church at the north end of State Street; the one that had been reopened with PAC approval as a Muslim prayer site for several years until the Friendly Forces ordered it closed. Others claimed that the monk had never been anything but what he was now, a mere relic of the old days best left behind in this new age of expected post-belief.

But despite the official disapproval, he remained, in vague sort of way, a symbol of something a bit otherworldly, something spiritual, yes, but harmless. The students felt drawn to his silly spiritual stuff because, unlike all of those PAC-defined insidious old religions that everyone in Arbor town was expected to agree had poisoned the past, he was nothing more than a safe, feel good, powerless token. What could be wrong in that?

The monk, now seemingly ready to resume his wanderings, worked himself slowly to his feet and smiling broadly at no one in particular, fumbled around for his belongings. Once all was in hand, he leaned heavily on his stick, edged himself about, and began shuffling away, mumbling all the while. It was hard to make out what he was saying, but it sounded something like a Tommy this and a Tommy that being some kind of savior or other. *Umm.* Maybe it was a song or poem or just some kind of old religious nonsense. Who knows what went on in his head? Crazy old man, it could be anything.

Although it was still early, the day was already getting hot, and so as he labored along, he lifted a shaking water bottle to his mouth for a drink. Unfortunately, it was empty.

Chapter Two

How Arbor University Is Rid of an Ungrateful Recipient

*F*inally, the waited for moment had arrived, and as the closely watched door at the back of the stage swung open, the accused was escorted out of the holding area between two guards … into a flurry of confusion. Some in the dome stood, some half stood, and some stayed seated. And as they all looked frantically about for direction, an anxious mumbling buzz welled-up, flowed swiftly across the dome, and then fell back, receding into a hush-tide as one by one the students and staff—all quietly and timidly following the example set for them by those on stage—took their seats. The colonel and all their leaders had remained seated, as surely they should have done. How disloyal to PAC it was to stand as if to honor the entry of a low-quotaed, ungrateful recipient!

The president waited patiently until those in the now muted audience had settled back into their seats, and then turning with a smile of determined triumph on her face, she nodded for the new entrants to approach the podium. And all eyes locked on the *Student of Lunacy* (SOL)—his official label—who temporarily wore full PAC guardian garb even though he was not a student-guardian. A quotaed white male, he was a very tall husky man who loomed even larger as he walked across the stage because he towered over his two PAC escorts, both frail-looking quota-correct females with graying hair, one walking with a slight limp, the taller one shuffling along with an uncertain, anxious look on her face. All three moved up until the president motioned for them to stop at the appropriate spot, where they turned to face the now eager but still hushed dome crowd.

The SOL looked to be about six-six or seven and weighed perhaps 270 to 290 pounds in the old units, big enough to have been a football player in the days before the integration of all sports when football had been abolished as too primitive and exclusive for our new era. But it wasn't only his size that caught the audience's attention; it was also his attitude. Standing up there at the front of the stage, looking down and out over the audience, his broad face with its striking blue eyes bore not a hint of the fear and humility he should have felt. Indeed, as the president solemnly tapped the mic before continuing to speak, the accused stood beside her with a broad grin on his face.

"Are we PAC-ready?" the president called out the required question, deliberately ignoring the grinning SOL as she looked at the ombudstera, who nodded PAC's approval. Smiling, she then turned to the audience and shouted, "PAC calls us ready, how say you?"

"We are ready," the loyal guardians screamed back as one. "Ready to serve PAC."

"Why are we called?" she shouted back in a loud, shrill, and triumphant voice.

"We are called to do justice," they replied, chanting, "justice! Justice! Justi …"

"Point of order!" Prof. Benjamin called out, and rising slowly amidst the din with a tired smile on his face, he leaned back against his chair and repeated, "Point of order."

"Point being?" the president snapped, turning an impatient scowl over at him.

"My quota group is now over-privileged on this stage, and I beg the president's permission to withdraw from this assembly in the name of PAC …" He smiled. "Justice."

"Over what?" The president looked suspiciously at him, but it then must have occurred to her that with the arrival of the defendant there were now two quotaed white males on the stage. So offering a thin smile, she sniffed. "Yes, I see. You are excused."

She then waited patiently, frozen smile and all, as the professor turned and after shaking hands with the commander of the Friendly Forces and nodding politely to the now approving and smiling PAC Ombudstera, left the stage. He kept his head down as he walked up the aisle toward the exit, smiling at the now happy audience's machine-like stamping feet and loud applauding gestures of approval that he was leaving.

"Is the subject of this inquiry present?" the president called out, and all fell quiet.

"He is, madam president," the taller escort replied in a small, halting voice, while nervously arm gesturing for the SOL to step forward.

"I am," the student also replied, looking first at the president and then once again out across the crowd. Still grinning, he actually seemed to be looking for someone out there, as incredible as that would be; surely he would find no friends in this audience.

"You will speak only when spoken to," the president snapped, scowling at him before going on to address his escorts. "Name the subject of this proceeding."

There was no reply. The crowd waited, and the subject waited, but there was no comment from either woman. Finally, the annoyed president, glaring at the SOL's two escorts, demanded, "One of you, will you PLEASE name this subject?"

"Oh, yes!" The taller one rushed to speak as both of the now very embarrassed escorts bit their lips and lowered their heads. "I didn't know you meant ..."

"Get on with it!" The president demanded, but then smiling nervously toward the colonel, she added in a softer voice. "Let's go forward in a seemly manner."

"Yes, ma'am, I mean doctor. I know you insist on being called doctor, not ma'am. I'm sorry. Yes. We'll get on with it, or I mean I will. His name is ..."

"Use the correct form of introduction," the president hissed through a tight smile.

"Before this honorable assembly stands one John Richard Wood, quotaed white male, a student of Arbor University." Blowing out a loud sigh of relief as she finished her lines, the woman looked pleadingly toward the president as if hoping to be excused.

"Thank you, madam escorts, you may be seated," the president replied, but as she turned toward the audience to continue, she heard extra movement behind her and looking around, saw that the SOL was walking across the stage toward the professor's now empty chair. He was planning to sit down right next to the colonel! Horrified, she shouted, "Not you, Student Wood. You are to remain standing over here, next to me!"

"Oh?" The SOL stopped, holding up his hands in confusion, and his face showed genuine concern as he smiled at the president and added, "Sorry ma'am, I thought …"

"Yes, you've *thought* a lot of things," she snipped, cutting off his comments. "That's why we're all here. You have thought wrongly about many, many things."

"Yes, ma'am," John replied, smiling self-consciously as he returned to his spot.

Rolling her eyes at his apology, she then turned to the audience and raised her hand to signal a solemn moment. The now hushed crowd then rose to join in the pledge:

All we here pledge to put aside the tainted
authority of the past and to follow only PAC.
Only PAC preserves what is just and true.
Only PAC serves us all as we serve PAC.

There then followed a moment of silence before the eager believers sat back down.

"The charges are as follows," said the president, and she began reading the items one by one, pausing briefly after each charge to peer grimly over her glasses at the SOL and then to look out across the audience with a studied air of oh-so-painful duty. "The first charge is …" And for this first charge only, she also turned a sad smile toward the colonel. "*Bigotism.* Charge two is … *sexism.* And charge three is … *elitism.*"

The hall erupted with stamping feet and shouts of "off-robe him! off-robe him!"

And as the din rose, his two escorts nervously moved up on either side of the SOL, but he stood calmly with his arms folded across his chest, that old smile now back on his face. Obviously not intimidated, he once again seemed to be searching through the audience.

"Order, please, order. We must have order to proceed," the president shouted, gaveling vigorously as she frowned out over the unruly crowd, holding up a trembling, pleading-for-quiet hand. When order was finally restored, she leaned around the podium, and looking directly down into the first row, asked, "Is the first priority *Charger* present?"

"Yes, madam president, I am she who charges first according to priority rule." A white female *Charger,* standing up in the first row, replied in a soft but serious voice.

"Then so charge."

"I charge this person—" she began, but was immediately interrupted.

"Be specific! How can justice be done if we don't know the quota groups?"

"My apologies. I, a quotaed-white female, European derived, charge this SOL, a quotaed-white male, European derived, with *bigotism!*" Her voice broke on that *evil* word as she rush-read it from a slip of paper, and after daring to say it, she halted to take a moment to regain control of her own emotions before going on. "That student standing up there before us has directed slander against our noble guest, the exalted yet humble commander of the Friendly Forces sent here to protect us from ourselves. Their cause is glorious, and their service is a deliverance. Indeed, we owe them so much!"

A murmur rose among those assembled as all eyes turned toward the commander; this was a very serious accusation. But the Chinese colonel himself continued to sit straight and relaxed in his chair, his neatly pressed and well-tailored uniform a sharp contrast to the untidy vests and capes over dungarees of those assembled. A quick smile flickered but then vanished as he offered a slight nod toward the accuser to indicate that he had heard the charge and to acknowledge the reference to his command and himself.

"It was scarce ten days ago that the SOL asked the question …" She paused, nervously swallowing and looking pleadingly toward the commander before finally continuing on in a thin voice that was freighted with anxiety. "And I am quoting him here. This is a quote, not my own words. He, that charged person up there, he asked, by what right do those he wrongly called *foreign soldiers* have to be here in Michigan?"

Boos and shouts followed, and the president, slowly shaking her now bowed head, withheld her gavel as she angrily waited for all in the dome to vent their very justified disapproval of that slur. She allowed two full minutes of protest, and then after smiling yet again toward the commander, she held up one hand, gaveling with the other. "Please, please, show some decorum to our honored guest. If the Student of Lunacy asked that question then he must be ignorant of our own long and bloody history as a miserable and unworthy people and of how peace finally came to us through the gracious intervention of the Friendly Forces, long may they prosper. We are fortunate they are here, and they and we are all so fortunate that they have a leader-commander such as Colonel Fu."

At those words, the assembly immediately rose as one to applaud the colonel who rewarded them by looking up briefly to smile and nod. The SOL, however, just yawned, glancing about as if the whole process bored him, but on this charge, there could be no rebuttal or chance to plead for mercy. John had been told earlier by one of his visitors that under the rules of the status of forces agreement then in place, he would be bound over to the Friendly Forces to answer that charge and his fate would be determined by them. If sent to Detroit, he could face a firing squad, as had well over three thousand others to date. If they spared him that, he could be detained in one of the many centers for political undesirables, as were some seven thousand others by current estimate.

"Please present the second charge," intoned the again grim-faced president.

"Sexism!" The new charger spit out the words, and while she very decidedly did not smile back at him as she stood to speak, the SOL did turn and smile at her, a quotaed Asian-American female.

As the SOL moved, he accidentally jostled his escorts, causing them to shuffle anxiously aside to make more room for this giant they were supposed to manage. They knew they had been selected based on their quotas and not their ability or size. Any challenge to their authority would be a total mismatch if it came to that, but the general rule was: PAC loyalty first and quota second, always; ability last, if it counted at all.

The Charger continued, "On the second day of this past June, the charged, newly arrived to replace one of his quota group who had passed on to oblivion, refused to accept his assigned roommate. He said, and pardon my language, I am quoting his words, that merely male said, 'She's a girl, and I can't handle having a girl as my roommate.'"

Once again the audience rose, shouting in protest, and once again the charged student smiled, and the president looked at him with disgust as she gaveled. "Order. We will have order. Let's get on with it. What are the particulars of the final charge?"

"Elitism!" A thin, solemn looking, quotaed-African-American female stood to announce the final charge. "On six occasions in one assigned first year summer class, the charged challenged our attempt to find a democratic consensus derived from a search for common truth, and he tried to impose himself as an authority. In fact, he made us all feel threatened and unsafe by demanding that an arbitrary measure of truth be used to replace our PAC sense of oneness and common consent, that measure being—books!"

"Books?" the president exclaimed, and gaveling again for order as the dome erupted, she turned to stare at the SOL and demanded, "Tell me how you, only a first year, indeed first summer, student got into a library? They're closed everywhere else, and the one here is reserved only for approved faculty and special students with tenure."

"Is it my turn to answer all of this?" the SOL replied, and as he stepped away from his guards it was obvious that his mood had shifted. Now standing just behind the president, he frowned out over the hall as he added, "I don't want to break any rules."

"Yes, we've seen how you try to avoid breaking rules," she replied, turning to look up at him more in annoyance than for any worry about her own safety, despite his size. "But that's beside the point, the charges have been read. How do you plead?"

"Oh, I don't plead at all, but I do have something to say." The student's frown had deepened, and there was now a focused and very serious expression on his face.

"You must follow form … and, oh yes, name your federal-ly-funded legal counsel."

"I don't need and won't use a lawyer. I just wanna say my piece and get going."

"Who has been appointed for the charged? This is serious, someone had better give me a name, right now!" The angry president looked all around until a note was quickly passed to her. After glancing down at it, she then turned back to the SOL and smiled as she announced, "Jason Roberts, quotaed-black male, is your lawyer."

"I've never seen him, don't need him, and don't want him."

"Well, so long as he's paid," the president snapped back. "This isn't all about you, it's about a society that works because it follows PAC fairness principles."

"May I speak now?"

"Of course, but only to the last two charges. You may not speak to the first charge about our honored and Friendly Forces. Only they may judge you on that."

"I've already said all I want to say about them. I have nothing personal against him. He looks like a good soldier, and I admire good soldiers, we used to have them too." And as Little John spoke, he turned half way around to offer a smile and nod toward the colonel, noting as he did so that the officer wore a highly polished holster just under his right elbow. Curiously, the colonel smiled and nodded back.

"Enough of that! You must stay on topic."

"I want to do that. May I go on?" the SOL replied, now think-ing about that holster as he turned back toward the president to con-tinue. "I'm called Little John, but I'm not very little and—"

"That!" the president interrupted him with a shout. "*That* is of no importance, get on with the specifics of the last two charges. We're not here to hear your life story. We're here to find you guilty of … I mean, you'll get a fair … well, just get on with it."

"Sorry, ma'am," John lied, and glancing around again, he noted that the colonel's chin was now down against his chest; either the old warrior was in deep thought, or more likely, he was bored. John smiled at that, but then had to pause to ask the president for help before going on. "Ah, what was that last charge, ma'am? No, wait, I got it. Yes. It was about my history class. You know, I love history and read a lot of it growing up. My parents were old-fashioned and kept books around, and I read them all. Of course, I'm not unusual. I'm from Clarkston, and we still have books there—oh!"

He stopped abruptly, thinking about what he had just said … and then looking grimly around he added, "Maybe I shouldn't have said that. Tomorrow a Brute Squad might be on the way to blow-up the only public library still open in Michigan." Shaking his head angrily, he blew out a deep breath and added, "Just one more PAC blessing."

"Get on with it and watch your language!" the president ordered angrily. "Such talk is threatening to us all and undermines PAC solidarity. It will not be tolerated."

"As you wish, ma'am. We were talking about my history class, although they didn't call it that, and there was no real history discussed. All we did was sit around and go on and on about how horrible things were in the old days and how PAC saved us. Our so-called instructor never said anything at all unless she decided that we'd say something not PAC-correct, and then she'd jump all over us. There was never a discussion about it when she corrected us. If she said we said it, we were supposed to just back off.

"Anyway, the class seemed to me to be a waste of time, and so I decided that we should get into some real history, and I brought up stuff I'd read, stuff none of them had a clue about, including our PAC-protecting, so-called, professor."

"You decided! I'm confused. By what right did you make such a decision?"

"Well, you know." John ran a big hand through his hair, and casually glancing back at the colonel again as he continued, he noted that the officer still wasn't showing much interest in their little show. "I figured I was in college, and I had a right to an education. Isn't that what's supposed to happen? I mean, why are we all here anyway?"

"Let me try to enlighten you, if that's possible," replied the president, and leaning back against the lectern, she scowled up at him. "You have a right to a degree, which can be yours after three years, no one is ever denied. But your education is bigger than just you. Your true education, if it is to have any meaning at all, must help you become fully part of the PAC community, to be part of the glorious ONE. *That* is why you are here, not for any selfish desires of your own." And then turning from him, she faced to the front and raising an index finger high above her head, shouted, "*Our new era!*"

"I came here to learn something!" John boomed back over the applause for that holiest of signs. "Getting right with PAC isn't the same thing as getting right with truth!"

"Our worthy students learn humility. We all learn PAC-truth by shared dialog, not by an appeal to outdated, wrong-thinking research or those old books you seem to worship … and certainly not by any reference to elitist, ancient, white-male authority. I need hear no more on this charge," she snapped, and angrily shaking her head, she turned to face the now very worked-up audience and called out, "How say you on this?"

"Guilty!" Their voices rang back as one across the dome.

Smiling as if in triumph, the president then turned back to face Little John and said, "You have been found guilty by your peers on this charge. We will await findings on the other charge, but you will at least have your classes closed and be denied federal edu-funds for one school year." Her smile broadened with every word as she spoke.

"OK, let's get on with this," the now tight-lipped John replied, stealing another glance at the colonel as he responded to the verdict. "As for the other charge, I'm as far from being a sexist as you can be, but I do find girls attractive, and I didn't think I could keep my mind on my studies with one prancing around my room full time, and I …"

"I think we've heard enough," the president cut-off his comments. "It may not have occurred to you that the so-called 'prancing girl' was not being provided for your enjoyment. She was there simply to share a room with you, to be your colleague, not your plaything. But why should I even bother going on? This is obvious," she muttered in disgust, and turning once again to face those assembled, she shouted out, "How say you?"

"Guilty!!" Came the roaring reply from the now revved-up gaggle of guardians.

"Well," John shouted back before the president could speak. "It did occur to me that many claim to live by that silly idea, but that few people actually do, biology being what it is. Of course, I'd have kept my hands off, but I couldn't have kept my mind off of her ... not for a long time, anyway, not unless we became real buddy-like friends."

"Sexist!" hissed several in the audience amidst a general churn of emotion.

"Sorry, I'm just a man," he snorted, teasing the president with his mock apology.

"You're not a man here, buster. You're a quotaed-white male, nothing more."

"And there's nothing less these days, but—whatever!" John shouted back at her, scowling now as he stepped back between his two very troubled guards, who quickly parted to make even more room for him.

"Guilt having been found on charges two and three, your student status is now revoked and you are ordered to release your student apparel at the conclusion of these proceedings. However, you will continue in detention until we hear from our honored friends of the Friendly Forces about charge one. If they declare you guilty, you will not only be turned-out of Arbor University, you will be bound over to them to face whatever action they choose. It is not for us to question them. Do you have any final words?"

"You bet I do," John replied, and as a strange smile formed on his face, he started edging back, seemingly toward the empty chair behind him. "I just wanted to be a good college student, to get a degree, and then find a job like Americans used to do in the old days. I'm a few years older because I had to help out at home. My family isn't well off and what with the economy in pits things haven't been very good. And of course, my kind, we're in a special crunch because we're so low quotaed that we never get the jobs or get into the cushy federal programs. Even to come here I had to wait until someone in my quota-group died before I could get in, and I ..."

Suddenly, the talking stopped, and as he just stood there, glowering out over the audience, slowly shaking his head from side to side, the audience fell silent—all eyes fully on him. And then, that big head jerked around, and snorting out a loud growl, Little John began stalking powerfully about like a prowling lion. His arms twisting and turning, his fists clenching and unclenching, he moved around the stage in two wide circles, all while staring up and out into space as if searching for some possible answer to all of this idiotic craziness— somewhere, out there. He stopped finally in front of Benjamin's now vacant chair, turned and ... and just quietly looked out over that by now fear-charged audience as if studying them, studying them as they very warily studied at him.

His nostrils flared as he revved up inside. He felt only contempt for that sea of upturned lemming faces and all they stood for, and he wanted to crush them, but he seemed to be waiting for the big hand on destiny's *do-it-now* clock to tick—just one more time—before doing it. And then, it must have done so, because Little John, clenching his now bared teeth, jerked up both fists to his chest, sucked in a deep breath, and let it all back out in a fists-pumping-the-air, audience-jolting roar that sent his own handlers and even the president stumbling over each other towards the other side of the stage.

And before anyone else could react, the big man spun around, and moving quickly to the unbelievably still dozing Colonel Fu, he seized his left shoulder with one huge hand and jerked him violently to his feet. Then with a look of pure fury on his face, he spun the very surprised officer around, deftly slipped his gun from its holster, and as the panicked audience watched in stunned and silent terror, he lifted the now futilely resisting older man completely off his feet and hurled him to one side, sending him on a facedown sprawl-slide across the stage, spinning head-toe, head-toe, full-stop.

During that whole, horrible ordeal, the audience held its breath, all eyes frozen on the hapless colonel, a shudder of fear racing up and down their PAC unstiffened spines. And then a collective sigh of—they would say—thankful relief followed when the abused officer rolled over to watch, but not to stop the unfolding show.

"*You* find *me* guilty," Little John boomed out at the audience. "Well, I find *all of you* guilty of being hollow shells ready for cracking, and that time's coming soon." Now looming high over them on the edge of the stage, he shook his head in total disgust, watching them shrivel back into themselves below him. And he started to leave at that point, but in an apparent afterthought, he instead jammed the colonel's gun into his belt and turned to the large lectern behind him. Reaching out, he snatched it up, and with arm muscles bulging, he lifted it high over his head, turned back to face them all again, and threw that huge thing out into the center aisle where its loud crashing sound was joined by the dome-wide whimpering of most of those cowering so-called "guardians."

They, all of those in that stunned audience, had flinched back in a reflex at first, trying to put some space between themselves and that madman, but now they fell silent, frozen upright in their chairs, watching in horror as John, pumping his arms over his head again, stomped down the stairs, bellowing out like a great ape. "I'm leavin'," he shouted as he moved up the aisle, "and I'll tear the head off of anyone trying to stop me!"

"You're a fool," the president spit-shouted after him from her cowering place beside the ombudstera. "You'll be hunted down. Don't you get it? You have assaulted a Friendly Forces colonel. You're now a war criminal. You're dead, you fool!"

"Hey!" John turned around to call back from halfway up the aisle, and laughing, he raised a hand in salute toward the now crouching colonel. "You know, if he's half the man I think he is, he's been assaulted before. I think he can take it."

With that, he also threw a salute at his two now crying escorts before resuming his march toward the door, pausing only briefly to brush aside the only student moving in the whole dome, a seemingly confused female who seemed to have blundered out into the aisle. No one noticed that a small slip of paper passed between them. No one noticed because the dome all around them was filled with dazed and very frightened PAC-ophiles, all now sitting stone-still, staring fearfully straight ahead, their only movement being in the form of the trauma tears, streaming down many of their tortured faces.

By the time John cleared the dome, the president was already swarming around the now standing colonel, apologizing and swearing to make things right. He, on the other hand, was wearing a socially correct smile on his face as he brushed himself off, more focused on pulling away from her than talking.

Outside the dome, Little John sniffing the air of his new freedom, frowned in disgust as he caught the smell of burning old desks and furniture. He shook his head; no doubt some idiots had once again set fire to the wood collected for winter heating. Why?

Why would anyone be so morally bankrupt that they'd sabotage their own people like that? Then, laughing out loud, he muttered, "Oh well, just par for the course these days."

Still muttering about all the idiots in his life and the PAC-driven insanity all about him, he strode across the campus, stripping off his hated student garb as he walked and "releasing" it as ordered, by dropping it all along the street—making sure to stomp on it after it fell. The now ex-student and new fugitive soon blended in with the people of Arbortown and became just another townie on his way, after drifting about a bit toward *ONE TRUTH Park*, its official name, or the Peoples' *Park*—one of its other names.

Despite being officially closed, the park was occupied by groups of folk singers almost every evening, especially in the summer, and by the crowds that came to watch them, to listen to them, and to sing forbidden songs. During those times, it actually was a peoples' park, but the signs were changed to read: *Hirve Park*.

John had been visiting the park to relax and get away from all the craziness of campus life since first arriving at school. But unlike most of the others, he knew the real story behind the name, the story of a small, brave nation using music to hold its people together and to help them through the long years of foreign control. How appropriate, he thought, maybe his new job should be to teach people enough history to help them see that what was going on now in America wasn't new and that other nations had faced the challenge of tyranny triumphant over and over again in the past. It really didn't matter whether it was their own fault—as he knew was the case this time in America—or the fault of evil, more powerful neighbors. When it happens to your country, you deal with it, or you let it deal with you—those are the only two real options.

Little John was the deal-with-it type. *Who knows*, he thought, *maybe even a little bit of real education beyond a steady diet of PAC-bilge could help the people of America turn this mess around. At the very least, a real knowledge of history, a balanced history, could provide some hope that if others have done it, we can too.* He frowned at that last thought, correcting himself out loud, "We *will* do it too."

Then, grinning with resolve and looking about with a new sense of appreciation in these first moments of his new life adventure, he moved on, silently celebrating his fresh-found freedom.

At one point in his stroll, without even bothering to look around, he tossed the Chinese officer's gun into a nearby large hole filled with trash, broken glass, and other junk. But just walking away, leaving it like that, didn't feel right, and so he stopped and turned to look back toward the hole again. Whoa, there was that the gun, way too visible, almost like a come-and-get-me advertisement. He knew he couldn't leave it like that. It could cause big trouble for some poor innocent slob, and that wouldn't be right.

Driven by that thought, he walked quickly back over to the hole and went to work. After unloading the gun and pocketing the bullets, he pushed it on deeper into the clutter, and then casting about, he began snatching up some of the other junk and debris scattered on the street all around him and tossed it in into the hole to complete the cover-up job.

Other people, going back and forth along the street, looked curiously over at him and all of his activity, and they probably wondered why that big guy thought it was his mission in life to clean things up. Wasn't that always someone else's job? Crazy!

Chapter Three

How Glenn Alleyne Stanton Steps Out into the World with a Roman Salute

*B*ack at the dome, there was utter chaos; a student had been cast out! Or more accurately, a student had elected to leave the shelter of perpetual life-tenure at a federally funded university—and had barreled out. It was incredible, especially the way he had done it, the sheer animalism of his exit. The audience had expected the usual lick-spittle groveling common among all those challenged by PAC, instead they got a straight-up, rampaging warrior who had left them stunned into silence, perhaps out of fear that he would return to do even worse. Or maybe, they were just struck dumb—set in there all drenched in their own chicken-hearted sweat, waitin' for nanny. It was hard to tell.

But predictably for such types, once they snapped out of their impotent cringe, playground-like posturing broke-out. And some ran amuck, shouting and screaming in wimpish anger and mock bravado, while others cried, tearing at their clothes and hair in tortured, righteous indignation. Such things were not supposed to happen, not here, not in this place, and not to them. Any display of anger here was always to be mere bluster, well-controlled and painfully PAC-correct. But that's not what happened. Not this time.

No. That brute had behaved like a barbarian straight out of the history books, not that the tenured-types present had ever read any real history books. But of course, some of them had heard about such utter barbaric types as the US Marines, Navy Seals, and the special operations troops from the other branches, all now banned under the terms of the *2028 Chicago Treaty of Forgiveness*, signed following that year's annual Presidential Apology for America World Tour. Such was the utter barbarity of these primitives that a mob of them was even now refusing orders to surrender Camp Pendleton in Southern California to the Mexico-Cartel coalition, and by so doing, they had become the western anchor of the growing resistance to the land giveaway PAC called the *Great Southern Peace Arc*, stretching from Texas to California. The president, following PAC guidance, had "returned" that whole area "peacefully" to Mexico by a mere executive order. As a result, the entire border was now a war zone.

But in truth, it wasn't the warriors that people loyal to PAC thought of first when images of violent and barbaric types came to mind. No, for most, it was those they called Christian extremists who, in their view, had tried to take over the country in the last half of the twentieth century. PAC's counter actions had facilitated its own final march to power.

And on this day, once the modern heirs of those marchers—now flailing about in the dome—had finished venting their feelings about the Student of Lunacy turned evil barbarian monster, they refocused their anger into a desire for vengeance. That renegade must be found and prosecuted. No, they should turn him over to the Friendly Forces; that would be much better, they had real firing squads, and they used them. The tenured ones didn't believe in capital punishment, of course, but this was different; this evil cast-out demon was an exception. He, more than anyone else, deserved—death!

While all of that righteous anger was morphing into a giant payback fantasy, the mussed-up commander of those firing squads finally extricated himself from all the smothering gushes of concern on the part of President Prudhomme and made his way out of the dome. Once outside, he paused to straighten his uniform and then turned to walk with a jaunty step on into town. He actually whistled as he walked, and if any in that frightened lot behind him had seen his face as he left their area, they would have been amazed and horrified. There had been no trace of fear or anger on Colonel Fu's face when he'd been sent sprawling across the stage, and there was none there now. Instead, he wore a mischievous grin and even had a twinkle in his eye as he made his way quickly toward a little Central European restaurant just off Main Street. It was a favorite of his, and when he was in town, he had his troops guard it to keep out the riff-raff, so he could enjoy it as a quiet retreat. He often ate there all alone, relaxing to the music, but on this day a broadly smiling Professor Benjamin rose to greet him as he walked in the door.

"Welcome, colonel. I trust you had a good time at the dome."

"You Americans." Colonel Fu laughed as they shook hands and sat down. "Just when I think I know what to expect, you throw something like that at me." He went on to brief the professor about what had happened, adding at the end, "I thought we had a plan."

"I'm sorry, colonel, I'd like to take credit for what sounds like a grand stunt, but in this case our young friend improvised. What you got wasn't theater, it was real."

"Well, either way, that Little John character is an animal, a real brute!" Colonel Fu said, rubbing the back of his neck and laughing again. "He snatched me up—like a rag doll, as I think you say. I wouldn't have been able to stop him even if I'd wanted to."

"Well, rag doll you're not, but what a trial!" Benjamin replied, also laughing.

....

"He loved it," the professor whispered to himself two hours later when he reached his office, and once inside, after carefully closing and locking the door, he leaned back against it and finally allowed himself to burst out into the loud gut-busting laugh he had held in for so long. "He loved it, Colonel Fu loved it. He got jerked around, and he just laughed!" he shouted out to the waiting student. "It was *beautiful*, oh so beautiful."

"You must have had a much better time than usual as the designated schmuck," the young man replied, grinning and eyeing his mentor curiously as he stood to greet him. "What went down that was all that beautiful?"

"Not what went down, Glenn Alleyne Stanton, but what went up, and I love it so much I can't stand it!" The older man laugh-shouted over to Glenn as he jerked off his cape and cap and flung them both across the room, and then, flopping back into his old wooden swivel chair, he threw up his feet and swung around twice before sitting back to plop them up on his equally old, well-worn, wooden desk. And then, grinning from ear to ear, he finally looked over at his companion and ordered, "My boy, mark your calendar. On this day, this glorious day, the curtain spectacularly went up—up, not down—on act three of our greatest American tragedy. We'll call this act, *The Good Guys Strike Back*, and believe me, my young friend, our play's denouement is now in sight. Oh, it's still a way's away, but I can see it coming. I can feel it in my bones, and I want you to know that it's oh so very glorious beginning was today!"

"I love that title, but come on! What happened? I want to enjoy this party too."

"It's what didn't happen, Glenn. It's what didn't happen," Benjamin declared, and as he paused thinking about it, he suddenly bent over, laughing again, laughing and coughing at the same time. But then, finally, after working hard to regain control by sucking in several deep breaths, he looked up with tears in his eyes and continued with his story ... in a near wheeze. "We already knew that this was going to be a great day because this is the day that you, Glenn Stanton, will leave your Uni-nest here to find your destiny in that great big and very damaged, yet still best of all possible worlds out there."

"Yes, but before we get to that, will you please tell me what happened?" Glenn asked again, half-laughing as he urged, "I want to know what happened at the dome!"

"Of course," the professor replied, and after sucking in one more deep breath, he very deliberately began to tend to business. First, as demanded, he updated Glenn about the dome events, ending it all with, "And I'm sure you know that if I had still been in there, I'd have had a hard time not jumping up and down and cheering on that Little John character as he tore up the place. But, Glenn, I hope I could have resisted that impulse and for better or worse, played out my usual pitiful role because that's what I have to do right now. It's my duty. Still, I'll tell you that even though I was ready to endure another PAC farce, I still bless him, that oh so very delightful young man. He rewrote the script and snatched victory from our usual ritual defeat. It's hard to believe—a capital *V* for Victory! A real victory! And that feels so good after way too long, so very good."

"I know how tired you must be of all of the game playing," Glenn said, smiling as he looked fondly over at the older man who had worked so hard to get him to this, his last day at Arbor U. He loved seeing him so upbeat and excited after oh so many other times, so many other relentlessly predictable PAC puppet-mastered gigs.

"Oh, yes. Of course, I'm very tired, but that's where we are right now. Many other people before us have had to endure the humiliation of occupation, but we may be the first people in all of the pages of human history to … well, a French philosopher, Jean-Francois Revel, said it best. He said, *'Democratic civilization is the first in history to blame itself because another power is trying to destroy it.'* Of course, he was speaking to a failure of all Western civilization and not just our own ignoble surrender to those much weaker than ourselves. But he was right. Our own hand brought us to this sorry state, and our fall is all the more shameful because we simply bowed down and meekly offered up ourselves as the mounting stool that lifted our enemies into seats of power over us."

"Wasn't there a captured Greek general who actually had to do that?"

"Yes, Valerian, a not too swift Roman emperor. It's been a while, but as I recall, he first defeated the Persians but then blundered into a trap and was captured. And at least he was a fighter. We didn't even fight—and that's the all-important difference."

"The difference between doing our duty and literally bowing to evil, I'd say."

"Very much so," Benjamin gave a short sad laugh and then added, "Did I tell you that Colonel Fu is a student of western culture and admires much of it, especially the old United States? He told me that he admired the way we were, but he didn't admire our wimpy, foolish self-blaming, and he couldn't understand our toleration for those inside our own country who divided us into in or out groups and ended up selling us out. And you know, he told me just today that he felt that everyone would suffer because of our ill-timed collapse. He believes that the world needed our example of many peoples truly coming together, trying to become one, and he certainly didn't mean PAC's fake *ONE*-finger routine. No, he meant real unity based on mutual respect, equality for all, and the freedom to speak our minds. He said that he believed people everywhere would now pay a high price because we allowed the PAC termites among us to chew away at our most basic right, the right to speak out peacefully without fear or favor."

"You've never talked much about him, but doesn't he think his own people are ready to step in and take the lead?" Glenn asked, shrugging. "That sounds weird to me. It seems like he'd be eager to press the advantage we've handed to him on a silver platter."

"No, I don't think it's weird at all. He knows that the present cozy arrangement between the tripartite powers won't last. Each one of them is eager to be all alone at the top, and sooner rather than later, Russia or China or India will move to pair off with one of the others to dump the third. Fu's guess is that the odd man out will be China because the other two fear her the most. Naturally, he thinks that China will come out on top and snatch up that silver platter of yours, but he also honestly believes that China would have been better positioned at home and around the world if the American collapse had waited for another decade or even two. I suspect that he may be part of a growing number of others among the elite there who would like to see China become freer and more open, more like we used to be before the rise of PAC."

"Well, I can buy his, two knock-off one and the last two fight it out to be the one in the position we were in before the fall," Glenn mused. But then, shaking his head, he looked at his professor and added, "Still, I don't know about the idea that China may have been on the verge of becoming truly free, do you agree with that?"

"What I believe is that unless we can step back in this whole mess will come tumbling down. I know that sounds extreme, but only India comes close to having the vision or the core values that are needed to build the kind of future we used to dream about. But India won't be the last dog standing, and right now neither of the other two can even begin to wrap their minds around our fumbled dream. I believe the colonel wants to see his country become freer, but without us, this old world will end up with nothing more than a clash of empires, followed by a sadly well-merited Dark Ages redux.

"Not that we got everything right. We've committed more than our share of well-meaning blunders. He told me that he found it incredible that we thought the way to use power was to run all over the place trying to save other people's democratic souls, even paying them for the privilege of trying to help them. He points out that conquerors have extracted tribute from those they controlled in the past; they didn't pay it. And he sees our nation-building and aid plans as being sort of like reverse Dane-geld plans that were destructive to both the giver and to the receiver—and I believe that he's partly right."

"Well, no one's getting any aid from us now, so whether we were stupid then or he's stupid now is a wash. What difference does it make? He's up, and we're down."

"Temporarily, yes, but he's not stupid, and I'd say, naive better describes us. But anyway, I don't begin to buy into all he says. I'm sure he's a good military man, but he's neither the philosopher nor the historian he thinks he is," Benjamin replied, and then smiling at his young ward, he added, "Meanwhile, the door's opening for us. All of the friendlies have overwhelming problems at home, and they'll have to fall back to take care of that business before they can square off against each other. When they leave here, it'll be up to us to retrieve our dream and to relight freedom's torch. If we fail to do that, this world will stumble downward and lose its best chance to regain our own and Aristotle's ancient vision of seeking to find the true *good* for all humankind. Thus, we'll be back to the old tired and tragic ways of conquer, exploit, and ruin—as I said, a new Dark Age."

"Sir." Glenn was glancing down at his watch, and although he hated to interrupt the professor, time wasn't standing still. "What we're talking about is important, but I'm sorry, I need to saddle up."

"Oh, of course! You're eager to go, and besides, we've rehashed all of this stuff hundreds of times, haven't we?" The professor grinned, fondly regarding the young man who now stood before him with his dungaree shirt buttoned to his chin, as was the travel fashion, and with the required copy of the red "PAC meditations" in his left breast pocket. But instead of the open sandals usually worn by students in the summer, he wore solid hiking boots, and a hefty backpack stood at his feet. "You're very ready aren't you?"

"Yes sir, I'm very ready."

"I hope so. Your father was one of my best friends, and he sacrificed himself fighting the rise of the very tyranny you're now going to face, both of your parents did."

"Yes, I know, and I'm eager to honor them by getting on with all this. So I still say, I'm very ready," Glenn repeated, smiling as he watched the older man's eyes harden. He didn't have to look down to know that the old warrior's fists would now be clinched as well, and that he was as primed as Glenn was for the launch.

"You'd better be, Glenn Stanton. You face a shattered country very much in the grip of the bad guys. Some of them are trying to destroy what we have left because they hate us and some just enjoy destruction; but mostly, Glenn, you go out now among a very confused people who need the truth you will learn to bring. They crave leaders to help get us all back to where we were and forward to where we deserve to be … to where the world needs us to be. And as you certainly know, that 'us' I speak of refers to freedom loving people around the world, not just Americans, but it's up to us to begin again, here."

"I know that, sir. My challenge is to join the Whig Partisan Alliance and to begin working with the Blue Company to help them get us back on that track, back to marching forward to where we all deserve to be—all of us, truly free and united as one people!"

"Do you have your certificates?"

"My federal-matching teaching permit."

"Diploma?"

"Master of social work," Glenn replied, and then he laughed. "But I don't have any paperwork to cover all my hours of training with you for the alliance."

"Yes, I know, Glenn." The professor also laughed. "And I look forward to a time when we can openly step out and state our true beliefs, when people of all opinions can coexist without being hunted down and driven out, but we aren't there yet. So right now, we need you to be able to flow through the system without much notice, and that means no blinking 'unbeliever' arrow that points to you wherever you go. How about passes?"

"Arbortown exit permit and Scholar's Sabbatical, and that's plus the friendlies' pass the colonel provided in case I need it. They're all stashed separately."

"Money?"

"Twenty-five hundred Unies."

"Good. United Nations Inefficient Economies Script is better than federal script. People have been suspicious of federal funny money since the dollar collapsed years ago. Nobody wants it," the professor said. "And how about the sign and password?"

"I know the sign and the password routine," Glenn said, and he went through the signing process. "Plus of course, my contact must know the chain of events."

"Sloppy signing, you can do better than that, but it's the chain that counts. The PAC security clowns will no doubt learn our words and hands routine, but they can't overcome our linking, narrative chain."

"Hey, I'll do better." Glenn laughed.

"You laugh now, but when the time comes you'd better do it well enough to convince your contact—or else." Benjamin gestured with an index finger across his neck, and the younger man threw up his hands in mock surrender.

"We will win!" He shouted out what this same professor had told him were his own father's last words as the PAC bad guys kicked the stool out from under his feet and left his tortured body twisting in agony on a thin rope in a tiny town in Australia called Grong-Grong. And then shifting his hands to the palms-out, fingers-splayed, thumbs-touching *W-W-W* sign, he closely watched his mentor's eyes as he repeated the Whig Partisan Alliance promise—not just a slogan, but a promise, "We will win!"

The older man, smiling proudly, turned his gaze over Glenn's head as the young man bent to heft his pack, and he looked out the window toward the PAC Union building where many years ago President Kennedy had announced the formation of what he had called the *Peace Corps*. *I wonder,* the professor thought sadly, *how that young president would have reacted if he had been told then that a later, weaker generation would rework the definition of peace, and that it would evolve over time to mean ...* surrender.

His tired old eyes then traveled around his office to the large picture of PAC Director-General J. F. Marcion hanging on the wall behind his desk. *What a joke,* he thought, *all who knew what was good for them might call her* dear leader, *but she was nothing more than a cat's paw for those who really controlled PAC, and PAC, itself, was nothing more than the pathetic virus that had weakened America—almost to death.*

He chuckled to himself then, because he knew that hanging on the wall behind that ugly picture was a plaque, one that he openly displayed when he was alone. It bore the silhouette of a soldier and a quote from that same Peace Corps president:

> *I believe in an America that is mov-*
> *ing, choosing, doing, dreaming,*
> *a strong America in a world of peace.*

He thought, maybe I should be displaying it now for this launching, but no, they had to hurry and the focus should be on Glenn and his mission. Besides, Glenn knew all about that plaque and he knew the righteous definition of peace. With that thought, the older man looked again at his eager student and snapped out, "Who controls this city?"

"I wish I knew." Glenn laughed, but he immediately regretted his flip response.

"Who controls this city?" the professor repeated, firmly, and there was no smile.

"PAC controls this city," Glenn replied, this time with a very serious expression.

"Who controls the Detroit Manufacturing Zone?"

"Friendly Forces, mostly Chinese troops, control the DMZ."

"Who controls the New York Economic Zone?"

"A UN Trust supported by Indian and Chinese troops controls the NY-EZ"

"And Washington DC?"

"The federals with Chinese, Indian, and Russian Army advisers, the Tripartites."

"And Florida?"

"Cuban Provisional Forces serving at the pleasure of the Tripartite Powers."

"And the Texas to California southern surrender arc?"

"PAC is pushing Mexico to move in, using some Russian help."

"And who agreed to the massive stand-down that made all of this possible?"

"The president of the United States working with an ever willing to roll over congress under the control of the PAC council."

"What is this PAC that controls so much?

"Officially, it's the *Peace, Accommodation, and Culture* party. Unofficially, it adds up to the peace of the weak, the accommodation of favored groups, and a rigid grip on our culture using thought control and social bullying. Philosophically it stands for all *Power at the Center*, for total power in the hands of an all-controlling ruling elite," Glenn recited. He paused then and shaking his head, added, "It's just one more head on the same multi-headed, totalitarian beast that once included the Fascists, the Nazis, and the Communists. And now, PAC peddles that same old dreary corporate state model to the world today, as do the Chinese and Russians, but not the Indians—at least, not yet."

"OK, that's what *is*, Glenn." The Professor stood directly in front of him now. "But why? Why, after the utter failure of these earlier 'heads,' have we allowed PAC?"

"Because we lost faith in ourselves as a people, we lost faith in our mission, we lost faith in our destiny; and we betrayed our calling. As you have said, we went from seeing ourselves as proud eagles, soaring up high toward the noble vision of a future of freedom that all the world could see and strive to join us in working toward, to blindly transforming ourselves into sad me-focused, entitlement gorged gooney-birds, waddling around in our own filth. We went from being *We the People*, finding our own way forward as responsible women and men with the character to govern ourselves in a free society, to allowing elites to soar over us and favored groups to emerge, leaving us with division instead of unity—all of us pathetically begging for steal-from-our kids' handouts that came only in return for PAC control." Glenn scowled on these last tragic words.

"Yes," the professor replied, shaking his head. "This, our land, lays open and wounded under the heel of its enemies because we failed it. But mark this well, the enemies who brought us down were not just PAC insiders. They had a lot of help. Useful innocents, including our own neighbors and friends, helped undermine us, but it is we, ourselves, who must each accept responsibility. We all allowed this to happen by not living up to our own individual calling as free citizens. But now, Glenn, you are starting this grand adventure to help undo that sorry bit of history, that colossal mistake. First, you will go to Whigville for training and to receive your commission, and then …" He stopped abruptly, staring at Glenn as a look of sudden realization formed on his face.

"But wait one! Hold it." The professor stood for a moment, almost floored by a sudden, OH-NO reality slap. Then, blowing out a deep breath, he sighed and laughingly shook his head as he explained, "You know, as much as I got a kick out of the way that Little John character turned our usual dome circus into a crazy-good gala, he complicated things for us more than you can imagine. And it's too late to make changes, the launch has already begun, and everyone's in motion. So ready or not, you need to leave now, and we both need to pray that your handlers can still make it all come together for you. I think they'll pull it off, but you're going to need to be even more careful and creative—and after that dome event, very lucky!" The professor added that last with a strange chuckle as he reached for Glenn's hand for their last handshake. The launch was on!

Glenn, although uncertain about what his mentor was talking about, still smiled confidently at him, and as their hands met and eyes locked, his breast swelled with pride. He didn't know what complications would come, but he wasn't worried; he was ready to go. Out there beyond Arbortown, the whole world swirled in turmoil beyond the help of a now crippled and occupied America. Things had come fully apart even as the babblers in Washington DC prattled on with cut and paste sound bites, offering up promises they knew they wouldn't and couldn't fulfill. Our great nation, once a beacon of hope, now lay wounded and bleeding, waiting for new and better leaders to claim their mantle.

"Sir, we the people of the United States are now called not just to reform, but to reform—to turn and force ourselves to once again put our feet on the road toward a more perfect union and to move beyond the squabble of group against group that has brought us down." Glenn spoke as he grasped his mentor's hand. "But as you've said before, it's really the same challenge that President Teddy Roosevelt warned America about over a century ago, and our great nation did the job it needed to do then to begin pulling the outgroups that he'd worried about into the fold. We accomplished that same kind of coming together again and again with people and classes … until the late 1960s and PAC's rise. Our cause now, the cause of the Whig Partisan Alliance, is to help our people move past that failure and to get back to building toward a new, enduring future of freedom for all."

"Go with God, my young friend. You are worthy of your parents, and they would have been very proud of you. Indeed, I'm sure they *are* very proud of you," the older man said, and his eyes were moist as he spoke those words. What a sight it was to watch this son of his old friends adjust his pack and with his young eyes sparking with resolve, to finally begin his mission after so many years of hard work preparing for this day.

"Nos morituri Te salutamus[1]." A choked up Glenn forced out the words that Roman gladiators once shouted to their emperor—who was sending them to their deaths for his own entertainment. But Glenn and others of the rising generations in freedom-seeking

---

[1] We, who are about to die, salute you.

countries around the world meant that salute to be heard not as a death cry, but as a vow to devote their whole lives—to the very day they died—to *living* for the cause of true freedom and as a sign of honor and respect to the next generation for sure, but also to their present supporters and to those all too few wonderful people among the recent older generations who had struggled to keep the flame of freedom and fairness for all flickering in a sadly darkening age.

"Sir, this time around, on the Whig Partisan Alliance watch, freedom's flame will be kept lit for ALL, not just for the politically correct puppy dog loyalists," Glenn vowed. "And that ALL must certainly include those in the swindled 'protected' groups that PAC has used and politically farmed to feather its own nest as well as the nests of all of those in its large supporting cast of enablers among the dark angel, cloud-dwelling PAC elite."

And then, after taking one last fond look around this room that had been such an important part of his life for so many years, he turned to leave. As he opened the door to step out, he smiled back at his mentor and whispered a throaty, "*E pluribus unum*!"

CHAPTER FOUR

How a Father's Plight Brings Two Travelers Together

Glenn paused briefly on the steps of Egg Hall, looking around and savoring the moment before setting off, whistling, toward the planned Liberty Street meeting with his contact. This was it! After ten years of secret study, dreaming of following in his parents' footsteps, his adventure had begun and he was on his way to Whigville. He felt like he would almost burst with the joy of it all, and looking at others around him on the street, he wished that they could see how full of life he was at this moment.

Of course, they were full of their own lives and not at all interested in this opening of a new chapter in his. He understood that, but he still wished that they knew what was happening to him right now or at least that he cared about them, because he did care about them. After all, as much as his fellow students, these good people had been part of the setting for his training as he prepared to join the Blue Company, and he had come to feel deeply about them. Their near hopeless PAC-driven situation motivated him.

But still, he knew that to those who bustled about all around him right then, he was just one more ordinary, everyday student. And it was as such a well-programmed ordinary student that he responded when an older man came up on the street behind him and in a halting, uncertain voice, very cautiously called out, "Brother?"

Brother! Almost choking on hearing that B-word, Glenn spun around to look not only at who said it, but also for who might have heard it, particularly when he saw that it was addressed to_*him*. At first, although he knew how idiotic the whole PAC-banned word list was, he wanted to scream back at the man, to separate himself lest some others might see him as being like that old man—a sexist! But he fought off that initial urge by reminding himself of the nature of his mission. After all, if he was going out to change things, why not start now? And so, with that thought in mind, he was able to force a nod and a faint-smiled welcome to the old guy as a sign that he would listen.

"It's my daughter." The father's words tumbled out, but he was so agitated that it was hard to understand him. "She come here fer nursing school, always wanted ta be a nurse, she did, but they said only men should be nurses an' she'd need to go to medical school instead. Don't know why they did that 'cause she don't want no medical school, if she can't be a nurse, she said she'd just come back home. Ya know what I'm sayin'?"

"Why not go to medical school?" Glenn replied. A bit confused, he wondered why she just didn't do her quota-assignment. "Pays more, not much, but some."

"That's just what I said to her. I told her we'd like to have her home, but what's she gonna do there? Things ain't good in Detroit, and it might be better to go to medical school even if you don't want to, I told her." More relaxed now, he paused, gingerly fingering his lower lip and pressing the back of his hand to his right eye, seemingly lost in thought.

"How'd you get that?" Glenn asked, finally noticing that the man had a black eye and cut lip. Of course, he knew muggings and assaults were a daily business all over Arbortown and that not much if anything was ever done about it.

"They got her this lawyer," the old man went on, ignoring the question, "I don't know why they'd do that. I'm her father, and I'm the one to help her if she needs it. And besides, she didn't want no help, she just wanted to come back home. Why'd they even wanta' go get her a lawyer anyways? Ya know what I'm sayin'?"

"The law requires a lawyer for all legal transactions, and everything about college, especially changing programs, requires a lawyer," Glenn replied, now torn between his Arbor U disgust at the old man's throwback notions about male responsibility and real concerns about others hearing all this and tying him into it. So he replied with a don't-you-know-anything-old-man tone to his voice that he regretted as soon as it came out.

"Well, the lawyer met with her, and was excited about her bein' left handed …"

"Met with her!" Glenn interrupted. "That's very unusual, a lawyer actually meeting with a client before a hearing doesn't happen very often. Usually they just fill out the fed-fee forms and leave all the decision making to the PAC legal guardians."

"Well, she did meet with her and got her this, here, paper," he said, holding up a form in front of Glenn's face. "She said there'd be no problem refusing her assignment because she wasn't PAC assigned to medical school, just okayed, said she'd do her a big favor 'n get her into the law school. Said she'd get her PAC endorsed there, and she did."

"Wow, congratulations," Glenn said, and he meant it; getting into law school would mean she'd qualify for federal assignments and the fees that went with them within a year. Of course, he knew this whole routine was only business as usual; the schools were always fighting each other for federal matching points. In this case they'd be slobbering all over themselves at the idea of getting a black, left-handed female from the Detroit Economic Zone—good for four Affirm-Points. The med-school people would be furious, of course, but no one cared. He almost laughed as he spoke to the father, "I don't know why this a problem, she's all set. I hope she'll do it. It's an easy gig."

"Well, she said she would, but it ain't that easy now." The man sighed, shaking his head. "It don't matter to me, but the law school said she'd have to deliver some kind of federal matchin' forms to 'em, and I had 'em, but I don't have 'em anymore."

"Well, where are they?" Glenn sighed; he was getting tired of this long story.

"I had 'em when I came here with the Brighton Convoy, believe me, but two feds cut me out of the group after we crossed the river, sayin' that I was breakin' the law by travelin' at night with no lantern ner night pass. N-I said to 'em that if I'm breakin' the law how about the forty other people with no lights in my convoy, and besides, I told 'em, look around, brothers, it's two in the afternoon and the sun's high in the sky; I don't need no lantern. Then they hit me— for no reason! How about all those other people? Hey, they just let 'em go, an' none of 'em had a lantern. Why'd they stop me and not them?"

"Well, sir." Glenn shook his head because even he, a recent graduate, couldn't help grimacing at the stupidity of what he was about to say. "I don't know where to start, but I'll try. First, her law- yer sold her to the law school. It happens all the time, but they still need the federal forms so they can get their points. As to the time, the Arbortown labor council has ruled that night begins at 1:00 p.m. That way everyone gets double federal matching for night work, and the work productivity reports look good to the feds. As for why you were stopped and not the others, let's face it, as an old male you're in a low quota group, and you were all alone and easy pickings. Of course, it'd have been even worse for you if you'd been an old white male, but old and male isn't good in our new age, whatever your other quota-group is. No one likes old males."

"Well, that's crazy, n-besides, they fined me on the spot and took everything I had on me, my fed-script, my ring, my watch, an' all the papers but the one I showed you. Heck fire, man, they even took my baloney sandwich—you know what I'm sayin'?" His lower lip trembled as he spoke, his eyes seeking Glenn's. "I don't know what to do, brother, and I thought you being a student, you'd know an' maybe you'd help me out."

"Look, we need to settle some things before we go any further with this," Glenn said, but as he held up a hand to shush the father, he paused, closely studying the old man and wondering, just for a fleeting moment, if he could be a PAC plant, testing his loyalty. But no, he decided, this guy was way too authentic and couldn't be that good an actor, and so he went on to offer some advice. "Sir, you need to quit using illegal terms like "brother." Don't you know that's probably the main reason they smacked you and why they had a right to smack you? You can't use sexist terms like that in our new society."

"Well, I call my daughter "sister," and nobody ever says nothin'.."

"And they won't, but just take my word for it, no more "brother." As for the money, it's gone. You might be able to get your papers back if you hurry, but I have to warn you, if those idiots realize what they have, they'll sell them to one of the other schools, and then you're stuck. Anyway, I really don't know what I can do to help."

"Can't you just talk to 'em? You're a student 'n maybe they'd listen to you."

"How would I ...?" He started to decline, but there was something about the old guy's face, and besides, there was still his man-on-a-mission to help others upend this whole crazy society notion that had caused him to listen in the first place. So why not start now with a real person and a real problem? It seemed clear cut now; he almost *had* to help, and so he plunged ahead, "OK, let's do it. Where'd you last see those guys?"

"They're over 'n the next block. I followed 'em there, and I watched 'em. I saw what they was doin'! They used my money fer a bottle, and they still got them papers 'cause they didn't search my pack. Know what I'm sayin'? They been too busy drinkin'.."

"Well, that was a while ago," Glenn replied, but he was grinning now and actually excited about this, his first new-life adventure. So slapping the old man on the back, he said, "Come on, show me where they are. We probably won't get your money back, but as for your pack ... who knows, we might get lucky, and if we don't, at least we tried."

And as Glenn followed, the old man eagerly turned and headed back down the street, stopping when he came to a long boarded-up construction site. Then, incredibly, after he bent over to look through a gap in the fence, the old guy just popped on through it before a stunned Glenn could stop him. Come on, no one these days would go through that kind of opening into who-knows-what on the other side! People were mugged right and left in the open streets—going behind a boarded-up fence didn't make good sense.

As Glenn held up, trying to decide what to do next, the father stuck his head back out through the hole he'd vanished into and excitedly motioning to him, hissed, "Hey, student, what-a ya doin'? Come on, they're still here, you kin talk to 'em right now."

"Na—OK," Glenn slurred his answer, and then, although not really liking this option, he blew out a long, deep breath … and eased himself on through the opening.

"There they are," the old man whispered, and grabbing Glenn's arm as he stood up inside the fence, he pointed to the two scurvy looking louts sprawled against the wall of the building off to the left side of the trash littered, trampled-down, weeded lot.

Glenn smiled when he saw that the feds' attention was completely on the bottle they were passing back and forth, but his smile was short-lived, fading away almost at once when he and the father moved away from the fence. As they started across the field, one of feds looked up, and cocking his head to one side in a bleary eyed stare, he studied the approaching men for a long minute before finally elbowing his drinking partner.

"Hey, ain't that the oldie who gave us all the trouble?" he called over to his bearded buddy, pointing toward the old man walking toward them with what looked to be a student. The other lout only peered lazily over at the two approaching men at first, but then, grinning broadly and rubbing his hands together, he nodded eagerly, and thinking about yet another easy score, he led the way as both drinkers labored to get on their feet.

"I brung this student here to explain things to you two men," the old man said.

"I'm just here to talk," Glenn cut-in, and forcing a smile on his face, he held up his two empty hands, hoping to reassure them. But he could see at once that he'd made a bad mistake by coming so far forward. One of the feds was already edging over to get between the two of them and their fence opening, and glancing quickly over toward the bordering street, Glen felt his heart begin racing as he saw that the bearded clown was now moving to cut that off as well. His first thought was that he could easily get away by making a run for it, but he couldn't just desert this old man. No, he was stuck here, boxed in between two brick walls with two bad guys now moving in on them, and all he had were his own two empty hands and this useless old father, tying him down.

What a great start this is to my adventure. I've covered maybe all of four blocks before bash and get robbed time, he thought, more disgusted with himself than afraid.

"So you're a shtuden.' Wow, big shtuff," the uglier one called out, mostly for his bearded buddy's benefit. Then, wide eyes dancing drunkenly and flashing a yellow, gap toothed grin, he produced a knife and slowly waved it toward Glenn as he slurred, "Yep, we're impreshed, man. Wow, ish crazy, we gettin' to talk to a real live shtudent—live fer a while anywaysh." Both feds roared with laughter at ugly's joke as they inched in even closer, their eyes locked firmly on Glenn.

"Yep, we're really impressed. I feel smarter already," the bearded one said, and gesturing toward where they'd been sitting with their bottle, he added, "Let's jest you two'n me move right over there fer a sit down? We'll give you a drink—er somethin'."

"Shomethin'! I like that," his partner exclaimed, barking out another loud laugh.

"No, I don't think that's a good idea." Glenn muttered a reply, his mind racing now, eyes darting from one clown to the other. "I think we'll stay right here. No offense, but we prefer to stand while we talk. Thanks anyway." He tried to smile, but failed.

"Oh, thish shtudent knows how to talk real proper. He shez thanks." The knife waver grinned, again flashing his yellowed teeth. "OK, you go right ahead 'n talk."

"I'm not here for trouble," Glenn said, still waving his empty hands and slowly shaking his head. "I just want to help with what I'm sure is only a misunderstanding."

"A misunderstanding! Whoa, we wouldn't want that, would we?" The bearded one spoke with mock seriousness, grinning again at his knife-wielding, laughing partner.

Glenn decided that the beard was the leader, and he didn't seem to have a weapon, so he'd be the one to go at first, if it came to that, and it looked like it *had* come to that.

"You're right, let's just the two of us talk?" Glenn smiled at the beard, trying to use an authoritative sounding but a not too offensive voice—which was a bit of a straddle. Not that it mattered; this guy wasn't buying it. So, knowing that their time was running out, Glenn slowly coiled to attack, eyeing them carefully and waiting. And then, out of the corner of his eye, he saw the knife holder look away. Something had distracted him.

That was his signal! After first feinting one quick step toward the place they had suggested, hoping to freeze them for even a second, he turned quickly toward the bearded fed, and screaming a loud battle cry at the top of his lungs, he jerked off his heavy pack and swung it like a bat as he attacked. The surprise worked, and he smashed that once leering but now wide-eyed face with his pack once, twice, and even a third time as the creep fell face down into the weeds. But there was no time to celebrate victory; yellow-teeth was on him, and as the knife blade swept across Glenn's line of vision, barely missing his face, he reached for his attacker's arm and grabbing hold, struggled to pull him around so he could disarm him before his bearded partner could get back up.

"Too long. I'm taking too long. Boozin's slowed him, but I'm taking too long," he panted to himself, working desperately to wrestle the knife loose. Then, out of the corner of his frantically searching eyes, he saw that the beard was now back on his feet and probably armed with a rock if nothing else. This is stupid, so stupid! He had so many very important things to do. He'd been warned to keep his mind on his task and to not get sidetracked, but here he was, caught up in this mess and not even out of town yet.

Then suddenly, the ugly lout jerked, stiffened, and mysteriously slumped like a drunk, causing Glenn to stumble backwards under the now limp man's full weight and despite his best effort, to go down ... with the bad guy on top—on top, but strangely still. In near panic, Glenn began twisting and turning, straining to move out from under all that dead weight, and all the while fear-jerking his head from side to side, trying to see where that bearded lout was, expecting him at any second. But instead of the beard, he saw the knife loose on the ground—just out of his reach. His panic spiked, and he started kicking and twisting even more wildly, pushing and shoving, desperately trying to get to that blade first, before the beard got to it. "I gotta shake this ton of ugly," he groaned, and he could almost feel a rock coming toward his head.

"Relax, friend. It was a good effort, but you were losing, and I think you're going to need a lot of help on your trip, an awful lot."

Glenn froze, his gut clutching at the sound of this new, strangely calm voice. And twisting quickly around, he saw the confusing sight of a mysterious giant leaning back against a protruding piece of construction drainage tile and grinning calmly down at him. At his feet, once again lying face down and very still, was the bearded federal leader.

"Who?" Glenn grunted out the word, as he finally pulled free of yellow teeth.

"John Richard Wood, ex-student of this once fine uni," the big guy said, stepping forward. And still smiling, he offered a hand that engulfed Glenn's own not so small hand and effortlessly pulled the embattled student to his feet. Laughing loudly as Glenn studied him, he added, "Everyone calls me Little John, like that Robin Hood character.

"You're the student who was ..."

"Yep, you got it, and I had you in my sights and was sort of drifting along behind you when you just vanished. I couldn't believe it, first you're talking to that old guy over there and then you're both gone." John laughed again. "I thought maybe I'd gone nuts or you were some kind of wizard. It took me awhile before I realized that you just might be dumb enough to go through that hole in the fence. No offense meant."

"None taken. It was a stupid thing to do. But why were you tailing me?"

"Because that's what the professor told me to do," John replied, now confused and frowning. "Didn't he say anything to you about meeting up with me?"

"Well, I knew I had a contact, but I didn't know it'd be you," Glenn replied, now mulling things over as he curiously studied Little John. Then, remembering what started this mess, he turned and called to the father, "Let's get our business done. Go through their stuff and get your papers and as much money as they have left, then we all need to get out of here. These are feds, and I don't want to try to explain why we killed them."

"Oh, they're not dead, but they'll be asleep for a bit and might wish they were dead when they wake up." John laughed, and reaching down, he effortlessly jerked up the bearded guy and began rummaging through his pockets. "Hey, this guy's got cash. It's only fed-script, but it's money," he shouted, and with his search completed, he let the still limp federal fall back to the ground, face first again, and turned to check on the others.

"You lucked out, my friend. The papers you need are still in your pack," Glenn shouted, holding them up for the father to see, and he smiled with delight when he saw the old man standing over yellow teeth, holding up his own watch, ring, and a big fist full of real money. "You know, those are unies, you're coming out way ahead on this deal, my man. Except, I guess, they must have eaten your baloney sandwich, sorry about that."

"That's OK. We've done good, and I thank you, two students. I thank you a lot." The old man was obviously delighted by it all, especially when they gave him the papers he'd lost and all the money they had collected. He was still thanking them when they shooed him away with instructions about where to go and what to do.

And as he started away, Little John shouted after him, "Hey, sir, thanks for all the help with that bearded guy, you had him under control when I got here. You had him so frustrated, I thought he could use some sleep, so I provided that." They all laughed, and looking at Glenn, John added, "That old guy's a fighter, I'll tell you—did a good job."

Glenn looked back over at the departing father with new eyes, recalling his own doubts about him, and then he and his rescuer moved off to a Main Street coffee shop to talk. It turned out that Little John had been contacted in his detention cell a week before by the professor, himself, and once he'd agreed to join the plan, he was told that he'd receive all of his contact instructions after the sentencing. "The professor told me to just keep my eyes open during the trial, and I'd see something I'd recognize on my contact's clothes."

"What was it?"

"She wore a sash that read, *Ms. Clarkston*, that's where I'm from." John laughed. "She jumped out in front of me when I left the dome and slipped me a note from him, telling me where and when to watch for you, and it had your description."

"Well, I knew we had a very broad plan in place, but I don't understand why I wasn't told that you'd be my contact, we certainly talked a lot about you. Unless this is my mentor's weird little joke, of course, and I'll bet it is." Glenn laughed, thinking he'd certainly take up this little twist in the plan with his old professor when they next met.

"I don't know about that, but I'll bet he didn't plan for you to help that old man."

"No, probably not," Glenn agreed. "Oh, by the way, who was the messenger?"

"No idea. I didn't see her face and," John replied, but then frowned, wondering about the big grin he saw forming on his new comrade's face. "What's with that grin?"

"I was just thinking about how worried I was about the poor, helpless, unfortunate student who was going to be devoured like a lamb by the PAC lions, some lamb!"

"Yeah, well really, some lions. What a bunch of losers. I can't understand how our country could have been taken over by a pack of wusses like those clowns."

"Burp!" Glenn muttered, laughing as he eyed John's reaction.

"Burp? Most people just do it; they don't say it. What're you talking about?"

"It's from my mentor. *BURP* stands for *Bully into submission* whom you can—wusses in our universities have always been easy marks for the winds of noxious change; *Undermine* your enemy—anyone who disagrees with PAC's new truth is an enemy to be taken out, not just someone with a different opinion;_*Raise* a protected class that'll need your help to keep the special stuff you give them—fairness being the first victim here; and last, *Protect* it all by erecting barriers for some and fast tracks for others. Wusses everywhere, slobbering to be on that safe insider fast track, have always been quick to sell out their neighbors to prove that they're loyal-to-the-bullies toadies."

"OK, yes, I see what you mean," John cut in. "But I don't understand how early PACies got away with jamming all of that nonsense through, why'd we allow it?"

"PAC's little divide and conquer cakewalk began during a confused time in the sixties. And I'm not sure why, but somehow, people just sat back and accepted it at first, including the birth of our very wuss-friendly *Hush-Now* creed that keeps it all in place. You know, that long list of things we haven't been allowed to talk about or to even think about in our new society since we embraced the great PAC-*Change!* And of course, that list grew and grew, leading to a mind-set that returned our colleges to a new round of Middle-Ages' era values. Inquisition 2.0—as you've seen. But it wasn't just wusses who allowed all of this. We've all contributed our part, mostly by going along to get along."

Both hungry, they stopped at that point and thinking that the big alarm for Little John wouldn't be out yet, decided it would be safe to adjourn their discussion to a local steak house to get better acquainted. Once there, they settled in over three huge Kobe burgers—two for John—fries, and coleslaw while Little John told Glenn about his trial, which he'd obviously enjoyed. Glenn laughed his way through the whole narrative and then filled in some details about his own milder history and their upcoming adventure.

That night, they stashed their next day's breakfast and lunch in an empty cupboard in a deserted house near the Peace River crossing and stretched out to sleep on the floor in one of its many empty rooms. Outside, they could hear the nightlong sounds of the times: screaming women, crashing bottles, and the drunken revelry of acting-out townspeople, students, or federals; they couldn't tell one from the other.

"This all sounds like an echo from the past, maybe back in the Old West before civilization arrived," Glenn muttered as he twisted around trying to get comfortable.

"Could be," John agreed, but after mulling it over, he added, "Or it could be more like the Middle Ages when the hotshot lords of the land and their wild and crazy knights ran roughshod through the fields and villages of the common people. You know, back in the early days of their jousting games, before all the rules came in to sorta civilize their new sport. Common folks like us were nothing back in those days. Of course, we don't add up to much now." John's drawled-out words got slower and slower as he spoke.

"You're right," Glenn whispered over to a near-asleep John. "It reminds me of what a guy named G. K. Chesterton once said, something about how the comedy of man survives the tragedy of man. I wonder if today's craziness is like what he had in mind?"

"Maybe," John mumbled. "Don't know … let's get … some … sleep."

"Anyway, I think he got it backwards—or we did. This time around, the comedy came first and swamped everything else. Civil rights progress, education, politics, everything was sabotaged as we gaga-eyed our way down a zany, straight to the cliff-edge path, leading us to today's tragedy. It was all so stupid—so many getting their views from TV talking-head jokers, the gurus of what? Information? Propaganda? PAC control!

"They say history repeats itself, but why did the rights for common folks like us have such a short run? I mean, why did we allow ourselves to be re-serfied by PAC—and laugh all the way down the drain? I don't know, but whatever it's been, comedy or tragedy, I don't want to be forced back to either the Old West or the Middle Ages." He whispered those last words, but just to himself by then.

He knew John was asleep, but he was too keyed up to relax, and so he laid back thinking about his mission and the Alliance dream, bouncing from one thought to another and back again. There should be no second-class citizens anywhere. Other peoples' misery is ours to help relieve, not just our government's. Free and caring people everywhere should reach out and make it a real people-to-people thing. Wasn't it John Quincy Adams who said something about how we should celebrate liberty everywhere but defend it only at home? What does that have to do with it? I'm going in circles!

Rolling over, trying to find a sweet spot for his head, he then wondered why we Americans had quit celebrating and defending the one-people ideal, and as he thought about that, he recalled the name of a very old song, "We Are the World." *Funny*, he thought, *it was from a time when young people dreamed of ... Well, who cares what they dreamed about? Their kid dreams dissolved into nothing more than a lot of silly adolescent acting out and navel-gazing fantasies that got subverted into what we have today: the banal evil of PAC-change, enforcing division instead of unity and reworking our old notion of real freedom to mean the freedom to have only "PAC-correct" opinions.*

He scowled, thinking that despite our loss to the bad guys, our failed dream *is* the way it should be. All people, everywhere, should be able to celebrate themselves as free individuals and have a shot at our old dream of *E pluribus unum* in their own cultures.

Oh sure, it may be utopian to think we can raise the banner of true freedom again and even to get it flying around the world, but that's the Whig Partisan Alliance creed and that's the Blue Company mission, so why not go for it?

"Young people of the world, unite!" he whispered, and smiling, added, "and old people ... and ... everyone ..." His eyes now very heavy, he finally drifted off to sleep, perhaps dreaming about freedom for all people, everywhere.

CHAPTER FIVE

How Two Friends Cozen the Guards at the Peace River Crossing

"*L*ittle John, we've got ourselves a problem," Glenn said, breaking a long silence in the first light of a beautiful Friday morning dawn. They were standing side by side, looking down at the Peace River ferry landing from under one of the few trees that had survived last winter's firewood hunt, and he was worried. "I've got a pass that'll cover every situation except you, you big galoot. After what you pulled in the dome yesterday, every clown in PAC-dom has been alerted by now, and they'll be swarming all over the place watching for you."

"Yep, look at 'em down there—federals, friendlies, and it looks like a passel of bounty hunters too," Little John replied, but then yawning loudly, he leaned back against their tree, sliding down to a sitting position as he added, "I had me a lot of fun yesterday with both of my exercise opportunities, and I'm not at all worried about today. I'm with a future leader of the Blue Company, a real life Whig Partisan Alliance hotshot, and I know that he'll come up with a plan. So all I have to do is just sit back, close my eyes for a spell, and wait."

"Yeah, sure, and when you wake up, you may find yourself alone, or worse, you could be looking up at a real gun in the hand of one of those friendlies," Glenn groused, and still keeping an eye on the action at the river, he eased down by his new buddy. But as he settled in, he thought over John's comment about all the characters down there and asked, "What's with all those bounty hunters? They're never seen around here."

"Probably after me. I imagine there's a big reward on my head."

"I don't doubt that, but where'd they come from and how'd they get here so fast?"

"Wow, you've been in the ivory tower too long; don't you know what goes on in the real world every day right across the river from you?" Leaning over beside him, John pointed at a cluster of four men standing off to the side on the dock. "Those guys right over there, the ones dressed even worse than the students, are like maggots on dead meat. They're all over the place and as mean as men can get. They don't care about anything but making a federal, and they terrorize the country everywhere outside the secure zones. My friend, you and I will have to get past a lot of them to get to where we're going, and yes, they may be after me, but they'll take you down just for the practice. On top of that, they'd probably score a pot full of real unies for killing you, just because you're with me. You might want to think about all of that before we go on with this trip."

"You're probably right." Glenn sighed, and casting a raised left eyebrow, scowl at his new friend. He continued, "Why didn't you just go along with the game plan? From what you said, the professor must have had it rigged for the colonel to pardon you, so you could do your thing with me. He must have had it set up so they'd release you if you just agreed to leave Arbortown within twenty-four hours, or something like that. So, zoom! You'd get out of here. It'd be clean, and we'd be good to go, right out in the open."

"Yep, probably did have a plan like that," John replied, and pursing his lips as he nodded at Glenn, he added, "But your buddy professor didn't tell me about the colonel part of the plan, and so I did my thing. I wasn't about to let those clowns get away with all their pathetic *Dance-With-Me-PACy* stuff. I don't dance to their PACy tune."

"OK, OK." Glenn laughed, shaking his head at his friend's iconoclastic comment.

People were supposed to show respect for PAC, and that song title and the word "PACy" were both beyond the pale. "You know, negative-attitude guy, I can see that I'm going to have trouble with you, but will you at least try to avoid sacrilege—in public anyway?"

"*This* is public?" John asked, shrugging as he made a big show of looking around.

"No, but the words came out too easily. You need to work on keeping your game face and your game mouth in place. We don't want to attract any attention to ourselves." Glenn spoke matter-of-factly, but then he paused, thinking about what he had just said. And after a bit, he turned to his friend and smiling broadly, added, "Or do we?"

"What?" John reacted to the seemingly devilish expression spreading across Glenn's now suddenly eager face. "You gotta plan? Let's hear it."

"Hold on, hold on," Glenn muttered, and slowly standing, he moved over to the edge of their hill where he stood, looking down at the landing below them and thinking, just thinking, but with a smile. A few minutes later, he returned, and kneeling down next to his now watching, wondering friend, he said he had a great idea that just might work. "But I need to check some things out in town. I'll fill you in when I get back."

He then left a mystified Little John on the hill with very strict instructions to stay completely out of sight, no matter what. "Even if the most beautiful girl in the world comes up here and sings a song of wanton desire in front of the bush where you're hiding, you stay put. No one must see you here, no one. That's very important. I'll be back in an hour or two, so watch the street for me."

Although unsure, John shrugged his acceptance, and after Glenn left, he moved over closer to the slope leading down to the street and eased in behind a bush, smiling as he did so and wishing that girl Glenn had mentioned would show up. Sadly, that didn't happen, and although he stayed out of sight in case someone came up to enjoy the view, that didn't happen either. During his long wait, all he witnessed was a single mugging on the street just below him; two punks roughed up a student and took some money. John shook his head; moron student, what was he doing walking alone out of the sight of those puny federal security clowns at the ferry? People are mugged all the time these days, and it was usually because they didn't use their brains. Grinning, he thought, of course, here he was very bored and sitting all alone just wishing some muggers would come up here after him. But that evil thought with all its presiding macho spirit faded instantly when he saw Glenn get out of a car on the street below. A real car!

"OK, big guy, I got what we need," Glenn spoke, breathing hard as he neared the top of their hill. Once there, he dropped the large sack he was carrying and rushed into a description of his trip in a strangely deliberate and casual manner, avoiding John's eyes as he spoke. But he need not have bothered; John's eyes were locked on that car below them. He hadn't driven a car since his Clarkston days, and he'd love to do it again.

"Wheels! I think I'm going to like this plan," John said, smiling until he finally turned his gaze over to the items Glenn was pulling out of the sack on the ground in front of him. "What's that, a dress? A great big dress. What's this all about?"

"Listen my friend, *this* will work," Glenn said, holding the dress up against John.

"For me?" John slapped the big purple tent aside, backing away. "Forget it!"

"Come on, you said you were going to trust me to come up with a plan, and I've got one. We're going to hide you in plain sight. I thought about dressing you as a huge federal or gorilla or some such, but that would attract lingering eyes, and we don't want that. This way not even bounty hunters will take a second look at you." Glenn tried hard to maintain a nonchalant pose and to keep a major grin off his face as he watched John's expression change from curious to more curious … and then, to flat refusal.

"No, no! It's not gonna happen." John stepped back, holding up both hands in front of his chest and scowling. "You're not getting me into a dress. That's stupid, who'd believe a guy lookin' like me could be a girl? It's stupid. You're stupid."

"Come on, you know there's a contact waiting for us on the other side, and we need to make the next crossing." Glenn replied sternly, trying to add a note of business-like urgency to his words even as he continued to work on keeping a straight face. And shoving the dress across to John, he insisted, "This is our plan unless you have a better one, and you know you don't. Just think about it. It's perfect. It's perfect because you're right, no one would think a man as big and ugly as you are would pretend to be a woman. People will look away when they see you so they don't get sick. It'll make them sick just thinking about how ugly you are. Come on, John, you know it'll work. So hurry and get dressed, my lady, your car awaits, and it cost me a hundred unies, not federals, to rent it. All of that, by the way, is so you can travel in the style of a great lady, so come on!"

"I'll tell you what, if any of them bounty hunters, federals, or friendlies—any of them—touches me, I'll tear their heads off." *Lady* John snarled from under his veil a few minutes later as he packed himself into the back seat of the car. But even though he still sounded mad, he liked being in the car, and this hiding-in-plain-sight notion did make a little sense. Besides, whether he liked the idea or not, he knew Glenn was right; they had a contact to meet, and he certainly didn't have a better plan, himself.

"Being touched is the last thing you'll have to worry about." Glenn laughed, and looking back at John in the mirror, he briefed him as he drove the short block to the river landing. "OK, we're here, so remember your lines and try to act like an important lady."

"What lines? I thought you said I was a mute."

"Good, you remembered, wait here for me." Glenn was still chuckling to himself as he left the car, heading toward the ticket booth, but there was only arrogance and not a trace of that smile left on his face when he reached the window. Once there, he pushed in and flashing his Friendly Forces Priority Pass, moved haughtily to the front of the line. The dull eyed, bored agent behind the glass was annoyed to have his routine disrupted—until he saw the pass, and then he immediately formed his biggest, most obsequious smile.

"Yes, sir, may I be of assistance to you in your travels, sir?" His eyes mooned with anticipation, and his face was almost pressing against the window of his little booth as he slobbered out his words, beaming in fulsome earnestness at this very important man. He would have kissed Glenn's hand if he could have reached it.

"Perhaps," Glenn muttered, and slowly looking all about with a pained look of studied disinterest on his face, he seemed unconcerned about the others in line, which troubled the agent and irritated them. At long last, deigning to continue, he scowled over at the agent. "As even you may recognize, I'm escorting a great lady—who will remain anonymous." He paused, looking around again as if to be sure that no one else could overhear, and then added in a low whisper, "She is the oldest daughter of the Mexican Consul General to the Detroit Manufacturing Zone." Then, eyeing the agent as if now deciding to trust him, he added, "She is indisposed and demands complete privacy."

"Of course, we will respect her every wish, and suitable accommodations will be arranged." The agent gushed his reply, and fluttering about in his cage, he was obviously uncertain about what to do first … or at all. But then, nodding his head quickly up and down, he made what in his mind was probably the most important decision of his career; he would take action to serve this great lady with the important pass. "If you can wait one moment, sir, I will go ahead of you and arrange private quarters," he said, and after submissively waiting to be sure, there were no objections, he turned to leave the booth.

"Remember, anonymous!" Glenn barked after him.

"Yes, sir, of course," the agent chirped, but he then paused uncomfortably at the now open door at the rear of his cage, looking nervously back toward Glenn. There was a matter that he needed to bring up; he didn't want to do it, but he knew that he had to ask about—money. He agonized at first, trying to find the courage to speak before finally risking a very strained, flinching, "Sir, will you be paying for the great lady's passage?"

"What? Why are you bothering me with mere details? Obviously, you will send your billing to Colonel Fu himself. I can't believe you'd even mentioned money to me."

"Of course. I mean, of course not, sir. I'll go now." Slurring his words as he spoke, the now humiliated agent bowed his head and hastily backed out the door.

A person behind Glenn in line chose that moment to loudly ask what was taking so long, and the clerk, hearing it, angrily rushed around the booth. Mopping his forehead, he smiled nervously toward Glenn without making eye contact and then spun to face the complainer. With his eyes blazing, he drew himself up to his full height and snapped at the man. "You'll wait your turn like everybody else. *And* this booth will be closed until I say it opens." With that, he sniffed, turned, and marched off toward the landing.

Once arrangements were set and under a swarm of curious eyes, Glenn made a major show of leading the veiled "great lady" from their fancy car to the landing where the now preening agent strutted as he waited to escort them up the gangplank. The agent didn't dare to look directly at the lady, but those who did, quickly looked away, and many of them then turned to stare open mouthed at each other and even up toward heaven.

Glenn, noting that none of them looked back at the lady a second time, struggled to keep a straight face, but he allowed himself to relax as they followed the clerk to the one enclosure on board, a small shack that accommodated special travelers. A Friendly Forces lieutenant had been sitting in there with two young ladies, but he vacated it at once when he heard who was coming—and the level of her pass. And he now stood ramrod straight by the door to greet the arriving celebrity.

"Welcome, madam," the young Chinese officer said, and although his voice trailed off and his eyes widened as he looked her; to his credit, he contained himself. "I trust,"—he broke off eye contact, coughing several times—"that you will be very comfortable."

"My lady appreciates your kind gesture," Glenn responded for her and shook the young officer's hand; the lieutenant looked to be about sixteen. "She is mute and cannot reply for herself, but you can be assured that she will inform Colonel Fu of your courtesy when they next dine together. What is your name, sir?"

Once they were situated and the boat in motion, Glenn decided to leave "the lady" alone in her unstately cabin and to walk about the deck to get a feel for the situation and the people; after all, this was his coming-out, and he wanted to savor every moment of it. He was particularly interested in the bounty hunters, thinking it curious that he knew so little about them, and so as he strolled about, seemingly admiring the view looking back over the water toward Arbortown, he angled over toward that particular knot of men who were joking around with each other off to the side.

"Who's that huge woman in the dress?" one of the bounty hunters called out to Glenn as he approached their place along the rail. "Don't see many dresses these days."

"Ugly!" sniped another one, and he turned his back, chuckling after saying it. Glenn pretended that he didn't hear, but noted that one of his buddies got in his face and pushed him farther away where they started arguing, with a little bumping and shoving. It was probably about the wisdom of saying stupid things about a woman traveling on a high level friendlies' pass. Not even bounty hunters would want to cross the friendlies. Glenn smiled, pleased with himself as he reflected on that fact.

"Hey, you deaf?" the first bounty hunter, ignoring the other two, still pressed his question. And now glowering, he leaned over closer to Glenn's face with a look of sour distaste that matched his breath. "I asked what's so important about that huge woman."

"No, you asked who she was," Glenn corrected him, now thinking that his little walk around the deck might not have been a good idea. But despite that, he didn't back down as he added in a firm, controlled voice, "And I chose not to reply. Who she is …"—he held the other man's eyes, taking his time—"… is none of your business."

"All I want …" The bounty hunter faltered. "I just want to know who …"

"Is there a problem here?" The friendlies officer joined them, and looking from one to the other but speaking to Glenn, he added, "Is this man bothering you, sir?"

"There's no problem," the bounty hunter said. "I'm not bothering him at all."

"I wasn't speaking to you," the officer replied, and he nodded over towards his men who were watching them, and the now worried clown, swallowing hard, stepped back as the troopers moved to their officer's side with their eyes now on all four of the bounty hunters. The lieutenant, smiling at Glenn, asked again, "Is there a problem, sir?"

"No, not at all." Glenn answered with what he hoped sounded like a relaxed, confident voice; things were getting tense and he didn't want tense. He wanted a nice peaceful trip across this stupid river, but now he was the one messing that up. With that thought on his mind, he nodded politely to both men and to the soldiers who were still closely eyeing the bounty hunters, and he turned and walked slowly and deliberately back toward the cabin. As he walked, he could feel all their eyes on him, every step of the way.

"Whew, I almost blew it out there," he said, sagging back against the closed door, once he was safely inside the cabin. "Those guys were ready to go at it, and you know, I think the bounty hunters would have pushed it if that officer hadn't been there."

"Yep, I agree. I was watching you," John replied. "For a minute I thought I'd have to bundle up these skirts under my arm and run out there to rescue you."

"Oh yes, that's all we'd need," Glenn mumbled.

"Anyway, forget that, there's a new pot brewing up at the front of the boat, some kind of scuffle between a few federals and a half dozen men. I can't make out all of what they're saying, but it's turned into some pushing and shoving," John whispered to Glenn, who moved over to the small front window to join him, looking out.

"Something about contraband," Glenn said and then muttered, "it's getting nasty."

As they watched, the shoving match turned into a fistfight. At first, it was four federals trying to isolate two travelers, but then the crowd grew to include many more travelers and the rest of the small federal security party. The punches got wilder and wilder and some of the badly outnumbered federal men were stomped on when they went down. That caught the attention of a curious friendlies sergeant who then walked over to the edge of the melee. He was probably just trying to decide whether or not to get into it when it happened; he was jostled—twice. Neither time was on purpose, but ...

"That was stupid." John whispered at once. "Now they've done it.

"Done what?" Glenn asked, and the words were no sooner out of his mouth when a shot rang out, and as he flinched back in surprise, Little John reached over and jerked him down to the floor just as a short burst, then a volley, followed that first shot.

Immediately, the barge erupted in loud shouts and screams as people scrambled first one way and then another, milling around in terror, some even jumping overboard. And then, suddenly, as quickly as it had started, it ended … and an eerie silence followed, broken only by fearful sobs, gasps of pain, and the moans of those injured or afraid.

Glenn and John stayed down until it seemed safe to move, and then after crawling back across the floor, they slowly eased themselves to their feet and peered hesitantly out the window toward the front of the boat.

Glenn was stunned by what he saw. The scene looked like the one in the *May 3rd Shooting*, a Napoleonic era war painting by Goya; he knew it because a print that he very much liked still hung in what was left of the university's art museum. As in that painting, the dead and injured there were strangely mingled while caring others crouched over them, sobbing as they cowered with a mix of anger and fear under the guns of faceless soldiers who stood primed, ready to fire again. The shooters this time were friendlies, but as in the painting, their victims seemed frozen, anxiously waiting for what might happen next.

Suddenly, a loud banging on the door behind the two jolted them both from their horror-struck gazes, and they spun around. John lunged forward, but Glenn flashed out a quick hand to grab his skirts and warn him away, and then he himself went to the door.

"Is the lady OK?" the lieutenant asked, his voice high and anxious, and this time he held his cap in both hands as he spoke. Glenn stared at him for a moment before he could muster an answer; the officer now looked like a worried twelve-year-old, and he and his men had just killed and wounded who knows how many people.

"Yes. Yes, lieutenant, we're safe, but what happened out there? My lady was trying to rest when there was all this noise. Did someone shoot at us?" Glenn asked, and he didn't have to act to add nervous feeling to his voice. "I hope not."

"No, sir, there was a disturbance with some regrettable violence, and my men had to quell it so that it wouldn't bother the lady. I trust the rest of her journey will be calm."

And with those words, he saluted and turned to go back to his men, who remained formed up along the side rail, standing in the at-the-ready position, their weapons still leveled and pointed toward the bunched-up, cowering passengers. Of course, no one else had guns, not even the federals, and so the friendlies had to have been the only ones firing.

"A couple look to be dead, several wounded," John muttered when Glenn closed the door. "One of the dead guys is the one who got caught with the contraband, wanta know what he died for?" John turned away from the window as he spoke, looking back toward Glenn who now stood in the middle of the room, sadly shaking his bowed head as he tried to sort out what had just happened.

"We both know what he died for. You heard what the officer said. They all died to protect the lady. They died to protect you," Glenn mumbled, and with his head still down, he walked over to the window where he stood quietly, just staring out, no longer aware of John. And he stood like that, breathing deeply for several seconds, lost in a study of the carnage, before adding, "What a brilliant plan I concocted."

"What do you mean? What are you talking about?"

"I mean all those people are dead and wounded because I created a great lady who needed to be protected." As he spoke, Glenn turned toward John, his eyes sad, his brow furrowed. "This is day two, blunder two, on my glorious mission to help people. I was supposed to help! I can't believe I've botched things so badly … right from the get-go."

"Come on, give me a break, Glenn." Little John held up a hand to stop him from going on. "That guy died for carrying contraband and for messing with the friendlies, and you'd better get used to this kind of thing. This and worse happens all the time. The rule is that if you get caught with contraband by the feds, you'd better expect to get beat up and maybe tossed in jail if you don't offer a payoff. This guy's mistake was resisting arrest when there were friendlies nearby.

Their motto is, 'Mess with the bull, you get the horn.' They shoot first and don't even bother to ask questions later. They don't have to. They're them, and we're only us. We're barely worth thinking about in their eyes, if you want the truth. Come on, this is all about where America is today, it's not about you."

"What are you talking about?"

"I'm talking about the real world you've come out into, Glenn." John reached out with his big hand, squeezing his friend's shoulder as he spoke. "Protecting an important lady will be nothing more than just a cynical paperwork excuse in that officer's report." Turning, he walked over to one of their chairs, and easing down into it, he tilted it back against the wall as he went on, "Now, you still haven't asked me about the contraband."

"OK, what was the big deal contraband that you say got that guy killed?"

"Hotdogs. Glenn, that guy was shot for smuggling hotdogs. But you know what else? He was actually shot for stiffing a federal who just wanted his usual payoff for looking the other way. Quota-crap, shootings, payoffs, and bounty hunters going after women wearing dresses—it's the way of life in this new world of ours. I guess this must be the big American *change*! the rest of world's all been waiting for, no more arrogance of power for us. That's been replaced by the subdued compliance of the shuffle-butt serf."

"Hotdogs? That doesn't make sense," Glenn started, but little John cut him off.

"No, you don't. You don't have the luxury of playing the guilt-trip, poor me for causing bad stuff game. This isn't about you or me. It's about the world of PAC and their decades long, steady drip-drip-drip, bleed America dry, take over here, even as some really bad guys outside our borders were moving to bring us down. But you know what? We shouldn't dwell on why we got where we are, our focus should be on the now and what we're going to do about it. I thought that was the Whig Partisan Alliance way."

"Of course. You're right," Glenn replied, and sighing and look-ing guiltily over at Little John, he slumped down onto the chair next to him, apologizing as they both turned to the lunch purchased yesterday. "I should have been the one saying everything you just said. This *is* our world now, and it's our job to suck it up and to deal with it the way it really is. This is where we are right now, and today is when we have to start if we're going to get back on track. We need to repeat that over and over until we almost can't stand it. There should be no looking back and no impotent self-doubt. We start where we are, right here, right now. Every day is another new first day for us, going forward."

"Yep! That's right. Just remember all that old-fashioned shining light on a hill stuff, and you'll stay right," John said, laughing his old laugh and flashing a WWW sign.

"To all that old shining light on the hill stuff," Glenn replied, and he too laughed, but then remembering where they were, he whispered a warning, "Hey, let's keep it down. Don't forget, you're a great lady, and great ladies don't have laughs that can be heard on both sides of this river—particularly mute great ladies. But you're right, my new friend. We will win."

At those words, John stood, and stepping back against the closed door, he lifted up the front of his dress, just a smidge … and curtsied.

Glenn, smothering a laugh, solemnly stood in response, and raising his right hand, he saluted his wise new friend with a sandwich—a hotdog, as it turned out.

Chapter Six

How an Angel Leads the Two to Meet a Worthy

The Peace River crossing was completed without further incident, but because of the problems on board, both the federals and friendlies formed up to provide an escort to protect the great lady when they landed. This left Glenn, who had not expected this turn of events, in a quandary; he had to find a way to ditch all of these guys. To buy time, he tried insisting that "the lady" had to stay in her cabin when they docked, saying that he needed to arrange transport. But that ploy died aborning with both sets of guardians beginning to grumble and the ferry schedule, itself, trumping everything. So he was back to square one—and time was not his friend. He needed a right-now plan, right now.

And then one seemed to just fall in his lap, when a dirty-faced local girl saved the day. Dressed in rags with a filthy looking yellow bag hanging limply from one slumped shoulder, she shuffled forward and holding her eyes respectfully down, pushed up to the Chinese lieutenant just as he was working up his courage to challenge Glenn. Explaining that she had made the crossing with them, she said she was concerned about the lady's comfort and especially worried that she might need to "rest" from her journey. Of course, such facilities were in short supply these days, but she told the officer that she knew of a place close by that offered the privacy needed. The lieutenant, eager to rejoin the ferry on its return voyage as planned, happily seized on the opportunity, and readily agreeing with her, he turned with a flourish to the federal sergeant and transferred all responsibility to him—whether he wanted or not. He didn't, but what could he do?

"Right this way, my lady," the girl chirped, and moving past the Chinese, now assembling on deck, and the federals, complaining their way down the gangplank, she led the confused great lady and Glenn ashore. Once there, the now three travelers turned to watch the friendlies sail away, and then after loudly announcing that she would show "her" the way to the restroom, the always-smiling townie reached for the great lady's very large hand. But Little John pulled away, groaning under his breath (everyone could hear him) as he shook his head and looked over to Glenn in a desperate plea for support.

Apparently the podium-throwing warrior didn't want to go to that intimate place with this young female, Glenn thought, laughing to himself. It was so funny that he did nothing at first except join the federals, all grinning at the amusing tug of war going on between the 290-pounder and the tiny little ragamuffin, just over a third her/his size; it made good theater. Everyone except John was enjoying the show, but only Glenn knew the whole story. Here was this big guy, who thrived on conflict, but yet couldn't handle the thought of being unmasked in the ladies' room by a small female townie.

Of course, Glenn knew that he had to help his buddy, so they could get on the road if for no other reason. But before he could decide when and how to make his move, the young girl once again asserted herself, and standing on tiptoe, she snuggled up to his panicked comrade and whispered something into his ear, something that caused his mood to shift in an instant. Suddenly, the big guy's anxiety seemed to just fade away, and as an unseen smile spread out under his dark veil, the now very relaxed lady waved off Glenn's unformed rescue plan and eagerly turning to follow the student, walked happily away.

With the tug-of-war over, the feds hesitated only briefly. They were still not happy to be stuck with this job, but they grudgingly fell in behind the two females, now heading off to their place of rest.

This left the still confused Glenn caught off guard, and not sure about what else to do, he settled for shuffling along behind them all. It was as if he was sort of cluelessly leading from behind—like a politician, he thought, grimacing.

They all trooped to a long closed gas station near the dock where the two ladies vanished inside. The federal sergeant then relaxed and turning to Glenn with a forced smile on his face, said, "Them women are lucky, finding a place with good water."

But Glenn, lost in thoughts about what to do next, ignored the sergeant's friendly gesture, leaving him feeling snubbed and angry. The fed started to challenge Glenn about it, but chose instead to head back to his men, loudly muttering, "Stupid friendlies lover."

Glenn, oblivious to his social error, moved off to the side just out of the feds' line of sight. Although a bit concerned about what might be going on right now in that old gas station, he was mostly focused on their situation. They needed a plan to get away from all these guys, but here he stood, stumped and coming up empty—yet again.

However, not to worry, people often say that good (and bad) things come in threes, and just as the dumping of the friendlies appeared to happen all on its own, the next two good things also just happened, or so it seemed, about fifteen minutes later.

"Sir." The sergeant reluctantly came back over to Glenn, and actually appeared to be trying to look squared away as he spoke, despite his scruffy clothes and week-long beard growth. "My squad's been ordered to escort the bodies and the wounded from the ferry shooting back into Arbortown on the next crossing. I've waited, thinking the lady might be ready by now, but she's not, and we have to get going to get there on time. Can I leave just two of my men here as escorts for the lady? I'm sure she'll be safe."

"Yes, of course, that'll be fine, sergeant," Glenn replied, a bit too quickly he feared. He didn't want this fed to see how relieved he was; two men they could easily manage, but not a whole squad.

And then, as he silently celebrated that break, a female student suddenly appeared behind the sergeant and reached past him to hand Glenn a note. As he took it, he noticed what seemed to be a pleased, maybe even smug, smile on her face, and he wondered what that was all about as he unfolded and read the message.

"I'm up the road, follow the student," it read, and although it was signed only with a smile face, Glenn guessed the author of those big, bold strokes. And so, although he had no idea what was going on, he decided to fake it. Turning to the sergeant, he told him that the great lady was tired and wished to sleep. They then agreed that two of the feds would remain at the rest area, allowing no one inside, and that while the lady slept, Glenn would follow this student to arrange further accommodations. With that done, the now smiling sergeant turned to organize his men, very pleased to be rid of what seemed to him to be a boring assignment, working with this arrogant friendlies-toady.

After watching the federal squad leave, a still confused Glenn played out the plan and nodding a goodbye to the two men left to guard the lady, he followed the student as she started walking away. Questions boiled about in his head, but he didn't speak until they were well down the road. Then, however, after glancing around to be sure the feds couldn't see them, he reached out for the young girl's narrow shoulder, and pulling her around to face him with a not too gentle grip, he finally vented his long bottled-up exasperation, "OK, I need some answers. Who are you, and where are the other two?

Let's have it, Miss whoever you are, what's going on here?"

"Got you on this one, didn't we?" she said, eyes dancing in a mischievous smile.

"What's this we-stuff? You got a frog in your pocket?" He was angry now.

"Wow, that's an oldie," she laughed, but then sensing that his frustration level just might be near the red mark, she flashed a quick WWW sign and added, "Sink me, I'm your contact on this side of the river. Call me J1, and hey, take a look at me! I came over with you on the ferry from Arbortown. Don't you recognize that dirty faced but very beautiful young townie who helped the great lady?"

Glenn, after studying her closely, finally nodded and said, "OOO-K, yes, I'll buy that." He was still confused, but now things did make some sense. He could see it; she was that girl. "How'd you do all of this? How'd you know us in the first place?"

"Despite that wonderful disguise?" she laughed again. "Actually, that great lady thing was a great idea! But anyway, to answer your question, I knew Little John from my first contact with him. I was the one who put him on your trail back at the dome."

She spoke with the easy mirth of a student, but Glenn caught something else in her eyes, and he realized that she was part of the bigger picture; she was the first link in the narrative chain Professor Benjamin had told him about. He'd said that the bad guys couldn't break it, and now he knew why. It was a chain with living links directing and watching over them as they traveled, keeping an eye on them as each new narrative event unfolded. They were sort of like guardian angels, angels who could adjust and respond to changing circumstances. It was a clever but very dangerous business, and so he knew they had to be special people, these angels. He smiled at that thought but didn't share it, not sure he should and wondering instead if he ought to apologize for his own behavior.

"OK, I'm beginning to see that there's a lot more to this than just an ex-student going to Whigville. A lot of planning has been done by a lot of people." Glenn frowned as he spoke, but at his own confusion, not at her, and then looking closely at J1, he added, "What I don't understand is, why? I'm certainly not important enough to—"

"Glenn, my old buddy!" A familiar voice cut off his comments, and he turned to see the old Little John approaching—back in his own clothes, but with bare feet.

"Where's your dress?" he asked, looking at John up and down. "And your boots?"

"That miserable outfit is stuffed up in the ceiling back at the station along with those big sequined flip-flops you forced me to wear," John replied gruffly. "I almost melted in the heat, I'll tell you, but I still kept my own clothes on under that tent you called a dress, except for my boots, that is. I guess my boots and gear are lost."

"You'll get your old gear back and some new boots at your next stop," J1 said. "But come on, tough guy, you can make it the way you are for the few blocks we still have to go. I'm sneaking you guys in the back way at a great place called the Two-Eyed Cyclops. But, John, remember that there are bounty hunters all over the place, and they'll all be very eager to collect on your head, dead or alive, preferably dead."

"They'd better make me dead, or they will be," John replied. "I'd like nothing better right now than a chance to shake off my mute time." He glowered over at Glenn.

"OK, fine, but why drop the disguise?" Glenn shot back, and ignoring John's look, he spoke to both of them. "How are we going to hide this clown now? The only thing bigger than he is, is that bounty on his head you mentioned. There'll be a hue and cry at our backs every step we take."

"You went off plan, and so we had to improvise. You did a great job of that, yourself, with your important lady bit, but that disguise wouldn't work going forward, and you don't need it. We think you'll be good once you're out of this area if you avoid the main roads. No one cares who PAC and the feds are looking for out here, and so just stay away from the bounty hunters, and you'll be home free—I hope. But you know what? Even if you do tangle with some bounty hunters, my money's on you two winning, just like in that vacant lot. But please promise me that next time you won't give them such an edge. Stay out of unsafe places!"

"We'll try, but with this guy along, every place is unsafe," Glenn said, laughing a very thin laugh; he was embarrassed by the poor choice he had made back in town.

"Not to worry, old buddy." John slapped him on the back. "We'll manage 'em."

Their walk, which seemed to be more a couple of miles than the promised couple of blocks, took them through mostly abandoned neighborhoods that bordered on Arbor University's vacant North Campus. All around them they saw what used to be great halls of learning now reduced to mere hollow-shelled, decaying ruins, living out their final purpose as stark and silent witnesses to what Glenn remembered his mentor calling the fey guardianship of the past several generations. It was their pathetic, self-serving hand on the plow that had bequeathed the harvest of this new day.

But something far more important than mere buildings caused that chill he felt going up and down his spine. As they trudged along, they could see young children off in the distance and could hear their cautious callings back and forth as they furtively flitted about among the rundown ruins. They were like wild things looking for scraps to eat or stuff to sell or just for a safe place to hide during the night. He had heard all about them from others. Called, "night callers," they were seen in PAC held areas all over the country—the fruit of PAC's long war on the old-fashioned family.

"Are we almost there?" John asked for the third time at least, and then grinning at the exasperated look J1 gave him, he added, "To be honest, I didn't know when I signed on to this gig that it included long periods of barefooted fasting. I'm not a good faster."

"You'll eat at the Two-Eyed Cyclops," she replied, casting him a mocking glare. "We call it the 'Clops,' and thankfully, that's where I get to unload you two moaners!"

"What do you think will happen to our guardians?" Glenn asked, choosing to ignore the back and forth bantering between the two. He wasn't in the mood for fun and games; the ferry killings still bugged him, and now those poor hungry kids all around them added to his down mood—with an even more sobering effect.

"They'll get slapped alongside the head." John laughed. "That sergeant will come back on the next crossing and find our two escorts sound asleep, and he'll think that we probably came out, saw them asleep, and left in disgust. I'll bet they'll all be very worried about being in a brew of friendlies' trouble over the whole thing."

"Yes, well, I suppose you're right about that, but I meant, what'll happen to those so-called friendlies who shot up the ferry?" Glenn replied. "I can't believe that even in this age of PAC's sham-peace a shooting like that would be ignored. Someone has to care. Do we even know for sure how many were killed? Or how many wounded?"

"Well, I was right in the middle of it, but I was too busy ducking for cover to see how it happened or how many were hit. I did hear some people talking though, saying that two died on the boat and several more were badly wounded and might die later. As to what will happen to the shooters, I'll tell you what. I'm going to let your next new friend speak to that," J1 replied, and as she spoke, she waved toward a thin, older man who sat waving back to them from what was left of an old gazebo just off the road.

It stood or rather sagged with flaking white paint under the weight of too many years and a too heavy vine, but it offered a shelter of sorts and the newish looking white plastic chairs it held were a welcome sight after their long walk. From Little John's point of view, however, the most important consideration was that the gazebo stood beside an empty parking lot, and on the other side of that parking lot was their much looked-forward-to eating place, the Two-Eyed Cyclops. They were there! Almost.

"Are we going to talk here or over a meal?" John asked, a bit afraid of the answer.

"Ah, you must be the now infamous Little John." The older man stood to greet them, smiling as he spoke. His voice had the cadence and rumble of an announcer or public speaker, neither of which he was or ever had been. "I've been looking forward to meeting both of you, but particularly this intimidator of intimidators."

"Sir, I give you Little John, of unfortunate great fame, and our other passenger, Glenn Alleyne Stanton," J1 said, stepping back to allow them all to reach across and shake hands as she introduced them. "And gentlemen, it's my pleasure to introduce you to Oren Mithandir, Worthy of Whigville and a Grong-Grong founder."

"My honor, sir." Glenn stepped ahead of his John to seize the older man's hand in both of his. "Professor Benjamin has told me ..."

"No names, Glenn," J1 corrected him. "You must get used to that. No names."

"I'm sorry," Glenn blushed. He knew the rule that each narrative must be kept separate and why that was important. "But I'm honored to meet a founding Worthy."

"Worthy?" John looked quizzically back and forth. "I guess I'm the only one here who has no idea what you're all talking about, and what's this Grong-Grong thing?"

"A Worthy is a leader of the resistance, and this gentleman is one of the founders of the Whig Partisan Alliance. Grong-Grong is just a small crossroads town in Australia, but it's one of our founding places," Glenn explained, and stepping back to allow John to get in his own handshake, he still continued to pursue his earlier question about the ferry shootings. "Sir, I wonder about the ferry shootings. Have you heard what happened?"

"Oh yes, news travels fast even in this collapsed-technology age," he replied. "But please, before we begin our talk, let me ask that you call me by my first name, Oren, and let's all sit down and relax. It's a hot day, but there's a bit of shade here and some water, but sorry to say ..." Glancing over at John, he smiled and shrugged. "No food."

J1 and Glenn both laughed at John's reaction to the food comment, and then she turned to leave as the others took their seat, calling back, "I'll go ahead to arrange for your ... *meal.*" She emphasized that very important last word just for John.

"That'd be great, and I hope it's not too far off." The big guy called after her, seemingly not at all embarrassed by his food-before-conversation attitude.

"The murders on the barge are of the same stuff that's being perpetrated all across this country by our so-called protectors," Oren said, frowning grimly and ignoring John's food focus as he spoke. "It's all part of the new morality given to us by PAC. We, in the Alliance, call it the *Cheshire Cat-Tiger Cage Ethic* or just plain *Tiger Cage.* It emerged in the sixties during the Vietnam War, and it's been used regularly ever since. That ethic, a sham really, involves overlooking any and all sins and crimes that are committed by those who opposed America then or by PAC today, while at the same time magnifying the slightest blemish or even the most minor mistakes made by our side. In Vietnam, our allies used such cages to hold prisoners, and those were held-up as stark examples of America's evil lack of humanity by the future power-at-the-center types. But when our allies lost that war, after being betrayed by our own congress, the rules shifted. And as if by magic, our critics' old outrage and high moral indignation about the "inhumanity" associated with such detentions vanished like a grinning Cheshire cat, even as the new rulers went on to imprison, torture, and kill thousands upon thousands of their own citizens. And what had been a handy political symbol to use against

America now became invisible to those of our elite who had stood against us in that war. Even worse, those same cages were offered up as humane alternatives to being shot, as if that was the only alternative; liberty, freedom, and justice were never mentioned or considered. The truth is that these budding power-at-the-center types could see then and do see now with only a single, ideological eye. Devoid of a balanced vision of truth or even our common humanity, they were and are half-blind to reality. Their pitiful peace signs and talk of love was smothered by the stench of the rotting bodies they had helped make possible.

"Those half-blind people, who were even then forming PAC, ignored the mass exodus of thousands of fearful Vietnamese who risked their lives to flee from that new tyranny in a desperate search for safety and freedom away from their homeland. And just as those we came to call Boat People were ignored by the emerging world of PAC-lovers, decades later a prison that had been drenched in blood and misery in Iraq for decades, with no notice nor even the slightest condemnation, suddenly became a symbol for PAC to broadcast about to the world as just one more example, for them, of American cruelty.

"'American' is the key word here. And you should never ever forget this all-important point: PAC held us up then and holds us up now to a narrow standard of perfection, not to really help others or improve us, but to empower themselves.

"Now, of course, we need to have, and always have had, very high standards for our own behavior. But there's a vast difference between self-criticism based on standards maintained as part of a healthy self-regard and those of PAC's sick and self-destructive, but very self-serving, neurotic criticisms. Today, PAC fosters 'blame America first' at every turn because such finger pointing keeps the focus off PAC's failures all around us.

"But friends, it's to *our own shame* that instead of doing an honest bump and go through them to tackle our problems head on, we settled instead for a pathetic *Poor us, all is lost,* wimp-waltz. This has allowed them to shut down all honest debate since then with their *HUSH-NOW* rules, forbidding Americans to look behind their sham-shame control curtain of 'settled-science' in any area, from race to economy—to thinking, itself."

"Yes, sir, and our fight now is to help our people get back on their feet and back on the road marching toward a PAC-less future." An enthused Glenn jumped in, speaking earnestly to both men, including a now suddenly very interested Little John.

"That's what the Alliance is all about," John contributed. "I may not know as much about history as you do, sir, but I do know a lot of it. I know that we came so very close to being what we could have been once, and we can do it again."

"We did come close, men, very close, but we got little credit for that among those who became PAC," Oren said, and standing, he began pacing back and forth as he continued. "There's an example that's passed down through our ranks that I want to share. In the years after World War II, there was a television program called the *Groucho Marx Show*. He was a famous comedian, and his show was very popular at the time, but it's been held up by PACies since as an example of our failure as a country because both the typical audience and contestants on that show were almost always white.

"Of course, that whiteness did reflect the tragic place where my own people were on the road to becoming an equal part of this good and great land, and I don't deny that.

But the criticism is unfair because it overlooks wonderful truths about America and about the progress we had made and were making even then toward a full *E pluribus unum*.

"That audience and the contestants included people from groups that had fought each other tooth and nail for over a thousand years in Europe, including just a few years before that show in the most destructive war in history. But they all now stood up there on TV as just plain, ordinary, everyday Americans—no hyphens. And think about this, a Jew hosted that show only a very few years after the world had witnessed the horror of an effort to murder every Jew in Europe. But to his viewers, that Jew was just a very funny and talented fellow American. Note, I said, American, to repeat, no hyphen was needed.

"What I'm saying is the great coming together that show represented should have been *the* lesson for us all, indeed a lesson to hold up to the whole world. But early PAC types were blind to the real lesson, and beginning in the 60s, they pointed to that show as an example of exclusion. Once again, with this as with so much else, what is really an American virtue was stood against the wall and condemned because we were not then, are not now, and never will be perfect. Of course, there's never been and never will be a perfect people—look, for example, at the tribal divisions in Africa, Asia, and the Middle East today. But *we* were on the road to making *from many, one* a reality for the first time in all of human history, anywhere. And my people had their foot on that road at last.

"Sad to say, our schools and universities quit teaching that fact when they quit teaching real history and literature. The great Roman philosopher Cicero warned that not knowing what happened before we are born leaves us always as children. Well, I say that it's just as bad to not know how other cultures stack up against your own in every area, including such things as minority or women's rights, because one-eyed Cyclops teachers are busy spooning out politically correct propaganda instead of teaching the truth about the world and our long march toward, we hope, *E pluribus unum*—worldwide!

"Of course, the beginnings of our decline now long predated the foolish sixties' children's crusade, but it was then that our elite, to borrow from G. K. Chesterton [Glenn smiled at that name], decided that our march toward being one people was too difficult—or really politically inconvenient—to be continued. Thus, the PAC-skids were greased. Oh, there was still some progress for a while, but our society faltered, and the pre-Power-at-the-Center zealots began their takeover. Their first step was to openly abandon our *E pluribus unum* dream by imposing a society-wide, one-eyed, *Hush-Now* inquisition. And from that came the inevitable slide into the tragic nightmare we see all around us today.

"As for my people, we more than most should have learned enough about our own history to protect and defend our path to full citizenship. We rose from slavery in America and elsewhere largely because British Christians in the nineteenth century decided to stop the slave trade, and for the first time in human history, slavery was being challenged. Throughout history, every people had taken slaves, and every people had suffered under slavery's lash, but even as it ended, it was my people who remained far more at risk, especially since the slave traders out of the Middle East could continue their trade for decades after it was stopped elsewhere. You see, they could still reach their African helpers and herd their captives back by land, away from the British gunboats.

"But we made many gains during the twentieth century in America, and so by the fifties we had our foot on the same road to full citizenship that many others had traveled before us. Within a very few years, thanks to the generous heart of America and to the courage and great leadership of so many great people, best symbolized by Martin Luther King Jr., we had begun to be fully accepted as one group of travelers among so many others, and we were on the verge of being just another part of that cheering throng of happy, caring Americans—no hyphen needed. But for PAC, my people had become too important as political fodder to be allowed to become merely another enriching addition to the whole, and PAC chose to do something about it.

"Think about it. We, as a nation, were at last—finally—becoming fully just one people, and no one had forced that on us. We, as Americans, had chosen to stand as one, and we did it for ourselves, all of ourselves. Then PAC intervened, and our road forward became littered with barriers for some and fast tracks for others, and King's dream of an America where it was character and not color or group that counted, faded. And sad to say, all of this was to the disadvantage of everyone, and all of us of every group are now paying a price for our failure to breath full life into our national motto. But, of course, our continuing division works to PAC's power advantage, as is and has been their plan.

"Now understand, we're all tempted to fail as PAC does by viewing others through a single eye of prejudice in favor of our own people or ideology, but the Whig Partisan Alliance Calling is symbolized by the name of the place where you'll soon be eating." He gestured across the parking lot. "We are called to help the world look beyond tribes and nations and ideologies with our God-given special soul-eye and to see not just what seems to be in our own self-interest, however we define that, but also—through our second soul-eye—to see that all human beings deserve the same full lives we deserve. Our animal eye looks out for self-interest and preservation, and we need that eye, but we're called to love and serve others as well … that's our two-eyed calling."

"We will win!" A fired up Glenn spoke the words with feeling, and reaching out to both of them for a handshake, he added, "I don't mean just America, the whole world needs freedom, and the whole world had freedom on the horizon until PAC happened."

"Time's flying gang," J1 called out, waving as she approached them carrying a pack and a pair of gigantic boots for Little John. "We retrieved all your gear except your boots, hungry man, so here are some new ones. You two need to saddle up and head for the back of the restaurant. Irma and Bev are waitresses here, and they're expecting you. But snap it up, you need to move out now. The crowd's growing, and they won't be able to hold your table for long without someone wondering why." She stopped, and smiling broadly at Little John, she added, "Besides, I know how hungry you are, little man."

In response, John hurriedly bent to his task, crouching to splash some water on his feet before pulling on his socks and boots. Then standing, he pulled her over, stooping to give her a big bear hug; he owed her a lot, and he knew it. She pulled away, laughing, and after sharing hugs with the other two, she turned to hurry back toward the dock.

"Thanks, angel!" Glenn shouted after her.

"Angel. Umm, I like that," Little John said. "Glad I thought of it. It's perfect."

"I like it too, Little John," Oren said, nodding. "And let me say thank you for listening to my little lecture. I know I was preaching to the choir, but I had to get it out."

"I loved your Chesterton quote, my mentor often mentioned him," Glenn said.

"You mentioned him yourself back in Arbortown," John cut in, and laughing at Glenn's surprised reaction, he added, "Didn't think I was listening, did you?"

They both wanted to continue their conversation with Oren, but they were able to talk only a few more minutes before needing to head toward the back of the restaurant. They asked him to join them for a meal, but he begged off, saying that he had one more traveler to see at the gazebo and places to get to that night. And then, after a smiling goodbye, he settled back in his chair to wait as they started out across the parking lot.

"Seems like a short talk for such an important man," John said as they hurried toward the rear of the restaurant. "Not that I'm complaining, I'm hungry."

"My guess is that he accomplished what he came to do before we got to him. And he probably just wanted to lay eyes on us as long as he was here, for future reference," Glenn said. But he kept looking back over his shoulder at the gazebo as they walked away, wondering about things. "But, John, I still can't figure why so much effort and so many people are involved to get us to Whigville. You know, there's been my old mentor, a friendlies colonel, and now, a real Worthy—if you can imagine that. Then, of course, we have our angel with maybe more of them coming. And it's not just the people we see, think of all the planning. There must be others. It just doesn't make sense to me."

"Yes, well you can wonder about all that clutter," John replied, looking over at their soon to be chow house as they walked around to the back. "But for right now, I'm more focused on eating."

"I hear you and agree, my man." Glenn laughed. "You're not the only hungry one here."

CHAPTER SEVEN

How Three Come Together at the Two-Eyed Cyclops

*T*he two companions stood sweating, it seemed for far too long, in the shade of the lone tree behind the Two-Eyed Cyclops, waiting for a signal to go inside. There was no breeze there, and they were hungry, which didn't help their cause. So by the time a young woman appeared at the back door to wave them in, they were more than ready.

"I'm starving, what took so long?" Little John grumbled as they reached the door, but his mood quickly changed when he saw their new ally—a beautiful young woman. She wore a T-shirt picturing a colorful Two-Eyed Cyclops across the front and ordinary blue jeans that were covered by a curious looking half-apron that immediately caught John's eye. Intrigued by it all, he said, "You know, I wondered what a Two-Eyed Cyclops would look like, and I love it, but what's with that great apron—all those colors?"

"Never mind all of that, just get in here—quickly!" She whispered, and stepping back past them after ushering them inside, she leaned out, peering cautiously around for any sign of troublesome eyes. Once satisfied that no one was lurking about out there, she turned, and after frowning first at John, she jabbed an air finger at them both and sternly warned, "You must stay quiet, you must be on your guard, and you must … not … draw unnecessary attention to yourselves. Please, that's very important—no undue attention!"

"Hi, my name is John. Some people call me Little John, but *you* can call me whatever you want to," the big man said, offering his best smile and his hand. But he had to settle for nothing but an impatient shrug in return as the young lady, ignoring him, his smile, and his hand, continued with her instructions.

"This place was teeming with bounty hunters and feds earlier, but they've all gone now, so we can get you seated. We've set up a good place that'll put this little challenge, whatever he said his name was, under the stairs and in the shadows." She nodded toward John as she acknowledged their dual problem—his size and wanted status. But then, after feigning a deep sigh, she finally gave in to his sad gaze and shaking her head as if truly reluctant to do so, smiled and added, "OK, I'm Irma. Bev and I will be on duty while you're here, and you should talk to no one else but us! No one else, do you understand?"

"Oh, I promise, you can count on me." John smiled back, again offering his hand.

"Thanks," Glenn cut in, and grinning at the interplay between the two as they shook hands, he added, "Don't worry, we'll be quiet. But I'm not sure about being in such a conspicuous place. This is as dangerous for you as it is for us."

"It's extremely dangerous. That's why I want our little acting-out friend here to behave," she replied sternly, but there was a twinkle in her eye as she spoke. And then, having made her point, she led them across the kitchen, temporarily emptied to make way for them, and on up to some swinging doors where she stopped to peer into the dining hall. Satisfied it was safe, she motioned for them to follow and pushed on into the room. The two men, keeping their faces averted, filed along the wall behind her, passing by the restrooms on the way to a table tucked into a small area under the open stairs. It was close to a staff-only door, and the only other table there was set up as a wait-table.

As John and Glenn sat down, Irma glanced around the room to be sure they weren't attracting unwanted attention and then said, "I'll be keeping an eye on things from up front, and Bev will be over to take your orders in a couple of minutes. So just kick back and enjoy, but please, please remember to stay put and stay quiet." She looked at

John. "I'll check back on you." And as she walked away, smiling and shaking her head, she obviously said something funny to Bev who passed by her on the way to their table.

"Hi, I'm Bev," the new waitress said, still trying to stifle a laugh and get serious as she spoke. "I know Irma explained things to you, but I'll add my two-feds worth, just for emphasis. All our necks are on the line right now, especially the boss's, so keep it quiet and do *not* attract attention to yourselves. OK, now if you think you've got that, I'll take your order; I know you must be hungry. We've got it all, and it's all good."

"Hi, I'm John and ..."

"I know who you are, Little John," she smiled politely. "But for right now, just place your order and stay quiet. And no matter what happens, stay in your seats."

"Let's order," Glenn cut in on the eye play going on between the other two, and as he looked over the menu, he wondered what kind of clown this Little John character was; he needed to focus on business, not flirting. "How about a steak burger, half-pound, with fries and a side of rings?" he ordered. "And toss in some coleslaw and ... oh yes, just water to drink right now, if it's good. I know it's hard to get good water these days."

"We have our own well and purification system, and it's very good," she replied as she turned her attention to Little John who was still studying the menu with a how-can-I-choose-only-one-meal expression on his face. It took him a while, but he finally sorted it all out and tossed the menu aside, looking up at her with a broad grin.

"I'll have the same, but make it two full-pounders, and whatever you've got dark on tap, and ah, oh yes, double the fries. But then, rethinking his order, he paused to look back at the menu. And after only a few seconds, he looked up with a big grin on his face and enthusiastically reordered, "Nope, scrap that. Make it four very big eggs, lightly scrambled, with those previous steaks tossed in, and make it mashed potatoes with a side of gravy and biscuits. No, change that. Make it a lot of gravy and just dump it all over everything, even the eggs and steaks, and switch the drink to cold water and a lot of black coffee—and keep it coming; I like coffee." He looked up with a grin as he finished, and handing Bev his menu, he winked and added, "And let's double his rings order too."

Once the ordering was finally over, Glenn leaned back to look around at the place, and as he studied that big room and the other patrons, he felt himself relax. They all looked like locals, probably business or trader types, and he guessed all were regulars. Playing with that thought, he decided that he really liked what he saw and would enjoy being a regular here, himself. It looked like a cowboy movie set with all its open beams and tons of stone and logs and heavy wooden tables and iron tools. But no, this stuff all looked like the real thing, especially those authentic looking branding irons. He grinned. Well, he couldn't tell for sure, but he wanted it all to be genuine real working ranch stuff.

And when Bev delivered the food, he asked, "What's the story here, particularly that fantastic looking long bar? It looks like the real thing, straight out of the old west."

"Yes, everyone loves it," she replied. "We call it our Texas Long Bar, but it's really from a place called Twenty-Nine Palms, which is somewhere in California. The boss used to work out there, but we don't talk about that these days." And then, turning with a broad smile and a playful sniff toward Little John, she added, "His name is Allen Peterson, but everyone here calls him … *Big* Al."

"Sounds like a good name, I like it," Little John said between bites, and then smiling appreciatively, he pointed to her apron. "I like this whole place, especially your aprons, but I don't think they're from the old west, at least not the old west in the USA."

"No, they're from a place called Estonia. Big Al's grandmother, I think it was, came from there when she was a little girl. Her family was fleeing some war, I don't know which, but Al said they were taken over by some other country," Bev said.

"Yes, they were," John replied. And still munching, but now suddenly serious, he put his fork back down and, pursing his lips in thought, added, "First, I think it was the Russians invading, then came the Germans, and then the Russians again. So, who his grandma—or probably great grandma—was fleeing depends on when she got out."

"Impressive!" Glenn sat back in his chair, looking at his friend with new eyes.

"Yes, it is. How do you know all of that?" Bev asked, and after glancing around the room to be sure no one else needed her, she slipped into a chair across from them. "We sing songs here that Big Al says are from there—or sung in the same old spirit, maybe, I'm not sure. He said that when his mother's people were taken over they used music to hold themselves together as a nation, and that same music helped them to rally later, so they could stand up to their occupiers. That's how they won their freedom."

"I'm surrounded by historians," Glenn said. "I don't know about this story, but I do know that vandals take over ONE TRUTH Park on campus every once in a while, and they rename it after a place somewhere over there. I've seen that happen a lot."

"Oh yes, we've heard about that park thing." Bev smiled and started to say more, but glancing over her shoulder, she saw Irma coming towards them with a businesslike look on her face, and she quickly stood up, whispering, "I'd better get back to work. I see Irma heading this way, and it looks like something's up."

"Hey guys, break it up," Irma said. "Bounty hunters are headed here, and to make it worse, Alton Pennington and his bunch may be coming too." And obviously worried, she added, "So stay down, stay quiet, and please, please, keep to your own business!"

John, sliding his chair farther back under the stairs, whispered to Irma with an embarrassed look on his face, "Sorry, but I gotta *go*, do you think it's too dangerous?"

"No, use that one." She nodded toward a door next to the wait-table. "It's really for staff, but you're OK to use it. Just try to be back before those guys get here, bounty hunters and Alton aren't a good mix. So, hurry up. I gotta get back to the door."

"You know," John said as he rejoined Glenn, "earlier today I used the ladies' room by the landing and now the women's toilet here. Is that a pattern of some kind?"

"Yes, it means you're evolving into a woman, a very ugly woman as we've seen." Glenn laughed. But then, ignoring John's annoyed grunt, he looked quickly around to be certain they didn't have eyes on them before leaning over their table with a serious look on his face to ask, "What's with you and all this history? How'd you know all that stuff?"

"I love history, always have, and I've read a lot of it on my own, not much else to do these days," John replied. "That was my biggest disappointment when I got to the uni, they don't teach history. They don't even know real history and don't want to know."

"Well, these days you don't have to learn all that old stuff. PAC gives you a truth script and you blindly follow it," Glenn said, recalling his own mentor's frustration with the state of things at Arbor U as he spoke.

"Yeah, that's the truth now, but these are the days and the ways that I want to help end. That's why I'm here," Little John replied, and then leaning back, he took a sip of coffee and scowled in disgust as he looked around at the still quiet but now threatened room. Just thinking about the mess his country was in, angered him. What a waste!

The quiet lasted so long that they were almost finished with their meal before the front door crashed open, and four men came swaggering in. Three were average height with big bellies hanging over wide belts that held sheathed fighting knives on one side and Billy clubs on the other. The fourth man was short and thin, and although he wore no weapons, his quota-category meant that he was in charge. And as they moved into the room, he scowled around, eyeing everyone, including the indistinct shadow-duo sitting behind the stairs, before motioning his men to a table where they could watch everything and everyone. Guessing them to be the warned about bounty hunters, John and Glenn sagged back even deeper into the shadows.

"We don't need no menus, we need our usual drinks and four full-pounders with double fries. You know how we like 'em," one of them barked at Irma, and after glancing around his own table for confirmation, he glowered over at three older men seated at a table next to them and snapped, "What're you fools lookin' at? We look funny to you?"

"The man asked you a question, and he needs a reply," snarled another big belly, turning threatening eyes on their now very uncomfortable neighbors.

"Nothing. We're not looking at anything," one of the obviously rattled older men replied, and he and his companions began nervously pulling their things together to leave.

"Stay seated!" A voice boomed out from the doorway behind them, and all eyes in the room turned in that direction. Big Al Peterson, about the same size and frame as Little John but a good thirty years older, stood there with his arms crossed over his chest, studying the four bounty hunters with contempt. Then, after a long minute, he moved to their table, his eyes never leaving them as he leaned down on it, bracing himself on his knuckles. Now looming over them, he glowered squarely at their leader, and nodding toward the three men they had attacked, he demanded, "You four will apologize to these good guests of mine, and you'll buy 'em a round of whatever they're drinking to bind it."

There was a stir at the bounty hunters' table, but their leader, trying to calm the situation, held up a hand to settle his men as he smiled up at Big Al and replied, "I'm not sure what you think we done, Al, but I guess we can afford to buy these good men a drink. After all, it never hurts to be friendly, and maybe they can buy us a round later."

"You won't be a later," Al replied, his eyes steady on their mark. "I've warned you about making trouble and chasing away my customers. You're out of here, for good."

"Hey, we got food comin' to us, and I'm hungry," one of them complained.

"Your food order's cancelled, but your drinks are comin' now, so finish 'em fast and get out," Al snapped. Then, standing up straight, he stepped back, rubbing his right fist knuckles in his left hand as he added, "I'm tired of you clowns, you're nothing but trouble-makin' riff-raff. I want you out, and I don't want you coming back—ever!"

"Yer the one makin' trouble, and fer yourself," the one facing him snarled.

"Hey, don't put off 'til tomorrow what you can fail to do today," Al replied, and now smiling broadly, he raised both hands with palms up, motioning "come on" with his fingers. But the bounty hunters, responding to a whisper from their leader, turned quietly to the drinks that had just arrived … and made no further eye contact with Big Al.

Back under the stairs, Glenn, releasing the hand he had on Little John's tensed arm, turned a tight calculating grin over at his friend. "Good job, you kept your cool, and you didn't attract attention our way," he said.

"Well, I wasn't going let four bad guys jump that one dude, who is he anyway?"

"My guess is that he is our current guardian, the owner of this place."

"Yep, I think you're right," John said, and then stretching his big arms out and back over his head, he laced his fingers behind his thick neck and rested his head back into them as he grinned over at Glenn and added, "I hope you wouldn't have tried to hold me back if they'd jumped him. You know you couldn't have done it, don't you?"

"Let me clarify something," Glenn replied, and after first looking sharply at his companion, he glanced around to be sure they weren't attracting attention before leaning over their table to continue, in a whisper. "I believe you're supposed to be my babysitter, not the other way around. You got a great start on that job over in Arbortown, so let's get back to that. We don't need two babysitters and no baby—if you get my meaning."

"Yes, you're saying that if you're going to do my job, you don't need me," John answered, meeting Glenn's eyes. But he wasn't grinning, and he was obviously sincere when he went on to add, "Look, I'm sorry, I know you're right and that I've complicated things for you, but I can do the job I'm supposed to do. We'll get to Whigville."

Across the room, the bounty hunters, after deliberately delaying for as long as they thought they could, finally finished their drinks and left without saying a word. A full hour then went by without another incident or any kind of contact attempt, and both John and Glenn grew increasingly impatient, eager to get on with whatever was supposed to happen next. On top of that, the room was filled now, and with all the tables occupied, they felt bad about holding down a spot that someone who would order something to eat or drink might use. But when they mentioned that to Bev, she brushed off their concerns, poured them some more coffee, and whispered, "Just relax and stay put. We're on plan."

"Hey, look at that." John laughed a few minutes later, pointing toward two tables near the front door where some drinkers had started stacking their cans. "My granddad was a military policeman back in the day, and he told me that the marines on his base used to stack real beer cans just like that. He loved it when they did that because it meant that he was going to get some action. Of course, these days, we only have those stupid looking clunky federal ration cans, but I'll bet this is all gonna end the same way."

"I've seen some of those old cans on display at the museum. They were very light and colorful," Glenn replied, nodding. "But what do you mean about the way it'll end?"

"Well, it might not. Those things don't stack very well," John said, and frowning over at Glenn, he complained, "I'm sick of everything being all the same color with no design or character, and I'm sick of seeing that ugly PAC seal on everything."

"Sure, I agree, but what might not? What are you talking about?" Glenn, by now also closely watching the can-stackers, spoke without looking at John. As the stacked empties grew higher, they grew wobblier and their stackers tried to steady them, leading to charges of holdin' from the other tables, something apparently not allowed. Glenn laughed, enjoying the action as arguments broke out at the tables about the difference between holdin' and steadyin'. "Come on, John," Glenn whispered, glancing away toward his buddy and then back again at the teetering towers. "What's going to happen?"

"Just watch," John whispered back, with a big grin spreading across his face. The tension was building with each added can, and a lot of good-natured bickering was going on as all eyes fixed on those two by now very shaky stacks and on their oh-so-careful stackers, huddling around their stacks, trying to add just … one … more … can.

Then, suddenly, two rogue cans came sailing in from the shadowy doorway, and the stacks exploded into a can-fall of clattering chaos. Cans went everywhere, spilling off both tables onto and around the floor, causing everyone in the place to jerk back in surprise, all looking about, still laughing but now wondering.

"That's it!" John shouted, but then quickly shushing himself, he slid farther back into the dark with an embarrassed glance over at Glenn, who was now sitting back, wide-eyed and laughing at all the excitement.

But that laugh ended abruptly, and his eyes narrowed when he saw who the can throwers were; the bounty hunters were back— and they were not alone. They had three federals with them, which meant that there were now seven possible problems haughtily looking around the room. And even worse, while all the feds looked a bit familiar, it was certain that one of them was the sergeant who had earlier led their escort from the ferry. And he was looking in their direction ... wearing a very broad, self-satisfied smile.

"Oh, no. Do you see who's here?" Glenn hissed over the chaos. The crowd was now on its feet in response to the assault on the cans, and Little John had eased himself halfway out of his chair. Glenn, noticing that, jumped up and reached over to grab the back of his friend's collar, shouting, "Stay put! It's the sergeant from the ferry, and I think he recognizes me. We're in big trouble if he puts everything together."

By then the room around them had erupted into a swarm of churning bodies with everyone seemingly going after everyone else at first, but sides soon began forming, and it became the bounty hunters and their federal friends against the rest. For a while it was no more than just the kind of good-natured pushing and shoving that Little John's marine MP grandfather had experienced all those years ago, and Big Al, who was standing with Irma behind the bar, didn't even bother to come out.

But when the numbers began to tell and the tide turned fully against them, the leader of the bounty hunters played his ace in hole. Pulling out a handgun, he raised it high over his head ... and fired one shot into the air. Instantly, the room fell quiet and everyone froze, stunned and afraid to move.

"Are you crazy, man?" Big Al's surprised voice boomed out over the suddenly very still room. "It's a firing squad offense if the friendlies catch you with that, and I don't tolerate weapons in my place. You drop it now, or I take it away from you!"

"Keyword's *catch*, Al," the bounty hunter leader jeered, grinning over toward the federal sergeant, who grinned back. "You can try to take my gun away, but right now, I gotta say, it's the owner of this place who's in trouble and not me. Al, you're guilty of harborin' fugitives and arrestin' federal fugitives is what me and my friends do."

"And shootin' vermin's what I do," a new voice came from behind the gun-holder, accompanied by the distinct sound of a weapon being cocked. "You, ugly, drop that puny little shooter right now, and all seven of you punks ... put your hands over your heads. And I mean reach 'em high and keep 'em high. Do it right now, not tomorrow!"

"You know what you're doin'?" The sergeant sputtered over his shoulder as his bounty hunter buddy's weapon clattered to the floor. But he flinched when he felt a firm, worrisome pressure in his back, and quickly jerking his eyes to the front and pushing his hands up even higher, he weakly added, "I'm a federal sergeant."

"You're a two-bit rent-a-punk," replied the voice, and as he spoke, he shoved them ahead of him, easing forward from the shadows where he'd been standing for the past several minutes. There was no gun visible, and noticing that, the bounty hunter leader eyed the weapon he'd too quickly dropped. It was on the floor still not far from his feet, but if he had plans to risk reaching down for it, he changed his mind when the man who had the drop on them threw off the thin travel cloak he wore, revealing the very real—and very illegal—dress jacket of a captain in the United States Marine Corps. The quiet that had gripped the room after the shot now deepened— all eyes on the captain.

"You can't be serious. You'll go to jail for wearin' that," the sergeant snapped, and eyeing the gun on the floor, he added. "And I'm gonna get that gun and arrest you."

"Too late, all the arrestin's been done," the captain replied, a big smile forming on his face as he looked calmly and deliberately around the room, scrutinizing the others there. Then, apparently satisfied with his survey, he gave a short laugh, and turning his eyes back to the still ceiling-reaching seven, he herded them a few more steps forward as he called out to the now hushed crowd, "OK, friends, you need to say goodbye to these jerks. Let's call 'em the 'migrating seven' from now on, because they're going to be migrated out of here to a holdin' place. You'll miss 'em, but you gotta let 'em go."

"You won't get away with this," the sergeant snarled, but he was careful to keep his hands up and his eyes forward as he spoke, choking out only a weak, "It's illegal."

"Oh wait, of course, you're right. I almost forgot PAC rules. How foolish of me to forget that two of you seven are due the *High Justice*." Pushing them forward another step, he looked around at the crowd with a grin on his face and called out, "These poor affirm-status fixated punks need to be made to feel more at ease about their fate. So I'm doing the numbers: I, a quotaed-black male, place you, a very poor excuse for a military sergeant and a quotaed-black male, and your bird-faced buddy, the leader of these bounty hunters, who looks like a quotaed-brown male, and all your low-quotaed white male crew under arrest." Then, laughing loudly, he waved a hand at the now approving, clapping crowd and added, "So there it is folks, all nice 'n neat 'n affirm-positive, PAC rules for PAC puppies, miserable misfits that they all are."

"What's with the migrating stuff?" Glenn whispered from where he'd ended up just behind the captain. "Where're they going? Why the uniform?"

"Migrating means they're being shipped out of here to some faraway place where they'll be watched for a while and kept out of trouble," the captain replied in a whispered aside. He was keeping his eyes on the crowd as they swarmed the captives, binding their hands and pushing them towards the door. But once they were gone, he looked around at Glenn and added, "I'm Captain Alexander Bullard Crosby, but people I like call me Alex. The uniform is mine, and I'm wearing it for effect."

"I'm Glenn ..."

"Yes, Glenn, I've been looking forward to meeting you," Alex cut him off, and nodding toward the stairs, he added, "And your buddy, sitting over there in the dark. I'm the third team member you've been waiting for."

"Team member? We knew we were waiting for a contact, but I didn't know we were waiting for a third team member," Glenn replied, his eyes still lingering on the doorway even though the prisoners were now gone. "You know, I'm not sure what's going on here. Won't these guys be missed? And I should ask, if our being here comes out, will we be blamed for it all?"

"That's an empty worry, my friend." Alex laughed. "Bounty hunters are always killing each other off, and no one cares. As for the federals, their desertion rate is so high no one even bothers to check any longer. So rest easy, you won't be blamed for those guys." Then, frowning, he studied Glenn for a moment before adding, "But you can be blamed for leaving your post. You were supposed to stay where we put you, and only one of you did that. Your moving could have made my job a lot harder."

"Yes, you're right. I'm sorry." Glenn whispered his reply. He was embarrassed to admit it, but he honestly didn't know how he'd gotten all the way across the room; somehow he'd just drifted over. He glanced sheepishly over at Little John to see how he was reacting to his buddy's mistake, but the big man wasn't reacting at all. Now with a glass of that something dark he had ordered earlier, he was leaning back with a big satisfied looking grin on his face, thoroughly enjoying the whole show.

The crowd outside roared as the seven bad guys were turned over to some of Alex's friends, who began marching them away just as Alton Pennington arrived. And Alton, bummed that he had missed all the action, made up for it by pulling everyone together and leading them all in a round of mostly illegal songs. He started them off with a very good version of the Marine Corps Hymn in honor of their new hero, followed by a medley of other old military, religious, and folk songs. And they wrapped up everything with several more songs in a foreign tongue that were belted out from behind the bar by Big Al, in honor of his grandmother and the freedom she had finally found.

Hours later, with the bounty hunters and their federal cohorts long since bundled off on their journey west and with the singing over, the now three comrades went upstairs to the rooms assigned to them and settled in with Big Al to talk and get better acquainted.

Meanwhile, downstairs, several people slipped quietly away, crossing the river to go do their usual mischief on the campus of Arbor U by turning ONE TRUTH Park into a place where real truth and freedom were both celebrated, a place to be called, for a time, Hirve Park.

CHAPTER EIGHT

How Three Comrades Become Three Outlaws

*J*ust ahead of dawn Saturday morning, before others were up and about, Big Al trundled the now three comrades out of town in the back of his covered supply wagon. And after a long rumbling, bumping ride, he unloaded them behind a thicket next to what remained of the old US23 expressway, just north of Arbortown. Laughing at them as they worked to unkink their backs after moaning their way out of his wagon, he pointed to a hill rising above the road on the other side of 23 and said, "OK, guys, you'll need to wait for your contact over there, she'll be coming along in an hour or two."

To avoid calling attention to Big Al's stopped wagon, they chatted only briefly, mostly thanking him for the risk he had taken for them. But he just laughed, waving off their thanks with a grunt, and as he lightly flipped the reins to get his horses moving, he shouted back a reminder, "Stay out of sight. If you're gonna get yourselves killed, be sure it's after you're out of my area. I like you too much to want you shot on my turf." The three jeered back at him, and grinning, he threw them a jeer-back salute as he rolled away.

"This isn't half bad," muttered a near asleep Glenn thirty minutes later. He was stretched out beneath a tree with one arm under his head and the other across his face to block the low morning sun, and rolling his head slightly to the side, he looked over at the others and added, "Great breakfast, free ride, and soakin' up rays. It's a pretty good life."

"Yep, good duty," Alex muttered, half asleep.

"I don't agree," John declared, and sitting up as he spoke, he pulled himself back against Glenn's tree to complain, "I signed on to this gig to see some action, not to lay in the sun. This is way too dull. And I didn't even get in a shot at the bad guys last night."

"A shot?" Alex mumbled sleepily, "You don't want to even think about shooting."

"You're the one with the gun, not me," John replied. "Not that I'm complaining, we would have been toast at the Clops if you hadn't come along with some firepower."

"What firepower?" Sitting up, Alex crossed his legs in front of him, squinting against the sun to look under the tree toward John. "You didn't see me with a gun."

"Well, of course not." John laughed. "I get what you're saying, but I ..."

"No, no, you don't get me at all," Alex cut him off, and moving around under the tree to get closer to the other two, he added, "You didn't see a gun because I don't have one. It'd be stupid to get caught with a gun, particularly for me. I'd get the *low justice*."

"Low justice? Why would you get low, you're quotaed-black?" Glenn muttered, and sitting up, he turned to face Alex. "What'd you do, leave the gun at the Clops?"

"Gentlemen, gentlemen, you didn't see a gun last night because ..." He turned away from them, and a moment later they were surprised to hear the sound of a gun being cocked, and yet he turned back to face them holding only a travel spoon and sheath knife in his hands. Grinning at their confusion, he clicked the two together again, this time with them watching him. "These two handy little items became the gun everyone heard."

"Doesn't come close to sounding like a gun," Little John said, and Glenn nodded.

"Doesn't when you can see 'em, but does when you hear a click and feel this in your back." He held up the round, flat pommel end of his knife. "Worked like a charm."

"That's incredible, talk about true grit!" John exclaimed with a big grin on his face as he leaned over to shake Alex's hand. "They could have blown you away, man."

"Not with their gun on the floor." Alex laughed as he accepted the handshake, and then turning to Glenn, he added, "You asked about me and low justice. Well, of course, you know that high justice is for non-whites and some white females, mostly compliant academics who play by PAC rules and honor the whole quota-groups farce, such as the fact that Asian males are treated as whites—unless the Chinese hear about it, of course. But white and Asian males actually get second or middle justice, even if most people think of it as low justice. Real low justice is reserved only for those who betray their higher quota-group. For example, Glenn, if you pretended to be a disbanded Marine and got caught wearing a uniform, you'd probably get flogged and maybe get put in a tiger cage for ten days or so. But I'm black, and I'm a real life Marine wearing my own old uniform. So if they caught me, I'd be thrown over to the friendlies and maybe get shot. If I had a gun on top of that, there'd be no, maybe, I'd be dead. That, my friends, is the real low justice, and it's reserved only for the people PAC fears most—top-quoted people who don't buy into all that quota group crap. It's been that way since the beginnings of their takeover in the seventies. We, chosen people, must sing the appropriate tune, or we're fish bait. And PAC-types have been viciously unforgiving about that; just look at the long list of minorities that were hung-out to dry over the last several decades simply because they dared to think for themselves. So what I'm saying is that you white guys can't get any worse than middle justice, nor of course, any better, but if I refuse to drink at the 'right' fountain, I threaten the PAC system, and so I'll end up getting the dead-low justice—emphasis on the word *dead*."

"I gotta shake your hand again," Little John said, his big grin even wider now.

But as John leaned forward, Glenn's urgent whisper cut off his move and his voice.

"Get down!" Glenn hissed, and they all hunkered down into the weeds under their tree. "I heard something weird. Someone's coming." Then … they all heard it.

"Woe, oh woe!" A pitiful, lamenting voice was calling out, immediately followed by a loud cracking sound. They stared at each other at first, but then slithered on their stomachs to the edge of the hilltop to look down the road and see what was happening.

They saw three men coming toward them, shuffling slowly along in line; and it was the two in front, the first one stooped and naked to his waist, who were offering up the moan sounds they'd heard, but those moans were crazy. They came each time the topless man himself or the guy just behind him, gently whisked his bareback with long white strands that looked to be made up of some kind of light cotton cord. Those cords were so light they floated in the air on their way to his back and shoulders, yet both men responded to each "blow" with loud and mournful moans as if they both were being hit by a real bullwhip. A third man, strutting along behind them, actually carried such a whip, which he was cracking just above his own head as he walked, but it was for sound effects only; it didn't come close to touching the other two.

"U-Statesians!" Alex spit out the words with an angry scowl on his face, and pulling back from the edge, he looked disgustedly at the other two. "They make me sick."

"U-Statesians?" Glenn frowned, looking at Alex, now crawling back to their tree.

"You know them. They're PAC-heads, weird holy-posing, anti-USA cultists," John snarled with a big frown on his face, and he too started back toward the tree, leaving Glenn alone, watching the three creeps whipping their way on down the road.

"Fascinating," Glenn whispered, continuing to watch as the cracking, whipping, and moaning cretins made their way on down the road. But as they were getting almost out of sight, they started chanting something that Glenn couldn't quite make out, and so he turned and called back to the others, "What're they saying?"

"Oh, their usual junk is something like, 'Woe is me and woe even more because I am a U-Statesian,'" Alex called back in disgust. "A lot of nonsense. But come on, get away from there; you're out in the open, and we need to be even more careful now."

"A lot of the PAC true believers use that name, so why so mad at these guys?"

"Duh!" mocked John. "Because they're the truest believers, most PACies don't think we should call ourselves Americans, but these clowns have made it a religion."

"Just come on back," Alex called out again, waving for him to get back under the tree. "You don't see those creeps far from the friendlies or the media. They'd get strung up without their nannies or nanny-kiss-ups around to protect them. No one can stand them." Both Alex and Little John were now waving him back, and so Glenn gave in.

"Well, OK, they're down the road and ..." He called back to them and was just pushing up to head back when a sudden loud roaring, whirring sound exploded on them from above! Flipping over in near panic, he found himself looking straight up at the light blue belly and pinwheel blur of a helicopter, rising menacingly over their hill.

"Get back here! NO, stay put, don't move!" Little John shouted to Glenn, waving both hands as a signal to lie flat and not move. "It's a media-copter."

"Too late, I'll distract them," Alex screamed above the noise, and grabbing his own pack and Glenn's, he turned to take off down the hill toward the woods. The copter, heeling over, zoomed out in front of him, spun around, and dipping down, began a return approach towards him at near grass-top level. It swung up when he dove off to one side into the weeds, but by the time he could regain his feet to head on down the hill, it had swung back around for another go at him. This time it came so close that its right wheel nudged him sharply from behind, sending him sprawling head over heels onto the road. And then, before he could recover and get back up, an unusual thing happened that was only partially caught by the media-copter's cameras for the evening news.

"No!" Little John had screamed as he jumped up when the copter made its first pass at his new friend. And looking frantically around for something, anything, he could use as a weapon, he found just what he needed by the time it swirled over him a second time. And as it came back around, sweeping just above the crest of the hill on its third pass, the big man ran forward, and rapidly swinging a large, heavy log like an Olympic hammer thrower, he thrust it up and out towards the enemy machine. And that huge projectile sailed up past the spinning rush of air from the blades and smashed into them, sending the copter fluttering toward the ground like a downed bird during hunting season. But instead of just flopping to the earth, it hit the ground skidding and grinding along the road, rolling over three, maybe four, times before settling upside down in a cloud of dust only about thirty feet from a wide-eyed Alex—crouching there, poised to jump away.

By the time all that dust had settled, all three comrades were off and charging down the opposite slope of the hill. Running like the devil himself was on their heels, they ran until they were deep into the woods where, gasping for breath, they collapsed in a dense thicket that offered shelter both from the sides and from above.

"Part of that's ... *whew* ... on camera." Alex managed to pant the words, and forcing a grin at the other two, he gasped. "Hey, wow, congrats guys. I'm whipped, and I'm a runner ... run all the time, and ... I'm done in, but you guys ... stayed with me."

"Not for much ... longer." Glenn wheezed. "And ... I run almost every day."

"Hey, I was ready ... to ... to ... to go down," John groaned, and grinning broadly, he added between continued deep breaths, "But I ... I don't ever ... exercise."

"Well, man, you certainly brought those clowns down," Alex said, his breathing already almost under control. "Saved my bacon. That's for sure. They had me cold."

"They had us all cold. I was stupid. Oh so stupid! Out there like that, right out in the open. Sightseeing!" Glenn muttered glumly. "How could I be so stupid?"

"Go easy on yourself, Glenn. Three 'stupids' is about right, but don't overdo it." Alex laughed; he had now fully recovered. "Besides, we were all out in the open way too long, and we should have heard it coming—I don't know how I missed hearing it. And you didn't know, how could you? Media-copters are everywhere, except in places like Arbortown. Out here in the real world, if they're not shooting pictures of some idiot U-Statesian cretins whipping themselves down the road and moaning about how sad it is to be born an American, they're doing human-fox hunts across the valley."

"Human-fox hunts?" Glenn sat back, looking quizzically at him. "What's that?"

"Don't you ever watch the PAC Broadcasting System?" Alex starred at him. "How do you think they got so good at the wheel nudging trick they pulled on me?"

"No, don't watch it," Glenn replied. "Come on, fill me in. What've I missed?"

"You know, it's like in old England, like when the swells would get all duded-up and ride on their horses with a whole herd of dogs to chase a fox across their estates," Alex said, and now back in form, he stood up and began a stretching routine as he spoke. "I think they used a real free-running fox in those days, and the poor critter probably had at least a chance to get away, but that's not true these days—not for human targets.

"PAC wouldn't approve of chasing animals like that in this new age, of course, but people? That's a different story, only the right people, naturally, proper quotas only. You know, only males who look like you two are fair game." He laughed, but they didn't. "But even at that, our PAC-media heroes don't risk free-running targets. Their preys are all hooked up to a monitoring system so they can track 'em wherever they go. They can run, but they can't hide."

"Well, frankly, I don't mind that if they're criminals," John said. "I've watched some of those chases on campus TV, and I don't feel sorry for those creeps. We don't want their kind loose. Some of their history profiles are pretty bad."

"Yes, pretty bad fiction. It may shock you to learn two things. First, they're only loose because the newsies want to have a show for us to watch. They cut them loose for media ratings and lackey-time entertainment. And second, the runners aren't criminals at all. They're guys locked up for violating quota rules, or for offending some PACy in some way, usually by not kissing up as energetically as she likes. In other words, John, they're white males like you—with a few Asian guys thrown in the mix here and there."

"I don't know why you say guys like me. I didn't see stuff like this happening over in Oakland County," Little John said. "Of course, nobody could own their own TV there, but the community centers had them, and in the stories I saw there, the runners always seemed to be criminals from the Detroit Manufacturing Zone … or Arbortown."

"Come on, look at what you did at Arbor U. If they'd caught you then, you could be running under one of those machines right now. Besides, you didn't see them running in Oakland County because the media has to operate in the shadow of the friendlies,"

Alex laughed. "They're like the U-Statesians. Can you imagine how long any of those clowns would last if they did their little walk and whip act anywhere in the real world? They'd feel a whip all right, but it wouldn't be made of cotton, and afterwards, they'd have plenty of real regrets, not phony baloney ones. It's the same with those so-called criminals. Like I said, most are nothing worse than PAC-bait, the criminal histories you saw were fiction. Anyway, forget all that, it's really not important for us right now, but I gotta tell you something that is important. We have before us a very real and very live, nonfiction problem to solve."

"Wow, a real problem!" Glenn laughed. "Are you suggesting we have only one?"

John joined in the laughter at first, but his laugh tapered off as his mind turned to Alex's comment about him. The marine was right, after that dome nonsense, he could've been just another poor slob being chased by a media-copter. Frowning, he felt angry at first, but then blew it off, laughingly thinking not to worry, I'd just crash it. But even with the laugh, he was still shrugging off that "running John" possibility when his self-focus was shoved to the back of his mind by Alex's answer to Glenn's next question.

"What do you mean by 'nonfiction' problem?"

"I mean nonfiction as in we have a real, right-now, true-life problem," Alex replied. "We're here in this nice safe thicket, but our contact will go to where we're supposed to be. In fact, our contact may end up getting arrested because of us, which means that we'll be left hanging here, wherever 'here' is, and our contact will be hanging, perhaps literally, back there—where we're supposed to be."

"Well, not quite hanging, but it could've happened that way," a woman's voice sounded from the bushes behind them, and the three men spun anxiously around to see a smiling federal ranger emerging from the undergrowth. "Hey, take it easy men. I'm your Pocahontas," she said, throwing up her hands to show the sign as they stood to face her.

"Password!" Alex demanded as they stood, eyeing her—and waiting.

"Sink-Me, you guys are tense aren't you?" She laughed as she re-flashed the sign and went on with her story. "You can call me J2, and relax, guys, we're back on plan. I arrived on the scene just in time to hear a loud crash and to see all three of you bailing down the hill—in the wrong direction, I might add. I had to break a sweat to keep up with you and then almost lost you in all this brush."

After introductions all around, they sat chatting about the crash and their run, and she brought them up to date on all the gossip about the hubbub last night by the river. "It seems that not only have some federals gone over the hill, but some bounty hunters have come up missing—not that anyone cares. On top of that, several witnesses have reported that they'd spotted that *vile,* most wanted student-barbarian. But the problem is that they saw him in a half-dozen different locations on both sides of the river."

Smiling at Little John, she then added, "Oh, don't you worry, big guy, he remains at large, but now there'll be an even bigger bounty offered for him. The good old news was that the first bounty was in federal script, and no one would work too hard to for it. But the bad news now is that, after what you did today on live TV, my friend, that reward will change, real quick. When they see that video of you ripping up a huge tree by its roots and tossing it up to crash their media-copter, PAC'll switch the reward to unies and make it even bigger. That'll grow the interest in collecting it—bigtime. So, good luck."

"Well, we can't control that, so what do we do now?" Alex asked, and nodding up at the sun, he added, "It's getting late, we're getting hungry, and my guess is we have a long way to go. Can we get back on track, or have we messed up too much?"

"Not too much, but we do have a way to go. Of course, if you'd had the good sense to just walk away in the right direction, we'd all be sitting over a good lunch right now. No one was chasing you except me, and I had to drop our lunch pack to keep up with you. So, you'll have to suffer until we get to where we need to be—in about an hour or so," she said, looking around at them and laughing at John's unquiet food-delay groan.

"That reminds me, speaking of packs," Glenn called out, looking over at Alex. "Thanks for carrying mine during our run."

"*That's* why you were able to keep up. I had two packs." Alex laughed, and glancing over at John, he added, "but that doesn't explain you, no-exercise guy."

"Hey, what can I say? It's a gift," the big guy replied, shrugging his shoulders.

They followed their federal ranger angel back through the forest, and in a little over two hours, a bit longer than she had promised, as only Little John commented on but was not the only one to notice, they arrived at a clearing near a small stream that ran just outside the town of Whitmore Lake. There they found a cozy cottage with the food they wanted and all the comforts of home. Well, food, clean beds, and shelter anyway.

Their long awaited meal would have tasted great even if they had not waited so long, and afterwards over coffee, they settled back, chatting about PAC and Arbortown—and about the resistance and the area they'd be moving through over the next few days.

But after a while, Little John changed the direction of the talk; he was interested in the angels who kept showing up. "Tell me about you guys, or I mean, gals," he self-corrected. "You're always just where we need you to be. Who are you and …"

"Little John, you don't have a need to know that," J2 replied, and looking over at him, she wore a smile, but her eyes held a serious look. She obviously wasn't joking, but Little John didn't catch that, at least, not at first.

"No, no. I'm really interested. I think it's amazing the way you're just where you need to be when you need to be there. And that's even when we go ..."

"Sorry to cut you off," she cut in, and standing, she walked over to a window where she stopped and stood looking out as if in thought. Then, turning back to face them a few seconds later, she continued, "I'll say only this, and you'll have to accept it. We're links in your trip's narrative chain. Our job is to keep you on plan and on track. When you go off, like today, it's our job—my job this time—to find you and to get you back on our plan. I've done that, and here we are ... on plan." She gestured around them.

"How do you get together for planning?" John asked, and standing, he walked over to where she was at the window, looking down at her as he waited for a reply.

"John, what part of 'you'll have to accept it' don't you under-stand?" she replied calmly. And leaning back against the wall, she looked up at the well-meaning almost giant, caught his eyes—and held them. Her usual steady smile was now gone.

"Well ..." he laughed nervously, looking at her first, then around at the other two and back to her. But then, still not giving up, he flashed his best big aw-shucks smile, and added, "I mean, I know what you're saying. I just don't understand what the big deal is. Why can't you tell us a little about you and how you work? We're all on the same side."

"You're right, John, we *are* all on the same side," Alex cut-in. "And our angel is trying to get it through your bone head that she can't tell you anymore. Charm away all you want, but 'all you need to know' is all you're going to get. So, let it go at that."

"I think we can leave it at that, can't we, buddy?" Glenn called over to his now embarrassed comrade. He shared his desire for more information, but his training had prepared him for the need to keep each part of an operation separate from the others, not that he was really good at that, himself. Then, trying to mellow out the sagging mood, he stood, walked over to Little John and slapped him on the back. "Come on, just step back. You two're looking downright weird facing off like this—like a horse and a cat."

"More like a donkey and a bobcat." Alex laughed, and he too walked over and slapped John on the shoulder. "Come on, man, this is a time to celebrate, not to tangle."

J2, laughing at their comments, offered her hand to John and said, "There's no tangle, I think we're more like two friends who just happened to disagree for a moment."

John's face reddened, and shaking his head, he accepted her hand and said, "Hey, I'm sorry. We—I—appreciate all you're doing for us. I may not agree with the rule in this case, but I don't have to agree with it. I know that, and I'm sorry I pushed."

"We need good pushers in the alliance, John. You have nothing to apologize for," she replied, and smiling around at all of them, she then added, "Well, I guess instead of one outlaw, we now have three. I can only imagine how big that reward is going to get."

They then sat back to discuss that change, which didn't really change very much. But not for long. Although it had not been a long day, it had been a hard one, and she could see that they were tired. So after chatting with them for a bit over an hour, she took her leave, telling them that she'd return in the morning to lead them on to their next transfer point. And she reminded them to lock the doors and to remain close to the cabin. They could use lights, but if they got an alert to go dark, they should do so at once.

"To our angels. Bless them all, but especially whichever one saves us when we go wrong!" John declared, raising a glass to J2 as Alex opened the door for her. A hearty cheer from the other two followed the toast.

But once she was gone, they turned first to their leftovers and not their beds. This was only their second meal that day, and they were all still hungry. And as usual, Little John ate heartily, but this time, with only one hand; he was busy massaging his feet with the other. He appreciated his new boots, but they'd take a while to break in, and today's long run and longer walk had not been kind to his feet.

As it grew dark outside, the near perfect Michigan summer night came to life with the sounds of the forest, and overhead, the stars glittered like diamonds across a cloudless sky. Many more stars were now clearly visible in this new city light-free era, which was the only good thing about these times, although nowhere near worth all that had been lost.

Inside the cabin, no one paid any attention to that beautiful night sky. All three men were soon sound asleep, and it wasn't until the next morning that they gave any thought to what was going on around them—and then for a very good reason.

CHAPTER NINE

How a Military Maid Twice Saves the Day

*T*he three comrades were jolted awaken, Sunday morning, by a loud pounding on their door, followed by an officious, screaming shout, "This is the Socmon of Whitmore Lake, and I demand that you open this door—now! Don't make me wait. I warn you!"

They all hit the floor, anxiously eyed one another, and then headed off in three different directions to check windows for possible escape routes. But all their desperate churning about was suddenly frozen in place by the sound of a loud whirling noise and several quick heavy thuds against their door—followed at once by a strange gasping gurgle that stayed them even longer in a waiting, listening mode. Then came, what? Well, it was like something heavy was pressing against the door and easing itself ever so slowly down its outside. Staring towards that sound and barely breathing, they silently prepared to respond to whatever came next. But it was just J2's near-casual voice that came next—and they still stood there, wide-eyed and dumbfounded.

"Hey guys, it's OK, you can come out now!" J2 repeated, but even the sound of her second call wasn't enough to relax their hold-'til-we-see-what's-next immobility—not at first, and so she followed up with her own round of rapid pounding, but hers included words of reassurance, "It's OK, it's OK. It's me. It's all clear. Come on out!"

Alex was the first to move. Easing the door open in an *at-the-ready* half-crouch, he cautiously looked around for hostile signs. But he saw only J2 kneeling with her back to him beside the very still body of some stranger. Confused, he whispered, "Is he . . ?"

"Oh no, he'll be OK," she replied, glancing over as he knelt beside her to inspect the fallen man. "He'll have a sore neck and a bad headache when he comes to, but my guess is that he'll be back at his usual disgusting trade before nightfall."

"What *is* that?" Glenn asked, speaking from the doorway. He was pointing to the thick cords with heavy balls tied to them that Alex was unwrapping from a man's neck.

"It's called a bola, and he's lucky. His head hit the door and so did the balls as they wrapped, so he didn't get the full force," J2 replied, and looking up, she laughed at Little John's expression as he craned his own bull neck to see over Glenn's head.

"Looks like I've missed all the action," the big man groused.

"If that's lucky, I wouldn't want to be unlucky with your bola thing," Glenn muttered, reaching down to give J2 a hand up. "We thought we were goners. Who is he?"

"As he said, he's the Socmon of Whitmore Lake," she replied, taking Glenn's hand and pulling up beside him. "And, my friends, he's a very important PAC-rat."

"Socman?" Little John pushed forward offering his own hand. "Hey, accept my thanks too and tell me about that doodad of yours—and what's the story with this guy?"

"Whoa, hold it." She laughed. "Let's do one question at a time, guys. First, it's Soc*mon*, not Soc*man*. They are all men, but PAC neutered that term years ago, and you haven't heard about them because they operate only near the marches. They're PAC enforcers who report to the local PAC ombudstera, who's always a woman, as you know. All of them are an unroyal pain, but this one in particular deserves whatever *pain* he ends up with after his dance with my bola. He's a real jerk."

"I've heard of them," John said, eyeing the devise, "a weapon and a tool, right?"

"What you see is what it is," she replied. "But listen up, my friends will take care of him. I need to get you guys out of here. Bad stuff's happening, and here's not good."

"You lead, mighty warrior. We'll follow," Glenn said, and laughed at her eye-roll.

"OK, guys," she replied. "First, I need to split you up. The heat's on bigtime now because of that media-copter." She glanced toward Little John, smiling and shaking her head as she began laying out the plan. "They're looking for three males but mostly you, big guy, and so it's into deep cover for you, which means"—she laughed out loud—"you'll have to get your new boots damp, wading through the wetlands to Brighton. And as for you, friend Alex, they have pictures, but they're not good ones, so we think it'll be safe for you to join the next Brighton Convoy on 23. You're quotaed high enough to make it by wearing different clothes. We'll get you three back together soon, but you two need to takeoff right now with my mates out there. They'll take good care of you, including getting you the clothes you need and some food. You'll both sleep in Brighton tonight. As for you, Glenn, we'll try to get you there tomorrow, but the next day for sure."

"So if they're traveling, what will I be up to today?" Glenn asked their angel, as they stood together a few minutes later, watching his friends disappear down the path.

"It's Sunday, and you're off to church," she replied. "Your buddies will have to miss out, but otherwise, we're still on plan. And so today, my friend, you'll experience the only version of Christian faith in action that PAC approves of in this glorious new age of ours. The church you'll visit is a perfect example of—well, you can decide what."

After a quick and cold breakfast and a shot of lukewarm coffee, Glenn followed J2 past the still snoozing PAC-rat to the promised church. It stood on a hillside next to a small lake, all tucked in between an apple grove and the edge of the woods he had just traveled through. She had to leave him there, and so he walked alone up the creaking wooden steps of the worn out old ruin and on into its dim, daylight-lit sanctuary. No one else was there, but that wasn't surprising because church attendance was discouraged, and most church buildings were now empty or converted to other uses. In Arbortown, they were often storage units, pubs, or stores. Not that it mattered; between Michigan's depopulation and PAC rules, there was little need for many real old-type church buildings.

PAC had worked long and hard to neutralize Christianity. Years ago, they even tried to make Sunday an official workday because it favored the Christian faith and to make Friday a weekend day. When that didn't fly, they got their revenge by pushing a "fairness" rule that called for three weekend days and also declared that all "historically privileged" places of worship—meaning only Christian churches—were public commons areas, which meant open displays of religious flags, crosses, and pictures were banned.

As he walked around inside, studying the decaying building, Glenn wondered why Christians had just rolled over year after year—indeed, decade after decade—and allowed so many things they didn't like or want to … to just happen. Of course, he knew there had been no effective opposition because the church was divided against itself.

It's funny, he thought, that sense of "we, the universal church" was talked about by Christians, but never a reality—all talk and no cigar, as people used to say. For most of us unity in faith was less important than not being like certain other *so-called* Christian groups. He shook his head. As a young man, it was hard for him to understand how that could happen, how believers could have let the culture swamp their faith so easily, with no real fight. It was weird how, instead of leading, everyone simply fell in line with PAC, following one new truth imposition after another, like sheep, sheep without a shepherd! Or like sheep following the big bad wolf, and that PAC wolf didn't even have to pretend.

He noted the torn, tattered American flag hanging limply on a dust encrusted old pole at the front, and then he looked over at the bare pole that once held a Christian flag. Some churches had found ways to rebel against the *religious freedom* laws, as they were called. A few had kept an ornate treasure-casket beside that empty pole with a Christian flag neatly folded inside, and some others had protested by going without any kind of flag up front at all. But no guts, no glory, he thought, sadly shaking his head. He knew that most Christians had simply rolled over about both the flag and the cross. Going along to get along became the twenty-first century's echo of St. Peter's denial.

"It's all so idiotic!" He snorted, recalling that his mentor often said that the old saw about a dog's bark being worse than its bite didn't apply to the church. And turning, he looked around at it all as he shout-quoted his old professor's words, "Our Christian rollover is more obvious than our puny little bark, and there's been no bite for decades!"

As Christians should have expected, these early laws were only the first shots in the final round of losses. Next, PAC decreed that all religious symbols were banned, specifically crosses on clothes and on jewelry, and it soon followed that sermons and songs had to be pre-approved by the local PAC ombudstera to be sure that they didn't cause division or offend any preferred group. Such demands were said to be for the public good, and the possibility that these actions might offend Christians was scoffed at. By 2029, only tame churches that met the *PAC freedom to worship* requirements were licensed to stay open or to be tax exempt. Not that taxes mattered much by then; the economic collapse was near complete, and most people had quit paying taxes either because the politicians had tried to buy their votes by adjusting the tax code to exclude them or because they hid their income. And sadly, too many people didn't pay taxes because they had no income at all. Meanwhile, in PAC-controlled areas, Christian churches simply began to wither away, led by those denominations that were already in steep decline. Believers who still chose to worship began attending house churches, as did Glenn in Arbortown. So far, these weren't considered part of the public square, and although PAC leaned on them, trying to punish them, their numbers kept growing.

"Glenn?"

"Yes, what!?" Lost in thought, Glenn flinched at the sound of his own name. But when he spun around to face the person calling to him, he was delighted to see that it was their Worthy, Oren Mithandir, smiling at him from just inside the door—under the only stained-glassed window fragment left in the building. "Good to see you, sir!"

"And you, my young friend. The original plan called for me to meet with all three of you, but I heard what happened both at the Two-Eyed Cyclops and with the media-copter. What tales you have!" he said, and laughing as he eased himself onto a bench, he nodded toward the one facing his. "But before we get to those stories, have a seat across from me here and tell me your take on what you see all around you."

"Well, I see a sad and empty shell of what was once a major force for good," Glenn said, gesturing around at the remnants of that Christian legacy as he settled onto the bench, facing the Worthy. "And I see what happens when people lose their faith and stray from the path. I mean, what's in here mirrors—or foreshadows--what's outside."

"And?"

"And it all makes me sad." Glenn went on, but then looking directly at Oren, he studied the older man's face for a reaction as he continued, "But mostly, I see a major challenge for us—in here and out there—to rally and to re-earn the almost place we'd reached only a few short years ago."

"Almost place? Interesting. I think I like that." Mithandir smiled. "But I like it only as long as you're clear in your heart and mind that we were nowhere near putting together anything approaching perfection. Still, we were a lot closer then to being what we could become than we are now, or than anyone else has been in all of human history."

"The term's not new with me," Glenn said. "I got it from that professor whose name I can't mention, and as you no doubt know, he wasn't foolish enough to think we'd reached perfection. But, wow! We had it good, or so I hear; that was all before my time."

"I know it was, Glenn, and I'm so sorry, you and your generation deserved better from your elders." Oren sighed. "I also know your professor, and I know that he's right. Things were very, very good in those days, but we let them become fat-cat good instead of lean-clean-servin'-machine good." Pausing then and looking all around, he shook his head as he added, "A big part of our fall came from shifting our eyes from serving others to the bankbook and an endless series of pathetic serving-the-self-in-the-mirror gimmicks. We became so engrossed in ourselves that we failed to preserve our community or our kids' future, and frankly, we've ended up soiling ourselves and undermining both."

"You're right, our age-old Eve and Adam dark side, serving self sin, is what took us down—again," Glenn whispered. And then, after praying together and sharing a brief meditation, they returned to their conversation. They talked for over an hour, but only briefly about that lost past; they were more interested in the present challenge.

And then, a symbol of their present challenge intruded. The sound of heavy boots stomping up the outside steps and up onto the warped old wooden floor surprised the two men, and they turned to watch as four scruffy looking big men, no doubt yet another pack of bounty hunters entered the church. Unsure what to do, the two chose to remain seated.

The intruders, stopping just inside the door to let their eyes get used to the lower light, didn't spot the two sitting up near the front at first. Once they did, they grinned their way down the aisle towards them. But those grins had vanished by the time they reached the two seated men, and the intruders just stood there, looming over Glenn and Oren like four dull-eyed, glowering towers. And then came ... nothing. The towers just stood, still glowering, but strangely quiet, apparently waiting for their leader to act.

That lead glowerer, however, seemed to be uncertain, and so it took a while. For several long seconds, he just stood, rocking back and forth on his heels, narrow-eyeing the two as he folded, unfolded, and refolded his arms across his chest. Then he coughed, seemly re-rethinking the situation—but still, zilch. Until, as his murmuring crew began shifting about with growing impatience, his beady eyes widened, and he grinned at each of his men in turn, his head bobbing up and down. He seemed to be ready! But no, it was fade to zilch again, and he lapsed back into his old rocking and glowering routine.

Having mastered that activity, he seemed to want to stay in his comfort zone, and so it took him a long time to move on from there. But at long last, his next move finally came to him, and his well-practiced glower changed to a broad, smug smile as a very self-satisfied expression formed on his face. This was it, finally, and his crew crowded up behind him, eager to hear what their leader had to say.

"What we got here is two ah them bad boys that crashed that media-copter."

"Whoa, yeah, right! I think we got ourselves a big, fat, *ree*-ward," said the tall, skinny, weasel-faced one.

"I'm countin' my share right now," the bulging, fat-faced follower added.

And the big muscle-bound, dumb looking one grinned, bobbing his head up and down, but he didn't say anythin' at all.

"Don't count your money yet," Glenn snapped back, and he started to stand, but Oren's hand eased over, taking him firmly by the elbow, and so he restrained himself.

"Welcome, gentlemen," Mithandir said, and gesturing for Glenn to relax, he was careful to make friendly eye contact as he calmly lounged back on his bench, speaking in a soft, unhurried voice. "Have a seat with us, please. We were just discussing what might have happened to this old church. I think it must have been a beautiful building once."

"Yeah, well, so what? Now you can discuss comin' with us to the feds," replied the leader. But as he spoke, he eased himself down next to Glenn, and casually waving for his three companions to back off, he chuckled with satisfaction at the sight of the now visibly frustrated student. Most of the people in his business hated students because of their privileges and self-righteousness, and this leader was no exception.

"I don't think you really want to take us to the federals," Mithandir continued in a calm, relaxed voice, still keeping an eye on Glenn. "My guess is that by now everyone in the state has hauled someone in, trying to collect that big—*ree*ward—as I think your man called it. My other guess is that the feds are pretty sick of the whole thing, and it doesn't go well for people who can't prove they have the real villains."

"The what?" The fat-cheeked man screwed up his face, looking confused.

"He means, we're non-perpetrators," Glenn said, thin-smiling at their confusion.

"Them two're trying to fancy talk their way out of this," weasel-face said, and with that the big, muscular fourth man, dumbly shaking his head in agreement, walked around behind Glenn, stopped and, flashing a gapped-toothed smile at his leader, slapped the back of the surprised student's head. And it wasn't a gentle slap, and Glenn's temper spiked, but he held himself in check, knowing that Oren was making an effort to control things, and that he wanted him to stay quietly seated. And so he did ... smolderingly.

"OK, I tried to save you." Mithandir spoke in what now sounded like a very sad and tired old voice. Then, shifting forward and leaning heavily on his staff, he slowly and with apparent great difficulty, pulled himself to his feet. Once he was standing, all stooped and swaying, he shuffled around to face the leader and added in tired wheeze, "It's up to you. You can take this very old man, quotaed black, and this very young man, quoted white, in to the federals, and you can explain how we did what you say we did. But first, tell me what you're going to say about it all, so we can support your story. Was it this student [he gestured toward Glenn] who reached up and jerked the copter out of the air, or did I, maybe, sock it down with, say, this weapon right here?" He held up his long, thin staff, his arm trembling with the effort. "We want to get our story right."

"Yeah," the big guy said. "We need our story right. Which one you think did it?"

"Don't be stupid," weasel face cut in. "No old man could've done that."

"You callin' me stupid? I'll knock yer head clean off!" The big guy turned angrily toward weasel face.

"You fools shut up," the leader snorted, eyeing them. "I'm takin' care of this."

"Of course, it's your call," Mithandir said, and smiling pleasantly at the leader, he nodded over toward Glenn as he went on. "My friend and I want to be helpful."

"Yeah, I'm sure. Well, you better believe that I'm doin' the callin'. But I didn't say it was the three of you—I mean, the two of you.

I never said that," the leader sputtered. But now, studying the feeble old black man in front of him, he felt unsure.

"The reports say there were *three* bad guys." A woman's voice came from behind them at that moment, and they all turned to see a federal ranger coming down the aisle. "I know these men, so maybe I was the third—villain, did someone say?" As she spoke, J2 made her way calmly towards the group, wearing a very disarming smile on her face.

Glenn turned at the sound of her voice, and leaning to look around the muscled oaf who had hit him, he grinned at the sight of their angel and decided to use her to get in a shot. "Oh no, it's our leader!" he shouted, with a mischievous glance toward Mithandir, "Do you think they'll guess she's the one who jerked that big copter out of the air?"

"OK, OK, don't get cute," the lout leader snapped, scowling at Glenn as he held up a hand to back off his buddies, all eager to take some kind of action. He was confused now, and there was more than a hint of uncertainty as he asked, "Who are you people?"

"I'm a professor at Arbor University, and I'm here with my student," Mithandir replied, very politely, pointing to Glenn. "And this federal ranger is our area guide. We came here to study old superstitions from U-Statesian history."

"Or to jerk media-copters out of the air, whichever seems like the most fun," J2 said, but then suddenly shifting from smirking to frowning, she added, "You four are looking pretty stupid, and you know what? I'm tired of all of this, tired of being abused by four white males."

"Now wait a minute!" The lout leader jumped to his feet, and holding up both hands, he began backing away up the aisle. "I'm quotaed-brown. I just look white, but that's not my fault; I hate it. Besides, you can't accuse us of somethin' we didn't do. We didn't do *anythin'* to you; we was just talkin' to these other two, and we didn't even know they was with a ranger. How could we? You wasn't even in here."

"Are you four males telling me, a quotaed-female ranger, what I can or can't do?"

"Like he said, we didn't know you was here," the fat-faced man nervously spoke up. "Besides, we was just leavin' when you got here. Why you so worked up?"

"Yeah, we was just leavin'," the lout leader said, and looking over at Mithandir and at Glenn, still seated but now relaxed and enjoying the show, he added, "Besides, we was jokin'. Who'd think an old man who can barely stand up and a student who don't know up from down could bring down a media-copter? It was a joke." With that, he motioned to the others, and they all turned to follow him, silently retreating out the door.

J2, now smiling again, walked over to a window to watch as the four clowns fled out of sight. After she was sure they were gone, she looked over at Oren, and although laughing, she admitted, "You know, I was worried when I spotted those guys in here."

"Worried?" Glenn looked at the two, confused. "We had it in hand, didn't we?"

"I think it's time to show you what's downstairs here, Glenn," Mithandir said, and motioning for them to follow, the now remarkably agile older man led the way.

They felt their way down a set of creaking, sagging steps into a dark, dusky, old-fashioned Michigan basement—real dirt walls and floor, with an impossible number of cobwebs hanging all over the place. As he followed them, Glenn looked uncomfortably about, wondering what was going on, but then, suddenly, he had to jump back out of the way as what seemed to be an age-encrusted set of ancient shelves swung out beside him, opening a doorway into a large, very clean, and well-equipped secret room.

And Glenn was amazed by what he saw when they entered that room. It seemed to have been cut from the basement into the hillside where it sloped toward the lake, but he recalled seeing no evidence of it from outside; there was nothing out there but a lot of useless rubbish. Yet now, from the inside, he stood looking through hidden ports that were intermingled with that junk, and he could see all around one side of the church and on out across the swampy area by the small lake all the way to the bordering woods.

"This is what we were concerned about," J2 whispered, motioning around the room, particularly at the four hooded men in shackles who sat silently facing away from them. She gave Glenn a chance to nose around a bit, and then, after nodding their thanks to an unseen guard, she led the two back into the basement. And as the shelving returned to its spot behind them, the three carefully made their way back up the stairs to their seats.

"Who?" Glenn started, but J2 motioned him to be quiet while she did a quick tour outside to be sure no one was lurking around.

"Three of them were part of your group of hotshots from the Two-Eyed Cyclops, and the other is a freelancer who got too close," the Worthy explained. "They're headed west where they'll be split up and assigned to various security groups. Very few choose to come back here, and those who do that we don't trust"—he laughed—"... go to California instead. Not sure what happens there, but I think some of them get volunteered into the resistance, fighting against the Russian supported Mexican army. Things are still crazy out there, as they have been for decades. As you know, California blindly led the way into America's one-eyed, amoral, don't-pay-as-you-go era of self-gratification."

"How do they get to Kansas or wherever, and what happens while they're there?" Glenn asked. "And I should add, by what authority do we take or kidnap these people?

Like them or not, they do have rights. Do we really want to be acting like PAC?"

"Oren will talk about that, Glenn," J2 said, walking up to the other two. "I just wanted to be present when you got your first look at what will likely be your future in the Blue Company—helping us run our growing underground and intelligence operations."

"Along with some combat assignments, I'm sure," Mithandir added, but he held up his response to Glenn's questions because J2 had signaled that it was time for her to leave. So they both walked with her to the door, and after Glenn offered a special thank you for saving him twice in a single day, Oren gave her a hug, laughing as he added, "Good job managing that crew, they left with tails between their legs."

"You two had them on the run when I got here, and Glenn, you guys could have managed that joker this morning. He'd have ended up like a pretzel, tangling with you three. My way actually was easier on him, but he's a colleague after all, and I'm really just a loyal, tender-hearted softy," she said, laughing as she walked away.

"I think we needed you both—or I mean, all three times, and I appreciate you and your sister-angel," Glenn called after her, laughingly adding, "Besides, if that bola is a sign of your gentle heart, remind me not to ask for evidence of your ungentle side."

Once J2 was gone, Oren went on to explain the migration process to Glenn. "All migrants are transported to a place where they will be made to work and be productive for the first time in many of their lives—the death of the work ethic being one of the things that went wrong with our society. They're far enough away out there that we don't have to worry about them easily returning here to cause trouble, but as I said, few have shown an interest in returning in the past. Life's pretty good out in Alliance country; it's almost normal away from all the PAC idiocy that we have to put up with here."

"How about families? Some of these guys must have families."

"If they're considered safe and want to get together, we see to it."

"And no one notices all these people just vanishing?" Glenn asked the question, but then regretted it; he already knew the answer, but he listened politely anyway.

"These days? Sad to say, people are vanishing all the time and few ask why, but I can tell you this; most people want to stay once they get out of here. They want to stay because, as I said, life's pretty good there. It's sort of like a return to the way things were in late nineteenth century America. Most people are making their living on farms and there's a feeling of the security that comes with a fair community-based authority that strives to live by Whig Partisan Alliance values—no quota garbage, no groups up or others down. There's almost no crime, and most people try to pull their own weight—some needing and getting a bit of encouragement. As to our authority, we're all working for the Blue Company, commissioned by and accountable to the Whig Partisan Alliance.

"Remember, Glenn, we're in a war, and you've chosen to go to Whigville and to work to gain a commission to help us win that war. Your work in that direction started before this trip, and we've invested a lot in you and hope for a lot back, but please understand this, you are being invited to join us. It's an opportunity, not a draft. We don't draft anyone. Well,"—he laughed—"except for those we think might be a potential danger, but those are few. The vast majority of us are volunteers. From the people out there in tree stands watching over us right now to those in the shooting wars in Alaska, North Carolina, and all around the Mexican border—we're all volunteers. And like them, you've been called. But it's up to you to decide how or even if you'll answer that call. It's a two-way street."

"Sir, I understand all of that, but I have one big question," Glenn said. "Why am I getting such treatment? I mean, for years I've had a privileged education with a founder and leader of the cause and so many others, and now I'm getting this special handling for my trip to Whigville. Why? What's going on? I can't see how I merit any of this."

"Good. You've learned lesson number one, and it's a biggie—one that got lost on the past few generations."

"OK, I don't even know what you mean by that."

"I mean, Glenn, you're right; you don't merit what you're getting. In fact, we Americans have never merited what we were given even from our very earliest days, but especially since World War II. It was a gift from our parents and grandparents, but it was a gift with strings. Those strings honor-bound us to serve the cause of freedom and to pass it on to our children first, and then to as many others in the world as possible—but surely to our own children. That was our calling, and it was our duty, but too many of us chose to serve our own—right now—selfish wants instead. As a result of that very real and tragic, play-now-pay-later (or not at all) sin, your generation, has been left with the mess we have today, and the cause of freedom has faltered around the world.

"Why'd we flop? I don't really understand it fully myself, but I guess it's because we're mere humans, and we're weak," Oren continued. "As we talked about earlier, we took everything that was passed on to us for granted as if, somehow, the world owed it to us, and we thought too little of the literally billions of others, including our own children, who counted on us to do our duty. Like the prodigal son, we chose to fritter away our inheritance in one, generations long, small-minded era of foolish hedonism, and that, my friend, is why we're where we are today and why we all have such a big job to do.

"As for you, now? The Blue Company chose you for its own reasons. You didn't choose us, at least not in the beginning. Soon, I hope, you will choose to move along the road of service that we've put you on, but all of that's in good time. Right now, you need to invest a few hours to prepare for tomorrow, and we have to get you to a safe house close to your first meeting at nine tomorrow morning, so you can do just that."

Twenty minutes later, the Worthy bid him goodbye, and Glenn hefted an extra backpack full of reading materials and followed the young guide, who had provided it all, off into the woods. Late that night, in yet another tucked away cottage, he put aside all that reading, and rubbing his tired eyes, he laid back in bed. He felt sad as he thought about the shell of a church he had visited and wondered what surprises the next morning would bring—would they be as grim? The readings had provided him with a lot of new information, but why did he need it? He was a master's level social worker, after all.

He laid there for a long time, tossing and turning and trying to get to sleep, a confused traveler who didn't really understand the personal *what* or *why* of the road he was traveling. How could he be sure it was the right road? *Bah*, that's nuts, he snorted, of course it was. He knew that, and he was determined to travel it. Then, smiling to himself, he recalled the Worthy's final words before leaving. He had asked Glenn if he had read C. S. Lewis's space trilogy.

Those stories were favorites of Professor Benjamin, and Glenn had read them all more than once. And thinking about them now, he laughed out loud and whispered, "I'm sorta like Ransom, the Lewis hero, facing a good-versus-evil adventure."

Smiling at that thought as he drifted off, he decided that, if nothing else, he had to see where this road he was on would take him … where it was taking America.

CHAPTER TEN

How a Confused Traveler Learns How PAC Cares about Kids

*D*espite what used to be called a cram-all-nighter, Glenn's eyes popped open early Monday morning. He was eager to get into the day's adventure—a tour of a major PAC educational facility— and although he was skeptical about the thought of PAC doing anything right, he squeezed in a final skim review of the reports on American education that he had plowed through the night before. Masters aside, he wanted to be prepared.

And he was ... awestruck! No other word could better describe his feelings when, at nine sharp with a good breakfast behind him and all reviewed, he found himself standing stunned before the most beautiful building he had ever seen. It was magnificent. It rooted him in place, his confidence faltering as he suddenly found himself feeling very unready to meet the kind of professionals who no doubt served in a palace like this one. According to his reading, this gorgeous edifice was variously called the *Clearing House, Ed-Central* or the *Center for Approved Learning Facility*, its official name. But his reading had also suggested other unofficial PAC-unfriendly names that were even more interesting: One was the *Golden Calf*, based on the formal name; another was *PAC-NICE,* for the *New Inquisition to Control Education;* and the last one was O*SHAPHT,* the eye-roll meaning of which he preferred to ignore but later came to understand.

Still, PAC friend or foe, no one could deny the true beauty of the building he now saw. Its broad cobblestone walkway led him between two enormous fountains featuring sculptured dolphins and sea gulls frolicking amidst a blue-white gush of shimmering water. It was exciting just to walk through it, turning in circles and gazing all around under the light mist it created. But not even that childlike adventure prepared him for what confronted him when he stepped past that mist onto the black granite terrace fronting the entrance.

At first, staring up, he gaped in wet-faced, open-mouthed wonder at the huge heavy wood and iron palace-like gates before him, and he felt dwarfed. His admiring eyes traveled lovingly over that wondrous portal as he searched it inch by inch for some sign of a mere mortal way into it, finally finding it in the double doors placed in the gates themselves. Although also ornate, they were sized to allow mere normal humans to enter.

The wonder of it all! With those gates plus the fountains, the sheer majesty of the whole experience was overwhelming. Surely in this, PAC was doing something right; a society that invested this much in the education of its children couldn't be as bad it often seemed from Arbortown; and it all gave him cause to wonder, however briefly, about his mission, even his own mind-set. Thinking now that perhaps he had been too negative, his right hand actually trembled when he reached out to tug open one of those beautiful doors.

"Master Stanton?" An attractive, late middle-aged woman with swept-back, gray hair greeted him with a smile as he stepped inside. She wore the sash of a teacher-in-chief, but her expression was less piously self-important than that of most of the PAC ed-chiefs he had known at Arbor U. And curiously, she seemed to be studying him very closely as they me—something that was soon explained when she flashed a WWW across her chest just before reaching out for his hand. And smiling at both him and his surprise as they shook hands, she introduced herself, "I'm Dr. Paula Cruz, quotaed Hispanic female, and we're pleased to welcome a masters-level scholar from Arbor University."

"Sink me," he whispered back, offering a quick return smile as they shook. Once they had squeezed the correct exchange sequence,

Glenn, who was still awed by the building, waved around at it and exclaimed, "What a place! I have never seen anything like it. The people of your community here must be very proud to be served by a facility like this, especially in these times. I can't get over it."

"Yes, we are twice blessed. First, by the good people we serve, and of course, by the generosity of PAC, which makes all of this possible," Dr. Cruz replied in such a loud voice that it seemed as if she thought she was speaking to a large group, which surprised Glenn, who reacted by looking around to confirm what he already knew: they were alone.

"This place is huge, how many students do you have here and what grades?" he asked her, and as he offered the question, he calculated, coming up with his own answer; there had to be somewhere between fifteen hundred to two thousand students here.

"Well, of course, none are on campus now because of summer break, which is so necessary for their growth and development, but directly and indirectly, we serve three hundred or so preschool and kindergarten through twelfth grade students on this campus," she replied. "But more on that later, let me show you our facility."

"Yes, thanks, I'd like that," he replied, and noting that she still spoke in a loud voice, he decided she must have a hearing problem and resolved to speak more loudly himself—to be polite. But that aside, he wondered about her numbers; they just didn't make sense … all of this for three hundred students? Should be many times that.

Apparently unaware of his confusion, she smiled again and, nodding for him to follow, led him off on what she said would be a quick tour on the way to her office. As they walked, she paused briefly to loudly identify each of the areas they passed through.

"The rooms on this hall are for psychological testing and research. We employ twenty PAC-certified psychologists. And this is for social work." She motioned down another hallway. "We have fifty social workers on our staff. And down the three halls over there are specialists such as occupational and physical therapists, speech, and other categories. But let's go this way, it'll take us through to the hub where my office is. This, by the way, is the teacher consultant hall, and at one hundred, it is our largest grouping."

"And this must be the hub you mentioned," Glenn called out as they reached the end of hall, his loud voice matching hers because he wanted to be supportive. But her response surprised him. Half turning, she looked quizzically back at him as if confused.

However, all of that was lost to him the moment he stepped into the hub itself. He was amazed by the stunning panorama before him; it was all like a page out of "Office Beautiful." The hub's luxuriously carpeted semi-circular floor area was bounded on the inside by four floors of glass-fronted offices with small balconies, all balanced by a wide ceiling to floor glass curved facing wall, showcasing yet another lavishly landscaped garden outside. And for the second time that day, he stared around in awe.

"This is simply spectacular," he whispered, but remembering her hearing problem, he continued in a louder voice. "This is spectacular. I guess all the classrooms have to be on the upper floors, but I've seen only one small elevator, and that escalator over there doesn't look big enough to accommodate even the three hundred students you mentioned. How do you manage to get them back and forth to classes?"

"Oh, Glenn, the students aren't housed in this building." Paula laughed, and gesturing toward the balconies above them, she went on to explain. "The fourth floor houses suites for our two top administrators and of course, the necessary PAC education ombudstera. The third floor is for forms and file storage, and the second is for meetings, demonstration projects, and our many supervisors." She paused, smiling as she added, "I should tell you that we do all evaluations as well as parent and other important meetings at this location. To better serve our population, all must come here, but they come a few at a time, and of course, we space them out." Waving a happy hand around, she went on, "And so, as I'm sure you can now see, while you may have thought we have a lot of extra space here, we're really very much squeezed." And with that comment still hanging in the air, she walked over to the window, and turning around to face him, she leaned back against the glass with a too broad by far smile on her face … as if waiting for questions.

"OOO-K." Glenn said, frowning as he also moved to the window. Outside, he saw a beautiful back lawn, more water works, and a low brick wall running in front of a long border of charming evergreen trees that blocked the view beyond. But as beautiful as it was, it didn't make sense. Turning back to Paula, he forced a polite laugh and asked, as diplomatically as he could, "Well, you've shown me where all the many professionals are housed and where the meetings take place and where all the paperwork is stored, but what about the kids? Where are their classrooms? Actually, I guess, where's the school?"

"Let's talk about that after coffee and donuts," she replied, and smiling happily with her hands up and out, she motioned all around as they walked. It was still as if she thought she had a crowd around her and was leading a tour, which by now was beginning to irritate Glenn. And then, as he was turning her glib words over in his mind and getting even more frustrated, she stopped—seemingly as an afterthought—by a large room right next to the rear exit. And stepping aside at the door, she motioned for him to look inside.

"Since you asked about how we serve our staff, here's one room in particular I want you to see before we take our break. We call this beautiful place the *TENT*, which stands for *Tenured Educators Not Teaching*, and it's one of my favorite places. It's for educators being disciplined and shows what good care we take of our professionals."

Glenn reluctantly glanced into the well-done carpeted room with its bookcases, lamp tables, and easy chairs, but he didn't comment on it. Instead, he just shook his head and turned to follow her as she walked away. He really didn't care about non-teaching teachers in trouble and their big den; this whole trip was turning into a real downer.

He was angry now, and when they arrived at Paula's office, just across the hub from the *TENT*, he finally burst out with, "What's going on? This place is magnificent, and it must have cost a fortune to build it, but all I hear about is staff, even those who don't work. How about the kids? What's here for them?"

"Why, Master Stanton, everything here is for the kids. Didn't you notice our motto written all across the front of the building?" She seemed to be different now, and although she continued to speak very loudly, she held his eyes and slowly shook her head from side to side as she passed him a coffee.

"Yes, I saw it. It said, *We Care About Kids.*" He was careful to continue in his loud voice, but deciding that her slow headshake might mean that right now wasn't a good time to talk, he shut up, took a big bite out of his donut, and waited for her lead.

"Yes, but did you notice that our *We Care About Kids* motto is written in exactly one hundred languages?" she asked and then surprised him by quietly adding, "But of course, we only allow kids and parents into this building a few at a time, for scheduled meetings and evaluations. When you finish your donut, we can talk about that, but please don't rush, I quite literally have nothing else to do today." After whispering that last part, she laughed and added in an even lower whisper, "You know, I might as well be over in the TENT collecting full pay for sitting all day doing ... well, whatever!"

"I didn't see anyone there—or anywhere else." Glenn muttered his reply as he took a sip of coffee, but then grinning at her in sudden realization, he added, "Don't tell me the non-teaching teachers are all off on their paid summer vacations, aren't they?"

"You got it," she whispered, and smiling, she sagged back in her seat, and they both sat quietly eating donuts and sipping coffee. Once they finished, Paula returned to her normal loud voice, saying, "And now, if you're ready, I'll show you our classrooms. We usually don't do this, but with the level of your pass, we wouldn't want to deny you a full tour. We want you to get a complete picture of a program we're very proud of." And on that note, she returned to form, leading him out of the building as if a crowd followed.

But everything changed minutes later when they stepped through the tree line. "Whoa! What's that ugly *mess*?" he called out, and stopping abruptly by a sagging wooden gate, he stood open mouthed, staring at an array of ten old and poorly maintained portable classroom units. But Paula grabbed his sleeve before he could say more, pulling him several steps off into the trees up to a large, fenced-in, electrical control unit.

"Glenn, you have to be careful what you say. This whole place is bugged, and you've been on camera inside," she explained, now talking in a surprisingly normal tone.

Confused, he frowned over at her, and she laughed and nodded upward. He followed her eyes as they shifted toward a camera fixed to a mounting far above them. It was pointed in their direction, but saw nothing because it had a red shirt draped over it.

"Shirt's been there for over a week, and it'll stay that way until the next scheduled service call next month, or even the month after, who knows? One of the benefits of this glorious new era of ours is bureaucratic inefficiency. But Glenn, watch what you say and do everywhere in PAC-dom and speak loudly only when you want them to hear what you're saying, because they are *always* listening and watching—or trying to at any rate."

"Hey, you don't have a hearing problem!" He laughed in sudden realization.

"No, I have a political problem, not a hearing problem." She smiled, and looking curiously at him, added. "I wondered why you were shouting at me, now I know."

"I wondered about you too, you seemed a bit schizo," he replied, grinning.

"Actually, I shouldn't be laughing. Everything's bizarre here, but it's not really funny," she said. "They come down hard on anyone they don't think is loyal, and I came too close to the line over coffee, but Glenn, sometimes I can't help it. I get so sick of the never-ending games. Anyway, as I'm sure you've guessed by now, all of this is why you were brought here. I wanted you to see this. I wanted this to be engraved in your heart and mind as you go on to Whigville. *This* is PAC education. Don't ever forget it!"

"Oh, it's engraved all right, and I'll never forget this whole mess, especially this side of the fence," Glenn said, gesturing at the run-down classroom trailer park.

"One equals the other, and you needed to see both." She frowned as she spoke.

"All that luxury for staff and big shots on the other side of the trees, and this is all you've got for the kids? There's not even a playground here."

"Your masters' degree is certainly not in education, Glenn, or you'd know that playgrounds were abolished as being too dangerously uncontrolled years ago," she replied. "But don't worry, the few kids who bother to come to school now don't get recess anyway. They're kept busy on endless PAC drills in their rooms—that's the only correct activity these days. Curiously, most girls make it fine in our less active schools, but a lot of boys don't, not that anyone really cares. The boys here, like all males in PAC zones, are headed for no work or low-level work futures anyway."

"But this is so stupid! It reminds me of a quote from John Witherspoon, the only pastor to sign our Declaration of Independence. He said, 'The best exercise in the world for children [that's boys *and* girls] is to let them romp and jump about as soon as they are able according to their fancy.' I don't understand why parents don't complain. Is love dead these days?" Then, laughing, he added, "On the other hand, I guess emersion in nothing but PAC-truth prepares their kids for Arbor U. and that probably makes it OK."

"Good quote, Glenn, but we started stealing our kids' romp time long before the rise of PAC. Our new betters just changed the whole thing from being the misguided but still caring helicoptering effort it was, to pure brain washing. As for our parents here, they're all Status Oners, and they do love their kids—even their boys—enough to want them to go to Arbor U. That means they have two choices: to be happy about what we do here or to lose fed-ed-credit status." She spoke matter-of-factly, not needing to explain that the Status Oners, voters certified as being loyal to PAC, were America's new elite.

"And so this is for the cream of the crop." Glenn sighed. "What a joke! Kids were better off in the old days, going to school in their own neighborhoods or to private or charter schools. Frankly, being home-schooled by caring, knowledgeable parents or even staying at home and playing marbles all day would be better than this monstrosity."

"What you have here is the ideal school, Glenn," Paula said with a bitter laugh.

"Ideal? From what you say, this place is mostly empty of kids even during the school year. They only come when they feel like it. How's that ideal?"

"Come on, Glenn, we educators have posh quarters and high salaries, and beyond doing the few evaluations required to bring in the fed money, most of us don't have to hassle with the inconvenience of actually working much with real kids. We don't have to actually teach them anything beyond the PAC drills—and that's only if and when they bother to show. The most important thing is the paperwork, always the right paperwork."

"I can understand why PAC prefers poorly educated sheep. They become reliably herd-compliant followers," Glenn said. "But at least some parents must want more. How are *their* kids educated?"

"Well, even though private education is outlawed in PAC-controlled areas, there's now a vital and growing underground all around us that educates our kids away from the barrage of 'Dear-Leader-style' PAC propaganda and education-lite," she replied.

"And that majestic building I just walked through?"

"There's an old Texas expression that was used in business in the old days: *Big Hat, No Cattle*. It signified having an important sounding job but not really having any power or authority over people. For educators these days, that adds up to 'Big Salaries, No Kids,' or in the vernacular, *'Big Feds, No Rug-Rats.'* The kids all belong to PAC in our glorious oh-so-correct schools today, and sadly, that's the way we seem to want it to be.

"It all started decades ago when education was taken over by the feds with the resulting build-up of middle managers who didn't focus on real education but did focus on a swarm of fed-rules, requiring an army of well-paid consultants. At first, parents responded by complaining, and for a short while, it looked like they might even retake the public schools. But the allure of "free" federal money was too strong, and both PAC and big government were able to easily consolidate their power by moving to a dumbed-down education model, favoring 'feel-goodedness' and PAC-approved loyalty. Right-thinking drills became the order of the day, and many people then just gave up and fled the public schools. We've been in this sad in-between era ever since, although since the friendlies came local control of schools has returned to the Heartland, away from PAC.

"Now, don't misunderstand, I'm not praising the friendlies. PAC would be out of power by now even here if it weren't for them and their guns, but for now anyway, they won't let PAC mess with our people out in the Heartland. I don't know their reasons for that, but we should be thankful. It gives us the time and the safe bases we need to get the Whig Partisan Alliance organized, up, and going across the country."

"OK, I understand all of that, but I'll never understand how we can justify giving our kids a lousy non-education but giving ourselves bigger monuments," Glenn replied. And with that, they turned and walked away in silence, going through the trees around that big fancy building instead of back through it. When they reached the path leading away, he offered Dr. Cruz a forced smile and his quiet but genuine 'thanks for the tour,' and they shook hands. He felt subdued and bit sick to his stomach as he walked away, and he didn't bother to look back at that big well-fountained palace with its empty motto.

"You don't look good." A woman's voice greeted him as he walked away. But he was in no mood for chitchat, and frowning, he barely glanced up as he tried to push on by her. All he wanted to do was to get back to the cabin, collect his gear, and move on. But the woman ignored his snub and fell in behind him, walking along for a few steps before calmly saying, "I don't think you know it, but you're going the wrong way."

"Who *are* you?" He snapped out the words, and scowling back at her, he started to walk even faster, just to get away—until he saw the WWW sign."

"Hold up, Glenn, I understand the mood, but you're still going the wrong way."

"Sink me, I'm sorry; I just had a bad experience," he mumbled, disconcerted as they shook hands. He now felt caught up on an emotional swinging bridge, off balance between the disappointment of his recent experience and now ... embarrassment.

"Yes, I know, and you look like it. But let's take a break over there," she said, gesturing toward a small clearing. "You'll feel better after you've had some lunch." Once in the clearing, she picked up one of the two large backpacks waiting for them there and opened it to reveal the personal gear he had left at the cabin, but it was the other pack that contained the really important stuff: a very welcome corned beef sandwich with chips, pickle, water, and a big red pop. Laughing at his obvious enthusiasm, she pointed at the lot of it and said, "This stuff is OK for right now, but later on today you'll do much better, much, much better—as you'll see." She winked, laughing. "You'll really see."

"Hey, I look forward to it, but this is great for right now. I love this kind of food. And I appreciate you getting my stuff," he added, grinning at her. "Of course, I know you're an angel, and I'm glad we connected, but I'm sorry, I didn't catch your name."

"I didn't throw it. You seemed otherwise occupied," she said, handing him a pop and sandwich. "I'm J3. We're all on the J-team, hence all of the *J* initials. My job is to debrief you on your last mission and to get you to your next adventure. Any thoughts?"

"I don't know," Glenn said. "Today's been crazy and very confusing for me, even though I know it all fits in perfectly with all the idiocy that's happened all over the place in America for the past seventy-eighty years or so. Funny, that's almost twice my age and yours put together." He flashed a grin with the lifetime comment, but quickly slipped back to a frown as he went on. "You and I have never known anything better, but it still doesn't make sense to me. And you know the craziest part? I believe that most of the one-eyed Cyclops junk that's gone on in our society was caused by good people honestly wanting to do the right things, but they just didn't think it through. At least, I believe that was true early on, before PAC jelled. That's the craziest part of this whole mess!"

"Our generation drew the short straw, that's for sure," J3 said. "And I agree that except for a few hardline power-at-the-center-at-all-costs types, most Americans went along with the cascade of well-meaning but destructive—what we call, dark angel—junk that brought us down by following along with honestly caring blind hearts and too easily manipulated brains. But we can't waste time feeling sorry for ourselves or for missing the merry-go-round years.

We need to get busy right now building a whole new playground. Nothing has gone wrong that can't be put right. Civilizations rise and fall, always have and always will. But Glenn, we don't want to put it all back the way it was. Something was bad wrong with our old wiring, or else how could generations of loving parents have so selfishly dumped on their own kids?"

They chitchatted about his experience at the mock school for some time, until J3 finally stood and gesturing toward the trail, announced, "Time to pick up and get rolling."

As they saddled up, Glenn went on with their theme, saying, "Every generation is called to be builders and not just consumers with their eyes only on themselves. And so I guess it falls to us now to begin moving our country back that way, by doing our duty to ourselves and certainly, to our kids. There's a short poem that I like that spells it all out. It's called:

Pass On the Good Stuff
What does one generation owe the next?
To pass on the good stuff and take care of the bad,
To offer their honor, treasure, and lives,
And to go to their graves giving all that they had."

"I don't know that poem, but I like it. We're stuck now with being on deck after more than a couple moral-scofflaw generations soaked up most of what that poem calls 'the good stuff.' They then happily kicked the empty cash-due can down the road for their own kids to pick up," she said. "But let's talk and walk. You have a contact to meet."

After a fifteen-minute walk, the woods opened to their highway, and J3 held up a hand, stopping them so they could huddle under a tree to look out and study the road and its travelers. "Careful what you say from here on. This'll be clogged by idiots, but your buddies and contact will be waiting just off this road, so I decided to run the risk."

Those words were still hanging in the air, and they were barely beyond the trees when their "risk" time came. "Unaccompanied male! Halt, you!" A large, slatternly looking, aging woman shouted out as she left a group of women sitting in the shade off the road and lumbered towards them. Breathing heavily when she arrived, she began shaking a heavy walking stick right under Glenn's nose. "Unaccompanied male, why are you on this road? There are rules to protect people like me from people like you."

"Are you crazy?" Glenn snapped back, but before he could say more or take the stick away from her, J3 pushed in, placing herself between him and the woman.

"You may have it right." She spoke back to Glenn, and picking up on his words, she seized the other woman's eyes and snapped, "She's either crazy or blind." But then, as if struck by a new thought, she added, "Or maybe I'm invisible. Maybe I can't be seen.

Oh, my, what will I do?" She ended her little spiel with a plaintive laugh.

"You get out of the way, I saw you go into that woods alone. You wasn't with this male then, and so he must have been unaccompanied, and that's illegal. Males are too dangerous to be allowed out without an escort." The old gal didn't back away.

"Well, that answers part of my question. If you saw me go into the woods, you must not be blind, and so that means that I'm either invisible right now, or you're crazy."

J3 spoke in a very calm voice, and then glancing playfully around at others going by, she added, "I'll ask that woman over there if she can see me. That'll settle it."

"Don't be silly," the older woman snapped. "I said I saw you, and you wasn't with this male when I saw you before."

"But you do see me with him now, is that right?"

"Yes, of course I do," the woman sputtered.

"Then, that settles it," J3 replied, and smiling over at Glenn, she motioned for him to follow as she turned to walk away, calling back, "She can see me, so I'm not invisible. That leaves only one option— she's crazy, and so we'll just ignore her and get on our way."

"You calling me crazy? Well, I ain't no crazy, old woman. I'll show you!"

"Listen, you crazy, old woman," The angel whirled to face her. "I'm saying that it's crazy to think you're in Brighton. It's the only town with rules about unaccompanied males. But look around. This is not Brighton. We *are* headed there, but as even you can see, when we get there, this male will not be unaccompanied. That means you're either crazy ... or stupid, but that's your problem, not ours. So, get out of our way!"

The woman stared open-mouthed at J3, thought about resisting, but instead turned to slink silently off to the side of the road, leaving Glenn, who'd watched the whole weird drama unfold, to gaze over at his companion with new appreciation. Laughing, he said, "Wow, glad you're on my side, but what's all this nonsense about escorts for males?"

"Brighton's a crossroads place, and so it gets pretty weird. PAC controls the officials, but to maintain that control, it has to swing wide and wild to accommodate some of the real nutcase groups congregated there. And as you'll soon see, there's no shortage of those in that town—the lunatic fringe is more than just a fringe there."

"So I'm going to be with you until tomorrow?"

"No," she replied. "We try not to bunch up too much, so you're only with me until I connect you with a good friend of mine and of course, your buddies. So come on, we'll need to hustle to get to the crossroads on time."

They managed to arrive within twenty minutes of their assigned time, and Glenn was delighted to see his friends lounging on the grass waiting for them when they got there. Indeed, he was so delighted that he decided to get them in trouble. "I note, J3," he announced with a very serious tone to his voice, "that these two very dangerous looking males are unaccompanied, and I'm shocked by that. Shocked! Something must be done!"

"What?" Little John looked up at him, frowning. "What're you talkin' about?"

"A clear violation of PAC rules," Glenn persisted, glancing toward their angel for confirmation as he spoke, but keeping an eye on them. He was eager to see their reaction when they heard about the unescorted male rule.

"Not really," J3 replied, to his surprise. "That crazy lady may have thought all males have to have a female escort, but the rule is that only lone males can't be trusted.

These two can watch each other. And they better do just that. There are no male gangs these days. You get caught breaking the law in a gang, and you're all off to Detroit and a friendly's prison—and they're not easy livin' places. They're follow-the-rules-or-get-shot places. So you see, at least some good has come out of our collapse. Our juvenile crime rate in America was a major crime in itself—generation after generation."

"What's this all about?" Alex chimed in.

After Glenn introduced them, they all plopped down on the grassy knoll near the intersection where she said they'd make their next contact. He then filled them in on both the crazy woman and his experience at PAC-NICE, as he had decided to call it, thinking of C. S. Lewis again. The other two then shared their own adventures, and they were just ready to ask her more about Brighton when their angel interrupted.

"There he is, that black gentleman walking by over there is your contact," she said, nodding toward an older man strolling along with another man and two women, all three white. "Don't be obvious about looking at him, just observe who he is. He's what we call a Masked Worthy, meaning he works completely within the PAC community, and of course, they don't know he's with us, and we want to keep it that way."

"Undercover! That's great, I love it," Little John said, grinning broadly. "You know our last angel was a …"

"Little John!" Alex and Glenn both cut in at once, and John stopped, embarrassed.

"Good, I'm glad you're glad." J3, choosing to ignore the near confidentiality slip, continued with her instructions, "You'll become part of his act later, and so watch for him to move out and then follow him—but he controls the time. He knows about you, and I know that you're going to love where he takes you tonight. But right now, before I take off, I'd like to hear your take on the unaccompanied male rule. What do you think?"

"It's idiotic, obviously, but it's only here, so no worries, right?" Glenn responded to her question, but the other two men just nodded, seemingly not all that interested.

"Well, it may spread from here, especially to college towns around the country. Academics and students are suckers for the latest wave of idiocy, from communism in the 1930s, to the adolescent self-abuse of the 1960s, and on to the 'blame America first' tripe that followed it and continues today," she replied. "PAC encourages this kind of thinking because it sets people against one another, which is what PAC likes most. They tolerate no loyalties above the party, and so they'll support this nonsense and allow its expansion."

"You gotta be kidding me," John said. "No one will tolerate that kind of junk!"

"Well, it's tolerated here, right now," she replied, and forming a wry smile, she then added, "And the same kind of thing has been tolerated around the world forever."

"What? Rules against unaccompanied males?" John stared at her. "I've never heard about that kind of craziness anywhere else."

"Think about it," she said, watching them closely as she continued, "Countries that represent a big chunk of the world's population have that rule right now, but with just one little twist: it applies to unaccompanied women, not men. The whole world tolerates that and always has, including our go-along-to-get-along leaders in the once dominant, pseudo-enlightened West. How is that any different?" She looked over at them, studying their faces, and they could see that she was very serious about this topic.

"Well, cultural differences, you know," Glenn fumbled around. "And of course, the custom has always been to let nations run their own internal affairs."

"You're right, but that doesn't make *it* right, and of course, it's not always about women," she said. "Religion is another area where we've fallen short as a people: too many countries allow the official and unofficial bad actors in their midst to persecute religious minorities. They kill them, imprison them, and subjected them to an unending torrent of daily abuse, and neither we nor any of the other so-called advanced countries have ever done much more than wring their hands over it—usually quietly. Thousands of men, women, and children—guilty only of being part of what in their killers' eyes is an inferior group—die every year, and we've looked the other way for ... well, forever.

"But for a few decades before our fall, our posturing had become only a sad, weaseling wimp-out excuse, because for the first time in history, people who claimed to be part of a culture of enlightenment had the power to punish the abuse of minorities and women in at least some and, actually, in most areas. But don't bother searching all the illegal history books for examples of our courage, you won't find them. Aside from our one success in South Africa, we did almost nothing as a nation or individually, nor did any of the other then privileged nations stand up for true equal justice. And even more tragically, our women's groups in the West were too busy spinning nice, safe, feel good, Janus-like webs at home to join in a real push for simple justice elsewhere. Male and female, we all simply refused to acknowledge the life-choking evil being visited on so many others, pretending that it was only an unpleasant reality, just one of those things.

"We ignored it because the victims were unimportant to us. Gals and guys, all of us were guilty of bowing down to a banner of evil rampant on a field of yellowed acedia. One writer named it the *Wilted Lilies of Forbidden Dreams* banner. But these ignored victims were men and women who deserved their dreams as much as we deserve ours."

She paused, studying them for a long moment and then, smiling grimly, added, "It's my belief that we're in this mess today because we've made too many decisions to blah our way through problems while the moral flesh of our civilization rotted away all around us. And generations of women had suffered far more than men for that neglect until the 70s when the collapse of the family left as many poor males as poor females of all races hanging out to dry. Then along came the PAC-types to make things worse."

"I don't think it's all that simple," Little John said, staring uncertainly at her.

146

"I won't argue with your examples, but to be fair, the rules about women and minorities go back a long way … to the beginning of time," Glenn joined in. "I'm not sure what we could have done before the fall, but now we have a new world to build, and I hope we'll make it better this time for everyone … all women as well as all men. The alliance is working for a freedom that includes everyone."

"I'll answer both of you. First, Glenn, if you mean that Americans couldn't push for a stronger moral position because of tradition, on the one hand, and the shameful neglect of our own poor, on the other, I don't agree. We should've had enough courage to honestly face up to our shortcomings and to also take a firm position on women and minority rights around the world. We don't have to be perfect to work toward making life better for people here *and* everywhere else. Better isn't perfect, but it certainly beats the horror of the status quo for those abused and left behind. We chose to bow our heads to that 'wilted dreams' banner, ignoring too much here and abroad. Tradition? Baloney!

"And, John, you say it's not that simple, but I think it's very simple. I believe that our many decisions to ignore the evil being visited on women and minorities back when we had the power to do something undermined our nation both morally and strategically.

"Morally, it undermined us within our own country, and it left us open to PAC poison.

"Strategically, it signaled weakness, and that's what drove the tripartite powers together.

"Of course, they weren't bothered by our weakness about women and minority rights, but they were concerned about the possibility that the puny radicals we were playing patty-cake within those days would increasingly become more of a problem for them. They waited, and they watched, and when they finally decided that we didn't have the will, despite all of our power to deal effectively with that feeble threat, they acted.

"When those same radicals tried their thin gruel of bluster and bombs against the tripartite powers, things changed fast. The terror-ists' old trump card of playing us off against our own values didn't work with China and Russia at all and had little impact on India.

The three came together, elbowed us aside, and then moved on to stomp the bad gnats, bigtime. And these days, we don't hear much about them at all. They seem to have vanished down history's sinkhole. It was simply a matter of our lack of the will to use the power that we actually had. Our new masters had that will, we did not."

"I think that's a bit of a reach, life is never that simple," Glenn said. "Besides, are you really excusing the friendlies for the horror they visited on Middle East?"

"I think she's right," said Alex, who'd been listening quietly to the others. "If we'd stood up to our responsibilities at home, the collapse of our family structure in particular, and really cared about all the suffering in the world we were so good at just wringing our hands over, we'd have a much better situation today for everyone. We had the power to do more than we did. We just didn't have the will. As for the tactics the friendlies used when they stepped in, they were horrible, and too many people were killed. But to be honest, it looks like the Middle East is more peaceful now than it's ever been, and so there may be a net gain in human life. Of course, I don't think things are better for women and minorities over there now, it's all just kept very quiet. The locals certainly don't want to attract more friendly attention, and so they're keeping a very low profile."

"Thanks, Alex. I can tell you for sure that things there are not better for women and minorities over there, but we no longer have the power or influence to do anything about it. We did once, but we don't now.

"Still, that's then, this is now," she said, and then shaking her head, she continued with a genuine, but sad-tinged laugh. "But listen, guys, I'm sorry. That's all in the past, and I believe with all my heart in the alliance creed: 'It's today, not yesterday, that we have; let's use today to go forward and build a brighter tomorrow.'

"Besides, you may not believe this, but I'm usually a more cheerful person. I'm like the guy in the story Boswell told about Samuel Johnson. A friend of Johnson's, whose name I've lost, told the great man that, despite all the sorrow he saw in the world, he couldn't be as glum as he, Johnson, was because, try as he would to be downcast, he couldn't hold on to it. Somehow, cheerfulness always broke in."

They all laughed, she joining them as she added, "That's usually true for me as well. I believe that things are truly very bad right now, but they've been bad in the past for us, and things are far worse for so many others around the world right now, especially women and minorities. I think a lot about all of that, but then I remember that it's our job to fix the problems, not to cry over them, and certainly not to feel sorry for ourselves. So I shift gears, and sure enough, that good old cheerfulness breaks in. What I'm saying is that, whether you can believe it or not, I'm essentially a very happy person."

"I like that, that part about cheerfulness breaking in," Little John said, tossing her a salute. "Thank you, you've given us some important things to think about."

"Thanks back to you, but we're going to make it better—for everyone. As to you guys, don't forget to let a little bit of cheerfulness break in, even as you go after the bad guys. But I see that your leader is on the move, and I have to get on the road too. So good luck and welcome aboard our very exciting, but oh so earthbound enterprise. I hope to see you again someday, but for now, stay close to the Worthy and wait for his signal. And guys, as I keep saying, you're gonna love where he takes you tonight."

What's his name?" John thought to ask. "Do we get to know his name?"

"Oh, I'm sorry. Yes, of course you do." She laughed. "Dr. Alexander Shampton, Professor Alexander Shampton—or, as he will prefer, just plain Al."

She was still laughing as she walked away, but then as an afterthought, she turned and shouted back, "Glenn, I don't excuse our occupiers for what they've done here or in any other place, but we left a power vacuum at home and around the world, and we're responsible for that. Our challenge now is to work together to earn another shot at the leadership opportunity we blew. We, and the rest of the world, deserve the kind of life and government that we all almost had. And you gotta' believe, we're going to do what we need to do to get that life back for ourselves ... and everyone. We will win!"

CHAPTER ELEVEN

How the Three Engage the Strange Firefly Annual

"*Y*es, we will win!" Glenn shouted back to their angel as she walked away, and all three watched her until she was out of sight. And then they turned to follow a Worthy to their next adventure, beginning with a place in Brighton called the *Sip N Surf.*

Angel 3 had promised a great experience, but this place was—unbelievable! Just walking in the door turned into an eye-popping experience for the younger men, but it was all old hat to Alex. And laughing at their reaction, he explained, "Hey, it's just like all the other PAC techno-clubs I've seen. You know, places where the elite meet to enjoy their standing at the top of the *We're-All-Equal-but don't-look-too-closely* pecking order."

Glenn, accustomed to the chronically power short, poorly maintained classrooms of Arbor U, nodded that he understood, but he had never seen anything like this, and he could not have imagined all this glitz and glamour in his wildest dreams. The color burst of the tall tables ringing the room around the dance floor drew his eyes first. Seemingly made to look like the front half of the surfboards he recalled seeing in old-time videos, they were all complemented by brightly colored, high swivel chairs that, as he whispered, "Wow, you guys, look at that. Everybody can talk at their own tables and then—zoom! They can spin all around to talk to anybody else they want. That's neat. It's really neat!"

And that room itself! It was eye candy with its lights and colors and angles, all folded into one by a parade of screens, flashing action-action from beauty pageants and sports events from around the world—except the banned American football. And of course, because this place existed to serve PAC's elite and lesser loyalists, there was no coverage of the worldwide depression, the endless wars, or the fighting going on across America. It was all fun and games, with nothing that might be viewed as PAC-unworthy.

Deciding to risk staying together, the three took a table close to the Worthy's, so they could watch for his instructions. But it was the technology on and above their table that captured Glenn and John's attention at first. With a press of a finger on a red tabletop *on-spot*, an eight inch crystal centerpiece cube rose to the surface while, at the same time, a canopy of colorful plastic rimmed by a shining metal ring descended from above them to a point just over their heads, close, but without seeming to press down on them. Alex explained that when activated, the canopy would spread a zone of silence around the table that kept outside noise out and inside noise in. This zone allowed people to chat privately—although PAC could hear—or to enjoy the shows of their choice: a full menu of PAC-OK entertainment presented right there by holographic images of six-inch high *Small-Singers* or comedians, called *Mini-Wits*.

Alex, enjoying his friends' enthusiasm, laughed as he explained, "Customers can choose not only the act, but also the level they prefer from the menu's HEM: *H* for hot, *E* for everyone, and *M* for mild. You raise the HEM to way hot for porn and lower it to smile-mild for kid shows. The middle level's for all tastes, but that's according to the usual politically correct fix on approved tastes. You know, PAC approves, we approve. PAC disapproves, we disapprove. One opinion serves—or actually,_*rules* us all."

Three of the four who gathered at the Worthy's table were also very familiar with the place and the set-up. Al Shampton, his wife, Roxanne, and her close friend, Nancy Boxer, had been here many times, and it was old stuff to them, but it was all very new to an ex-colleague of Al's from Arbor U who had joined them at the last minute. Not socially tuned in at his best, their guest was not at his best on this day, and he was not making a good impression on the two women present, particularly Nancy.

He had never seen a display of opulence like this before, and he didn't like what he saw now ... or the fact of the place itself. "Come on, Al! How do you think PAC justifies all this techno-palace crap?" Jim Richards asked, and after taking another long sip of his drink, he leaned over the table, closely eyeing his friend as he darkly added, "Think about it. All this technology is ... well, it's like before the Great Fall."

"If I told you that the owners are all PAC clerics, would that help you understand?" Al replied, laughing at first, until he realized that the women were not laughing with him.

"I don't find that humorous at all," Nancy snapped, and looking first at Al, whom she had known for a long time, and then to his friend, she added, "It would be best for you to just enjoy what you're given and to avoid comments like those. They border on PAC-bashing, and that's not what we're all about. We owe too much to PAC for that."

"Yes, everything I am now I owe to PAC, and I certainly wouldn't want to be a PAC-basher," Jim replied grimly, and finishing his drink, he signaled for another. "But I have to wonder how this palace can operate in such a before the Great Fall fashion when the businesses all around us"—he paused to burp—"are lucky to have any electricity at all, even for a few hours a day. The technology I see here is incredible. They *have* to be using more than their *fair-use quota*. Am I missing something? Isn't saving the planet a big deal any longer, or are there special rights for special people?" He looked defiantly around, waiting for even one of them to defend this "palace."

"Jim, don't go there," Al side-whispered to his friend, hoping to protect him. There were things that aren't talked about, and this was definitely one of them. Then, glancing at the women, he loudly added, "Let's all just relax and have a good time."

"Jim, you shouldn't drink heavily before you come out into public." Nancy sniffed as she watched him take another long 'sip' from his glass, but then smiling, she added, "And I'm sure that the so-called 'Great Fall' that you mentioned was the 1930s' depression and not our present temporary readjustment."

"Temperrry?" He slurred. "Near thirty years off the PAC cliff's temperrry?"

"Come on folks, let's sit back and enjoy ourselves." Al was worried. This was getting nasty and it wasn't even like Jim who had always been a very laidback, above the world, scholarly type. Of course, that was in the old days, and Al hadn't seen him since his involuntarily retirement some years ago. Jim had left Arbortown after that, and Al had lost track of him. He still didn't know where he'd been, but he looked different now. The once dumpy, disheveled academic looked fit and well-pulled-together—except for the obvious fact that he'd had too much to drink before joining them for the evening.

"Listen to me, Al, Roxanne and I are offended by Dr. Richard's silly spiel and his whole manner, and you should be too," Nancy snapped, interrupting his thoughts and scowling meaningfully at him as she spoke, "You'll note that Rox and I are *not* smiling."

Rox, saying nothing, was not smiling, just sort of borderline frowning hesitantly.

"Come on, gang, it's all in the eye of the beholder, or in this case, the be-listener," Al said, grinning as he always did before starting one of his infamous stories. "There's an old tale about a preacher. You remember those people, don't you?" The women's eyes rolled, but he went on anyway. "Well, he was walking alone down a country road one day, back during that 1930s' depression you two mentioned." He paused to smile at both Jim and Nancy before continuing, "And coming upon a farmer in his field, he shouted out that the Lord had richly blessed him with a good crop. Well, that farmer, who was a crusty old soul, came back with 'You shoulda seen this field when the Lord had it all by his self. I did all the work that got this worthless piece of land to produce what little it does, and no matter what you think, preacher, I'm gonna take all the credit.'

"Of course, the preacher didn't like that, and so looking up to heaven, he shouted out in a loud and powerful voice, 'I guess you gotta show 'm, Lord!'

"And you know, those words were no sooner out of his mouth than there came a mighty boom followed by a great wind, and that now terrified farmer instantly found himself teetering on the edge of the last bit of Newtonian matter this side of an immense dark void. And I'll tell you, that old boy's clinching toes curled in his boots as he tried to balance and keep himself on our side of the subatomic realm that now lay gaping open before him, even as the sheer dark nullfulness of all that is without the hand of God seemed to be reaching up, trying to tug him down and away.

"But thankfully, that old farmer repented in time and was allowed to stumble backwards where he rolled over onto his knees, falling at once into a fervent prayer of thanksgiving. And as he prayed, that great void gave way once again to our little four percent world of particles and waves and to a farmland blessed by a good crop."

After finishing his story, Al sat back, grinning around the table, expecting to see smiles and less tension, but he drew blanks instead. Not one of the three smiled or even looked at him. Instead, Rox and Jim just sat there, stiffly and quietly staring down at the tabletop while Nancy glowered over at Al as he finished, slowly shaking her head.

"I don't understand that story," Roxanne finally mumbled and then surprised her husband by adding, "Nobody believes in all that God stuff anymore ... do they?"

"No, they don't," Nancy cut in briskly before Al could answer, her face now wearing an angry crush-the-nasty-bug look. "Of course you don't understand. It's a stupid story about stupid people back in a stupid time." Turning, she then scowled over at Al and snapped, "And what's all that gibberish about a four percent world anyway?"

"Ah, well ..." Al also frowned, but not at her. Nancy mad and on the warpath wasn't good. And then, sighing deeply and concerned about where all this was going, he answered her question. "Scientists believe that ninety-six percent of the universe is dark matter and energy—the four percent is the world we know. But, Nancy, please listen ..."

"Act-shlly, thish story's 'bout us," Jim cut in, his drinks now catching up with him. But seemingly feeling that he was on a roll, he picked up on Nancy's stupid people and stupid times comment, and slumping back in his chair with a self-satisfied look on his face, he cleared his throat, smiled blearily around the table, and mumbled, "Don't chou get it? Itch about PAC 'n 'bout us! That farmer wuz lookin' at our reeeality. If he'd jusht turned 'round, he'd 'ave seen the Garden uff Eden we left behind when we shtumbled up to the edge of thish bottomless PAC-pit 'r country—all uf ush—fell into … yearsh ago."

"Come on, Jim, that's not what the story's about at all," Al nervously protested.

"I'm sick of all of this. PAC inherited the so-called pit you're so worried about, and PAC will pull us out of it," Nancy snapped back. "You are a depressing throwback to the days of white male privilege. It's your kind who caused the mess we have today."

"Well, ya know … I 'gree wish you. We let PAC happen … 'n coulda shtoped it. N-thach … a umpardonable shin … in my book." His voice then, becoming even more garbled, trailed off into a whisper as, sighing deeply, he slumped back into his seat, the last words of his failing gambit almost lost, "Power-n … no will … ish …"

And that was it. Unable to finish, he fell silent, perhaps running out of gas, or more likely, the drinks got to him. Either way, he now sat slumped in place with his head bowed, blearily staring down at the table.

"I'm dialing up some entertainment to drown out all this PAC badmouthing," Nancy sniped, and eyeing her now sagging adversary with contempt, she reached out to hit the *on-spot* to bring up the cube. "I'll dial *M* to make Jim-boy, over there, happy."

With that, they all sat back to sip drinks, eat their meals, and to watch forty long minutes of frenetic mindlessness. Al forced himself to endure the drivel once again because the women loved the Mini-Wits, but he could see that Jim's gaze and mind were both somewhere else. Whether that was all because of drink or just life, Al didn't know.

But he felt guilty now as he studied his old friend, wondering what had brought him back to Brighton. He'd arrived unannounced at their door, just as they were leaving to meet Nancy, and Al could think of nothing else but to invite him to join them. Jim had asked to meet with him alone first, but Al didn't take the time to do it, and now the whole evening had turned into a disaster. But then, just as he leaned back trying to think of a good way to help his old friend, a sudden loud drumroll interrupted everything. And as every eye in the place turned as one towards that sound, all the domes moved up and all of the cubes went blank as they slid back down. PAC had taken charge of the tables.

"We are honored to have with us ten inductees into the PAC Sisterhood," said a woman announcer, wearing the usual jeans with the now popular red high heels and black top hat and tails look. Gesturing toward a table of chattering and laughing young women, she went on, "They are fortunate to be inducted just in time to choose to become *BUGs* in tonight's *Firefly Annual,* and to help them launch their new lives, they're asking that all sisters here present come forward for a laying-on of the *Hands of Relatedness.* Please, all sisters in the audience, let's help them celebrate this moment. Come on up!"

"Sisterhood? Bugs? Fireflies? What're they talking about?" John asked, looking across at a shoulder shrugging Glenn. But Alex took the question, and shifting forward with a *you're-gonna-love-this* glint in his eye, he motioned for them to huddle up.

"Well, it's all just another PAC values redo. The sisterhood's another group of true believers," he said, and the smile on his face faded to a dark, humorless snort as he added, "And as sisters, they're above old-fashioned things like chastity or a commitment to marriage vows, and so the gala that'll take place later tonight is really an orgy."

"Why do they want to be called *bugs*?" John asked. "That seems degrading."

"The *B* is for 'beauties,' and the *G* is for 'gallants,' an old term for men of culture and romance. The *U* in the middle is what tonight's all about, it stands for 'Urging,' and there'll be a lot of that going on when the sun goes down." Alex's mood had shifted to sour by the time he had finished his brief description, and so he closed with, "The whole thing is just one more PAC insult to the idea of family and to humanity's future."

After that, although still confused about all the BUG nonsense, both Glenn and John sat back with Alex to watch the show—and to keep an eye on Shampton's table. Some kind of trouble seemed to be brewing there, but they could only see and not hear what was happening, and so the big blow-up at the end of the sisters' hands ceremony took all three of them by surprise. They ended up, however, with their own ringside seat, watching Nancy strut her stuff and become a champion of the sisterhood.

"Merely-male, swine!" Nancy screamed, apparently reacting to a comment from Jim. She then strode purposefully around their table to his chair and without warning, pounced on him and began to pummel his head and shoulders with both fists. Professor Shampton, springing up to hold his wife back when she moved to help her friend, noted that others all around them were also on their feet, but no one dared to try to break up the woman-on-man attack. And the table of New Sisters, without even knowing what was said or all that had happened before, loyally applauded, cheering on their sister.

Their applause swelled and was joined by others when Nancy finally stepped back from Jim, who had only blocked and not returned her blows. And pumping both hands in the air, she shouted, "This merely-male throwback called us all, whores! That's what he said our *Hands of Relatedness* stands for. Can you believe it? Can we tolerate that? No!"

At those words, the whole room went up for grabs, and the women at the table of the New Sisters, springing from their seats, rushed to surround the offending man and to keep him there until the police could arrive. He was guilty of a hate crime!

Once on scene, the police went about their routine in a brisk and PAC-friendly manner. The obviously unrepentant but now charged-up and grinning Jim Richards was quickly arrested for disturbing the peace by reckless sexism and then whisked away.

No charges were filed against Nancy who was now the belle of the ball—and was loving it! She hugged Rox, and the two of them, joined by all of the cheering sisters and many others in the room, began dance-marching around the tables in a mad, triumphant conga-line, loudly shouting the sacred sisterhood chant: "Eve-ah! Eve-ah! Eve-ah!"

The three comrades, elbowing their way along behind Shampton through all that chaos, followed the police as they pushed Jim Richards beyond the raucous crowd and on out the door. But even after he was taken away, they still held back, waiting for a signal from Shampton as J3 had instructed, but he didn't signal. Instead, as they stood watching in confusion, he spoke briefly with his wife and then turned and slowly moved away to a bench under a close-by streetlight. And without looking around for them, he slumped down there and dropped his face into his hands, obviously reacting to something, but what? Could it be just his friend's arrest? That didn't seem likely, but what else?

They didn't know, but keeping their instructions in mind, they decided to just wait, giving him some space and time. There were no other benches close by, and so they settled down side by side on the curb, close to where he was, but not too close. They didn't talk while they waited, glancing occasionally toward Shampton. But he just there, leaning forward with his elbows on his knees and his face in his hands, not moving.

Finally, after what seemed to be a decent interval, Glenn stood, and approaching the professor cautiously, he politely cleared his throat and whispered, "Excuse me, sir ..."

"Yes, yes. Give me a second." The still head down Shampton whispered back almost at once. His voice was very husky, but after he too cleared his throat, he sighed deeply and then very slowly raised his weary head to look up at the younger man.

Glenn, looking down at this, an alliance leader, was impressed by what he saw in the dim light of the street lamp. Even though the professor's eyes were rimmed red and his cheeks still moist, he seemed well on the way to regaining his composure, and within just a few seconds, he morphed from a look of dejection and defeat to what soon became a confident command presence. It was incredible. Whatever tragic news had caused his pain and discomfort must still be there, but he was putting it aside for them, ready to do his duty. That was the Whig Partisan Alliance way!

The professor, now forcing a smile, sighed and slowly running a hand through the wisp of white hair on his near bald head, nodded towards the others. "Tell our friends over there to join us," he said. "And I guess I should begin by saying Sink-Me, even though, honestly, part of me already feels totally, completely sunk right now, very sunk."

Glenn, unsure what else to do, settled for nodding solemnly as he motioned to his now standing friends to join them, and by the time their contact routine was completed, the professor was greeting each of them by name with the poise and bearing of a true Worthy. He told them that Richards would remain in police custody until his background was checked out, and then he would have to leave Brighton. He also told them how changed Jim was now from the old days when he had been a good scholar and professor of history, now only a small part of a pseudo-department called Antiquated Core Studies.

"Jim was let go when history was cutback and politically corrected—a process that'd been going on for years—and it doesn't look like he's found a new academic way for himself, although physically he looks to be in better shape than he used to be. Maybe he's been doing some manual labor, but whatever it is, he looks the better for it. I hope that means he's connected somewhere, but I'm still going to contact some people for him and see about getting him relocated to a happier place, one that's far less PAC-marked in other words." He smiled sadly as he said it, but then frowning deeply, he looked directly at Alex and added, "I know for a fact that it should've been me getting that retirement and not him, but I out-quotaed him. He'd published more, he'd done more and frankly better research, and he was far better with the students than I was ... or am. But these days two things rule: loyalty to PAC is a big number one, and if they think that's in place, then the quota-score is number two. There is nothing more—and as for competence, ha!"

"Well, professor, I'm sure that's true here, but when they shut down the Marine Corps they didn't offer any of us a place anywhere, and my quota didn't matter. We were all poison," Alex replied, and then after pausing to think about it, he added, "But we didn't care about color because, in the Corps, there's only one color—green. We're all just plain marines no matter what our color or our quota-group is—or at least, we used to be. And you know, the way we were is the way it should be. The way it needs to be again."

"I agree with you, my young friend, and that's what the Blue Company is all about," Shampton said, and flashing a genuine smile this time, he slapped Alex on the back. "But at least you, in the Corps, were allowed to keep your honor. The other services were reduced to being mere shadows of their former selves, and then to make matters even worse, women replaced all the male officers by the decree of a_military czar who had no notion of, nor really cared about the historic missions of each branch, what they once stood for, or even about the enemies we faced. Your tour of duty ended with honor, but the other branches are now prisoners in the tragic lemming-like suicide run that is PAC's reign. The people remaining in those services are victims of a failure of will on the part of their old leaders and of political PAC puppets outside their services." He paused, looking at them. "But not for much longer, and ..."

But then, after glancing down at his watch, he took a deep breath and looked over at his new friends with a mix of sadness and embarrassment on his face. He now seemed to be unsure of himself, fumbling for words and searching their eyes for a reaction as he went on to a new topic. "Unfortunately, I have some other things, some business I have to conduct tonight—and this is awkward, and well, I'm sorry ... But I'll just have to lay it out for you, and hope you won't mind, maybe a personal favor. I need your help."

He then went on to give them a thumbnail sketch of the BUG fiasco he faced that night, one that he had learned about just a short time before. "This whole crazy BUG ritual started years ago when a PAC leader saw a TV show about fireflies and how those little things attracted mates by sending flashing light signals in a code that only the right mate would be able to decode and respond to, or maybe it was a bevy of possible mates, she wasn't sure. But from that bit of natural science—authentic or not, I don't know—came this whole BUG nonsense. Of course, it goes without saying that, as with so much else these days, it's based on the usual *poor-us-the-victims* notion that, after all the centuries of being dominated everywhere by men's signals, all women should now be liberated to signal any mate they choose and to have him fight his way to her."

"Is that new?" Little John mused. "Sounds like the way it's always been to me."

"To them it's a very new and liberating idea, and it fits with the military shift that I just mentioned. In other words, as with the officer corps, so too is this an exercise in male-phobic idiocy: there are no good males, only what they call, mere-males. So being quotaed-black doesn't help me here; all males are equally bad," Shampton spoke with a deep frown on his face. "Of course, I knew all about that nonsense, but I had filed it away in my bulging *PAC-idiocy to be endured* file, never dreaming it would touch me directly. So it was a big surprise for me to learn, just tonight, that my wife had signed on to it. And by law, I have to either participate or be dumped in favor of anyone she chooses among the men who make it to her tonight or anyone else she wants. It's all disgusting, and I'm disgusted with her and with myself for being part of it, but I can't just step back. Call it pride or stupidity or both, but I've got to try to find my wife tonight."

"Well, not to be mean, but I wasn't all that impressed by her," Little John said, and then, ducking his head under the withering glares of his companions, he made it worse by adding, "I mean that you could do better, sir. I mean that, after all, you're ..."

"What do you want us to do, sir?" Alex cut in before John could say something even more uncalled for. "We'll help in any way we can, but I have no idea what you need."

"She, at least, gave me her code, which should mean that I'll be the one who finds her. She claims this is all just a romantic adventure for her, and that I'm gone so much that she got lonely and joined the sisterhood on a lark. Well, I don't believe that it is just a lark. I think she's a PAC convert and that Nancy Boxer and her friends have heavily influenced her and now own her. But, Little John, I don't want to end my marriage this way. It may not seem like I have much to you. In fact, it may not be much, but it's what I've got, what I've had for a lot of years, and I don't want it to end like this."

Shampton then filled them in on the full BUG routine and showed them the map that Rox had given him during their brief conversation while the police were working on Jim. "She marked the location where I can position myself to look for her signal." He pointed to it and went on to explain that all the so-called gallants were to move forward only when they saw the right signal. "We're not supposed to compete with one another, but two things ruin that peaceful little plan: guys being guys, some idiots will think it'd be fun to poach on another man's signal, and they'll follow along until a woman is found and then cut the other guy out. And of course, gals being gals, some of them will give the signal to several men and reward whoever takes out the others on his way to her."

He looked up at the three men. "I'm asking you three to be my insurance against just such a setup. I don't trust my wife now, and if she violates our vows by giving the signal to others, I want to be ready. I may be an old fool for doing this." He glanced toward Little John, who looked quickly away. "But I'm not a total fool."

....

Dark found them all squatting in the grass, watching signals and counting flashes. Men all around them were moving out in response to their "lucky" codes, crawling along in the grass and keeping an eye out for others as they went. Of course, the first fight broke out within minutes of the first flashes, and fights soon spread along the whole line.

But the four stayed back, waiting. In fact, they waited so long that they all began to think that Rox had provided a bogus signal or changed her mind about participating. If the latter, she may have gone home, but if the former, she probably—well, Shampton didn't want to think about that, and the others kept quiet.

Then came the signal, and they all eagerly dropped to the grass and started forward, watching all around as they crawled but particularly in front because that's where the other men would be by now. They had been the last to leave, or close to it, and so if someone planned to make a move to take out Shampton, it would happen up ahead.

They moved along on hands and knees under the watchful eyes of the Crawl-Form Referees—the lowest form of PAC male enforcers—who were there only to count crawlers and to be sure the men were humble and really crawling, not to give assistance or break up fights. But the four ignored those creeps, and led by flashes, they worked their way across a small valley and began moving up their target hill. Then, whoa!

Just when they had almost reached the top, the flashing ended.

They paused to decide what to do, certain that they were close to where she had to be. The light had come from a place just off to the side away over there, and it didn't look like anyone else had moved up their slope with them. If true, that was good, and they were now only minutes away, and the professor's marriage had been saved!

Glenn had felt the excitement of the hunt from the very beginning, or at least that's how he thought of it. The grass under his hands, the dirt, and the smell of being that close to the earth had his adrenalin flowing, and he was actually enjoying what seemed to be a great adventure. But he chastised himself. His adventure was coming at the expense of another man's pride, a Worthy's pride, and he reminded himself that his adolescent thrill about having an adventure was nothing compared to the loss that man faced. Yet, that thrill was still running through him, especially when they reached the stonewall at the very top of the hill where the professor chose to go forward alone.

"Rox, I'm so glad I found you. I'm too old for this, and I was getting pretty tired.

If I had a vote, I'll tell you, I'd vote against the rule that says a man has to crawl all the way." Shampton had called into the darkness, half-laughing as he panted out the words and stepped away from the wall. Still breathing hard, he paused to look around, but it was now so dark that he had to squint to see and could barely make out Roxanne as she emerged from under a nearby large tree, seemingly adjusting her clothes as she came towards him. But she was pulling them back together, not undoing them ... and looming just behind her, the old professor could make out another figure—a very large figure.

"I didn't expect you, Al. I was sure that you'd be too proud to go through all of this just for me," she whispered the words, shyly, half giggling and nervously looking down as she tried to catch her breath ... and button her blouse. But then, as her confused husband watched in exhausted amazement, she remembered who she now was, and her attitude suddenly shifted, morphing from that of the gentle wife of so many years to an all too true a *Sister*. And it was as such a liberated *womon* that she added, "Why am I even apologizing to you? You lost the race. I don't have to apologize to you, now, or ever!"

After that outburst, she hesitated again as if unsure of herself. But her will faded for only a moment, and then, after taking a deep, very measured breath, she steadied herself, and tossing her head in defiance, she turned her back to Shampton and nodded toward the giant shadow still waiting in the dark behind her.

That shadow stirred, and the three comrades' eyes widened when they saw that it was a bull of a man who stepped out into the dim light to shuffle silently toward the now stunned and seemingly defenseless professor, now sitting open-mouthed on the wall.

But it wasn't the expected easy-mark, elderly professor that the sneering hulk encountered, and the struggle was brief and near deadly for that failed conquering hero.

By a combination of surprise and sheer power, Little John made short work of Rox's new, but now very battered, bruised, and unconscious playmate.

Shampton, feeling humiliated, watched the short battle unfold from his place on the wall, and when it was over, he slowly raised himself to his feet. And although very disgusted by the sickness of it all, he forced himself to stand tall, and with his head up and his eyes narrowed in resolve, he crossed the short space to Rox, now sprawled alone in the dirt, staring straight ahead and sobbing. Her red blouse was still undone and one side of her black brassiere hung down across her lap, but he ignored all of that.

Standing over her, he paused for just a moment, silently looking down at this, his wife of so many years, and he waited … waited for some sign of hope. When she didn't acknowledge him or even look up, he took a deep breath, steadied himself, and bending to reach down, he very gently laid his wedding ring on her bare thigh. Then, lost in a flood of grief, he stood up straight again, turned, and walked slowly and very unsteadily away, without looking back. Tears were streaming down his face.

His now ex-wife, according to PAC event rules, didn't object or even watch as her discarded husband walked away from her. Instead, still sobbing, she crawled over on hands and knees to lay herself across the body of the unconscious man who was now her legal companion—until she decided otherwise.

The ring? It lay lost and forgotten in the weeds and the dirt. Their long marriage, based upon thousands of years of now discarded tradition about the bonds of marriage and husband and wife loyalty, was history. PAC, ever a jealous ruler, was triumphant: loyalty to PAC was to be the only enduring loyalty.

CHAPTER TWELVE

How Glenn Is Twice Awarded at the PAC Academy

The three comrades stayed up half the night talking with Al Shampton in the hayloft of a big red barn just outside Brighton, but they didn't waste much time on the sisterhood craziness they had experienced, nor much about our PAC inspired calamity.

Not that the professor ignored the failure of will that made it happen, he hit it hard and to the point. "The post-WWII generations were called to be the free guardians of liberty—as we all still are—but they chose to be mere government lackeys. Called to be self-disciplined builders, working toward a better future, they chose the selfish pleasure of PAC's beggar-the-future house of mirrors. Thus, they enjoyed a merry decades-long "free" feast and left their own children with the table scraps ... and the bill.

"That wimp hubris put us in this fine mess," Shampton went on, seemingly ready to wrap up, but then studying their reaction and not liking what he saw, he quickly added a warning. "But wait-one, don't make the same self-centered mistake they made! They saw themselves as being so uniquely wonderful that unpaid bills didn't matter, but there are rules about bills: they *must* be paid. And our elders didn't pay as they partied, and so it's left it to us to face the music and to deal with the chaos we've inherited. But before you get too caught up in self-pity, you need to remember that we aren't close to being the first group of generations to be left holding a bag full of past-due bills—not at all.

"Think of the Civil War," he declared. "How many generations kicked the can down the road about slavery? And let's not forget the generations that gave up on the faltering effort at the Reconstruction that was supposed to move us past that war. They condemned black citizens to long decades of second-class citizenship—and not just in the south. And the unintended consequence of that was to leave the whole south, black and white, to endure a near century of poverty outside the mainstream of American progress.

"The causes for that failure started in the late 1800s with the birth of two new political evils. First, the early pre-PACies joined and adopted the ideas of the just born progressive movement, ideas that divided humans according to specious theories about race and ability. At the same time, the old southern aristocracy, working to shore up the power it had near-lost at the end of the Civil war, used progressive theories to lock in the support of poor whites by creating *Jim Crow* laws to roll back the new rights gained by our black ancestors. Progressive racial theories and Jim Crow both soiled our history then and on into the present, but with a new twist in your grandparents' time.

"In the 1960s, the now emerging PACies began pushing the same segregationist model that the southern aristocracy had used almost a century before, but with that twist I mentioned. They flipped the colors of their victims by jamming poor, unconnected whites into the backseats once reserved for blacks on the bus. Thus, at a time when we had both the financial and moral capital needed to begin building a truly race-neutral society with a strong focus on lifting *all of our poor* by improving their neighborhoods and schools, we chose to create *protected classes* with special privileges. For example, we favored both rich and poor minority children over those of poor, unconnected whites, including kids of the production workers whose unions actually supported that discrimination. Go figure.

"Of course, the PAC elite didn't care any more about the minorities they fast-tracked than the old southern aristocrats cared about poor whites. PAC built then and maintains its power now by dividing people into tribes, just as those aristocrats had done, and in both cases their shameful privilege-mongering led to ruin.

"Today, that means foreign occupation and a PAC death-grip on our quotaed throats. We're paying that blood price because of PAC, just as the south paid a price all those lost years earlier. The difference is that, outside the south, America boomed in the nineteenth and twentieth centuries, and that boom finally found its way south. But today, the world teeters on the edge of a new Dark Ages, and unless the alliance can get America back in the game, there'll be no boom coming to lift any of us back up to the future we deserve."

He paused to study their faces at that point, grinning as he added, "Me thinks I can hear the poor-me chorus rising in your noggins, singing your own version of PAC's two favorite songs: 'White-White, Wicked White' and 'Ustatesia The Bad, You We Subdue.' But don't dance to a flipside version of those lie-based, self-destructive tunes. PAC wrong-headedness isn't corrected by blindly following their path of division and exploitation. It's corrected by reaching for the sunshine of *E pluribus unum*—for us all.

"There has never been a better society than ours in Asia, Africa, or anywhere, but so what? Our calling now is to not only help ourselves, but to help willing others find the freedom they deserve. And I believe that there are enough right thinking people all around this glorious world"—he sketched a circle in the air with right index finger—"for us all to begin working together toward a time when true justice will be delivered fairly and equally to all, with all striving to do their own part, and with no preferred tribal groups tolerated. But, my friends, that bridge to the future must be built by addition, not division, and by viewing all people as … well, as simply, people."

He smiled then, watching their eyes as he added, "Some say, we're either one or we're done. I say, we're either one—or our work's not done." He stood up at that point, happily gesturing as he went on, "Our dream of a world where all men and women can stand together as equals and not as mere appendages of groups, classes, tribes or even religions or politically correct groups is the only dream worth having. And mark this,"—he emphasized by pointing at them—"And I mean, really mark it. It's important! I believe that we, in the Whig Partisan Alliance, are charged to be that dreamed-for-future's pro-lepsis. It falls to us to live and model that dream right now, right here in our present day, very damaged America, and then to offer it—as a model—to the world.

"Our model should be based on helping others help themselves and not by playing Wizard of OZ. We've tried the fake pinning of medals on a chest and handing out empty awards game by allowing people into schools and programs based on their membership in favored groupings. That has caused damage to the lives of many of those so favored and to the lives of many of those who lost a slot they had rightfully earned."

They talked on through the evening about our future and the challenge before us, but even good things end and there finally came a time to sleep, a sleep that ended way too soon with a very early morning wake-up call. Not even the chickens were up when a shaken awake, moaning Glenn joined the other two, slow crawling, groggy and cotton-mouthed, quite literally out of the hay. And the excitement of last night's sharing was now lost in a thick brain-fog as the three comrades shuffled blearily to the breakfast table where they slumped down as directed to silently munch their way through a good, but unappreciated meal.

Shampton was also up, but incredibly enough; the older man wasn't just present, he was also fresh and alert, and he had no mercy on them, pressing the three to eat fast and to get their gear together. "Little John," he said, "You were seen last night at the Sip N Surf along with two other men that PAC couldn't identify." He smiled toward Alex and Glenn. "And so we need to get you guys out of here ahead of any prying eyes or the fed patrols. Being feds, they'll sleep away most of the morning, and so you have a window, let's not waste it. You need to leave right now so you can get well-clear of this area."

"Ah, my public wants me wherever I go," John mumbled. But it was a hollow sounding, self-mocking comment, and although he grinned weakly at the others as he spoke, he was obviously unsettled as he left the table to go brush his teeth at the basin by the side door. Rejoining them after pulling his gear together, he looked around with a dispirited smile and apologized, "Look, I'm sorry. I know I'm a problem, and it might be dangerous for us to stay together. I think you guys will be better off without me along, painting a target on your backs, and so I'm just going to take off on my own."

"We wouldn't have been better off last night," Shampton reminded him, and smiling, he reached over and slapped John on the back, "nor on at least two other of this little effort's adventures. But you're right about not staying together, and so I'm going to split up your happy little trio to get you clear of this area. The feds don't communicate very well with each other much less with the bounty hunters, and so once you're out of here, you'll be able to get back together. Meanwhile, trust your next angel, and I'll make you a promise. I think it's a sure thing that you'll enjoy the adventure she'll connect you with later today far better than the dark angel dance you had to endure with me last night."

"Last night was—" Glenn started, but he was cut off.

"Last night's over, come on, you gotta get out of here now, or you'll lose that next adventure. And oh yes, Glenn, you have one angel and one brief stop the others will now have to miss until a later time. So it's into this first wagon for you! Jump up and cover up. We'll send your buddies along about fifteen minutes behind you."

With those words, he walked down the line, firmly shaking hands and looking into the eyes of each one of them in turn and with just a trace of moisture in his own. "You're good men and a good team, but you still have to get from being just me to we—sort of like our country does. I look forward to seeing all of you again soon, but for now, you gotta get out of here!" He shouted out those last words, laughing as he shoved them ahead of him towards their wagons.

"Thank you, sir, looking forward to next time," Glenn shouted back as he climbed into an old covered wagon and on up to the top of a high lumpy load of hard potato sacks. Moving to the front, he wrestled several sacks up behind him as a shield before settling back to endure the ride. Endure being the right word, the trip seemed longer than it really was because the horses had to pick their way along what was left of the potholed road, and the wheels missed very few of those potholes. But finally, at long-jarring last, they arrived near the I-96 overpass where Glenn got his very welcome signal to dismount.

He was happy to leave that lumpy ride and potato smell behind him as he jumped down. And gear in hand, he stooped low in the pre-dawn light to run across the wide, beat-up old highway, slipping into the bushes on the other side. Once there, he began bending and stretching to unkink his back as he watched his ride lumber on without him.

After it vanished, he turned to explore his hiding place, looking in all directions, observing his surroundings. There were no people in sight, but down the hill from where he stood, he could just make out what was left of a small strip mall. It looked empty, as most of them were these days, with its buildings falling into ruin and giving in to nature. But wait! At the far end of its weed-grown parking lot, he could now see signs that one building was still in use.

"Whoa, that might mean trouble!" he whispered to himself, and hunkering down in the bushes, he slowly looked around again, studying all possible approaches to be sure he was alone. It was quiet now, but he knew that with at least one open building down there, some people would be coming and going in this area before long.

Still, he felt safe behind his bush for now, and so he leaned back against one of the trees and slid down to sit and wait for his contact. A big yawn came as he relaxed, and closing his eyes, he let his mind drift back to last night and to Al Shampton.

That man had been incredible. He had taken a real emotional body blow but rose above it to do what needed to be done. There had been no hint of the pain he must have felt about the betrayal of his marriage as he talked with them. None. It was all about them and the need for them to become part of the effort to help America and the alliance move forward. What a man! What a model of how to focus on duty!

To Glenn, that proved that Al lived what he preached; he actually lived the "as if" alliance attitude that he'd reminded them of last night. He'd said, "Our call is to elbow around each and every distraction and to focus on working hard inside and outside the system to lead our people back toward the culture they and the world deserves. That'll mean accepting the need for ego-stressing compromises along the way, but so what! It's all doable, including unpleasant realities like

the need to bow and tug our forelocks in feigned deference to PAC
from time to time. Our fix must be on our mission, period."

He was right, of course, and others were already laying their
lives on the line. The hot-war battle for change had started, and
Shampton and Alex had briefed them on the spreading rebellion. No
longer just defending the Heartland, fighters for the alliance were
now on offense across the country, and open battles were going on
in many places.

They had described the struggle across the whole range of the
PAC-Southern Surrender Zone, as the alliance called PAC's new version of our southern border. A weak kneed president of the United
States had unconstitutionally ceded a very real part of our country
to Mexico and the cartels, but leaders from all of the border states
had joined to reject what they called the *Cowardly Cretin's Cession*
and raised up large armies to challenge anyone who tried to cross
their border from anywhere, which included, most especially, from
Washington DC. To the east, the Texas rallying cry was a hearty: "Not
one inch of Texas / Given away / Today, a free Texas / Tomorrow,
USA / … USA, USA."

In the west, the California Orange County irregulars had formed
and were joined by other groups, including the Modesto Militia, to
support the marines and elite units from other services now refusing
the order to stand down and close the Camp Pendleton Marine base.
Volunteers were streaming in from everywhere, and there was even
talk that they were getting ready to push south to retake San Diego,
now in ruins and to regain control all the way to the old Mexican
border. And even in the northwest, units of irregulars in Washington
and Oregon had joined with Alaskans and Canadians to deny Russia
an easy occupation by pinning it against the coast in Alaska.

And so it was everywhere from coast to coast, citizens were dig-
ging out of from under the debris of decades of personal and societal
malaise. Raising the *Don't-Tread-On-Me* flag, they declared that the
old *Rip Van Winkle era* was over and promised to fight to end the
days of the tyranny of *PAC-3: Promises-Plunder-Politburo*.

"You seem to be in deep in thought," a woman's voice jolted
him back to the now.

"What?" Caught off guard and embarrassed that someone could have just walked up on him, Glenn looked up in near panic at first, but he quickly relaxed when he saw the smiling face of what he took to be their next angel. After they went through the contact routine, the new angel, to be known as J4, plopped down by his tree to brief him about what was coming. He was to visit the PAC Leadership Academy, just below them in the old mall, and while there, he would receive an award.

"Award? I just started this trip. I haven't done anything yet," he said, sitting back and looking at her in genuine surprise. "Besides, do I want that kind of publicity?"

"It's a tradeoff. Your Friendly Forces pass has been used too close to some very questionable events that we don't want to you to be identified with, and so you'll get a new pass, at an even higher level. But don't worry, there'll be no publicity."

"So you're saying that I'm not being awarded for something wonderful that I've done that I just can't recall, but no one cares anyway?" he joked as they stood to leave.

"Have you actually ever done anything to be awarded for?" she quipped, but then quickly added, "I'm sorry, but I couldn't resist. Anyway, just think of it as you're being awarded for your potential greatness and try to forget that it's nothing more than an insider gesture. Anyway, other than things like sports, does anyone ever get an award for real accomplishments? I think the general rule is that insiders reward right thinking, not deeds or proven talent, and they swap all their little awards around with each other."

On that happy note, they headed on down the hill, and as they approached the buildings, Glenn thought it was curious that this hotshot academy looked more like a rundown warehouse than a major PAC facility, a huge stepdown from the pseudo-ed center he had seen earlier. Turning to J4, he said, "This place is a dump. It's more like the real life student classrooms I saw on the slum side of the fence at Whitmore Lake than the Taj-like money pit for professionals and PAC honchos amidst the fountains there.

J4 agreed, laughing as she went on to explain why this place was so different. "That is quite a palace. I've seen it. But we've been temporary here for over a decade because the power brokers can't agree on where our own Taj should be built. Each one of them wants it in her own backyard, and until that gets settled, it'll stay here, crumbling into ruin while they try to out wait each other."

"Sounds familiar," Glenn replied. "Reminds me of Arbor U politics.

"Oh, speaking of Arbor U," she said, after checking them both in with the 'I-could-care-less' guard at the door. "Your old professor has provided us with an impressive list of your publications and a glowing report about your work as a master's level student. Your paper on … let's see, what is it? Hold on just a minute. Let me find it. I know it's somewhere in my pack here. Ah, yes, I've got it." Smiling, she held up a copy of what was apparently an old paper he had written. "Here it is, and now let me see, it's called, *On Transcendental Metameritocracy.* That certainly sounds impressive. It's perfect."

"You're kidding me! It's gibberish, that was a joke." Glenn laughed nervously. "It wasn't supposed to have been seen outside the professor's office. Come on, it makes fun of PAC, for crying out loud! If that gets out, we're both going to be hung out to dry."

"Hey, I know what you're saying. I've read it, and it is a bit of a risk, but he and I decided that it was worth the fun," she replied. Then, laughing at his reaction, she added, "Now don't worry, you won't face a firing squad. No one else here's read it, and no one is likely to read it. In fact, I can't think of anyone in this building who'd guess that you were PAC-bashing even if they did read it. Believe me, the students and staff here are on the low side of the scholarship curve, but don't worry about them. They're all way up high on the oh-so-very-important political connections and slavish devotion to PAC curve."

The angel was right about the perfunctory nature of the event, but for three hitches the short ceremony would have been over in less than a minute. Those hitches came because the PAC official who presided over the event in the almost empty building was "helped" by three other officials called subalterns. They represented the contending parties in the endless power game going on to control the planning for the final building.

"We're called together—" the official began, but was immediately interrupted.

"Praise PAC," sub-A called out, and she lifted both hands in praise.

"Praise PAC, blessed be its name," shouted sub-B, hands also raised.

"Praise PAC and blessed be its name and glory to *Our New Era*, ONE," called out sub-C, raising the holy single index finger sign for ONE, thus trumping the other two.

"Yes, of course, praise and blessings, now let's continue," the official mumbled, hardly missing a beat. She was used to all of this, and she had a schedule to keep.

The three jostled with each other to be the one closest to Glenn as he received his award, pushing up around him when he posed for pictures. But the official herself seemed more concerned about meeting some colleagues for what she called an early (and probably late) business brunch than she was with honoring Glenn. After rushing through the set-piece routine, she presented him with a large certificate and more importantly, gave him his new Friendly Forces pass. Then, grabbing her things, she turned to leave.

"Wait," called out sub-C. "We forgot to thank PAC."

"Of course, hail PAC," the official called out and again started for the door.

"We should probably—" sub-A started but was cut off by sub-B.

"Praise be to PAC—" sub-B started, but she was cut off by the official.

"We have said hail, and that ends the ceremony," the official insisted. "You defame PAC by doing the praise after the—" Then, she too was cut off.

"To the revered PAC praise," shouted sub-A.

"To the most revered ..." called out sub-C.

"To the most revered praise, and I salute its holy name," outshouted sub-B.

"This meeting is adjourned," the official outshouted them all, dashing through the door just ahead of their protests. This left Glenn, stunned by the farce-faced sham, to turn and join J4, both laughing at the sheer tawdriness of the whole thing.

"Maybe we should be more careful," Glenn whispered, eyeing the three subs.

"Don't worry about them. All they can think about is your high connection to the friendlies," she replied. "They'll try to stay close but won't dare to bother you. And so, we'll pretty much have free reign while you're here."

"Well, you were right on about the ceremony … It was a joke," Glenn said.

"Yes, a bad joke with no style and less class." J4 laughed, and then turning to the three subalterns who now stood grinning just behind them, she sighed deeply, and being very careful to smile—these were well connected loyalists, after all—she said, "Master Stanton and I will now tour our building, just the two of us. You three are to remain here."

The three subs looked nervously at one another. They wanted to be close to this friendlies-connected guy but didn't want to offend him by challenging J4's tour plans.

What right did she have to make such plans anyway? They were miffed, and as the two walked away on their tour, the subalterns were left to mill about, trying to decide what to do. Sub-A suggested that she should go along to explain the facility's history and the plans her group had for it. Sub-C quickly shouldered in and announced that there could be no tour without her approval. But then, sub-B claimed foul and announced that she was reporting them all—including Glenn's angel. With that, she huffed away to contact her superiors, leaving the other two to just stare at each other at first, but then fearing that if she contacted her superiors, and they had not contacted and briefed their own, they'd be in deep trouble, they both rushed after her to make their own toady calls.

"Are you going to get in trouble for this, and what'll you do if those clowns show up again?" Glenn asked.

"I'll be fine. They won't dare risk making you mad," she replied, and Glenn noted later that when the three did reappear, they were careful to stay back, tagging along shoulder to shoulder in the distance. If one pressed forward, they all did. If one turned to move away, so did the other two, but they always tried to keep Glenn in view.

"All three," J4 explained, "will write reports about how they themselves had honored an important PAC functionary with major friendlies' contacts. None of the reports will even mention the other two cyphers nor, probably, the official who ran the meeting. It'll be all about me-me and only me-me in each one's report."

Without the comic relief, the tour wasn't very exciting because there wasn't much to see. Glenn looked into a lot of empty rooms, but there were no libraries or labs or ... well, name what should have been there and rest assured that it wasn't. The rival powers were obviously blocking money for anything but the bare necessities. There was space to meet, a few students were allowed into the school to maintain the appearance of a level of need, and some supplies were provided, but only when desperately begged for and even then only after a lot of political turf event arm-wrestling.

"How do you stand it here?" Glenn asked when they finally arrived at J4's office, the three subs taking up posts just down the hall.

"How'd you stand Arbor U?" she replied and then quickly added, "I'm sorry, there I go again, my bad. You asked a valid question, and I should answer it. The truth is, I love the challenge here. I believe with all my heart that what I'm doing is important, and I like teaching the students we have. You might have a hard time believing this, but I actually do get some real information besides propaganda into their truth-starved heads."

"Not your bad, mine," Glenn replied. "That's a solid reason, and you know, I have to confess that I enjoyed being at Arbor U. The classes themselves were mostly just praise-PAC bull sessions and not very challenging, but like a surprisingly large number of others, I found a way to learn a lot and liked most of the people I met there, especially the people of Arbortown. I think the students, staff, and townies, deserve better than they're getting, but most of them don't think about that at all. As for the students, most flow mindlessly along like run-off water down PAC's ritual academic slopes, even lapping up the empty awards and certificates that are handed out all the time—like candy.

"But remember, they only have PAC, and I was lucky enough to have a mentor to help keep my focus on a broader reality. Because of him, I had the excitement of feeling like I was on a mission to change things for the better, and what young person wouldn't love that? Anyway, I agree with you, what you're doing is important, very important."

"Well, winning a new future for our country and the world is the goal that keeps us all going." J4 rummaged around in her desk, looking for something as she spoke, and finding it, she smiled broadly as she handed it to him, saying, "This booklet fits what we've been talking about, but you must give it back to me. You can't take it with you."

"Sounds mysterious," he said, but then glancing at the cover as he took it, he read the title out loud, "*The Protocols of the Elders of PAC*. Is this a joke?"

"Think of it as sort of an inadvertent modern version of C. S. Lewis's *Screwtape Letters*," J4 replied. "Of course, that's from our point of view, not PAC's. They think it's all good stuff, and believe it or not, they take it all very seriously."

"That's crazy. The title itself should be tip-off enough. It's from a centuries old con-job," he muttered, and settling back into his seat, he began to browse through it. A few minutes later, he called out, "Hey, this *is* crazy, I need a copy to show to my buddies."

"I'm sure you want one, but you get caught with this on you, and you get shot," she replied, very seriously. "And not to be too self-serving, but even worse, I'd get shot too. All the copies are numbered, and that one is signed out to me. PAC may be very inefficient, but I'm not going to bet my life on them not being able to read the numbers."

"How about running an unnumbered copy, can it be that big-a-deal? You're right here in the middle of them, and it's in your desk for all to see, yet you're very much alive. What's the problem?"

"That's part of the craziness here. We all have a copy, and we're required to teach it. Isn't that wild? They require us to teach this stuff because they honestly think these protocols will turn all of our students into good little PACies," she said, laughing. "Don't you get it? They see these as genuine. I told you they're not bright, and, Glenn, that gives us an edge. I can actually work within this system to do what I need to do."

"So you teach them about the importance of … let me see." He glanced through the pamphlet, grinning as he read out loud, "*Raising the PAC flag of submissive diversity by rewording diversity slogans to undermine thought error*? Does that make any sense? And you gotta love this, '*Grooming the media to act as right-thought-minding surrogates.*' And how about this beauty? '*Truth depends on controlling the meaning of Is.*' I can't even guess what that means. I don't believe all this!"

"Yep. I teach my students that PAC's major truths require multiple and very flexible definitions of dependent minor truths and how we can only understand these by deferring to PAC guidance. I suppose you've read about Orwell's—*we're all equal, but some are more equal than others.* Well, my students and colleagues don't read much, and so they end up living a present day version of his *Pigocracy*, and don't even know it."

"OK, I see what you're saying. But come on, let me take a copy with me."

"Well, you don't have a snowball's chance, if you catch my drift. You can look through it here, but don't forget, we have a deadline to meet," she said, glancing down at her watch as she spoke. "And oh yes, pay close attention to the section on religion and the need to centralize control over it through cultural shaming, an anti-religious media, and a false choice values squeeze. But hurry, I've got to get you back on the road."

Twenty minutes later, after solemnly shaking hands with each of the three sub-clowns, and assuring each of them that she had made his visit a great success, Glenn walked back up the hill with the angel. As they walked, he thought about all that he had just seen, and when they reached the top of the hill, he turned to her and said, "I admire you for what you're doing and what you're enduring, but I feel sorry for you. At least I had allies around me at Arbor University. You have only the Three Stooges."

"Far more than three, Glenn, and it is all crazy, but look around you, this is where we are for now. Yes, of course, it is a challenge, but we're all called to contribute where we're planted, and I believe that what I do here has real meaning. How we do our jobs in the present *now*, whatever those jobs are, will determine the next generation's better *now*. I have a role to play just as you do, and as crazy as it might sound, I find a way to feel good about it and to enjoy it."

"Well, my hat's off to you, but let me ask one other thing," Glenn said. "I've been warned in other places to be careful because PAC is always listening, but you don't seem to be worried about that."

"Well, thankfully, the three stooges take care of that. They rip out each other's mikes, leaving me free to do the same and blame it on them. On top of that, it takes forever to replace the bulky things available these days, and with their eyes *and* mine looking, we find them right after they're replaced—and they're always replaced.

"But speaking of high technology, I have something else for you, something that you've never heard of before. It's called a Citizens' Band radio. You like illegal? This little thing is sooo illegal. Although I don't think it's firing squad illegal, or at least, I hope not." Smiling at him as he reflected on that thought, she rummaged in her pack, found what she needed, and then handed him a funny- looking bulky device that looked like it came from the fifties or sixties. "This'll help on the next leg of your journey."

"What'd you call it?"

"It's called a CB, a Citizens Band radio, and your next contact will show you how to use it." She watched him as he turned it all around, looking it over and studying it, and then added, "The good news is, it can't be traced to me. So if you get caught, I'm clear."

"Well, I'm sure we're both glad that only one of us will get hung!" Glenn said, glancing over at her as he squeezed the devise into his pack, and they both laughed.

From there she led him to his next contact point, on Hacker, where she situated him under yet another tree. "Try to stay alert.

Your next angel, as I hear you guys call us, will be along soon. She'll explain the CB, and this next gig's gonna be a lot of fun."

"Thanks for all you've done. We do call you guys angels, and in my book that's just what you are. Someday, I hope to be able to meet up with each one of you again and to have some time to really get acquainted."

"That day's coming, Glenn. But right now, I've got a lot of walking to do to get your buddies into position at their own pick-up spots for the next leg of your adventure."

They said their goodbyes, and then, after watching her rush away, Glenn settled down on the grass to eat the chips and sandwiches provided that morning, washing it all down with a warm root beer. Once he finished eating, the drag-me-down impact of their early morning get-up call finally hit him, and leaning back against a tree, he closed his eyes and was soon asleep. As he drifted off, his last thoughts were about how ironic it was that PAC had awarded him, a budding Blue Company guy, twice in one day.

CHAPTER THIRTEEN

How the Three Are Joined to the Yellow Cog

"*U*p and at 'em, Sir Buzz Saw!"

For the second time that day, Glenn was aroused from deep thought by a woman's voice; although this time it came to him through the pleasant fog of sleep accompanied by a swift kick to his sprawled-out feet. He resisted his first impulse, which was to jump up and engage the kicker. Instead, feigning an innocent, grinning idleness, he peered lazily up and about as he moved his head slowly from side to side—but only very slightly.

What he saw was a woman standing over him, and for some reason, she was dressed in what looked to be a costume version of the chainmail of an old time knight. And pressing in behind her were others also wearing strange, but more colorful clothes. Some looked to have on jesters' outfits, but most seemed to be decked out as villagers—from the Middle Ages, he guessed. Barely moving his lips, he chuckled to himself, thinking that these 'ye olde' costumes actually look better than the garb we wear today, a lot cleaner and certainly brighter. But what's up here? Who are these people?

He was still trying to decide what to do against the odds he faced when he spotted a new kick coming. Ah, decision made! Quickly waving his hand, he sat up to stop it.

"I'm awake, I'm awake," he called out, and offering what he hoped would be taken as a peaceful look, he nodded all around at the crowd standing over him. What were they up to? If they were bad guys, he hoped they'd write him off as just another drifter and ignore the obvious fact that he was an unaccompanied male. He didn't want to have to use his new pass right here in Brighton; it was way too soon for that.

The kicker studied him skeptically for a moment before turning to motion the others away. Glenn, unsure about what to do, settled for just watching with her as she watched her companions laughing and joking their way back towards a strange looking array of color-ful wagons, each lined up behind horses along the road. Once they reached them, they waved back to the kicker and moved out, appar-ently continuing their journey.

With that, the lady knight turned her eyes back to Glenn and faux-frowning down at him, said, "We could hear you snoring a mile away, that's why I dubbed you Sir Buzz Saw. You're a real rack-et-maker, which sorta complicates our plan to make you an under-cover agent." With that comment, she laughed out loud and flashing the contact sign, reached a hand down to help him to his feet. "I'm J5, but you can call me Joan."

"OK, Joan it is, but tell me, is this 2036 or 1436? I feel like I'm a few hundred years out of sync," he said, grinning as he accepted her hand. And once he was on his feet, he gave the countersign, frowned, and added, "Seriously, what's going on here?"

"Well, you can take your choice. Our costumes are from the Middle Ages, but our own society is collapsing back into the nine-teenth century. So, you pick. Do you want 2036 regressing to 1836 or 1436? Myself, I'd go with the nineteenth century. I think I could survive in a remake of that era, but things were way too crude back beyond that."

"I'll buy that." Glenn shrugged. "But I'm not ready to bail on 2036 just yet."

"You got it, my literal friend. 2036 it is, and you're about to travel with the not yet famous Yellow Cog. We're a federally funded traveling troupe of entertainers—you know, part of the temporary stimulus package that's been with us since our parents were our age." And mirroring his shrug, she gave a short laugh and continued, "Now, don't get me wrong, I'm not knocking this gig; I actually like it. It's not only a living, it's a lot of fun, *and* it provides the cover of all covers for my real mission in life, which is to help lop the ugly head off of that slithering snake we call PAC."

"OK, but just who or what are you supposed to be, and what does your troupe do?"

"Come on, I told you, I'm Joan, you know, Joan of Arc. It's my stage name, and the sheriff of Nottingham drags me to a pile of wood and burns me at the stake once a day, three or four days a week, depending on our travel schedule and the weather. And when I'm not being torched, I run this operation and work for the same cause you do."

"The sheriff of Nottingham burning Joan of Arc?" He laughed. "I think you're mixing up your stories a little bit. I can hardly wait for Little John to hear about this."

"Hey, I'm looking forward to meeting that copter killer, but as to my story line, what other evil English official do you suggest? Besides, no one these days knows the difference," she replied. "And as to this little gig, I think you're going to like what you see, most of those here are dead sick of PAC, but just like so many others in the country these days, they don't think they can do anything about it." And nodding affectionately toward the group ahead of them on the road, she added, "My people are the usual mix of those who spout off a lot, posturing as independent thinkers, and a majority who just sigh and go with the flow. And of course, there's no doubt that we've got at least one person who's a mole for PAC and reports everything that goes on in our little family." By this time, they were both hustling down the road after the troupe.

"So we have to be careful," Glenn replied, shaking his head.

"We have to be very careful," she said. "In the old days, all roads led to Rome. These days all words get back to PAC. With that, she increased her speed, motioning for him to follow so they could catch the wagons. And as they closed on her noisy troupe, she shouted a reminder back over her shoulder, "Remember, you and your friends must seem to meet for the first time with us. We're always absorbing people who want to earn easy federals, so that won't raise any suspicions. But rule number one is that while you're all here none of you should take any action that isn't coordinated through us."

"Sounds good, but who's this, us?" He called out his question as he moved up beside her, but instead of an answer he got a warning to walk quietly. They were now moving in among the wagons, mingling with the others, and many of them were giving Glenn a good look-over. Fortunately, no one tried to approach them, which left him free to return their look-over, studying them closely as he strolled silently along beside J5.

"Yes," he whispered over to Joan once it seemed safe. "This is a perfect setup, just the kind of cover we need. And they look like interesting people, people I think I'd like to meet. So tell me more about this whole traveling show setup, and you said, us. Who're the others? How many contacts do we have here?"

"Well, first, there's no *we* for you here," she replied as she moved them off to the side of the caravan away from the others. "You don't know the next two people who'll be joining our troupe. As far as you're concerned, there's just you, and for right now, all you need to know is that you're with me. The rest will come when it comes."

With those words, she turned to shout over to a large woman, walking or rather shuffling all alone beside a gaudy looking purple and white wagon that appeared to be a big tissue box on wheels. She was dressed, Glenn decided, as a village trollop. "Judy," Joan called over, "can you give me a hand here, please? This recruit needs to find an outfit and an act that'll put some zip into his rather flat personality."

As Judy waved back and started in their direction, Joan grinned broadly at "flat" Glenn's scowl, slapped him on the back and said, "It's OK. You'll like Judy. She'll help you put together an act and get you outfitted while I tend to some other duties."

With that, she left him, and Glenn turned to watch the trollop, laboring her way towards him across the busted-up old black top road. She wore a forbidding scowl that seemed to be pasted on her jowly face, but she turned out to be an interesting and colorful person. In no time at all, Glenn learned that she was a very outgoing, boisterous, and even when out of character, a vulgar woman who was a bit too familiar and pushy for his tastes, even calling him "Glenn honey" from the first moment. But somehow, he quickly came to like her; she was one sharp cookie—with a lot going on behind that scowl of hers.

And that "a lot going on" came out almost at once after she invited him into her moving costume wagon to sort through all the garb there, looking for both a costume and a character he could play. She had a tale to tell, and as she told it, he saw her other side and heard a story that he had not heard even a whisper about back at Arbor U. It all took him by surprise, not because it illustrated a failure in PAC's imperfect educational and medical care systems, everyone knew both to be corrupt, crony-driven monstrosities, but because Judy as a female Hispanic should have been riding cloud-high in the PAC quota system. Yet here she was, marooned with this troupe, and feeling trampled underfoot.

He had studied under Professor Benjamin in the Department of Antiquated Core Studies, but that was a non-degree program, thus he also had been enrolled in the Social Work/Education Department and had completed graduate work there. So he should have heard rumors, at least, about her kind of problem, but he had heard nothing—which had to mean that such things were being politically hushed up. Now, listening in surprise to her story, he began to think that America's own nightmare *Animal Farm* era might be reaching its next phase: a time when even the top groups were beginning to be sorted out. Certainly, her story showed that there were now people on the very top rungs of the PAC privilege ladder, as she certainly should have been, who were being pulled down.

"I was a teacher, fully federally-funded and certified, but I got on the wrong side of the *PAC HaF-TO* program," she said, but then paused to make sure that he knew what she was talking about. "You do know about HaF-TO, don't you?"

"Yes, *Health and Fitness—Team up or Opt-out,*" Glenn replied, noting that now, as they settled back to talk, she seemed to change. Something was different, but what?

"Well, I was up for promotion to lead-teacher, and I wanted that job. I felt like I deserved it, and I thought I'd get it because the

other candidate was only quotaed gender and race. I equaled her gender and race, but I also had handicapper points." She paused, shaking
her head sadly, and then added, "Two years ago, I'd have been in, no
sweat. But times are changing, and although the handicapper points
are still there, now they can be challenged. And that's what that other
dame did. She challenged me!"

"What'd she do, say you weren't handicapped?" he asked, choosing to ignore her use of the word *dame*, which would have seen him
tossed into a tiger cage for using. He was genuinely confused and
wanted to know more about this latest PAC snarl.

"Nope, she couldn't do that. Come on, it's obvious, I'm way
more than fifty pounds over the fed standard for my height, race,
and gender. No, she got me on the new rule," she muttered, and
anticipating his coming question, she answered it. "The new rule is
that handicapper points can be used only by those who have a hand-
icap that's not an expression of their own choices. That means she
was able to claim that I *chose* to be weight-handicapped in order to
get the points. Her mother's a hotshot high PAC official, and so, not
surprisingly, the board agreed with her complaint, and that got me
shoved into that lousy HaF-TO program."

"OOOK." Glenn spoke slowly, studying her. He still wondered
about her change, but her story intrigued him enough to cautiously
go on. "As I said, I know a little about it, and from what I've heard,
it … well, it actually sounds like a pretty good idea, you know, helping people get back on track, or at least, that's the theory"

"When it's voluntary maybe, but it becomes compulsory for
anyone who claims points and is challenged. My lack of exercise was
what took me down, and I knew that might happen. My friends
warned me to give up on the job, and I finally tried to do that, but it
was too late. The board ruled against me and put me on an improve-
ment plan."

"That sounds fair enough," Glenn said. "You get help managing
your weight and fitness, and after meeting your goal, you'll get a shot
at the next promotion."

"Glenn, you've been breathing in too much Arbor U smoke.
What it really means is that you get assigned to someone who gets

paid to help you but never shows up, while you get a deadline that *does* show up. In the end, they ruled that I'd had my chance and that not only did I not take that chance, I *chose* to stay overweight and out of shape. The board said that meant that, from their point-of-view, I was willing to put the whole PAC economy and the environment of the entire nation—even the whole world—at risk. And,"—her eyes widened with anger—"there's no appeal to that ruling, and my quota didn't matter.

So I not only didn't get my new job, I lost my old one, and I got myself branded as an *environmental criminal.* But wait, there's more. As a criminal, I've also lost all of my federal health benefits. AND to top things off, I'm on a Haf-TO offenders' watch list."

"Come on, what are they going do, not treat you if you get sick? If there's one thing we have in this society, it's universal health benefits. We may have to wait forever to get even the most routine outdated service, but you still get some kind of help."

"You must be from another planet," Judy laughed bitterly. "You don't seem to understand what 'opt-out' means. It means I'm out of the system, so the only medical service I get is emergency first aid and palliative care. It means I'm in what is called the *Futile Care* category, so any care I request above my new category has to be approved by the *Free Use Czar for the Unscheduled,* just like people who are too old and others who have used up their *Points Offered for Treatment* services. I'll tell you, I don't have a POT left, and when you don't have a POT, you're out of luck because everyone wants you to just go away somewhere—and die. That's why I'm here. I have a master's degree in teaching with years of experience, but I have to work as an actor on a federal subsidy that barely pays for my food and fees. That's *my* PAC HaF-TO plan."

"I'm sorry. I didn't know," he said, and although he thought about adding some other comments about PAC justice, he decided not to. Who knows, he didn't think so, but she could be a PAC snoop, hoping to gain back some privileges by pointing a finger at him. That could be the strange difference he saw in her, and he could even understand why she'd stoop to that, if what she said was true, and he believed it was.

So, he stayed focused on the business of trying on the outfits she offered and finally settled on one that fit what Joan had called his "flat" personality: the rather blah-looking white robes of an abbey-clerk. It should be easy, he thought; all he'd have to do is walk around with a beneficent looking smile on his face, keeping his hands clasped in front of him as if in constant prayer. He shrugged, accepting the outfit with a resigned sigh and a mumbled modest response, "OK, I'm no actor, but I guess I can do it."

"From what I see you can't do anything else, but you know what? I can take care of that. I'll get Joan to ask one of the others to teach you to juggle. If you get really good, you might get promoted to court jester, and that'll be more fun. Besides, it's a skilled trade and pays a lot more. It's only in federals, of course, but money's money."

"Thanks, that sounds like fun—a lot more active. I'd like to try it," he replied. But although he was excited about the idea, he thought it curious to consider a move from spiritual leader to fool as being a promotion. How very twenty-first century that kind of thinking was! But still, holy clerk or fool, he'd take what he could get.

Once dressed in his new skullcap, sandals, and loose fitting white robe—wearing his own clothes under it all—he left Judy at the costume wagon. Although still unsure about trusting her, he genuinely felt sorry for her. But now, he had a role to learn, so he refocused to that and began practicing his proper facial expressions and prayer-hands positions as he mingled with the other performers alongside the slow moving wagons.

It's funny how interesting it is getting into a role, he thought, and how relaxing it was to be able to forget about everything and to just focus on something as simple as the way he held his face and hands. But it wasn't easy. Maintaining what he thought was the right look was tough for him, and he carefully studied the others for some clue as to how he was doing as he walked by them. When, every once in a while, one of them seemed to frown at him, he worried that he wasn't getting it right and that maybe he was looking more consti-pated than religious.

He grinned at that thought, but quickly refocused to regain his beneficent looking holy-smile-above-clasped-hands look. And he thought he was doing well until one of the passing frowners approached him, calling out, "Hey, you got a minute there, student?"

"Of course," Glenn called back and stopped, nervously studying the short, ruddy faced, scrappy-looking man walking up to him. "How're you doing?"

"I'm doing fine, man, but what'a you up to?" The man pushed up close, too close, and as Glenn stepped back, giving way, he wondered what this guy knew about him. But that worry faded as his new companion laughed and added, "I'm with this crummy gig because I gotta be, but you're a student, at least. So why're you here doin' this 'n not layin' about all the time collectin' big easy feds and being tended to? I don't get it."

"Well, I know it looks strange," Glenn replied, and he forced a laugh as he blundered on with what he hoped would work as an explanation. "And you're right, I am a student, or I was until I graduated a couple weeks ago, but I needed a break away from all that Arbor U crap, and this looked like it'd be a lot of fun. Thought I might learn to juggle and just hangout for a bit with normal people. My name's, Glenn, Glenn Stanton."

"I'm Archie Bringey." The other man's reply came slowly as he looked Glenn up and down, seemingly thinking about the student's explanation, but then, laughing, he held out a hand. "Yeah, I'd get sick of all that Arbor U stuff, myself. I don't know how you guys put up with it. I'd be takin' some of them pompous, uni-nut professors down real hard if I had to be around 'em long. I stay away from there, place makes me sick." He spit off to the side, and as he turned to leave, he added, "You're OK. Welcome aboard."

A bit later, the troupe came upon another candidate, standing beside the road with his cap clutched in the huge paw that was his left hand. And Glenn watched with concern as Joan waved for everyone else to keep moving along the road while she walked over to interview this new potential member. Judy had told him earlier that two quotaed white males had just been dropped from the troupe in Lansing because their group was overrepresented. By adding him, they had already added one back, and so, even though he knew Joan was expecting Little John, he was afraid she might have a problem adding another white guy. But it all seemed to work out, and Glenn was both surprised and relieved to see her leading the big guy in a brisk walk to catch up with them from behind. As is usual with the alliance, Joan had come up with a plan that fit even this situation.

"Hold up, everyone," Joan shouted as she approached with Little John, and the whole troupe stopped so everyone could gather around for introductions. Puzzled, Glenn wondered about that; she had introduced him only to Judy. But the "shoulda-guessed" reason for the different process became evident when she announced, "We are honored to have John Pontiac as a novice with our little company. John's family traces itself directly back to the famous Chief Pontiac from the nineteenth century or so. He helps us with our Native American male quota, and we are very pleased to have him with us."

The troupe applauded vigorously, and each in turn shook the new member's hand with the still mostly ignored Glenn, too sweet smile, praying hands and all, last in line. Catching John's eye as they shook hands, he winked and said, "I welcome you, honored descendant of so great a chief." And he almost laughed out loud at his friend's eye-roll.

"I've heard of him, but I don't know much about him. To me, Pontiac's just a town," John whispered back. "I told her that I was from Oakland County, and she comes up with this story! What do I say if someone asks me something about my heritage?"

"Lie, my friend, lie. I'm told that lying about being a Native American has been a cottage industry since the nineteen-sixties. Probably no group has had more people lying to get into it than your new quota group. Besides, no one'll know the difference, just don't say too much because you don't know much, and you'll give yourself away."

Shortly afterwards, despite his admiration for their angel's fast footwork to get John into camp, petty jealousy raised its ugly head when that same new John Pontiac was immediately named a juggler trainee. Why did he get it so fast, and I have to wait? Glenn wondered. And matters deteriorated even more when Alex, the next new member they encountered on the road, was also welcomed with a warm handshake greeting by the whole troupe and then immediately elevated to "jugglerhood" based on no proven talents.

"What's going on here?" Glenn asked Joan. "These guys get the grand welcome and are in as jugglers from second-number-one … and I'm on a waiting list?"

"Umm, you know, I've never had a competition for juggler before. But, Glenn, even you can see that, although they are strangers to you, these two men are both higher quotaed than you are, and we make a big deal of welcoming them because they help us meet our quota goals—you white guys are a dime a dozen. So they get what they want when they want it, but you'll have to wait until there's another opening with no higher quotaed person in line for it," she replied. Then, smiling broadly, she rushed on to add, "Which, not by coincidence, is now. So come on, there's someone I want you to meet."

After his pouting complaint, Glenn felt like a foolish little kid as he trailed along behind her through the now stopped camp. The real adults in the troupe were all busy unwrapping tents and unloading supplies to set up for the night. They would use the extra time they got by the early stop to polish their acts so they'd be ready to perform at a big fair in nearby Parshallville the next day.

"Glenn, it's my privilege to introduce you to one the finest jugglers in the federal performance system," Joan said, after stopping him at a clearing just on the edge of their campsite. And as she spoke, she swept an exaggerated hand wave toward an approaching older clown, wearing a large fake hump on his back.

Glenn, caught by surprise, stared with a you-gotta-be-kiddin'-me expression on his face as the old man, his supposed to be juggling instructor, came shuffling up to them, flashing a toothy smile. Leaning heavily on a crude, homemade crutch, he looked like he would need help, not give it. But Joan ignored Glenn's attitude and smiling broadly at the older clown, went on with her introductions, "Dell-X, Glenn. Glenn, Dell-X."

"Hark!" Dell-X, teetering unsteadily from side to side and raising an open hand behind his right ear, leaned forward as if trying to hear—and see. He squinted, Magoo-like, as he spoke. "Me thinks

I hear a sweet and melodious voice, the voice of an angel, pure and innocent, but who is this at her side? Do I see a preacher, a true holy man of some kind? Oh, how curious that would be in this new age of unbelief! But I'm not particular. I accept all, padre or madre, believer in the eternal or believer in self and a mere mud-ball world, it matters not to this old soul. All the world's a stage, and you preachers also have a right to your own, all be they rather dated, entrances and exits—mostly exits these days, me thinks, now that merely voting 'present' instead of standing up tall to be counted for what you believe in has been urged upon us by the times. Ah, yes, these glorious PAC-blessed times!"

And with that strange response barely out of his mouth, he flashed a showman's smile, spun about, and after deftly lifting Joan's sword from her belt, he tossed it, his crutch, and his own belt-knife high into the air in front of a stunned Glenn. And then, after bouncing them all about for several rotations, he returned each item to its rightful place ... finishing it all by bowing deeply and stepping back.

That once tottering, humpbacked old man and his incredible act left both Joan and Glenn surprised and Glenn even a bit rattled. So much so that, after it ended, he just stood there, rooted in place for a long moment with a gaping mouth that widened even more when Dell-X followed his routine with an artfully flourished WWW sign. His back was to the other troupe members milling around them, and so only Joan and Glenn could see his hands as he did the sign.

However, after signing, Dell-X made very sure to turn so that everyone milling around could see him plop two leather balls into Glenn's fumbling hands and hear him order the young man to work with 'em overnight to get the "feel." And with that, he waved to the crowd, and as he shuffled away, the character of the hunchbacked old man replaced the master juggler. He was once again stooped, shuffling, and now, whistling.

And just before vanishing into the throng of the still laughing and applauding bystanders, that artful clown turned back around to face Glenn again, and cupping his hands beside his mouth, he shouted out a single word to that still stunned young man: "Practice!"

CHAPTER FOURTEEN

How the Three Save a Juggler and Free a Worthy

*W*ednesday morning brought yet another pre-dawn wake-up call, and as he joined his campmates preparing to head for Parshallville, Glenn was captured by the excitement of it all, beginning with the wolfed-down breakfast and camp-coffee-burned lips. The smell of the early morning breakfast fires scattered about their encampment, the laughing and the shouting while they lifted and loaded up, and the easy camaraderie of the troupe, all charged his spirits as he rushed about in the early light, helping his fellow performers get their show on the road. He loved it, and by the time they moved out to the north he had embraced a sense that most of these were good people and that this was how life should be: people, politics aside, working together toward a common goal.

To top it all off, after they had been rolling only a few minutes, Joan drifted over to walk with him, saying she wanted to brief him on what to expect that day and to make sure he had been practicing with the juggling balls Dell-X had given him the night before.

"Work on your act, you need to look authentic. The crowds are always good here, but we have to be careful. We don't know who's who," she said. "This is a crossover point for a lot people and stuff moving between the feds who control Lansing and outliers of all types who're vying for control of everything north of here. So even though most of the people will be just regular folks wanting to have a good time, some will be unfriendly to the alliance—you know, spies and the usual bevy of rowdy lowlifes and bounty hunters. That means you have to be on your guard, and as I've said to your two buddies, stay away from each other. There'll be a lot of eyes out there, just lookin' and watchin', so you need to fade into the mob and give 'em nothing to see or talk about."

"Yes, of course." Glenn replied. He wanted to be polite, but he could barely hide his impatience. He didn't want to talk about all that stuff, it was obvious; he wanted to hear about that old guy who'd plopped two leather balls in his hand and then vanished last night right after an amazing juggling act. So bypassing diplomacy, he just came out with it, "Who's this Dell-X character besides a walk-on juggler, and what does he have to do with me—and why is he giving me orders?"

"You, my friend, have been entertained by a Founding Worthy," Joan replied, laughing at his frustration-driven litany. "Can you believe it? One of the founders of the Whig Partisan Alliance is your *juggling* instructor. You asked for it, and beginning this morning, you've got it—in spades. So I hope you've been practicing. We gotta impress the boss, and Glenn, he *is* your boss ... and mine." She laughed at his stunned reaction, and then waving goodbye she moved off to connect with others in the troupe.

An hour later, Glenn greeted the now fully up morning sun with Dell-X at his side and two now familiar juggling balls bouncing in his hands. His teacher had found him right after Jen had moved on and immediately put him to work, bouncing the two balls just the right way, up and down, in and between each hand—to get "the feel," so he said.

"I'd hoped you'd have practiced more last night." Dell-X had groused when he first arrived, but then eyeing the uncomfortable, but sincere younger man, he smiled and added, "I guess you can make it up today if you keep working at it. But it takes work, you gotta work at it, preacher. So go to it, and I'll be back." He had called that last part over his shoulder as he walked away, leaving a chastened Glenn to his practice. About a half hour later, Dell-X arrived again to check his progress, and after offering comments and a couple of suggestions, he left—a pattern that kept repeating itself. Each time it was the same routine; he'd watch briefly, look disappointed, and then after a comment or two and a quick demonstration, he'd leave. Not once did he offer a compliment to Glenn on his progress or engage him personally; it was always a work-focused, "Mmm, keep at it."

"Sir, I think I'm more than ready to try something else," Glenn suggested when Dell-X returned for the third or fourth time. He felt intimidated by being under the eye of a Worthy and was reluctant to say anything, but this routine was getting very old.

"OK, yes, you're almost there. It'll be a bit longer, but you're getting close to that third ball," Dell-X said, and then as he circled away for what Glenn hoped would be the last time, he called back, "Keep 'em going, play 'em up and around—work at it! Keep them both in the air at once, but higher. Try to toss them higher."

Glenn had to fight back a strong need to protest. This *was* a Worthy after all.

"OK, let's see what you can do now." Dell-X shouted ahead of himself as he came walking back up to Glenn thirty minutes later, just as the troupe was arriving at their show site.

"It's now or never," Glenn whispered to himself, and he was so wound up that he flinched when Dell-X slapped him on the back. But he recovered quickly, pasting on a smile and censoring his many complaints about the long, dull, training routine. Joan had said they had to impress the boss, and he was determined to do just that.

Anyway, there was something about the self-assured expression the Worthy always wore that ... well, that made Glenn not want to cross him. So while everyone else bustled about changing from a travel to a setup routine, and even though he yearned to be part of all of that activity again, Glenn allowed himself to be led off by his trainer in search of a practice place for yet more dull training—but now with that third ball!

Dell-X announced that they had found just the right spot, not by words but by quickly stepping out ahead of Glenn and dramatically turning to face him, holding out an empty, palm-up, left hand. Glenn, hooked despite himself, stared first at the proffered hand and then refocused to watch the smooth swing of his teacher's also empty right hand as it flowed in an easy, even, underhand arc from back to front, ending suddenly with a loud *smack* against the underside of his still outstretched left hand.

"And, PRESTO!" Dell-X shouted as his hands connected, sending a third ball blurpopping up and out toward a surprised and completely unprepared Glenn.

"What? Wait!" Glenn shouted, and dropping the two balls he had in hand, he dove forward trying to catch that new ball. And missing it, he scrambled across the grass, groping around like a little kid trying to retrieve thrown parade candy.

"Whoa, you gotta catch those, preacher."

"Sorry," Glenn shouted, scowling as he continued doing his clumsy pick-up act even as his smiling teacher calmly slid down against a tree trunk to sit and watch.

When Glenn finally got himself pulled together, Dell-X put him to work at once, offering the needed instruction and encouragement from his comfortable new spot under his tree. It all looked so easy for him. First came the hated two ball drills, but then, after repeated demonstrations, Dell-X got him started on that longed for third ball.

An increasingly frustrated Glenn enjoyed very little early success, mostly because he had trouble keeping his focus. As he worked, members of the troupe were hustling about, doing their set-ups just across the clearing from his training spot, and many of them offered well-intentioned encouragement, along with not a few laughs.

The lack of progress embarrassed Glenn, and he nearly gave up, thinking again and again about how much he would rather be out there with the others than messing with these idiot balls. Those other people were doing real work while here he was fumbling and bumbling about like a child. He wasn't going to be ready to do his silly act at all; he was certain of that. Still, he continued working at it.

"You'll get it. Just be patient," Dell-X assured him, and Glenn, swallowing his frustration, worked at it and worked at it, until … slowly but surely, he began to keep the three balls in motion. Of course, early on, he did it only by running first this way and then that way to stay with them. But finally, and it seemed suddenly, he had it!

He had that mysterious "feel" Dell-X had talked about; he actually felt it. And once he had found his touch, it all began to flow. Of course he couldn't duplicate his teacher's example, but now he had a real act, and small step by small step, less and less awkwardly, he was actually juggling. It was thrilling! *He* was a juggler, a very proud juggler.

"This is great," shouted Glenn, keeping his eyes on the balls. "I can do this."

"I think you've got it, preacher," Dell-X agreed, and laughing loudly, he nodded toward a tree near where he was sitting, "Have a sit-down right over there. Let's take a break and talk a bit now before the crowd gets too large."

"Sounds good," Glenn replied, moving towards the tree. Although now eager to continue developing his new talent, he was tired and really did want to talk to this guy.

As Glenn eased down across from him, Dell-X handed over the water skin, and glancing about for unwanted eyes, asked, "Before I begin, do you have any questions?"

"Yes, many, but first, why do you call me preacher?" And gesturing down at his clerics' gown as he spoke, he added, "This is only a costume, you know who I am."

"Ah, but who are any of us, really?" Dell-X replied, in character, but then smiling broadly, he quickly added, "OK, if it bugs you, I'll stop at once. But as long as you've brought up religion, I have a question of my own. May I ask, are you religious?"

"No. I mean, yes. What I meant was that, no, it doesn't bug me, but it seems to be unnecessary for you to call me that when it's just the two of us." Glenn had fumbled his reply because he wasn't sure how he wanted to answer that question. He knew that an honest answer, if heard by the wrong people, would mark him as an enemy of PAC. But that shouldn't be true of this man, he was a Worthy, as unlikely as that seemed right now, and that should mean that he'd follow the alliance creed by accepting Glenn's right to believe or not believe according to his own conscience. Besides, Joan had cleared him, and that's all he really needed, and so he added, "Yes, I am a believer, how about you?"

"Well …" Dell-X smiled at him. "As you've just demonstrated, there's a tricky one."

"Oh, it's not tricky. I was just confused. There are only two possibilities."

"If it were only that simple," Dell-X sat up, and leaning forward over his crossed legs, he continued. "I am a believer, but one of the things I believe is that we Christians have been more a part of the problem than a part of the solution over my lifetime."

"What do you mean?" Glenn asked, but as he said it, he decided that he knew what Dell-X meant and tried to correct himself, "No, wait, I know what you mean …"

"Well, why don't you let me tell you what I think I mean, first, and then you offer your version, and we can argue later about who's right." Dell-X laughed.

Standing then, he raised his right hand high over his head, and moving it in a small circle, extended index finger pointing down, he said, "I believe that we believers, all of us, including this one, have failed to live our beliefs well enough to keep unbelief from flourishing. We've been like the rich young ruler in the Bible, thinking that we had it made as long as we kept our heads down and followed a few rules. So we ended up by *baa*-ing with our chosen flock while passively accepting the emergence of today's crazy array of PAC intolerance. Intolerance! The question is, why? Why'd we let it happen?

"I think there are two reasons: on the one hand, those who became PACies or PAC-toadies wanted to be modern, and that meant being too cool to stand up for square things like self-reliance, self-respect, or even basic things like living within our means or old family values. So our surrender-monkey elders split between those who just gave in to the modernizers in order to go with the PAC flow and those who actively twisted our essential faith message from a focus on disciplining ourselves to help others as servant-believers, to either becoming PAC-collaborators or—on the other side—to a fixation on personal prosperity and getting rich … because, 'God wanted us to prosper.' Either way, believers shifted from 'feed my sheep,' to 'belly up to the table to serve yourself.' All sides, by focusing on self, openly or tacitly abandoned the public square to PAC control."

"That sounds a little too much like self-hate, don't you think? We certainly didn't stand tall, but we're where we are because PAC undermined our culture."

"Ha! That's like saying you got VD because PAC legalized prostitution. I don't think what I said is self-hateful at all. Earlier generations delivered us to an era where *E pluribus unum* was becoming a reality, but we fiddled as it was all undermined by PAC."

Glenn smiled at the *from many, one* reference, an alliance favorite, but he still protested, "Why just, *we*? How about, *they*?" You're laying everything on believers."

"No, I'm not. I said we, and that means all the usual suspects—including us. The alliance philosophy is that we hold ourselves and our own close groups responsible first, and then we move out from our own base to do our job, which is to be our brothers' keeper—a term Cain, ironically enough, introduced. We, the believers of America, have drifted along with the cultural winds and accommodated and appeased year after year, even when it should have become obvious early in this century that we were at a final tipping point. In the space of the coming of age and move to senescence of a single generation, we went from being close to having a free public square that reflected the values of our people to one controlled first by a purposeful chaos and then by PAC." He snapped his fingers, "just like that—and practically that quick, really."

"So, you're bashing the Boomers? And what do you mean by purposeful chaos? Do you have some kind of long-term conspiracy in mind?" But even as Glenn asked that question, he searched his mind. He had heard that term somewhere, but where?

"Conspiracy? Not in the usual march to conquest sense, but more like Napoleon's takeover in France. At its beginning, PAC was just a loose collection of 'we're better 'n the common folk,' riffraff, mostly confined to a motley group of self-focused wannabe real revolutionaries types. But things changed during the social chaos of the thirties when more of our people became open to a kind of progressive control from the center thinking that fogged its way into our colleges and some of our churches and even took over part of the labor movement. From there, that evil grew and evolved into—well,

1 ofnull BLUE COMPANY

really into a new religion for power at the center types and to the formal birth of PAC.

"It was an easy dance step in the sixties for those early PAC fifth columnists to soft-shoe their way into the mix of a new era of clueless youth who had begun disrupting the public square. Of course, those kids were enabled by the fact that their elders were understandably exhausted from the trials of the Depression and the utter horror of WWII. This allowed them to do what earlier generations of young people probably wanted to do: to strip off the old values and beliefs and replace them with naive playground-kid wisdom.

"Usually, the adults win that struggle, and the kids grow up. But in this case, the guardians of our admittedly imperfect society were just plain worn out. So instead of a gentle or not so gentle redirection of those foolish young people, the adults just stood by, watching as much of what had been gained for us over the previous couple hundred years was flushed down history's drain pipes, all in the name of some kind of vague change!

"Think about it, that slogan is stupid on its face, change to what? Hitler, Stalin, Mao, the Inquisition? They all produced very real change. Change? Come on, it's a hucksters' slogan, greasing the skids for devious power grabs, a la Napoleon. He started as his people's savior and went on to bring years of horrifying change to all of Europe. And now, in our time, PAC has become a similar change agent by coopting the 'P' of the Boomers naïve *peace* and changing it to mean iron-edged, *power*! Full Power-At-the-Center always leads to 'destroy all who stand in the way'—always has and always will. Unless the people have the guts and brains to rule themselves, they will be ruled by whatever nutcase dolts bubble to the top. Today, those dolts happen to be PAC idiots.

"Why'd it happen? I frankly can't understand why, Glenn. Couldn't then, can't now. Oh, it's easy to blame our politicians for serving themselves instead of us, but why did we, the heads-on-straight, upright, good people, settle for doing the *Poor Willy/Wilma Waltz* and let it all, just happen? And even worse, why did we join in with outstretched palms while our leaders shoveled out the cash for

null 201

all those oh so feel-good entitlement programs? Why didn't we think about our kids and grandkids? I flat out don't know."

"OK, OK." Glenn threw up his hands, laughing at first at Dell-X's intensity. But he sobered up quickly when he remembered that church he had visited … or really, that once-church. Dell-X was right about our failed responsibility, and Glenn knew it.

"Let me add just a couple of other things." Dell-X also laughed. He was on a roll, and he wanted to finish. "Those sixties kids thought they'd create a naked public square, a blank slate on which to write a thrilling new chapter based on their new-only-to-them free and easy adolescent philosophy. But PAC, now mature and ready to take over, moved in to impose its own new and gloriously unfair egalitarianism on us all.

"So, what those youthful acting outers thought would be a grand new day for their kind of equality, a new time when all kids would be equal and get to play all day long with no adult supervision, became … well, I'm sure you know all about Orwell's farm. Some people and their values will always be made more equal than others, if we allow it, and we allowed it. Our *New Truth,* another term I'm sure you know, became what the PAC elite, and only they, decided it was: who's up and who's down, what words mean and don't mean. But hey, those sixties kids had their fun—just like Hansel and Gretel.

"Leaders who once *pretended* to serve the people, now rule as petty czars. Even our entertainment industry, which once performed *for* us and at least *pretended* to respect our values has drifted to the clouds above us all and now openly imposes their amoral, profits-before-all, *circus for the peasants,* style on us. And of course, all that dump-on-the-dull-folks-back-home, free-swinging freedom the kids loved didn't last long, but it wasn't the good common folk, standing up for enduring values, who caused all these misguided libertines to back down. No, it was PAC that dropped the hammer, and our entertainers, now freed of our old values, are all owned and controlled, indeed, near-enslaved by new masters with new, non-negotiable rules—thus, our new change!"

"OK. I've read Orwell, he comes up all the time these days, and I can see … "

"Hold it!" Dell-X held up an urgent hand. "We need to continue this later; we're attracting attention we don't want right now." He nodded toward three bounty hunter types who stood eyeing them from over by a hot dog stand. "You go do your act."

They quickly broke up, and Glenn, trying to look holy, melded into the now large crowd and began wandering about. As he walked along, bouncing two balls in the air, he became more and more sure of himself, until finally, he just had to try his new act. And so, after confidently pulling out that long awaited third ball, and with all three in hand, he loudly proclaimed his intent to the laughing, jovial throng pressing in all around him.

He had done it with Dell-X and was spot on as he started, but his so-called act very quickly turned into a fumbling, show 'em what you can't do, routine. Unprepared for the impact on his concentration that all the people pressing so close around him would have, he lost his groove ... and his control. The crowd, no doubt thinking it was all part of his act, laughed and jeered as he stumbled all about, bobbling and dropping balls, but he soldiered on despite it all—until he lost one. It had probably just rolled under a nearby stand, but he was done by then and gave up without even bothering to try to retrieve it.

Yet, despite his very real embarrassment, he was determined to keep up at least a semblance of his act, and so he pressed his hands together, lowered his head, and moved away into the crowd with a genuinely prayerful look on his face—because he really was praying. Behind him, he could hear a loud round of laughter and applause, but he didn't care about that or about where he went—he just wanted to get away.

At first, he wandered about with no particular plan in mind, but then he began wondering about his two comrades and how they were doing, and so he started drifting around, sort of looking for them. Of course, Joan had warned them all to stay apart, but he decided that it wouldn't be too risky to just walk by them and take a quick look at their acts. If they were still performing, they were probably having trouble just as he'd had. And so he circled the grounds, twice, keeping his eyes open for them but mainly just enjoying himself. He even took a break under a tree with a couple of juicy hotdogs and a big lemonade, all the while telling himself that he wasn't really disobeying orders.

About thirty minutes later, full and relaxed, he finally came across his buddies. Both were performing in the same general area—and they were incredible. He was amazed by how good they had become so fast; Dell-X must have worked with them too. Alex not only had good ball control, but also kept up a glib and entertaining patter while he easily whipped three balls up, around; and about. John was less eloquent, but he was trying to move beyond just bouncing balls, and he drew a lot of laughs when his big assortment of clubs and even a hotdog came crashing down all around him. Glenn also noted that they both had caps brimming with federals laying on the ground in front of them, and as he walked away, embarrassed, he unconsciously lifted a hand to touch his own skull cap, still on his head and very empty. Oh well, he didn't like juggling anyway.

His blah mood shifted when he wandered into the show place of the fairground, an old cider mill. Built a century and a half ago with beautiful huge rocks and blocks supported by massive wooden beams, its heavy, well-worn thick plank flooring was crowded with big bulky iron contraptions, and creative stitching displays and old posters filled the walls. On top of that, the whole place smelled of apples and fresh made donuts even this early in the season. He grinned, knowing that in just a few short weeks they'd be cranking out gallons of fresh, delicious cider, and he hoped he could come back here then to sample it all. He was still standing there, basking in the smell and feel of the place, munching on a donut and sipping hot cider, when Joan found him.

"Glenn, there's a problem brewing, and I need you," she called out, reaching around the man behind him to tug at his sleeve. Nodding, he took another bite and was raising his cup for a drink when she jabbed him sharply in the ribs. "I need you, now!"

"What's so urgent?" he asked once they had reached a quiet place under some trees away from the mill, and as he spoke, he curiously looked out over her head at the milling crowd, scanning it for signs of a problem. "Everything looks normal."

"Dell-X may have been outed," she whispered back, ignoring his comment and obviously worried. "This means a change of plans, and you'll need to help me get him off the grounds. I've set up your two buddies as back-ups if there's trouble getting away."

"Let's go," he said, turning quickly to move out, but she redirected him.

"No, hold it! You stay back and come forward only if I signal you," she ordered, and as they began walking, she added, "You may need one of your friendlies' passes, so get the best one out and be ready. And I probably don't need to tell you this, but if you do use a pass, be arrogant and don't confuse your roles—no more meek and mild monk."

By the time they arrived back at Joan's wagon, a crowd had gathered, and Dell-X was standing alone, facing a semicircle of bounty hunters and federals. He seemed calm, but the situation was very tense. A federal officer, standing just in front of her men, was shouting loudly at him and apparently trying to arouse the crowd by holding up a paper of some kind. The situation felt like it was near the boiling point.

"Do you deny that the person in this paper is you?" she challenged Dell-X.

"I don't deny that I am the person standing in front of you, but I can't be in two places, so that can't be me in your hand, besides, I'd have to be pretty skinny to fit into that slip of paper." He laughed—but no one joined him. The crowd was on edge.

"This is out of your travel pack, do you deny that?"

"I have a lot of things in my pack, but I'm not them, and they aren't me."

"Don't try to use your silly clown-talk on me," she snapped, and then looking around at the crowd, she added, "And you ain't the only one in trouble here. We know this whole troupe is filled with PAC haters, especially that big guy over there." She pointed toward Little John, who was standing off to her left, decidedly not blending in.

And those words were no sooner out of her mouth than "that big guy" screamed out a mighty roaring call to arms and charged toward her and her group, shouting, "PAC rats! Bring 'em down!"

Others, quickly answering his call, surged forward, and that caught the federals and their allies completely off guard. They had not expected a sudden assault, nor even less, the crowd's support of those they were trying to arrest.

"Stay back! You are violating PAC privilege, stay back!" The leader screamed.

"PAC rats! Bring 'em down!" replied others from the troupe and crowd as many of them swarmed forward behind Little John who had bounded across the space between himself and the federal leader, sweeping her off her feet with one big arm. And then, after knocking her down, he turned with a snarl and plunged into the line of her still startled and frozen allies, his face now glowing with a look of sheer joy as he began knocking heads. And many others from the crowd, either because they were supporters rallying to the call or just for the fun of it all, also jumped into the fray and began taking down the federals, bounty hunters, and anyone who defended them.

In the midst of it all, Joan looked for and somehow found Dell-X's now dropped documents, and then, after slipping off to the side and checking to be sure it was all clear, she signaled Glenn and Dell-X that it was time to leave. And all three of them, pulling their cloaks around their faces, moved quickly back through the fairgrounds and away from the fight. At first, it was slow going because they were moving against a strong tide of revelers rushing to the sound of battle, but they soon broke past the crowd and were out in the open. A few running minutes later, Joan stopped them at the place where she earlier had stashed their gear. After they quickly saddled up, she returned Dell-X's papers, and brushing aside his thanks, led them off to the north through the woods. They walked along a river until they came to a bridge where she finally allowed them to stop.

"I'll need to leave you here," she said, laughing as she reached out to give them both hugs. "I don't know when I've had so much fun, what happened back there, or why. But both Alex and Little John followed our plan to get us out of trouble, and so now I need to get back to make sure that big galoot and the captain also get away."

She passed on instructions to continue north on Linden to Center Road. "It'll be just past the PAC training site on the old golf course, but don't worry about the PACies there, they won't bother you. Head east on Center, but before you do, use your CB to send this message." She handed Glenn a slip of paper. "Say only the words on the paper and listen to the reply. Then turn off the CB, tear up the note, and leave the phone in the rusty old mailbox that we've left under a tree northeast of the intersection. Oh, speaking of the CB, I need to show you how to use it or there'll be no message."

Glenn had forgotten that he even had the thing, and as he fumbled for the CB and handed it to her, he wondered what would have happened if he'd been caught with it back there. Oh well, he shrugged, thinking it could have been bad, but didn't happen. Then he turned to watch as Joan showed him how to use the devise.

"So all you have to do is hold down this little button [she pointed to it], read your message and release the button. We're good to receive at the other end. There'll be a brief response telling you what to do. Then turn it off. Modern technology isn't only in PAC hands, even though they're trying mightily to make it that way—all in the name of protecting us from ourselves, of course." Joan then gave each of them another hug and reminded them to change back into their own clothes and to hide their costumes under the bridge before they moved on; she'd collect them later. After that, she turned and quickly headed back toward the fairgrounds to check on "that big galoot" and Alex.

Dell-X was unusually quiet as they moved along the road Joan had put them on, and Glenn, who was worried about his two buddies, didn't feel much like talking, himself, so few words were exchanged on the walk toward Center Road. Once there, Glenn called on the CB and left the message required. He then listened to the very short, strange reply before ditching the illegal device in the mailbox behind the tree as instructed. From there they moved east on Center toward whatever new contact experience the message would bring. The two had no idea what would happen next, and the message they heard was too cryptic to help: "Sweeping south, secure self 23 west side."

"I want to explain …" Dell-X started to go over what had just happened, but before he could do that, they were caught up short. Up ahead, they spotted a squad of armed federals standing on the old

US 23 Bridge, all looking directly at them. Indeed, their leader, who stood well in front of his men, was pointing at the two of them ... and he was holding a familiar looking CB radio in his hand. Dell-X and Glenn looked at each other, slowing their pace, but they had no real choice about what to do. They were right beside the PAC training center at that moment and so neither fighting nor running was an option when there was an army of feds right there, available to chase them down.

Unhappily, that left nothing to do but to face these guys and brazen it out. So as they continued walking, Glenn fumbled for his pass and wondered how they had found his radio and arrived here ahead of them. It didn't seem possible.

"Let me handle this, sir," he whispered to Dell-X, laughing to himself as he recalled Joan's unnecessary instructions about attitude. "I can manage these guys."

"Well, what do we have here, a couple of runaways?" The leader of the federals shouted out, flashing a smug grin as they labored up the slope towards him. He wore no insignia of service or rank, but he was obviously full of himself and the one in charge. Holding up the CB, he added, "Did you think you could outrun modern technology?"

The other federals eyed the two travelers with wide grins. They were used to such contacts, and expected to shortly end up with either reward money or a bribe.

"That looks decidedly unmodern to me, where'd you get it, at a pawn shop?" Glenn replied in a matter-of-fact, almost bored tone of voice. Ignoring the others, he sharply eyed their leader as he spoke, and although he seemed to only glance at the CB, he actually studied it, but to no avail. He couldn't tell if was his old one or not.

"Don't you worry about where I got it, you just worry about showin' me the right papers," the leader growled back, but he was more guarded now. Glenn's attitude and voice gave him pause, and he wasn't as sure of himself as he had been. These two fit the description that had been radioed to his company, but for some reason they didn't act like they were worried about being stopped. That bothered him.

"I trust these will do?" Glenn replied, pushing his Friendly Forces VIP pass into the leader's face and smiling as he noted the man's sudden change in demeanor. It was fun watching the fed's eyes widened as he studied the pass, reading such key phrases as *to be passed without question, to be treated with every courtesy, to be given any and all provisions required.*

"Do you understand what you're reading?" Glenn snapped.

"Yes, sir!" The leader shouted his reply in a tight-throated hoarse voice, and now cringing under Glenn's contemptuous gaze, he nervously licked his lips as he added, "Is there anything we can do to help you on your journey, sirs?"

As he spoke, he gestured frantically to his men who had been idling off to the side only half interested in what was going on; they had expected their leader to handle it. But now, responding to his flailing gestures, they shuffled into a semblance of an orderly line and stood with their eyes on Glenn, worrying about what might happen next.

Glenn, after accepting all of their food and water, loudly complained about the delay as he wrote down their names and ranks. This was all fun, and he was enjoying himself, but business had to come first. So after letting them stew in their own error-juice for a bit, he nodded his acceptance and ordered them to escort him and his friend across the overpass. Once they reached the other side, he instructed them to go directly to the fairgrounds where, he sarcastically suggested, they were really needed.

But then, just as a relieved Glenn was beginning to congratulate himself on a scam well executed and the feds were forming up to depart, but before they could move out, Dell-X stunned them all by reaching out to snatch the CB from the fed leader's hand and to smash it against the nearby cement wall. And then, without offering a word of explanation, the older man turned with a big smile on his face and began walking away.

"Not to worry!" a very surprised Glenn, recovering quickly, rushed to account for that strange behavior before the federal could screw up enough courage to take some kind of action himself. "Even though such radios are illegal," he continued, sternly eyeing the other man, "I'll not report you because you've been so cooperative. But right now, all of you, get going to the fairgrounds and do not stop anywhere along the way!"

The now very confused federals followed those orders without hesitation, leaving behind them Glenn and Dell-X, both blowing out deep sighs of relief.

Grinning, Dell-X then whispered, "Good pickup on my move. I didn't want to risk them getting some last minute instructions to hold us. Now, we'll be long gone before they can find out that we're the runaways they wanted, if they ever do."

Agreeing, Glenn laughed, and they slapped hands before turning to continue their journey. Unfortunately, their upbeat mood was to be short lived. As they started down the hill to reconnect with their road on the east side of the bridge, they saw a column of a dozen or so federals approaching them from the south.

It was then, as they reached the bottom of the slope leading down from the bridge, that Glenn realized that he had forgotten to retrieve his friendlies' pass from that stupid fed sergeant!

"Whoa," he muttered to himself, "What a moron I am, what a complete moron! From now on the word moron should be spelled, G-L-E-N-N."

CHAPTER FIFTEEN

How Captain Alexander Bullard Crosby Gains a New Commission

"Get down! Get down right where you are and crawl back to us!" The hissed-out, urgent sounding orders, coming just as they finished their walk-slide down the hill from the overpass, caught Dell-X and Glenn off guard, and although they both thought they knew that voice, they still turned, preparing to confront a new threat—this *was* a fed hot-bed, after all. Crouching down, they squinted warily into the darkness under the bridge and relaxed only when they saw that, yes that really was just Alex calling out to them. Relieved, they stood up and, grinning and waving, started walking towards him.

But his reaction froze them. And he wasn't just waving now; he was flat-out flailing, but why? They looked at each other, their grins of recognition now fading into another round of confusion. He seemed to want them to get down again, but wait! No, not just seemed, he very much wanted them to get down.

"Down!" He hissed, much louder this time, and rapidly shaking his head in frustration, he motioned for them to get all the way down in the grass. "Drop all the way down. Don't look back here, just get down where you are."

At that, Dell-X, following orders, dropped like a rock, but then seeing that Glenn was still standing, he reached up and jerked him down, shushing the confused younger man as he looked anxiously back towards Alex for new instructions.

Glenn, now even more bewildered, looked first at Dell-X and then back toward the dark underpass where a shadowy Alex seemed to be gesturing for them to either stay down or to come toward him. He wasn't sure which, and so he chose to half-stand so he could look back to check on the feds they had seen coming down the road. And because he looked away, craning his neck to peer back over the tall grass between them and the road, he didn't notice Dell-X do a fast crouch-run toward Alex. It took Glenn less than a minute to decide that if he couldn't see the feds that he knew were on that road, then they couldn't see him. But when he turned to share that thought, he saw that Dell-X was gone, and so he shrugged and began his own belated run-crawl up the slope to Alex.

By then Dell-X had joined both Alex and the now visible Little John, and all three stood impatiently waiting for Glenn. He was grinning when he reached them, but he saw right away that his buddies didn't share his good cheer; they were obviously annoyed.

Still, there wasn't time to deal with his foul-up. Feds were approaching, and with that PAC school so close, they were concerned about being trapped between the two. If they were caught there, what would they say? Would they dare to use one of Glenn's passes again in the same place and virtually at the same time as the last one? Should they just cut and run? They whispered all of this back and forth as they looked out at the now fast closing feds, all the while ignoring the now chastened Glenn whose own smile had faded as he crouched there, listening to their whispers—about his now gone only pass.

"I thought I'd to have to come out there and get you," Alex groused as he finally reached down for Glenn's hand. "Come on! That's the third time on this trip that you've put yourself in position to be spotted, but there's no excuse this time. If you're gonna be on the team, you have to follow orders. You were standing out there like that sign-post you called yourself last time. I can't believe it."

"You come on, give me a break! We saw the feds when we came down the hill, and they probably saw us. I was just trying to figure out what was going on," Glenn replied, wondering why all the fuss. These guys needed to mellow out, and he started to say so, but decided instead to just let it die. After all, he knew that he'd be under the gun again when they discovered that he no longer had a friendlies' pass to show, his only one` being on its way to the fairgrounds with that sergeant. He smiled grimly, thinking about his botched retrieval, and he started to confess but decided to change the subject instead. "Say, how'd you get here ahead of us?"

"What was going on is that you blew off an order," Alex continued, and his voice still had an edge, but he lightened up as he replied to Glenn's question. "We just angled across country with Joan's guys—left right after you and had a shorter trip."

"How'd you miss the feds who stopped us?" Glenn asked.

"That's the key. We spotted them targeting you two, and so we circled around here in case you needed back-up," Alex replied, his eyes still on the approaching feds. "But forget all that, it's old news. Right now, it looks like we may need to use one of your passes—so be prepared."

"Well, that'll be a problem," Glenn replied, and looking sheepishly around at the others, he finally confessed. "I forgot to retrieve the only pass I had from that last clown."

"Forgot?" Alex and Dell-X spoke at once, but Little John just shook his head and grinned as Dell-X continued. "He wouldn't have had the guts to hold it. Are you sure?"

"Yes, of course, I'm very sure," Glenn replied, and holding up both hands in the universal surrender sign, he shook his head and apologized. "I'm sorry. It's all on me, and you're right, he was way too shook up to challenge me by holding on to my pass on purpose. I just forgot to take it back. My bad. I don't know what I was thinking."

"That seems to be a recurring theme," Alex muttered, and he stared at Glenn for a long moment but said nothing else. The others, looking from the approaching feds to Glenn and back again, also said nothing at first … until Little John broke the ice.

"What happened back there?" he asked, and leaning in between his two comrades, he plopped his big hands on both their shoulders, squeezing them hard and flashing a generous smile all around. "What's done is done, but how'd we get into this fix?"

"Sorry, I was just trying to figure out what was going on," Glenn mumbled.

"No, not here, I saw all of that." John snorted. "I mean back at the fair."

"I'd better answer that," Dell-X spoke up, and gesturing for the others to join him, he moved over closer to the edge of the shadows. "Stand over here with me so we can keep an eye on the feds out there while I explain."

"Oh great!" Alex interrupted as they lined up to talk. He'd glanced away from the feds, looking north. "There's another merry band coming at us from the other way!"

But it's what they had not seen that would have worried them even more. Long before the comrades saw the new group, two figures had split away and moved across US 23 to head south. That meant they might be coming up behind the still bickering gang at any time!

"Well, it looks like we have two problems closing in, and they're both on me. My bad, not Glenn's, and I owe you guys an explanation," Dell-X said, shaking his head. "But we're running out of time, so I'll make it brief now and fill in the details later."

"Joan said that you were outed, whatever that means," Glenn said.

"Well, Glenn, it means that you aren't the only one here who has to wonder what he was thinking. I plead guilty as well. Simply put, my own foolishness almost cost us our mission," Dell-X began, looking around at each one of them with a regretful frown as he spoke. "Call it foolish pride or just plain stupidity, but I've always kept a few personal papers with me over the years, and Judy came across some of them. Not her fault really, she didn't know what she'd found, but the papers revealed that I'm wanted for violating the Internet Freedom Act, you know, the one that gave the feds then and now PAC full control of the whole ball of digital age wax, thus guaranteeing our technology collapse."

"You?" Little John studied the other man. "How'd you violate? And besides, the web's been down for all us commoners forever. How old are you anyway?"

214

"Yes, well, the feds began collecting the web addresses of people who were into what they called 'fishy' content way before the web went down," Dell-X went on with his explanation, ignoring Little John's age request. "Over the years, they've developed a huge database of PAC enemies, and I've been on that list since the beginning. Luckily, I've managed to duck them because they couldn't ID me—until today."

"So, Judy recognized you and turned you in?" Alex spoke while keeping his eyes on the two approaching fed gangs, but he was now studying the northern one with a great deal of interest. There was something about it that didn't seem right to him.

"No, I think it was more a combination of accident, curiosity, and maybe PAC loyalty," Dell-X replied. "Apparently she was moving some stuff I'd tossed off to one side while I was practicing. That included my ball pouch, and she looked inside—just to look, I think, but maybe she was hoping to find a federal note or two. Anyway, she found my secret pocket and worked it open. It contained some old news clips about me and my activities with a group that helped birth our Whig Partisan Alliance, a group that became very illegal. It even included my picture, wanted status, and real name."

"Real name?" Little John looked at him. "You're not Dell-X?"

"Here we go again with who I am." Dell-X laughed. "I thought I'd run out that string with the fed officer. Yes, I am Dell-X, but that's my stage name. The clip Judy found gave the real one and my status, and so she went to Joan. Joan downplayed it as just ancient history and pretty well convinced her to put my papers back where she found them and to forget about it, but unfortunately, other ears were involved. A bounty hunter overheard, figured there might still be a reward, and brought in the feds. That's where you guys came in, and I'm very lucky that you were around. Without you, I could be crouching in a tiger cage right now, waiting to be bundled off to the friendlies."

"What'd you think they'd do to you, and why would they want you, the friendlies, that is?" Alex kept his eyes forward, still studying the coming federals as he asked his question. The four could see the feds before they could see each other, but Alex knew it wouldn't be long before the two war parties met and joined up to find them. So even as he asked the question, his mind had shifted away from Dell-X to those two groups.

The more he watched them, the more he wondered. And so, without waiting for an answer to his questions, he added, "Dell-X, what do you think? Are they both feds? If they are, it'll be pretty easy for them to find us under here, hiding almost in plain sight."

"Yes, I agree, that northern group looks very un-federal," Dell-X said, looking toward them as he answered Alex's other question. "As to the friendlies, I don't know what they'd do with me after all this time, but I don't want to risk finding out.

"Anyway, guys, don't be too hard on the clowns in front of us." Dell-X continued, and as he spoke, he turned to watch the three for their reaction, "I want you to try to wrap your minds around another way to think about them. Of course, we all view our feds, today, as a rag-tag sorry collection of what's left of our military. But they have a lot of good people, and they have the potential to be more than they are. Their main problem is that they're burdened by inept PAC-whipped leaders who don't have a clue, and by the resulting poor training and lack of discipline. But all of that could be changed."

"They're getting close," Alex mumbled, and scowling over at Dell-X, he snorted, "I don't see how the feds are ever gonna change. They're just a mob, and mobs don't get better on their own, they just keep getting worse. Who's going to help them do it, and why'd we even want them to get better? They're just going to be coming after us."

"Well, it's our hope that you and others like you will be willing to help them with that change, Captain Crosby, because we need those people—and they may not know it yet, but they need us. They need you and all of the other Whig Partisan Alliance, Blue Company warriors to be their trainers—and their role models." Dell-X spoke softly but with an, I'm serious nod at the now confused young officer. And then, before Alex or the others could respond, a woman's voice chimed in from the shadows behind them.

"That is, if you're ready to accept a new commission, Captain Crosby." And as she spoke, the woman behind that voice stepped out in the open so they all could see both her smile ... and her proudly flashed, WWW.

"Who *are* you?" Alex snapped, embarrassed that they'd been surprised.

"It's OK; we're all on the same team. Although, speaking of leadership, I'm surprised to find you on this side of 23. You were supposed to wait on the west side."

"That'd be another mark against me." Glenn admitted as he stepped forward to offer a hand. "We had a bit of a dust up with a group of federals, and I guess we went wrong from there, my fault. I'm Glenn Stanton, the one who sent the CB message."

"Well, you're with one of my bosses, so how can I complain?" She laughed as she shook his hand but then quickly moved by him to embrace Dell-X. "It's so good to see you again, sir. It's been five or six years. Camp Pendleton last time, as I recall.

"You two were at Pendleton six years ago?" Alex's jaw dropped. "That was the turning point; that's when the Marines took command and refused to surrender the base."

"And you, old friend." Dell-X returned the embrace, and beaming, he held her back at arm's length as he announced, "Men, this is J6, our new angel, and if anyone can get us back on track, she can— or at least, I hope so." And shaking his head as he stepped back, he smiled and asked, "Is our plan still workable, or did I mess us up too much?"

"No worries, we're good," she said. "But right now, I want to meet this big guy I've heard so much about, the hero who downed that media-copter, the copter killer, as everyone's calling him." And turning as she spoke, she extending a hand to Little John, who had shape-shifted away from his initial 'knock-heads' posture and now stood there grinning and blushing like a schoolboy.

"Well, ma'am," he finally said, his grin broadening as he stepped up to shake her hand, "It was really more luck than anything."

"Hey, don't be so modest and don't call me ma'am. I've worked hard to earn J6," she said, laughing at her own faux ego-posturing. "I'm looking forward to hearing about the copter, and of course, that dress. I understand you set a whole new standard in formal wear for women." The others all laughed at that—and at John's annoyed expression.

"I have two questions," Glenn cut in, ignoring John's glower glance at him. "What'll happen to Joan after all this? And are we on to Whigville or doing something else out here first?"

"That's three questions, Glenn," J6 smiled. "And the answers in reverse order are: yes, yes, and don't worry about Joan. She'll do fine. She has a good cover story and a lot of high-level protection. They won't lay a glove on her.

"As for the other two questions, Glenn, you're to remain here with me to observe PAC in action again, and then it'll be on to Whigville for all three of you. But before we go on, I want to introduce all of you to the man who'll soon lead the rest of you lot off to a safe house while Glenn and I visit that old golf course you passed on the way here. It's not a show place, but it's as major as PAC gets in these parts right now, and Glenn, it'll give you one more glance into the reality of the mysterious PAC mind—and soul."

She then motioned toward the shadows, and a jovial looking short, husky man in his mid-thirties stepped out to greet them with a deep Texas drawl. "Howdy folks, I'm pleased to meet you, and I've been looking forward to talking to you all, especially that copter killer over there. I salute you, my man. You've become famous."

"Guys …" J6 laughed at that greeting. "I want you to say hello to the 'Howdy' man, Lt. Colonel Howard 'Howdy' Lopez of the Alliance Forces. He came here from helping organize the resistance in Texas and will do the commissioning honors for us."

"But first, let me answer your earlier question, Alex," Howdy said, reaching for Alex's hand as he spoke. "For sure, those two were at Pendleton. They helped get the ball rolling out there, and it's a good story, but we'll save it for tonight at the safe house. Right now, I'm here to swear you in, and we need to do that before all the key-stone kops action starts between those two grand armies out there." He laughed. "Of course, as you may have guessed, one of them's our people—the sharper group, marchin' south."

"Well, I'm glad one of them's ours, but neither one looks very grand," Glenn said, smiling as he reached for Howdy's hand. "But what's all this about a commissioning? Are we really close enough to Whigville for that?"

"Thanks for your good words, but I don't feel famous," Little John cut in, warmly shaking hands with Howdy before turning to ask J6, "Do I get commissioned now too?"

"Yeah, commissioned as our designated basher," Alex said, and they all laughed.

"No, better than that. You'll earn a real one," she replied. "All three of you will go on to Whigville and enter the WPA academy. And you, big guy, will become part of our officer training program."

"So, we're all training together?" Little John said, grinning over at his friends.

"Well, not really." Howdy laughed and explained. "Alex is already an officer, so he'll be going to our senior command school. After that, who knows? He may deploy to one of our new bases as a senior federal officer or … whatever. And Glenn'll get to go through a special military-like boot camp, then be shifted to federal intelligence training."

"Federal! They'll be federals? Are we back to that theme again?" Little John scoffed. "It'll take a great big step down to become one of those slobs! We need to be taking them down, not stepping down to join them."

"Little John, all three of you will be federals," Dell-X said, and as he spoke he gently squeezed his comrade's shoulder in a gesture of reassurance. "We're marching toward a new day, and with it will come a whole new federal force. Our military was once the best in the world, and it's going to be that again. That identity belongs to all of us, to a new reunited American people, not to the PAC parasites who divided and almost destroyed us. Fed deserters are flooding in to us from all over right now, and that's good.

"We've put the word out that if they come in, they'll get a chance to begin again. Of course, they'll start as TP's first. That stands for 'transition personnel' and not toilet paper, by the way, but they may feel almost that low when they first start retraining. And then they'll be folded into our new reconstituted federal forces—all the old branches and traditions are coming back. And let me add that

I mean that they'll all be rebooted to be even better than they used to be. You're too young to know, but our military was heavily politicized just before the Fall, and so we're going to do a major delousing process to weed out the knee-bending PAC toadies. *And* we're reclaiming our old warrior spirit."

"Tell that to the friendlies running the Pentagon right now," John muttered. "Or tell it to the people in Clarkston who were savaged by those barbaric slobs."

"Correct me if I'm wrong, Dell-X," Glenn chimed in because he knew that John was talking about his own hometown, and he knew how bitter the big guy was about the PAC crimes there. "But can't we think of ourselves as being like the Free French were during World War II? You know, we'll put together a shadow government first, but later on, the people will welcome us as a liberating and uniting force—and we're all one again."

"I like that example," Dell-X said. "But, of course, you're right, John. There is a political puppet problem, and that's why I say that our main effort will be to de-politicize those coming over to us and to refocus and properly train them. Our new military headquarters is in Oklahoma City, and the plan and command control needed to end the sad politically correct rule of the absurd that has been the PAC era will come from there.

"Right now, we don't know what we'll do after the liberation, borrowing Glenn's term. We may or may not keep the military headquarters in Oklahoma, but I can assure you of one thing for certain. The whole inbred bundle of domestic federal mis-operations will be reformed into a new constitutionally friendly size and be scattered permanently around the country. You know, commerce in Michigan, education in North Carolina, and the like. We've learned our lesson. There'll be no more clustering of all our civil servants in one place. That nonsense mis-socializes even the best of them and makes it too easy for the bad apples to go wrong-rogue on us, and it leads to a tedious careerist culture that shoulders out accountability. Going forward, they'll be kept closer to the people—and accountable to the people, not the elites. No more casual-careerist lifer-types, fiddling away time and ignoring the peoples' interests allowed. It'll be meet the mark or out the door, fairly, but quickly. And, for sure, there'll be no more jumping into the special-interest gravy bowl for a big loyalty payoff after their exit from service.

"In our new day, that'll be true of congress as well. We'll make it illegal to go to work for any special interest for at least ten years after leaving office, and we'll term-limit them all—congress, courts, and all the rest. *And mark this*: we'll make sure of two other things. First, every one of our 'public servants' will be subject to the same laws they push on to us, and we'll pull the plug on their high flying—we pay, they go, junketeering high above all the rest of us. And second, we'll root out and punish those who use their office to target people and groups they don't like. That kind of partisan targeting is as bad as treason, an unforgiveable crime against both the people targeted and our whole order of government. Targeters will be tried, and if found guilty, they'll be fired, stripped of benefits, and then be heavily fined and sent to jail. *They* are an utter disgrace!"

"Let's do this!" Howdy interrupted. "Things are ready to lift off. We've got good seats for this show, so let's finish our work and save the talk for later."

"Alex, raise your right hand," J6 said, holding out a Bible for him to rest his left hand on. Howdy, keeping one eye on the gathering conflict near them, then read a brief but moving charge, and Alex solemnly took the oath.

"Congratulations, *Major* Alexander Bullard Crosby. Welcome to our growing Blue Company, Whig Partisan Alliance team," Dell-X said, and turning to Little John, he added, "John, you're next, but don't try to hold out for major. You'll start at the starting point … as a not so mere officer candidate."

"Just get me on the team, and let me at 'em," Little John replied—with feeling.

The ceremony was just wrapping up when the shouts from the two confronting forces broke in, and they all quickly moved closer to the edge of the shadows to watch as fifteen federals lined up facing north along the southern edge of Center Road with what looked to be a Chinese major standing off to one side. The federal leader, a sergeant, stood in the middle of the road with his head thrown back and chin thrust out, rocking back and forth on his heels and toes in a commanding, arms crossed, legs apart posture.

Facing him was a very thin elderly woman who, although slightly stooped, stood with her head up and her eyes firmly fixed on the federal leader. Behind her stood eight elderly men, apparently all soldiers—as improbable as that seemed. And they also stood tall, if a bit hunched, and seemed as unflinching and determined as their leader did. She, although not in uniform, wore the bars of a federal captain—a rather old federal captain.

"I'm ordering you to prove your loyalty to PAC," the sergeant shouted at her, and ignoring the bars, he glowered over at the company behind her and added, "That means all of you. I want to see your papers, and I want to see them now!"

"I challenge your right as a quotaed black male sergeant to give that order, and I demand a salute," the woman barked. "Right now!"

"I'm not going to ..." The sergeant started to refuse—she seemed to be only an old woman, not an officer. But fearing a gender mistake, he stood straight and saluted.

"I further demand the right guaranteed under PAC rules to speak to the ranking quotaed female," snapped the woman claiming to be a captain, speaking in a reedy but steady voice as she returned his salute. Her troop was standing firmly but quietly behind her while the federals, suddenly now all in a dither, began whispering and arguing in rank.

"You know federal officers don't go on patrol," the sergeant replied, glancing nervously over at the Chinese officer for support. But when none was forthcoming, he turned again to the "captain" and in a near whine asked, "Please. You must have papers on you, would you just show them to me? We'll make this all short and sweet."

"I will do nothing but take your names," the woman said, and throwing back her head and raising up on tiptoes, she glowered around him at his men and added in a loud and confident, although crackly, voice, "And I mean that I want the names of all the men in your troop. Every man-jack of you is in serious violation of PAC rules."

"That's Vivian for you, eighty plus and still a force. I'm proud of her." A smiling J6 spoke in a soft whisper, and as the others nodded, she added, "She's a jewel."

"Look, please," the federal sergeant stepped back with both hands up and a big forced smile on his face. "I'll tell you what, let's pretend that we didn't meet. We'll just go on over to the training center like we never saw you. Saves us all a lot of time."

"I don't know," Vivian replied, stepping back as if to study his suggestion. And then, after glancing around at her squad, she finally agreed, "OK, but only if you go back the way you came. You can't use Center Road."

"What? The training center is just across 23, right here, why go all the way back?"

"Your call, sergeant. I'm trying to be cooperative. You go back, or you give me names, and I mean right now!" With those words, she moved up almost head-to-chest with the federal leader, and as she glowered up at him, she noted his nervously bobbing Adam's apple and knew that she had won the game. But the sergeant still wasn't sure.

Not sure that is until the Chinese major walked over to them and said, "I suggest that you accept this gracious captain's offer, but with her permission, I won't be going back with you. I'll go to the center from here, and you can join me there in an hour or two." He nodded politely to the captain as he spoke and then stepped aside, smiling.

"What!" Little John hissed when he heard that. "Is he coming this way?"

"Yes, but he won't notice you guys," J6 whispered back, adding, "So, you four can go on over to the northwest side and relax on the grass right now." Then, glancing at Glenn, she couldn't resist adding, "Which is where you were supposed to be waiting."

"How can he possibly miss us?" Little John insisted, bewildered.

"Sometimes you see only what you're supposed to see. Everything is going according to plan, so go on," she winked and, smiling, shooed them off on their way.

Five minutes later the federals were bickering their way south back down the road that they'd just come north on while the other group was straggling north on that same road. And the Chinese officer, who had introduced himself as Major Han, was walking toward the training center, chatting with J6 and Glenn. He didn't even glance at the four men as he passed them, sitting in their previously assigned place on the grass.

But at least two of those men let out a big sigh of relief once the officer was gone, and then all four sat back for a while to take a short break and to enjoy the sunshine ending of what had turned out to be a beautiful day. And as they unwound, all marveled at the not quite equal beauty of God's good earth and the Alliance's good planning.

Ten minutes later, Howdy signaled that it was time to follow him and Dell-X back under the highway and on to a cottage by a nearby small lake. The plan was that Alex and Little John would spend the next two days relaxing a bit with plenty of good food and a lot to study while they waited for Glenn to finish his new adventure at the PAC training center. Their work, in fact, began that evening with a long conversation, after which Howdy and Dell-X left them to go on ahead into Whigville.

Once their leaders were gone, Alex and Little John browsed through some of the materials that had been brought to prep them for their coming adventure, but they decided to have another snack and to get some shut-eye before plunging into it. The plunge could wait for the next day. Right now, it was savor the moment time. They were close, and they knew it. Whigville and all that waited for them there was just one or two peaceful nights away. Meanwhile, all was good at their cozy little lakeside safe-house: the food, the drink— indeed, life itself!

CHAPTER SIXTEEN

How Glenn Stanton Encounters PAC-Truth

A groaning Glenn Stanton crawled out of his sagging bunk on Thursday morning with yet another reason to hate PAC. What kind of guest quarters were these? Steerage came to mind, but considering that the other guests here were a Chinese major and J6, a high level PAC something or other, he decided he'd probably just drawn the short straw that his low quota commanded. Grumbling at that thought, he shifted himself to the floor, and after working his way through some much-needed standing-sitting stretches, he got ready to start the day. He had a lot on his mind, but by the time he showered and dressed, his nagging stomach had overridden everything ... except breakfast.

"Welcome," Major Han greeted him from a small table by the window as Glenn walked into their large, very well-accommodated, shared sitting room. "Come, join me for breakfast. I'm starved after my morning run. A good run is the best way to start a day, and it felt great out there, running along in the fresh air, watching the sun come up over the hills—almost as good as being back in China."

"Thank you, sir. I know what you mean about running. It *is* a great day-starter, but I haven't run much lately," Glenn said, deciding not to mention that his last run was away from a downed media-copter. After shaking hands with the major, he walked over to the coffee pot and had just started filling his cup when their door opened and two men entered, carrying large trays of what had to be their break-

225

fast. Great timing, he thought, smiling as he carried his cup over to their table. But that smile turned to a frown when he saw the meal; this wasn't the kind of breakfast he had expected.

"*Harrumph!*" The major was also passing judgment on the food, but with worse than a frown; he was scowling. Glowering over at Glenn, he shook his head and darkly muttered, "First class, this isn't. It isn't even close, and I expect first class. I demand it!"

"I think we must have the honor of eating what the trainees and troops are eating," Glenn ventured, offering a feeble excuse as he studied the miserable collection of cold toast, lukewarm fake eggs, and a clump of what looked to be only a gesture toward hash brown potatoes—also room temperature. But then, after an oh-well shrug, he took a short sip of his coffee, and pausing, looked down into his cup and added, "Um, not good, but it tastes better than our food looks, and at least it's hot enough, don't you think?"

"Good by some standards," the major replied, and setting down his cup, he gave a thin smile and added, "If my orderly gave me something like this, she'd get a beating."

"Whoa, better watch comments like that," Glenn said, laughing nervously as he looked over at the major. He was surprised by his sexism, but eyeing the officer, he was sure that the comment wasn't meant to be taken lightly, and so he started to explain what his own gentle correction meant, "Nothing against you, sir, but this is PAC and …"

"And I'm not subject to your silly PAC rules." The major snapped back, finishing Glenn's sentence for him. He obviously didn't like being served a trainee's meal, and the younger man was certain that he wasn't going to let it go. Lunch should be very different, he thought, smiling and looking forward to that difference as he began eating—alone.

....

"I have bad news, very bad news," J6 whispered thirty minutes later as she settled heavily into the chair beside Glenn on the side porch. He had chosen the most comfortable deck chair he could find just around the corner from the federal troops, now gathering information on the parking lot parade ground. And still tired after last night's lousy sleep, he had almost nodded off in the warm summer sun, but the tone of J6's husky whisper, snapped him fully awake, and he looked anxiously over at her.

"Someone spot me?" he asked, sitting up and quickly glancing around.

"No, but that might happen. Some of the trainees were at the campground during your little adventure there, and they're on their way back here. But unfortunately, that's not my bad news." And then, swallowing hard and obviously distressed, she held up a hand to stop him when he started to speak again. "No, Glenn, let me talk. I got the word earlier this morning that Professor Shampton had been arrested, but now ... and oh, this is so hard! Just ten minutes ago this came." And as she held out a scrap of paper, she finally surrendered to grief, shaking her head sadly and turning away with a muffled sob.

Taking the note, he read it in a low whisper, "Secure all boats; Dunkirk has fallen."

"Boats? Dunkirk?" He looked up from the message, confused and wanting to know more. But she was in such obvious distress that he didn't feel right about pushing her, and so he settled for reaching out and gently patting her arm as he sat back to wait.

"Glenn, the professor was Dunkirk," she said, blinking back tears as she searched his eyes. Then, swallowing, she turned away and whispered, "But now—he's dead!"

"Dead? Oh, I'm so sorry," he said, and as he leaned over to comfort her, he felt overwhelmed himself, blinking back his own tears. He was stunned. Their Worthy, Professor Alexander Shampton, that vital driving force, was dead? "But how? Why?"

"He was my very dear friend. We knew he was in danger. We even discussed pulling him out, but sent in an agent instead. And now ... now, it's too late." And with those words, she slumped back in her chair and, giving into her feelings, softly sobbed.

Glenn, quietly waiting until she was ready to talk again, thought back to his own memories of this man he had known so briefly, the man he'd met just days before, and the man he had come to admire so much. And finally, when she looked ready, he asked, "If he's Dunkirk, who are the boats? People like Little John, Alex, and me?"

"Close." She turned a tight, gentle smile toward him, "But no, the boats are people like, well, your angels. You guys are our passengers. The message means that we need to break off contact with Brighton until we can get another control in place, and ..."

"What's going on here?" A sharp, demanding voice interrupted them before she could finish, and they both looked up in surprise, but only Glenn, cowed by his Arbor U conditioning, stood up. He recognized the man challenging them as yesterday's hotshot federal sergeant, the loser in the confrontation with Vivian Clancy at the underpass.

"Mind your manners!" J6 snapped back, not caring who he was and certainly not cowed. Already angry with PAC and all it represented, she needed very little to fuel her fury. This clod's interruption would have been stupid on its face at any time, but right now she was in no mood to suffer PAC fools lightly, and so, while remaining seated and without even bothering to look at him, she thrust her ID card up into his ugly face. This left Glenn, who stood facing the man, to struggle to hold back a laugh as he watched the federal buffoon's repeat of yesterday's groveling retreat in the face of PAC power. But there was no smile on J6's face. Her eyes sparking with rage, she ignored the man's pathetic apology and dismissed the fawning creature with a mere flick-away gesture.

"May I see that?" Glenn whispered, nodding at her ID card as the sergeant slunk away. He immediately regretted his impulsive question, thinking it might annoy her, but she surprised him, and after studying him closely as he sat back down, she shrugged and held out her card—being careful to cover the name with her thumb. Still embarrassed, he only glanced at it, but spotting her rank, he let out a soft, low whistle that almost, but not quite, got a smile out of her. Hoping that near-smile meant that she was on her way back to form, he then risked a silently mouthed, "impressive," meaning both her control *and* her rank. "A high-ranking PAC-honcho, I had guessed, but not how high."

"The question may soon be, how *high* will they hang you?" she replied, moving them grimly back to the business at hand; although now recovered, she still wasn't in the mood for banter. "You're out of here early tomorrow, and so all of your observations will have to happen today. But it's still a risk, so keep a low profile once you get inside."

"How about you? If the professor was outed, maybe you angels are next."

"Maybe, but I doubt it. I heard about the thing with his wife, silly twit that she is. My guess is that the sisterhood went after him without knowing who he really was. It was probably a twisted revenge thing, one we should have anticipated and headed off."

"Not your fault, everything's crazy there," Glenn insisted. "But, you know, I barely knew him and still came to admire him as very impressive man—and mind."

"And soul, Glenn. He was a very impressive soul. We were more than friends; he was my mentor and confidant. Without him, I don't think I'd have survived all the PAC nonsense when I was first recruited for this assignment. I'd have done something stupid and ended up dead or jailed after a round of foolish, self-serving, rookie posturing. He helped me to stay focused on our plan. He helped me keep my head together."

"Posturing? What do you mean by that?" Glenn asked. "Surely almost any protest against PAC would be the real thing and not just posturing."

"Glenn, as lost as America is right now, our country needs disciplined loyalists to step up and help us win our way back. Self-righteous martyrs won't get that job done. God knows we've had enough real martyrs already without more of us diving into the fire on purpose for no good reason. It gains nothing, and it hurts the cause. Posturing to vent anger or frustration or, even worse, to satisfy immature ego needs provides us with only a useless feel-good moment. It's a waste," she said, now looking directly at him, shaking her head. "What we do, we need to do with purpose and as part of a plan. Anything less is foolish ego massaging at best, and at worst, it undermines our effort."

"But how ..." He started, but another interruption stopped him. This time it was the ancient parade ground speakers, announcing formation time, and they both stood in response and walked around to watch as forty or so federals slouched into position. It was a painful sight even for Glenn who had never seen a real military formation. The troopers just seemed to shuffle aimlessly about until they finally stood in a slap-dab line, all facing forward with their fists crossed over their chests, ready to recite the PAC pledge:

"All we here pledge to put aside the tainted
authority of the past and to follow only PAC.
Only PAC preserves what is just and true.
Only PAC serves us all as we serve PAC.
All honor be to PAC and to our exalted
leader, Chairwomon Marcion."

"Ah, the glorious Third Pledge to PAC, my least favorite," Glenn side-whispered to J6, smiling as he added, "Of course they're all my least favorite, if that's possible."

She laughed at that, gently slapping his shoulder. "I not only think it's possible, I think it's a majority opinion. Look at those guys out there, do you really think any of them would stand and die for PAC?"

Then, as they turned to walk away, she glanced at her watch, groaned, and said, "As much as I'd rather sit and talk longer with you, I have to get to my duties. You can continue to relax for a while, but you're here for a reason. You'll need to join me before long; so give it about an hour and then come on inside." With those words, she took his hand in hers, firmly squeezing it as she turned to go. She was back on her game, ready for duty, and she even left him smiling with her last words as she walked away, "You'll learn a lot before this day is over, an awful lot—emphasis on the word, awful."

He was still laughing to himself about her comment as he settled back into his chair and began looking around. It was a beautiful day, and the grounds of this old golf course, although long neglected, still seemed lovely and relaxing to him.

But inevitably, his mind turned to their martyred friend. If they had known that he was in danger, perhaps they could have helped. He couldn't think of how, but maybe they should have pushed him to just give up on his wife as John had suggested. And how about that Jim Richards guy, the professor's friend? Could he have been the agent sent to warn Shampton that J6 had mentioned? If so, his effort became an example of an agent getting too caught up in his own problems to complete his mission.

It was incredible to think that the professor might have died not because of his noble efforts to save his country from PAC, but because his silly wife had surrendered to the times and found a new playmate. Was it a revenge killing because her lover got roughed-up? No way to know, but what a waste! Sure, the alliance would fill the gap left by his murder, but the man himself, that unique and gifted man couldn't be replaced.

"You seem deep in thought, my young friend," a voice interrupted him.

"What?" A startled Glenn, looking up in surprise at the smiling face looming over him, saw that it was the major, and he rushed to get to his feet. "Yes, sir!"

"No, no, stay seated," the major said. "You look comfortable. May I join you?"

"Of course," Glenn replied, and as he settled uneasily back down, he wondered what this guy was up to and how he should manage himself. This was a Chinese officer, after all, and so trying to be polite, he smiled and said, "I was just looking over these old golf club grounds. They're beautiful even now, but they must have been incredible once."

"You looked so relaxed here that I wanted to join you for a bit before going back inside," the major said as he settled into the chair J6 had occupied. "And yes, this place is beautiful. I can see its potential even now, and it probably was very special once. Too bad they let it go." He glanced over at Glenn, "I love golf. Do you play?"

"No, golf has pretty well died out here except for courses like this one that are reserved for PAC leaders and their guests. I've never played."

"Too bad. It's a great game, very popular in China. You may know that most of the top players these days are Chinese," the major said, smiling proudly as he settled back into his chair. And then they both sat silently for a while, for quite a while, long enough that Glenn wondered if he should be trying harder to offer polite conversation.

The officer had rejected their pathetic morning meal, leaving Glenn to eat alone, and so there had been no talk then. And now it seemed to be up to Glenn, but unable to think of anything to say, he just sat there, nervously waiting ... until, finally, it was the major who spoke again.

"Perhaps, Glenn, all of this can be seen as a symbol of what has happened to your country," the officer ventured, speaking slowly and deliberately, while still gazing out over the grounds before them. And although Glenn didn't look directly at him, he now guessed that the officer had sat down next to him for a purpose, and that purpose was about to come out. As he turned to reply, he wondered why a Chinese colonel back in Arbortown and now this major, who knew and had asked after that colonel, were both helping him by providing papers, protection, and now, it seemed, conversation.

"If you mean, sir, that a lot of good has been temporarily lost, you're certainly right," Glenn said. He recalled J6's warning to stay with the plan, but he wasn't getting into the old *apologize for America* game either. "But we have high hopes for the future."

"Yes, of course you do," the major replied, and pausing, he seemed to study the younger man for a moment as if he was trying to take his measure before deciding how far to push him. And then, his decision apparently made, he turned back to their view, sighing comfortably as he continued, "You have a very lot to regain to get back to that future, my young friend. You Americans once had everything. More people prospered here than anywhere at any time in history; more people were able to follow their own dreams here than anywhere, ever, and you had more power than any other people in the history of the human race. In fact, you had the world at your feet, but you let it all come to this, almost overnight, and all without ... well, without even putting-up much of a real fight to save yourselves. I don't understand that. Why would a people let such power go, such glory, and such access to all that's good, just like that,"—he snapped his fingers—"and without a fight to the death. Why?"

"Well, sir, I think that we, like Rome, let our politicians begin to buy us and to play us off against each other," Glenn replied, and then, after casting a cautious glance toward his companion, he decided to hazard a gentle verbal elbow. "And perhaps it would help you understand if you compared us to your own history to Chinese history. Like your own people did long ago, we turned inward late in the last century and became preoccupied with our own petty group against group divisions—think of the Warlords who came to control much of China in the early twentieth century. Well, in our case, we justified our own idiocy by weaving serving-self fantasies about how we deserved it all, whatever it all was—now. NOW, emerged as a near-holy word, and we became so focused on serving ourselves that we ducked our obligations to our own children and to the cause of freedom. And finally, we let our politicians force-feed us with lies about the nature of those in the world all around us, some savage barbarians included. Thus, we abandoned both our friends and our responsibilities to the world. In short, we failed to conscientiously govern ourselves, ourselves."

A bit nervous about how his words would be taken, Glenn looked away from the major and out across the golf course as he spoke. He was talking to a Chinese officer, and remembering J6's warning about posturing protests, he didn't want to offend him. So, swallowing hard, he tried to choose his words carefully as he went on, "But major, most importantly, all of this is because we temporarily lost our faith in ourselves both as individuals and as a people, and sad to say, we lost our faith in God and the challenge given to us to become one people, united in the cause of freedom at home and abroad.

Thus hobbled and divided, we couldn't muster the gumption to save ourselves."

"Ah, such noble words, but they're just words, as it turns out, what we would call, *fang go pi*—that's, dog fart, in English." He laughed then and raised a hand to cut off Glenn's protest, "Now don't get me wrong. You're the first American to be so honest with me, and I appreciate that. I can see that you're sincere, and I will show you the courtesy of also being sincere. I even agree with you that it's an old, old story, one that's been told and retold around the world throughout history. Self-serving politicians always offer up the bread and circuses or the much-loved 'free lunch,' as you call it here. But aside from what I'll call your noble, *stinky air*, explanation, why did you let them do it? Why didn't you raise up a champion to help you self-correct, a hero to lead you?" But then, he stopped, as if thinking again about what he, himself, had just said.

"No, champion or not, it wouldn't have worked," he continued, but now with a pitying smile on his face. "You were doomed to fail even when you were at your peak because your biggest problem wasn't a lack of faith, as you say my young friend. It was a lack of the will to bend your knee to the obligations of power. You had the power. You had it all, and the whole world waited for leadership, but after the Cold War, you fell into a nattering mass of self-seeking division and self-doubt, and your decline was swift."

"I don't agree with you, major," Glenn said, and smiling nervously, he turned to look directly at the other man as he continued. "And sir, you may not be aware of it, but you're coming across as sort of an accidental theologian with your comments."

"What do you mean by that? I'm not religious."

"Well, Christians believe that Christ was tempted in the wilderness with three things: food or material goods, safety or security, and power or prestige, the world at our feet, as you say. He refused all three and pointed to God alone as the one and only true empowerment source. So you see, from our point of view, you're right and wrong at the same time. You're right, and I'll admit that we Americans did cave to two of those three temptations. We, particularly the privileged generations after World War II, were mostly complete suckers for the free lunches you mentioned, and we were so tuned into security that we wrapped our souls in the tattered blanket promises of government as nanny. But I doubt that more than a handful of us ever cared about all that power you mentioned.

"Yet, on the other hand," Glenn paused, wary of the major's stinky air comment. "From your point of view, I can see what you mean about bending our knee to what you see as the obligations that come with power. But, sir, at least until we began our collapse into ourselves in the sixties, we didn't bend our knee because we didn't want power in your sense. We, most of us, wanted others at our side, not our feet! We were the first powerful people in history to actually want to share the dream of a free world where all people, everywhere, would be left alone to live their own lives and to let others do the same. I know that sounds stupid and naive now, but—"

"Interesting myth," the major cut in. "I don't know about all that superstitious stuff, but I do know what needs to be in place for one country to stand above all others. We Chinese know that real leadership requires that the soft power of the velvet glove of harmony and benevolence as taught by Confucius must be worn over the iron fist of the legalism of Han Fei. Both men lived long before your Jesus, and we honor them today by building on their teachings to create a stable and enduring society. And anyway, you Americans celebrated perpetual adolescence above that God you talk about, and you now face the consequences of your foolishness—a grown-up reality rub and a very dim future."

"Sir, I agree with you about us being stuck in our silly adolescent preoccupations," Glenn cut in, thinking of his experience, moving from holy man to court jester. "A huge chunk of us did abandon adulthood and begin to form our social and political views based on what air-headed entertainers had to say. *Comedians* became our opinion leaders!"

"Yes, but that's not the whole story. You failed, not only because of that or any noble dream of yours, but because you were wrong about power, the power real leaders must exercise to control and serve their people, and the power a nation must exercise to control or destroy its enemies. I don't see how you can deny that. The proof is all around us." Pausing at that point, he glanced down at his watch and frowned. Then, he stood, smiled, and said, "I'm sorry. I'd like to continue this, but I must get to my duties."

Glenn, smiling at the combination of that chair and watches, almost let it go at that, but he couldn't. And so as casually as he could, he stood up beside the major to offer a final question, "What about your partners, the Russians and the Indians?"

"A good question from a courageous young student," the major said, laughing at both the tone and the question. "It's a question I could take offense to, but I'll answer it. Very simply, in the end, the Middle Kingdom will stand alone at the top, and we will stay there because we have the will do what needs to be done to do so, and we will do it."

"And the Russians, Indians, or how about the Kurds, Jews, and other minorities?"

"Who cares about minorities?" The major shook his head, now frowning at Glenn. "Your foolish American sentimentality, that's another big thing that brought you down.

We will let any country do anything it wishes to do to its own people or its neighbors as long as it doesn't threaten us. On the other hand, the world knows that if our interests are harmed, we will crush our enemies. We will grind them down and then let them spend generations picking-up the pieces by themselves. That will be their price to pay each and every time. If we are attacked by or even from a country, we will destroy that country. We will destroy any city or village that houses those who attack us. We will kill their families. We will hunt down their leaders and kill them. We will grind their faces in our victory and force them to acknowledge it. And the whole world will see all of that take place, and the whole world will learn from those lessons.

"And Glenn, understand this, we will make them all believers in our power, and they will come to know that it will be we, the victors, who will receive and not provide tribute. We will not provide tribute in any form, and that includes your so-called foreign aid. What a joke! It did more harm than good in most places—but it made your leaders feel good about themselves, which was really all they cared about. When we give money or assistance, Glenn, it is in exchange for a service from the recipients, and they'd better appreciate that fact and deliver as promised. So we both gain.

"As for minorities, there is never a shortage of such historical debris, but they'll have to find peace within their own areas. That's not our concern unless for some reason we have them under our protection. And if we choose to intervene, it will not be with false redlines. We will overwhelm and be victorious, not humble-bumble from behind.

"As for the Russians and Indians, their only place in the future will be to rule areas as our surrogates, nothing more. You Americans failed because you failed the will-to-power test. We will never fail that test, we welcome it."

Glenn, shaken after the major left, sat back wondering how even the alliance could succeed against such a dedication to power and to such a will to use and retain it. Reflecting back to his earlier thoughts about the why of all the Chinese had done to help him along so far, he now felt he knew the answer: everything had been done to enhance and maintain their own power. Why had we failed to do the same? Was it really because power wasn't our main purpose? Scowling, he thought, if that's true, were we wrong? It certainly seems now that history may be showing that, in the end, the will to use and to bend your knee to the responsibilities of power is the winning way.

That thought was still weighing on his mind when he went inside to join J6. And as she pointedly looked down at her watch when he walked up to her, he offered back only a weak grin at her near-scowl. He felt a bit guilty, but still, he was almost on time.

Her duties included watching over the credentialing and the manual maintenance activities of the trainees. The manuals themselves were twentieth century throwbacks: huge three ring binders that contained up-to-date PAC training materials and regulations. As there were frequent changes, it was the job of the trainees to pull out the old pages and to put in the new, and although he was still mulling over the major's words, Glenn had to laugh at the pompous style of the PAC compliance officer. So very full of herself and thirsting for adulation, she stalked slowly back and forth on top of the three long end-to-end training tables, shouting instructions to the gathered eager-to-please trainees.

"Rip out those old pages! Wad them up! Throw them on the floor! I said, throw them on the floor, not lay them on the floor! They are to be treated as soiled tissues of lies, as used toilet paper," she shouted. "These old pages are disgusting shades of wrong thought. They are not PAC truth, rip them out and tear them up! Throw them on the floor. Throw them!" She repeated the words again and again as she stomped from table end to table end, pausing occasionally to kick piles of discards onto the floor in disgust.

The wonderful new pages, on the other hand, offering the latest version of PAC-truth about events in Ustatesia (as, of course, they called America) and its ever-changing relationships with the rest of the world, and all pages about the Friendly Forces of China, India, and Russia were handled with extreme care and profound respect. White cotton gloves were used to insert the new pages, and for that holy job, the crude table-dancer turned into a now caring counsel-or-leader who moved quietly and reverently across the floor from person to person, white-glove-helping and supporting each trainee with soft whispered instructions in sincere and solemn tones.

The table-dancing trainer wasn't the only PACy watching over this glorious event. Detrisha Eckert, the senior editor of PAC's national newsletter and the presiding ombudstera for this area joined her, and there were four other trainers, plus the angel and Major Han, prowling among the tables as the trainees performed their holy duties.

Glenn, watching that insane show, felt himself becoming increasingly interested. At first, he had trailed listlessly along behind the others, the conversation with the major lingering on his mind. It took some time before, he could shrug off all of that and begin to take in the crazy, but very PAC-normal, drama that was unfolding around him. Once involved, though, he quickly noted one thing in particular: many trainees were upset with the changes they were mak-ing. Perhaps they just wanted to hold on to old familiar ways or old loyalties; he didn't know, but he smiled as he watched them because these young people could become potential alliance recruits.

As he got more into the activity, he could see that there was some good stuff in these manuals, using the term "good" to mean either "very interesting," or "crazy." For example, now that Vietnam had joined the Chinese co-prosperity community, it was being relisted as a long-time ally and friend of PAC. As a result, the Montagnards, whose ancestors had fled to America from Vietnam after a long ago war there, had been downgraded from being a quotaed minority on the old pages to being listed on the new pages as long time PAC enemies, and they were given the worse of all labels, that of a white male-identifying minority group. This change took away quota rights they'd had up until a few weeks ago; rights that were now lost in the black hole of PAC truth, a hole that bulged with the debris of generations of PAC-friendly political correctness.

This didn't surprise Glenn because he'd heard from Professor Benjamin that a group of them had joined with the army holdouts and local alliance supporters who were now in control of Fort Bragg in North Carolina. They were doing this despite very strong federal demands that it be turned over to the commander of the Friendly Forces. That friendlies' commander, a Russian officer, had been rudely bundled up and sent back to DC in a sealed cargo container the same day he arrived at the base to take command.

"Glenn," J6 called over to him after only half an hour. "I think you'll find the credentialing process in the next room to be interesting; why don't you observe that?"

"Of course," he replied, and as they walked away, she whispered that the trainees who had been at the campgrounds were due, and that he should stay in the other training room and plan to take his lunch in his own quarters. With that stimulating thought now spiking his adrenalin, he changed rooms, wondering how long he had before the ax fell.

Inside the credentialing room, he saw two tables set up along one wall with three PAC officials, now including the ombudstera, seated behind them busily poring over files. Several smaller tables were arranged about the room, but without chairs, which meant that the dozen or so candidates filling out forms had to kneel beside the tables to do their work. Glenn, pausing at the door to look around, decided that he deserved a chair, and after dragging one in from the other room, he carefully positioned it beside the ombudstera. She and the other two officials there frowned as he joined them, but they didn't correct him for moving the chair, nor did they offer a welcome.

He, on the other hand, leaned forward to make eye contact, nodding to each of them in turn as he sat down.

After all he'd seen on his journey so far, he wasn't surprised to find that the whole credentialing process in this room was yet another exercise in form without substance. To make matters worse, most of the candidates, all from high quota groups or with very tight PAC connections, were flat out pathetic. While it certainly wasn't their fault, given the state of education, or really non-education in the country now, the fact was that so far only two of them had successfully completed the forms by themselves—and all of them were going to be *teachers*! It was left to Glenn and the other helpers to become scribes, filling out simple forms that were over the heads of most of these soon to be "educators."

The process was made even more frustrating because of the stark truth that the only important part of the whole thing was the PAC endorsement. Each candidate had presented the committee with a seven-page PAC document that essentially spelled out what the credentialing officials were supposed to do, and that's exactly what was done. Thus, for example, even though candidate A couldn't read or write beyond a sixth grade level, she was credentialed at a master's level teacher—because of her master's degree in PAC studies. Candidate B could actually read and write at an eighth grade level and also had a PAC studies masters, but her lower PAC rating, for whatever reason—most likely because she had fewer PAC connections—meant that she was credentialed only at a bachelor teacher level. Candidate C, on the other hand, could read and write at a college level, but she was from a country town outside the secure PAC zone and had been homeschooled, and so she was made a teaching assistant. Her PAC studies master's degree didn't help. However, her ability did not go unrecognized, and she was given one other duty. She was to act as interim mentor-scribe for the other two until they settled into their new jobs at the same school. It was an unpaid honor that she gratefully accepted.

"Thank you for this opportunity to serve PAC and my fellow teachers," she said when the job assignments were presented. "I hope to prove myself worthy."

"Didn't you fill out the forms for the other two?" Glenn asked her off to the side.

"Yes, but only to help out," she replied. "They were busy with more important things and didn't have time for mere paperwork. They'll both be excellent teachers. My goodness, we all know that PAC chooses only the best."

"So it's teaching assistant for you," he mused. "Is that enough?"

"PAC's will is my will." She added the last as she walked away, and she seemed to be deliriously happy—and with good reason these days. She, at least, had a job.

The process went on and on until it became a blur to Glenn. All that mattered was the decision made weeks ago by some PAC functionary in Arbortown who neither knew nor cared about anything but PAC connections and quotas. It was all a sad charade.

Later, over lunch in his room, he discussed his feelings about it with Angel-6, and she agreed with him about the lockstep foolishness of it all, but told him that he should be thankful because he at least got to see some males—several of whom were Asians.

"The Asians are here because the major was going to be here to be certain that they would be, particularly after the Arbor U fiasco. But most of the time, Asian males are treated as whites and don't get the quota breaks. And, oh yes, the males here today came as a group, as small as it is, because we process males only in groups large enough to garner a crew of PAC-Tenders to keep order. So, you lucked out. They found eight guys eager to serve PAC, although only three of them are back-of-the-bus whites guys."

"Maintain order? Are males that unruly?" Glenn asked with a grim smile.

"Well, the history of crime in this country suggests that, yes, guys really are that unruly, but of course, crime stats have nothing to do with it here. That, at least, would be a bit logical, but PAC is only ideological, never logical. Crime has less to do with the low male status than PAC's devotion to multicultural humbug. Remember the idiot Brighton story and the crazy escorted male rule?" she laughed. "Well, that very same ombudstera visiting us today is that Brighton pseudo-leader, and she runs a tight ship. It was tough getting you in, and frankly, my rank plus all your friendly and PAC endorsements wouldn't have been enough if you hadn't arrived with the major. You'd have been banned without him. That woman hates men."

"Well, she's an idiot, that's for sure. But let me ask you this, why does the Whig Partisan Alliance work so closely with the Chinese?" Glenn frowned as he asked the question, unsure of both his reason for asking it and why it bothered him right now.

"One hand washes the other," she replied. "We cooperate, but it's because we have to cooperate; we certainly aren't one with them. They're barbarian warlords, and they'll take the march of civilization back two hundred years, at least. However, right now, they're trying to check the Russian influence on the federals, and … well, you know what we're trying to do. They also know what we're trying to do, and although they support us for now, they'll turn on us as soon as they think we're getting too big."

"I guess I can understand that. I don't like it, but I think I can understand it."

"Let me throw one more item on the table for your don't-like-it file," she said. "I had a long talk with the ombudstera, and she was very frank about their educational effort here—pure propaganda. I asked her why we don't make this a real educational experience for these young people. After all, they're going off to be educators, and they come to us with no more qualifications than most of our politicians. The old gal got a big laugh out of my politician example, and she was pretty open, saying that PAC's one and only goal was to ingrain a single, grand rule of scholarly process in what she called, 'their servant minds.' That is, first and foremost, they must learn to seek out PAC's position on every issue; then, second, they must learn to collect only data that supports PAC beliefs; and, third, they must insist that any and all choices made by them once they start teaching will add up to a total confirmation of PAC-Truth as taught here; and finally, they are to attack and destroy anyone who disagrees with that process or that truth.

"You know, Glen, that sounded funny coming from a frail, weak brained old woman who couldn't destroy a wet paper bag on her own. But it's the weak ones, like this gal, who cling to PAC for strength and support. They and their simple kind have been the standing army of useful idiot enablers for evil causes for eons."

"Incredible, but not surprising and as you say, hardly new," Glenn said. "It wasn't even new when Hitler outlined the same approach a hundred years ago. And much more recently, even before our universities openly became PAC-controlled, they'd moved to that 'one-eyed Cyclops' position in most areas of inquiry, even launching a new form of the old—one belief and only one belief—Inquisition in our age of supposed nonbelief. But of course, their inquisition was directed against thoughts unacceptable to PACies, not against supposed religious heretics, and from the sixties on, those early-identifiers brushed aside such Old Enlightenment inspired ideas as tolerance for free thought and free inquiry and replaced them with their twentieth century PAC-friendly version of the Old Scholastic model from the Middle Ages. And sadly, those early herd-conforming radicals became low-hanging fruit for PAC to pick and use, and it was almost impossible for them to resist because PAC is a jealous god, and unlike the real God, PAC does not espouse free will. Their staunch defenders must all become like well-programed, remotely controlled zombies, robots, or mad dogs. Pick your own term, but as you know, even weak bodied and slow-minded people like our ombudstera will try to tear you apart if you stray from PAC truth."

J6, laughing at his enthusiasm, raised a hand to cut him off, "Hold it, you're preaching to the choir, my young passenger. I'm with you, chapter and verse, but we do have a world out there that needs just that message, so keep working on it until you've got your speaking-truth-to-freedom lovers style down pat."

Standing then to get back to her duties, she waved aside his effort to keep her in conversation and left, carrying back his claim to be ill. That allowed him to skip the afternoon and evening training activities and thus avoid bumping into trainees who might remember him from the fairgrounds. The only down side, from his point of view was that his absence no doubt made that old buzzard ombudstera happy. He regretted that.

The new plan left him alone in his room all afternoon and evening, which could have been boring, but wasn't. He used the time to think about the major's comments at first, but then angry thoughts about the real mad-dog defenders of PAC, who had killed a great man, took over, and he reflected again on that Worthy's charge to them to help make the Whig Partisan Alliance the prolepsis for the new beginning both here and around the whole world that everyone deserved. The best way to honor him was to continue his work, and with that in mind, he settled back to write in his journal.

When they reconnected that evening, he and the major exchanged only chitchat pleasantries back and forth between rooms, but they didn't reopen their earlier talk, all of which was fine with Glenn. He didn't really want to listen to more major-talk.

On the way to bed that night, Glenn decided to leave early the next day, right after breakfast. Or on the other hand, recalling this morning's breakfast, maybe he should skip it and leave before. But no, that didn't make sense, both the lunch that he'd taken in his room with the angel and his supper alone had been very good, a fact that he knew was thanks to the major, and so he might as well go for a good meal one more time.

With that happy thought in mind, he settled back into his still lumpy bed, and as he closed his eyes, he renewed his vow to work even harder to build the "We-team" that the now dead Brighton Worthy had urged on them, telling them that it would take team-work to get our country and the world back on the road toward, *E pluribus unum.*

CHAPTER SEVENTEEN

How Three Comrades Slip through the Whigville Marches

After a second night of sagging bed tossing and turning wakefulness, Glenn rose early Friday morning to a gnawing sense of urgency, and the worry that had stalked his sleep now left him convinced to get out early to avoid unfriendly eyes. That decided, he rose and quietly began gathering his things. As he did so, he heard movement from next door and shook his head, smiling. As early as he was, he had not beaten the major, over there in his room noisily getting ready to head out for his morning run. With no enemies to worry him, he simply slammed his way out the door without a care in the world even as Glenn was tiptoeing about, ever so carefully, preparing for his own much quieter exit.

But more than worry about noise troubled him. He was caught up in a go-no-go argument with himself that continued even after he had finished packing. Now sagging back onto his bed, he felt fed up with his own dilly-dallying. "Come on," he snarled at himself, "Focus! Focus on the safe thing to do. Forget all of this back and forth. I could be outed here. So I need to get out the door and to get as far away as I can before first light. It'd be stupid to take a chance on getting caught here."

But was that really the best plan? He leaned forward on the bed, elbows on his knees and chin on his hands, considering it all again … one-more-time. After all, a good breakfast might be in order, and the major expected him to be here and might take it as a personal affront if he left early without saying anything, and that's not a good thing. "OK," he muttered to himself, "I'll eat first. If I leave early, it might be a while before I reconnect with the alliance, and that could mess up everything. So I'll just relax over a good meal, and wait for my next angel-contact. I need to trust the alliance."

Grinning then at his own foolishness, he chuckled, feeling good about having made yet another "final" decision. But of course, it wasn't over. As he lay back on the bed for the next half-hour, waiting for mealtime, he reflected on his trip so far, especially the loss of the Brighton Worthy, and his doubts (fears?) came seeping back in.

He was ready to go and could leave right away, so why not just do it, just get up and go? Of course, as he had thought countless, boring times before, that would take him off plan and complicate things for the alliance; but it would be easier for them to find him out there running free than to have to figure out how to get him out of a tiger cage if he was nailed here. Out there, he'd find a way to stay visible to the good guys and avoid the bad. Who knows, he might even be able to find Alex and Little John. J6 had said that they'd be on a lake close by. Of course, there were many lakes, and he couldn't remember its name, and even if he could, finding it on his own was unlikely. And how about Whigville? Taking off now might edge it farther away. He didn't want that, but ...

"Come on, what's wrong with me? I'm sick of all this wimp-waffling," he angrily whispered to himself, and this time he stood up and reached for his gear. "This is it. I hope I don't mess things up too badly, but no more back and forth. I'm out of here!"

But at that moment, before he could heft his already packed gear or go back around his boring old-decision-waffle track again, a loud pounding, followed by the violent rattling of his doorknob stopped him in his tracks. He caught his breath ... and held it. Someone out there wanted in who didn't feel a need to ask, and to his dismay, he recognized the voice when it came. It was that blundering fed sergeant, for a third time!

"You, in there! Open in the name of PAC and the PAC ombudstera. Open now!"

Quickly shouldering his gear, a now panicked Glenn moved through the door that connected his room with the major's much larger and more comfortable quarters; they had left it unlocked so they could chat back and forth. Once inside, he quietly slid the bolt home and turned to rush toward the window—he had to get out of here. But wait! There were men talking and moving about out there. Stymied, he sagged back against the major's side of their door, muttering, "Great, plan B's out, and there *is* no plan C".

"We warned you!" And that shout was followed by a loud crash as they kicked his door open. Stunned, he pressed his ear against the major's door, listening to them as they muttered and fumbled about on the other side. Then the sergeant shouted, "Get your head back in here! Did those fools out there see him? I said, did anyone out there see him? What do you mean you don't know? (The voices got very loud now.) Did you have to unlock the window to look out? You don't remember! Come on, you gotta be kidding me. He may be in, he may be out, but you don't know!" Glenn smiled.

After that, there was no talking, only quiet movement, and then the doorknob at Glenn's elbow turned, ever so slowly, and shook, just a bit. This was a Chinese major's room, and they were being cautious. Glenn, sucking in his own breath, listened as their frustrated whispers receded into a long silence—too long. They were listening too!

Afraid he would make some small noise and betray himself, Glenn held his breath until he could hold it no longer, fought back a cough, and even worried that they might hear his racing heart. "Come 'n get me," he wanted to yell, but he didn't. He just stood there, waiting, waiting until at long last he heard the sound of footsteps leaving his room.

Of course, he knew that sooner or later they'd try to check the major's room, and driven by that thought and his own panic, he began looking around, searching in the now dim light for something, anything, that he could use as a weapon. His eyes fixed on first one thing and then another until, finally, just over there, what is that?

A walking stick? Yes, the major had a very solid looking walking stick, and a now smiling Glenn snatched it up, and turning it over, he hefted it, looking it up and down. It was perfect! He admired the beauty of its carving, but mostly, he loved the fact that it was a very solid piece of heavy hardwood, a real head-knocker. He almost laughed out loud as he slapped it several times against his palm, thinking, yes, he'd finally go down, but he'd take some bloody heads with him.

But his brief moment of warrior anticipation was interrupted only seconds later by an oh-so-gentle knock at the major's main door, followed by a very respectful quiet delay, and then, finally, by a painfully halting, kiss-up voice. "Sir, we don't mean to disturb you [pause]. But there's a fugitive at large [pause]. Would you mind, sir [pause], mind just letting us come in to check [pause] your room … just in case he's in hiding there? Not that we think you would hide him [pause], but he may have slipped in while you were asleep, or you know [long pause], while you were out or something, and …"

"What is going on here?" the major's loud voice interrupted the sergeant's lilting plea. "Can't I even go out for my morning run without losing my privacy?"

"No sir! I mean, yes, sir!"

Glenn relaxed, smiling as he listened to that poor federal sap apologizing and begging for forgiveness for bothering so worthy a gentleman. But although loving this timely turn of events, he still measured his breath, finally letting it out in silent relief only when he heard the major brusquely order the whimpering feds to leave his living space, followed immediately by their toadying assent and the welcome sound of retreating feet.

But as relieved as he was, he knew another shoe still had to drop, and swallowing hard, he prepared himself to deal with that shoe. And its droptime came very quickly with the sound of a key turning to unlock the major's main door. Glenn tensed, freezing at the sound and nervously licking his lips as the question about what he would do was settled by his inaction. He just stood there, doing nothing, as the major entered the room.

"Sorry sir, there seems to be a misunderstanding about me." Glenn spoke up at once, and blinking his eyes when the light was flicked on, he forced a tight nervous smile as he very gently and self-consciously laid the major's walking stick off to one side.

The officer, glancing casually around the room as he entered, brushed off Glenn's comment by saying, "Oh, I don't think there's a misunderstanding. I think that seedy clod who just left knows all he needs to know about you. He knows that you're a fugitive from some kind of big dust-up nearby, and he knows that you and your friends are all wanted for questioning about a number of things, including the downing of a big *media-copter* a few days ago." He grinned as he stressed that key term, *media-copter*.

"But, sir ..."

"No, no, don't try to explain. I'd like to know more about all of that, but time may be a problem for us. You'll need to get on the road and ..." He stopped then, his eyes on his walking stick. And looking at Glenn, he smiled and added, "As for that stick, you keep it. It was a gift, and it's a great stick, but you're going to need it more than I will."

Glenn was surprised by the gift, and he quickly thanked the major, but as he bent to retrieve what was now his stick, he wondering what was going on. What were the Chinese up to, helping him? He was still sorting it all out, when the officer shifted gears.

Glancing yet again at his watch, the major, held up a hand and, smiling at Glenn, said, "On second thought, you have a long journey ahead of you, and you'll need a solid meal under your belt. So, we'll eat first and enjoy a good chat. You can tell me your copter killer story and then be on your way."

With that, and without waiting for Glenn's reply, the major turned and walked to the outer door where he leaned out, ordered breakfast for two and complained about the noise outside his window. Within minutes the noisy people were gone, and a very short time later, breakfast arrived. Glenn smiled as he looked it over, very much appreciating the delicious fact that this meal was one worthy of a Chinese major.

"This was excellent," Glenn said when they finished eating, but then smiling, he nodded toward the outside door and noted the obvious. "Of course, ordering a meal for two might be seen as a clue by some, and my guess is that my new friends will all still be out there waiting for me when I leave. This was great, and I thank you, but as

I'll have to face those clowns out there sooner or later, I might as well make it sooner." With that, he stood and reached for his gear.

"Tut-tut, my doubting friend, just enjoy the now and deal with the sooner or later, later," the major replied, and with a broad smile on his face, he rubbed his own very flat stomach as he added, "I'm well known for my hearty appetite, and those men have other duties. They have a morning formation to attend—and *all of them* will be there."

Glenn stared at him. Their breakfast conversation had turned out to be mere small talk with no mention of the media-copter and with none of yesterday's very open sharing. And now the major seemed to be acting out a part of some kind, but his acting wasn't all that good. Seemingly following a script, he took another quick look at his watch, stood, and after a long, slow stretch, he walked over to the window, pulled up the shade, and raised the sash. Glenn shook his head in wonder as he watched the clumsy routine. After leaning out to take a few scripted deep breaths, the major pulled back inside and, turning around with a broad smile on his face, headed for the door. What was going on here?

"I need to step out for a bit," the officer announced. "Formation is due to start, and I want to be there. You'll be fine here." With that, he waved and walked out the door.

Glenn, now reseated, stared curiously after him. The meal, the stick, the strange ritual at the window, what did it all mean? The major had learned nothing from Glenn about anything, and yet he still seemed very pleased about something. What? Why?

Before he could begin to sort-out the major's behavior, a sound from outside spun him around. Something's up, he thought, and snatching-up his new walking stick, he positioned himself by the still open window in the at-the-ready to swing position just as a dark figure came crawling stealthily into the room, one leg first, and then the head. His big stick held high, Glenn eased forward, tensing to swing as that now slowly standing figure turned to face him. But whoa! Just as he started his swing, a wide-eyed woman, shooting-up both hands to ward-off the coming blow, let out a whispered near-shout.

"Hold it, Glenn! We will win! We-Will-Win!" She shouted it twice, rapidly flashing the WWW sign as she spoke. "I'm J7! Hold it. You don't need that stick. I'm your new angel, but I'm not ready to become a real one yet." Her words gushed out.

"What? Who?" Glenn gasped, and then as her words registered, he slumped back into the closest chair, with a deep sigh of relief. "I gotta get my heart rate back down. Why didn't you give me a warning? Why didn't the major?"

"Well, think about it; I just met you." She tried to laugh, but had to take a couple of deep breaths first, sagging back on to the bed to recover as she continued, "And the major knows nothing about you or any of this. He's never seen me, and needless to say, he has no idea who you are or that you might have hid in his room—not that those pawns out there would dare to confront him about it anyway. But, hey, let's get out of here; we need to make our move while they're all still in formation. So saddle up!"

"You're kidding me! It's light out now, and this place is crawling with federals!" Glenn protested, but she had turned and was already climbing back through the window.

"Come on, follow me," she whisper-ordered. "Follow me now, right now!"

"You're the angel," he sighed doubtfully, and although not liking to do it, he grabbed his pack—and his new stick—and followed her out. She then led him in a slow jog across the back lawn to the old golf course, and angling wide to the south away from the clubhouse and then east, they moved toward US 23. As they ran, Glenn looked back and was surprised to see a much larger formation of troops in front of the building this morning than there had been the day before; it looked like close to a hundred.

"Big stuff seems to be going on back there," he shouted ahead as they ran.

"Hold it!" She called back as she led him into a grove bordering the ditch that ran along the old expressway. "We'll need to crash here for a bit to wait to be cleared for our move across the highway—it's wide open out there, so we gotta be sure. But yes, you're right, the feds are gearing up as you'll soon see, and it may be bad for us. Let's hope not."

"I was afraid I'd have to go solo," Glenn said as they plopped down. "But you angels always seem to come through. What is it, mostly luck or good planning?"

"Well, we scored some breaks maybe, but luck doesn't have much to do with it. I had to rework my schedule bigtime to get here a lot earlier than planned, but we're used to that. We reset plans when events change, and with you guys, change is a habit."

"Sorry," Glenn smiled, adding, "Do we need to worry about that huge formation?"

"Well, the feds have shipped a ton of new troops into the area, trying to seal off the Whigville marches, and there's a big move of some kind coming soon—all very hush, hush. Of course, there's also a very big deal being made about a high value renegade and his two friends, something about a media-copter," she said, and turning, she eyed Glenn with a broad smile. "How'd you three get to be so important?"

"I have no idea. I don't think I am. My guess is that they want my buddies, and especially the one they think brought down the media-copter. I'm just along for the ride."

"Well, not really, you're all important. We all are, everyone in the alliance," she replied sleepily, and settling back, she yawned and closed her eyes. They were leaning against trees now with their faces turned toward the slow rising morning sun, feeling very relaxed in its warmth. "Let's rest," she muttered, continuing to speak without looking at Glenn. "Feds are coming from as far away as their hub down in Toledo, and I've heard they just hit Fenton with friendlies' air to soften us up. I don't know how hard they hit, but something big's about to happen, and we're all going to be in on it."

"Good, I'm ready. I want to get to Whigville, and I know it's close. I can feel it," he said, looking impatiently over at her as he spoke. He wanted to get moving again.

"Close, but still a way," she murmured, seemingly near asleep. And much to Glenn's dismay, thirty minutes went by before she stood to look around again, and then something off in the distance must have caught her eye because she waved Glenn to his feet. "We're good to go, and you're about to get a little closer to good old Whigville. Come on, we've got our window to cross—but it's a close squeeze. Let's do it!"

Glenn, looking about for her signal, saw nothing as they stoop-ran across the crumbled south and northbound lanes and ducked down quickly into the ditch on the other side—duck being the appropriate word. The ditch still had a little water left in it from the last rain, which was something J7 allowed for, but Glenn didn't. He'd flung himself into the weeds without looking and was now soaked up and down his left side.

"Oh, great!" he shouted. "Thanks for the warning."

"I didn't know," she laughed. "But, come on, it's only water—and little mud."

"I'll bet you didn't know," Glenn replied, but he couldn't help laughing with her as he added, "I notice you're still very dry."

"I look before I leap," she joked back, but then, glancing over his head, she instantly sobered up and waved for him to lie flat. "Listen, the feds coming in have guns, and that's a big deal. We can't outrun bullets, so we have to avoid their patrols. And it looks like one's got us in its sights right now. You'll need to do exactly what I say."

"Feds?" Glenn whispered, rolling over in the grass to look. "Did they spot us?"

"Stay down!" she ordered, and squinting down the road, she said, "There are five of them, but the good news is … I don't think they're feds, so no guns. But they are bounty hunters, so listen to me real good, stay down, no matter what happens, stay!"

With those words, she stood up in plain sight, brushed herself off, and walked out of the ditch like she was leaving a swanky restaurant. Once up on the road, she paused to look around, seemingly for something to the north, and after a brief look that way, she turned, ever so slowly, still looking, until she seemed to spot the men coming up from the south for the first time. Smiling broadly, she then stood on tiptoe, waving both hands for them to come to her, even as she drifted to the north, away from Glenn's position.

"Who are you?" the apparent boss of the bounty hunters demanded as they huffed up to her. "What're you doing out here anyway, don't you know there's a day-curfew on? The feds've just hit Fenton, and they're swarming all over the place now."

"Why would that bother me?" she replied with a laugh. "I'm just pickin' flowers."

"It'll bother you if they see you," the boss snapped, staring at her in disbelief.

"Oh, I didn't know. I just came for a walk 'n thought I'd pick me some flowers. Ditches are a good place to look for flowers because they stay wet longer." She smiled off in Glenn's direction. "But if I'm not supposed to be out, I'll just head back to the major."

"Major?" the largest bounty hunter came forward with a not-so-strange grin on his face. "What can a little ole federal major offer a gal like you?"

"Oh, my major isn't a federal, he's Chinese, you know, Friendly Forces." She smiled back at the oaf, noting that he stopped his approach at those keywords.

"Chinese? You gotta be kiddin' me," he muttered, but he stayed stopped.

"Not kidding you, big guy. Here's my pass signed by the major himself just a couple hours ago." She handed the pass toward the big man, but the leader snapped it up.

"Where'd you get this?"

"Right over there where he's staying," she gestured over her shoulder.

"Is that right? Well, mah-dam," the leader mocked her title, scowling at her. "I don't begin to believe you, so you're comin' with us. We'll see about that major stuff."

"No, I won't be going with you." Her once musical voice now changed to a cold and commanding tone, and she locked her eyes firmly on the leader. "I'll continue on my search for some lunch flowers, the major likes flowers, and you'll get out of my way."

"She's lyin'," the big guy said. "I don't believe a word of it."

"Get out of my way, now!" J7 snapped, and glaring at him, she stuffed her pass back into her cargo pants and started walking directly at them. Glenn, watching from the weeds only yards away, knew that he was supposed to stay down no matter what, but he wasn't going leave J7 without some backup, and he clenched his walking stick tightly as her act unfolded. His eyes were on the leader, who was staring in disbelief as J7 came at him, but when the big man behind the leader made a move to cut her off, Glenn tensed.

"Well, I still don't believe you," the leader said, and reluctantly giving ground, he nodded for the others to stand aside. "You'd better believe we're going over there, and if we don't see a Chinese major, we'll be back and make you eat your stupid flowers."

"How sweet. You tell the major that little ole me said to not start lunch alone."

She called out that comment over her shoulder to the retreating bounty hunters as she walked away, her cute-talking voice now back in full bloom. She knew they wouldn't dare approach the major ... and even if they did, she was covered.

Laughing at that thought, she headed north in a near skip as a very relieved Glenn blew out a long breath and relaxed his hand on his stick. The five bounty hunters had left without even looking in his direction; they were too busy arguing with each other as they crossed the decaying old expressway. Glenn waited until they were well gone, and then he stood and, keeping his head down, crouch-ran up the road after the still moving J7.

Once he thought it safe, he stood up straight, picking up his pace to catch her. "I can't believe you," he said when he finally came alongside her. "You had them talking about flowers as if you actually had some in your hand." Then, thinking for a moment, he looked all around them and laughed, "Or that there were flowers to be seen, anywhere."

"It's called acting, Glenn, good acting, and ..." But then, hold-ing up her hand, she slowed down, scanning the east side of the road. Something there concerned her enough to cause her to lead the way across a shallow ditch and on into the edge of the woods where she knelt to study the trail and to think about what she was seeing.

"Glenn, this is where we need to leave the road, but there are signs that someone else is using our trail, so stay close. If we're stopped, you take your cue from me, and do exactly what I tell you to do, no questions. And, oh yes, no talking from here on."

They walked in dead silence for over an hour, stopping frequently to listen and to wait on a path that wound up and down, tracking north and a bit east. She's moving us in the right direction, Glenn thought, and so maybe she'll pick-up the other two on that lake, whatever it's called. But meanwhile, the sun was getting high, it was hot now and water was running low. Even water like that back in the ditch would seem good very soon.

"Welcome to Sherwood Forest, my name is Robin Hood," Alex's friendly voice greeted them at a sharp bend in the tree-shadowed trail. But as a delighted Glenn started to step forward to greet him, he was jerked off his feet from behind by a booming laugh and two bulging arms that pinned his own to his side. He struggled at first, but relaxed when he realized the others were all having too good a time at his expense.

"OK, oaf." He laughed once he was back on his feet and had regained some of his dignity. "It looks like I need to remind you who's in charge of this operation."

"Why it's me," both of his companions said at once, but then, quickly correcting themselves, they pointed to their angel and said, "No, it's she."

"I'll go along with that." Glenn laughed. "You should have seen her manage the gang of bounty hunters we ran into." And turning towards her with a big grin, he shook his head, still in wonder, as he added, "In fact, all seven of you angels have been—I have to say it, magnificent. Where'd they find people like you? How'd they train you?"

"Who's this, they? I thought we were all part of a new 'we.' Anyway, I don't know and don't want to know who the other so-called angels are," she replied and went on to remind him, "I thought you knew that things are compartmentalized in the alliance with crisscrossing security lines to keep everything running in service to the whole."

Then, turning to look back down their trail, she said, "Of course, it's natural to wonder about such things, but let's let it go at that. No speculating, just acceptance."

"Of course. I'm just impressed by how you respond to changes," Glenn went on.

"Yes, and in this case I'll fudge the rules a bit. It was our air-head ombudstera, herself, who let their plans about you slip. She thought she was making points with a friendly and didn't realize that right now the Chinese are making a move on the Russians, and, for some mysterious reason, helping us fits into that plan. My guess is that they have aims on Alaska, but whatever their motivation, we had to move fast to get all you out. I won't even tell you what I had to go through to get to you a day early. The feds are swarming, and all the usual ways across the Whigville marches are closed off."

"Yep, she came by our cabin last night and got us out just before PAC hit the place," Little John said. "We'd barely cleared our stuff out of the cabin and hid in the bushes when they hit. They moved in just before dawn, and they weren't gentle, and they weren't taking any chances—came in with guns blazing bigtime—real guns, not pellet guns. We wouldn't have known what hit us."

"Hey, you can't blame them. They thought they'd be running into the guy who brought down a media-copter with his bare hands." Their angel laughed. "Cut them some slack, they were afraid."

"I'll buy that." Alex laughed. "But how are we doing now, are we OK and back on track? If so, we have to be getting pretty close to Whigville by my calculations."

"You're very right, major, and I think we're about to get some new information," she replied, pointing to a young boy running toward them along their back trail.

About ten or twelve years old, the kid came running directly up to J7, loudly calling out, "The federals are coming. The federals are coming."

Then without waiting for directions or a reaction, he shot around them and raced on to spread the news up ahead while they all moved quickly to saddled-up and resume their trip. After about twenty minutes of very fast walking in deep silence, Glenn moved up alongside J6 and said, "If you tell me that kid's name is Paul, I won't believe you."

"Well, Glenn, as a matter of fact," she whispered back, smiling. "It may or may not be. I don't know. But I do know he's one of us, he flashed the sign."

"I didn't see our sign," Alex said from close behind them.

"I didn't say our sign, I said *the* sign. One my contacts gave it to him not more than an hour ago. Remember, the alliance is compartmentalized. I knew—you didn't."

"How could you know it, you've been with us?" asked John, now joining them.

"Because my contact is still my contact; we've never been out of touch. That's why, gentlemen, I knew which way for us to run last night at your cabin." She smiled at them. "And right now he's telling me the federals are lagging far behind us. So we can relax a bit, even take a breath and enjoy some of the water you two have with you."

"I forgot how thirsty I was," Glenn said, looking around for the water bottles.

"And food, we've got sandwiches and chips and a big piece of cake, and I don't know about you guys." John grinned. "But I think eatin' it is better than carryin' it."

"OK, OK." Alex laughed. "Enough talk, you're driving me crazy. Let's eat, if it's safe and if we have the time." He looked over at J7, and she nodded.

After they ate a quick bite, Glenn was ready to hit the trail again. They were almost there, and he wanted very much to be there. But J7 held them up for almost two hours because a federal patrol was wandering around just north of them, according to her information from someone, somewhere; Glenn could never figure out the who or where.

And unfortunately, once they finally got started, they were stopped again, and that start-stop-start pattern continued for the rest of the day. Later, not wanting to risk running blindly into federals on the trail between camp sites as darkness loomed, they camped for the night in a well-concealed spot that had been set up for them only a short time before. It had sleeping bags and enough food for an evening meal and breakfast the next day.

The trip had been more stress inducing than physically exhausting, but it had left them all tired and so there was little talk. After a couple of sandwiches, an apple, and a handful of nuts, washed down with fresh water, the three were ready to get some sleep.

Whigville would have to wait one more day.

Glenn was the first one to hit the sack, but he didn't go right to sleep. Instead, he sorted through the day's adventure, trying to make sense of things. He had questions to ask, a lot of them, but he'd have to deal with them later, he decided, and rolling over to go to sleep, he called out, "I suppose Dell-X and Howdy are already in Whigville."

"Oh, I'm sure they are," Alex whispered back. He was still sitting up, poking around at the fire. Little John didn't reply; he'd gone to sleep the instant he stretched out.

"Yes, they'd be there by now; that's great," Glenn murmured, more to himself than to Alex, and rolling over onto his right side, he too gave in to sleep, a very contented sleep, far better than on that sagging cot of the last two nights. They were almost there.

Above them, small clouds rushed over the face of the moon, and all around them were the sounds of night. It all seemed so peaceful, and yet there were predators slipping silently about in the surrounding woods, hunting, killing, or being killed, just as they have been doing since the dawn of time.

CHAPTER EIGHTEEN

How The Three Find a Whigville under Siege

*E*xhausted from the day before, Glenn overslept and had to hop to it, eating on the run in order to get saddled up on time, and so he didn't notice until they were ready to go that J7 wasn't with them. "Hey, where's our angel?" he asked, looking at the other two.

"Don't know, not here when I got up," Alex replied. He was standing across the fire sipping a coffee, and as he spoke, he poured the dregs into the flames and turned to poke his cup into his pack. "Don't worry, she'll show; she knows today's the day."

"Haven't seen her." Little John shrugged from his squatting spot by the fire. All packed, he was still working on breakfast. "We're close," he munched. "She'll be here."

"You're both right, and we're a lot closer to the finish line than you know," J7's familiar voice chimed in from behind them, and they all turned around, smiling. But their smiles quickly vanished, replaced by confused wariness and a shift from a welcome to a ready to fight mode when they saw her. She was wearing a federal majors' uniform.

"Hey, take it easy," she said, and laughingly lifting her hands, she gestured down at her uniform, adding, "Don't you like my clothes? Come on, that makes me sad."

"You get caught with that outfit on, you'll be more than sad, you'll be dead,"

Little John said, warily taking a last sip of coffee. "You shouldn't take that kind of risk."

"Actually, my friend, I'm very safe. You see, I'm a real federal, and I can tell you now that I recall all the nasty things you guys have said about us." She spoke with an unusual edge to her voice and had a very serious look on her face ... at first. But she couldn't hold the pose, and a chuckle broke through as she added, "And, of course, I agreed with each and every one of those things." With that she broke into a full laugh, and moving on into camp, added a tilted head, tongue out, cross-eyed, sloppy salute.

Seeing her shift, a smiling Little John stood, and slowly moving his hand from behind his back, he revealed a huge rock, which he meaningfully bounced up and down, in his not small palm. "You're one lucky federal. I was ready to take your head off."

Alex, laughing at the sight of John's rock, held up a long thin throwing knife that he had cupped in his own hand and said, "But first, you'd have had this in your gut."

"Whoa, you guys are prepared," she said, looking expectantly over at Glenn, who grinned back sheepishly and held up two empty hands. The walking stick he had raised against her at the golf course yesterday morning was now leaning unthought-of on his pack two steps behind him.

"Well, two warriors out of three," Alex said, and shaking his head sadly, he turned back to J7 and added, "But I'm sure he had a plan; he was probably going to talk you to death with a long story about organizational dynamics or some such stuff."

"Or worse," John chimed in, "He'd have lulled you off guard with his story about the ant and the bee ... or was it a wasp? You'd fall asleep listening to it—I know I did. Of course, he kept on waking me up, yammering along and laughing at his own story."

"Yes, I'm glad you brought that up. It's a great story," Glenn chimed in with a feigned look of excitement on his face. "You see, it's a metaphor for our times about an ant, a spider, and a honeybee. Sir Francis Bacon was talking about ..." They all jeered him into a laughing silence.

"OK guys, this is fun, but you need to get going," J7 said, and still laughing, she knelt down by the fire and began unfolding a crude map. "Gather around and take a look at this sketch of where you are now and where you want to go. We walked in a big loop yesterday, and so you're close. Well, come to think about it, you're really inside greater Whigville right now—different county, but same spirit and alliance-controlled." At those words, they eagerly crowded around to look over her shoulder as she continued.

"You're here in a place called Seven Lakes, not that it matters what it's called, no signs are left these days," she said, pointing to the map. "You'll be going north to the first road, here, and then left or west until you come to a camp on this small lake, right here. It's a short walk, and you shouldn't miss it, but if you do, they won't miss you. Anyway, don't worry, you're inside Whigville lines, and everyone you see should be a friend—we hope. The feds are all over here [she pointed] in Fenton, and as you can see, that's quite a bit south of the camp you want. And they seem to be staying in town for now, even pulled back their patrols late last night, but I've heard their air did hit a couple days ago and that may mean a big move's coming. We don't know, but the word on both sides right now is to watch and wait. That gives you time to get where you're going."

She stood up then with a big smile on her face, and after shaking hands, she gave a big hug to each one of them and said, "Guys, it's been fun getting to know you, and I look forward to coming back home in the near future to see how you're doing. By then, I hope we'll have a victory or two to celebrate, but for right now, you need to move out." With that, she snapped off a major angel to major Alex salute, turned, and hurried away.

"Thanks for everything," Glenn called out as she walked away, and although the three were eager to get going, they waited, watching until she was out of sight. And then, it was an eager Glenn who was the first to grab and shoulder his pack with a "Come on, saddle up, I can feel it deep down in my soul; we're within aura-distance of Whigville."

"What kind of distance?" Little John asked.

"Don't encourage him." Alex laughed. "But he's right, let's roll."

On that order and with a new spring in their step, the three comrades started off, striding proudly toward their goal with their shoulders thrown back and zip-a-dee-doo-dah in their—well, at least in Glenn's heart. And if he hadn't been afraid of attracting feds, he would have sung that good old song out loud because, right now, at this very moment, his life-long dream was coming true. He was entering Whigville!

None of the three had been here before, although Little John had grown up only a few miles away, in a town called Clarkston—a town now held very literally under the sword by friendlies backed federals who had terrorized the village and forced his own family off their land. The only compensation offered for their lost property was the free admission into Arbor U for their, too low quotaed to otherwise ever be selected son. What a payment that turned out to be. What a joke! Little John hated them all.

As the they moved along, maintaining a steady but easy pace, they began to see signs of life, and an excited Glenn, speeding up, shouted, "I see smoke. That means we must be safely inside Whigville for sure, and I'm more than ready. For one thing, I could use a place to relax and shower."

"I'll see your shower and raise you a good hot meal," Little John shouted, but he didn't need to; he had easily matched Glenn's new pace, and they were side by side.

"_I'll_ see that and raise you both for some real safety. In case you haven't noticed, we're being watched, and by a lot of eyes," Alex whispered as he moved up beside them, and he nodded towards the tree line on both sides of their road. "They're all around us, and we'd better hope that you're right about us being inside Whigville lines."

"We're there, my doubting friend. We're in Whigville, I can feel it," Glenn said, ignoring the caution. But his joy ended on the word, it, as twelve staff-toting, sullen looking men, suddenly converged on them from the bushes and trees on both sides of the road, blocking their way forward, or back—and they didn't look friendly.

"You three headed someplace?" a short barrel of a man, bald with a ruddy face and dark serious eyes under bushy brows, stepped out in front of the others to challenge the travelers. Unsure of what to do, the three waited, watching cautiously as their new apparent foes' leader silently looked them slowly up and down, taking his own sweet time. At last, whether satisfied or dissatisfied, they couldn't tell, he snapped at them in a commanding voice, "You deaf and dumb? Don't just stand there, answer my question!"

"I'll answer your question," Alex said, stepping forward to present himself as the senior military officer. "We're your friends, and we'll cooperate, but first, you need to tell your buddies to lower their weapons. You can see that we're unarmed."

"That's funny, you had weapons when you were chatting up that federal major less than an hour ago," the leader said, and a slow 'gotcha' smile spread across his face. The three friends glanced uncomfortably at each other—unsure about how to respond to this seemingly angry man now pushing up to Alex and glaring around at all three of them.

He had stepped forward when Alex had presented himself, and they were now almost touching as the leader scowled up at the taller man with what looked to be … a twinkle in his eye? Cocking an eyebrow after a long pause, he then pressed Alex, "How do you explain that little fact, oh man of peace? Did all those nasty old weapons just disappear? How about that student's walking stick, did it walk away, or is it still in his hands?" He nodded toward Glenn, and as he spoke, his almost smile vanished, replaced by a firm, threatening glare as he motioned for his followers to move in. They quickly did so, without speaking … or lowering their weapons, and none of them were smiling.

"His stick is just that, a stick. Unlike all of yours, his isn't intended as a weapon," Alex insisted, his eyes darting from one man to another, watching for their next move. There were a lot of them, his reply had been lame, and he couldn't see an easy way out of this, but who were these guys anyway and, if enemies, why this far inside Whigville?

"Ah yes, weaponless hands." A genuine smile now slowly formed on the leader's face and his ruddy seriousness melted away, giving in to a loud laugh, which was joined immediately by the men behind him. "All the better for us to shake hands with, Major Crosby.

Welcome to Whigville, and by the way, you handled our little joke very well."

Alex blew out a relieved gasp, which broke into a hearty laugh, and as he reached out to accept the offered hand, he was pulled forward into the now very friendly, hugging, backslapping and hand-shaking crowd.

His two comrades, however, were a bit slow figuring out what was happening. Glenn was caught looking down at the walking stick in his hand, wondering why he hadn't thought to go after it as a weapon when J7 reappeared as a surprise federal. Why had he been ready to use it earlier at the golf course, but not then, or even now?

And half crouching beside him, Little John's mind remained fixed on a rock in the road that he had begun nudging loose with his boot when these men first appeared. He had heard the laughter around him as the noise of a battle beginning and was halfway bent, reaching down to jerk up that very rock, before he realized what was happening.

"Whoa, almost forgot! Welcome Major Crosby," the leader called out as he stepped back to snap-off a brisk salute. "This is to you as both a marine captain and as our major. I'm Lt. Don King of the Hill Road Rifles and these are some of my warriors."

Alex, pausing to stand tall, snapped off a return salute at the lieutenant. He then offered an informal salute toward the alliance men and joined his two comrades; they all walked through the now welcoming ranks, shaking hands and slapping backs. These were all their buddies, real life Blue Company warriors.

"This is exactly the greeting I expected, the second part of it anyway," Glenn mused out loud to no one in particular as he walked, shaking hands and looking happily around. Off to his left, he saw that Little John was drifting off with a group of new fans, telling them the media-copter story, hand motions and all. He laughed at the sight of the big guy holding court but decided not to butt-in; he liked the story, but it was John's story. Alex, on the other hand, had moved off into the shade with the lieutenant, and thinking they'd be talking business, Glenn decided to join them.

"This is fantastic, lieutenant. It's great to be here at last," Alex was saying when Glenn walked up. "But I've been out of the loop for a while and need to get up to speed about what's going on. Do I get my briefing from you or at HQ, if we have one nearby?"

"Sir, there's always a headquarters. It's over by the big lake, and we're instructed to get you there as soon as possible. The feds just scored a big hit here, driving us out of downtown Fenton, and they've even tried a few exploratory thrusts against us out on this side of town. So it looks like their move on Whigville is coming and coming soon."

"You mentioned rifles," Alex said. "I don't see any here, but I should warn you, the feds are now heavily armed and supported by Chinese air."

"And Alex and Little John almost came under fire yesterday," Glenn chimed in as he squatted down next to them. "So they saw those fed weapons up close."

"Yes, well, you've seen them, but as I said, we've experienced their fire power. Fenton is now loaded with well-armed federals, and there's word that some copters have been flown in, but we haven't seen any gunships yet," King said, and then pausing, he looked at each of them with a distressed look on his face. "We've had a taste of what they can dish out. Their air hit us a few days ago, and then a huge pack of fed-rats rampaged through town in a burning and looting frenzy. If those jets return on another bombing and strafing run, I don't know what we'll do. We're just not ready for that, not yet."

His face was grim as he spoke, and he had to pause for a moment to regroup. But then, shrugging it off, he helped himself to lighten up by turning around and yelling over at Little John, "If those jets come back, we'll be glad we've got us a one-man copter killer with us; I hope you can bring down one of those big babies."

"I'll try," Little John shouted back, laughingly posing and flexing his muscles.

"Congratulations, Little John. Sounds like you're, the man," Glenn shouted at John, and then slapped Alex on the shoulder and eased down on the grass beside him.

As the laughter ended, Don turned back to Alex and Glenn to continue with his report in a businesslike, but still emotional near whisper. "It was bad. They hit us hard, a lot of our people dead or hurt bad—a lot of damage. But we didn't have anything to use to stop 'em. We hear what we need is coming, but it's not here yet, and we're naked."

Glenn leaned over, nodding in sympathy. Concerned about what had happened, he was even more eager now to get into action, and looking at Don, he said, "We'd heard that something big came down, but no details. Can you give us the whole story? And do you have an assignment for me yet? I want to get into this thing."

"Whoa, slow down, sir." Don smiled, reaching over to grasp the eager young student's hand. "I'm sorry; I was so caught up with the major and the military situation, I forgot that we had a special traveler on this run. It's very good to have you with us."

"Well, I don't think I'm special, but I was told that I'd have a job to do. I just don't know what it is," Glenn replied. Embarrassed by the "special" tag and unsure how to deal with it, he was still thinking about how to respond when, suddenly, a loud ear-jolting roar exploded all around them. And the men there all reacted differently, Glenn and Alex both jerked their eyes up to the sky, but remained in place, watching as a big jet thundered by them just over treetop level a hundred yards to their west. However, to the men of the Hill Road Rifles, these jets meant death and destruction, and the memory of the bombing, strafing attack on Fenton just days ago sent them scattering for cover.

But for Glenn, flyovers had been part of the PAC-Deliverance Day celebration every year back in Arbortown, and he knew the intimidating thrill of that huge sound but viewed the jets as nothing more than big noise-making machines. So he didn't move.

Little John had never seen a jet up close, and so he just stood rooted in place with his head thrown back, and staring after it, he shouted, "Wow, feel that power!"

The two officers didn't stare up or run for cover, but they did spring to their feet and Don began shouting orders, "Put out all fires. That guy's probably on a recon or intimidation run, but he might try to hit us next time around. We're all sitting ducks out here. Get with it. Saddle up! Come on men, up 'n at 'em! Move. Now!"

After watching the plane out of sight, Alex nodded a signal to John and Glenn, and they joined the others, preparing to move out. Fortunately, the plane didn't return, and after they had all jumped to follow Don's orders, the three and the Hill Road Rifles men were soon route stepping away, leaving a clean, well-policed area behind them.

This is it, Glenn thought. They were part of the Alliance now, and as he walked along with them, he savored the feeling that came with the sights and sounds all around him. Yes, this was his place, and these were his people. And he had reached the day he had worked so hard to get to for so long—the day of his new beginning. He was about to join the alliance that both his mother and father had given their lives to help start.

He thought about that as they marched along a well-planned circular route towards the HQ, but he was also aware of the hidden sentries watching them every step of the way to their destination which, as it turned out, was not right on the big lake. They stopped instead just off a crumbling Fenton Road, about a quarter mile short of that lake, in a big long closed retail complex now disguised to still look empty and unused.

Once on site, Don sent his men to take-up positions to the south and then led the three comrades up a wooden walkway toward the HQ's doors. And Glenn, glancing around as he followed Don towards those doors, was surprised and delighted to see that all of the now disappearing Hill Road Rifle troopers were actually carrying *rifles*. And he stared after them, wondering where all those guns had come from, so soon—and how?

"Presto change-o," a familiar voice spoke. "I see you've noticed the rifles."

"Dell-X! You made it," Glenn said, and as he turned to greet the other man, he shouted to his companions who were already disappearing inside, "Hey, Dell-X is here!"

After greetings all around, they assembled in what once had been a large sales display room but was now their war room, complete with blackout-curtains covering the four boarded-over windows. And then, after joining the others hustling about to light the kerosene lanterns scattered around the room, Dell-X walked up to the big white board hanging on the front wall. At first, it seemed to Glenn to be just a mish-mash of lines and numbers, but he finally figured out that it had to be their Whigville defense plan ... and that the action was centered right here on their Fenton location. He smiled, liking that.

"Here's a rough picture of where things are right now, but of course, it all changes by the second," Dell-X said, picking up a pointer. "As you know, well-armed federals hit Fenton hard two days ago, forcing us to pull back. So they now control everything from here [he moved the pointer] ... to here, and they're positioned to attack Whigville in a three-pronged attack, along these lines." The four men followed his pointer, nodding.

"The word we have from inside sources is that there's to be a diversionary move here, heading north along this highway from their forward positions at Groveland Oaks and Mt. Holly, right here," he said, naming the two locations. "But the scoop we have says they can't sustain that move for long because they don't have the firepower or the local support they need. Of course, they know that too, and so we believe that any move from there will be only an effort to distract us from their main thrusts, which we think will be right here, through us at Lake Fenton and also through Holly, just over here."

"They don't have any local support in Oakland County, zilch!" Little John shouted from the back of the room. "Their entire line from Pontiac north will turn into a shooting gallery once this thing starts—with them as the targets. They tried to disarm us for years, but they couldn't get it done. Everyone's still got guns and plenty of ammo."

"Thank you, John, that's what we hope will happen, if it comes to that," Dell-X called back, acknowledging his friend with a smile as he went on. "But either way, our own main concern is here with these two approaches." He traced out a line along Grange Hall to Holly Road and then on into Grand Blanc and another line along Thompson to Halsey and then on to Baldwin and Holly Roads and on into Grand Blanc. "Their plan is for these two prongs to converge here to complete the destruction of a big hospital that their air hit the other day at Baldwin and Holly, right here. They then plan to intimidate the locals by burning their way through the city of Grand Blanc before moving on north to attack the Whigville training command location." He moved the pointer to show those moves all the way to the Whigville site.

"They did that in Clarkston, and it intimidated no one!" Little John shouted again.

"And it will intimidate no one in Grand Blanc, Little John," Alex called out. "But it could take a lot of lives, and it'll scatter the people. I'm sure that's what they want—to get the people running in panic. So how are we responding to all of this, Dell-X?"

"We have a solid plan in place, but events are still unfolding, and …"—he looked around at them—"… our planned military response is on hold for now." Dell-X stopped, obviously aware of the stunned gasp and the baffled looks on the faces of the four men in front of him when he added that last part. Yet he stuck with his instructions. "Right now, all I can tell you is that we have a plan to stop these attacks if they get under way, and that the people we need are in place to deal with whatever happens, including any Dixie Highway thrust. But …" He blew out a deep, resigned sigh, "I'm truly sorry to say that's it for now. I hope to give you more later today, once events now under way have moved forward. But, for right now, we're asking that you just standby, at the ready."

Then, pursing his lips, he stepped back from the whiteboard and added, "And I'm sorry, but I can't even take questions now. Please be patient and know that things are in flux, and I'll tell you more when I know more … in just an hour or two, we hope."

"What is this? This isn't a plan. It's just a description of the mess we're in. Are we relying on fairy dust, or do we have a real plan?" Little John stood up, protesting. "I was in Clarkston when they hit two years ago. They were barbaric. They killed. They looted. They raped. And then they had this witch-ombudstera come in and tell us how lucky we were to finally be part of the glorious new PAC change. Our dead were still unburied, the coals were still glowing in our firebombed homes, and she was telling us how PAC was there for us—that PAC was the dream we'd all been waiting for. Let me tell you [Now there were tears in the big man's eyes], we wanted to kill her. Her change was the change that barbarians have brought to civilizations since the dawn of time; we wanted to kill her, but we didn't. We just stood there and took it. We took it because we were afraid, afraid that they weren't through with their own killing yet, and we'd already lost too many, and we had our dead to bury. So please, please don't tell me we're going to just sit back and wait to see what happens. That's what was done in Clarkston!"

"I hear you, Little John," Dell-X went over to him, and taking John's huge hand in both of his, he shook it, looking firmly into his eyes as he continued. "Our counter moves are under way, but I can't describe them to you, not yet. Our job, for now, is to be ready to form up to support those moves, but if they fall through, we are to stop any fed advance along Thompson and Grange Hall roads. We have Don's guys—he smiled at Don—and other troops to stop them; the woods around here are full of well-armed troops, and they'll fight for every inch of territory. If the feds move to hit Holly and Grand Blanc, there's a surprise waiting for them, but I can't say more now, except that they will never get by the Great Lakes Veteran's Cemetery, and they will not get to Whigville."

"Their air got to Fenton, and no one protected Clarkston," Little John protested, and sagging back into his chair, grim-faced, he sadly shook his head, "Give me a break!"

"Yes, John, you're right. And they also hit the Grand Blanc hospital. But Clarkston is outside our zone of defense right now, and we weren't equipped to deal with the air hits in Fenton and Grand Blanc," Dell-X replied, sadly searching John's face as he spoke and wishing he could reassure him. "Their air attack surprised us, but we'll not be surprised next time, and the Chinese know from other places that, once we're properly supplied, they won't be able to trade planes for bombing runs. Stuff's arriving now that will make them pay, but we need a little time to make it operational. So I'm sorry to say, that's it. I've shown you all of the plan—or description—I can; you'll get more info when you join your units. But let me add that I have every reason to believe that you'll all look back on what's about to happen and feel that you've had a rewarding day today."

At that, Dell-X left the room and Don, hoping to alleviate the tension, leaned over and whispered to the three discouraged men, "There's food in the room next door. You'd better eat up and get some rest. If things go right, this could be a long day's adventure."

"Adventure!" Little John scowled as he followed him through the door. "I came here to make war against PAC. And *that* is the only adventure I care about!"

"John." Don took his new comrade firmly by the arm. "You're in the alliance now, we all are. We follow orders, even when they don't make sense to us."

"That's right, John," Alex called over on his way out the door. "Keep the faith!"

"There's a bigger picture, John, and we have to trust our leaders," Glenn called through the doorway from the table where he was picking up a plate. "And if Don is right, this might be our last meal for a while. Besides, it *is* our first meal in Whigville. Eat up!"

Little John was still not convinced, but he did like the sight of the food, and so he moved over to the table and grabbed a plate. As he began filling it, he muttered a sharp correction to Glenn, with no sign of humor, "Actually, to be accurate, this is our second meal in Whigville, counting breakfast."

Glenn grinned over at his distraught friend but decided not to say more; the big guy just needed some time. John had memories of blood and loss that Glenn knew about, fresh memories that gave him a good reason—many good reasons—to despise PAC.

Alex, who had followed Dell-X out the door at the end of their meeting, returned a short time later with a big smile on his face, and the first thing he did was to walk over to a now eating Little John, and slapping the big guy on the back, he said, "I think we have a shot at a very big and very satisfactory day today, my friend. And believe me, you're going to be real happy with the way it all works out. Just trust the alliance."

"Is that right? Well, I'll trust all right, but like one of our greater presidents once said, I'll trust, but verify. Or, maybe I should say that

I'll trust when I can verify. I need more than just words," Little John groused back.

"Patience, my friend, patience." Alex laughed as he began filling his own plate. "All good things come to those who wait and trust … and eat."

John didn't reply, but he did seem to enjoy his meal more from then on.

CHAPTER NINETEEN

How the Rampaging Lilliputians Fall Back

"*Plucked eagle* on the move. *Soaring Eagle* respond now!" A shout rang through the HQ and surrounding areas, setting everyone in motion, including the recently briefed and just fed three comrades. At long last, it was going to be nose-to-nose time.

"You're with me, sir," Lt. King shouted to Alex, and turning to Little John with a big grin on his face, he added, "We'll need that strong right arm of yours too, big guy."

Glenn, looking up with a charge of anticipation, tossed aside the thick Whig Partisan Alliance guidebook that he'd been reading and jumped up in anticipation. This is it, he thought, and watching as the others saddled up, he knew he'd get his own call soon. But as the men of the Hill Road Rifles, joined by Alex and John, finished pulling their gear together, they moved on outside to begin falling in, and still no word came for him. Instead, he soon found himself standing alone in the now empty room with a what-about-me look on his face. What was going on?

At first, he just stood there, listening to all of the excitement outside and feeling both confused and angry. But he was too eager to be part of the action to settle for that, and so, deciding that it would be best to stay visible, he walked out the door and crossed the porch, taking a position in plain view against one of its posts. From there, he watched as the others completed their preparations and began to move out.

"Lieutenant!" He shouted over at Lt. King as his unit marched by, and the officer turned, waved, and cupped one hand to his ear as Glenn called out, "Anything for me?"

But his question drew only a "sorry" headshake and a sad shrug as they moved off between the buildings, leaving Glenn muttering to himself in disappointment. He stayed on the porch after they left, leaning back against his post and repositioning himself from time to time by propping up first one foot and then the other for support. But that didn't satisfy him, and he soon began pacing back and forth, thinking about how he should respond. And he would respond; that was certain. He would not be left out!

He didn't blame Lt. King for not including him; the man had orders to follow. Maybe they saw him only as a student, and he wasn't being overlooked; he just wasn't needed. After all, what skills could he offer? He wasn't a warrior and had never really done anything worthwhile at all. But no, that can't be it, he decided, and he wandered back inside to poke around at the food table, munching on some carrots and many more chips. But the quiet in the room soon got to him, and he drifted back outside, his mind now beginning to play with radical, even subversive thoughts. "I may be only a student, but I can contribute, and I'll prove it. I'll go after them on my own right now. All I have to do is to start walking; they can't stop me," he muttered out loud, and he actually started to go down the steps, intending to do just that, but then …

"No, that'd be stupid. The alliance plan has worked beautifully so far." He was back to muttering again. "Despite all our foul-ups, they've kept an eye on us and been there for us. They know where I am right now, and they'll have a job for me to do." He grinned as he thought about all the times their angels had tracked them down and rescued them. "Yep," he called out very loudly, "and it'll be an important job. I know will!"

So as hard as it was, he continued to wait. He waited, pacing back and forth, in and out, for about half an hour. Then, after fighting back a new surge of frustration and self-doubt, he waited some more. That next half hour was the real test, one he almost failed. But thanks be to some guiding mind in the alliance, just as he had reconvinced himself to pitch in his hand and to blunder out into the field after the others, he was saved by the sound of an opening door, and he turned eagerly to welcome his possible rescuer.

"I'm looking for Glenn Alleyne Stanton," a young man announced, and as he came on into the room, he looked all around as if it was thronging with people and he had to sort through a crowd to find his man. Then, his eyes fell on … Glenn's walking stick? And as Glenn watched in total surprise, his contact, smiling broadly, seemed to forget his search. Instead, he studied that stick for a long moment as if he wasn't even aware that there was a real person attached to it. And when his eyes did finally move up to fix on Glenn, the guy just grunted—or so it seemed to Glenn—and without any expression or real zeal, he blahfully mumbled, "And I believe, I've found him."

After those words, uttered from only a half step inside the door, Glenn's contact turned as if to leave—without an introduction or any real interaction at all beyond a stark over the shoulder order, "You're supposed to come with me; I'll fill you in as we go."

Glenn, his own earlier welcoming smile now well-slipped from his face, felt his blood pressure spike as he glared at the man's turning back. This clown's ham-fisted approach, on top of the long wait, was too much. He felt like an unwanted lost dog being retrieved from a kennel, and he wasn't going to let that go.

"Hold it!" He snapped out the words as he approached the door, angrily scowling first at the man, then down at his own stick, and finally back up at his contact. But as the guy turned, facing him with an innocently questioning look on his face, Glenn faltered.

"Oh, nuts," he mumbled to himself. He couldn't stay angry at this stick-fixated kid. He looked to be too nice to have intended anything bad, and now he was obviously confused by Glenn's look and harsh voice—not a good start to their time together. And so, although part of him still wanted to rip this clown up one side and down the other, his frown softened, and he offered a hand instead of a fist. After all, the guy meant no harm; he was just inexperienced.

Sure, Glenn didn't like the way he was being retrieved—he hated it, but so what? He was in Whigville with important work to do. So he just needed to flush all that "stuff" marching through his gut and head and get on with it. That decided, he felt better, and there was only a very slight edge remaining in his voice when they shook hands.

"Before we go," he said, but with a smile as they shook hands. "I need to know who you are, under whose orders you're acting, and where I'm supposed to be going."

"Of course, I'm sorry, sir." The young man blushed, but he still winked as he introduced himself; this guy was embarrassed, but not intimidated, and Glenn liked that. "I got side-tracked by your stick, everybody knows those sticks, but let me do it right; I'm Don Pearson, your Blue Company liaison for today," he said, and grinning broadly, he added, "You know, I really do believe that we will win our county back, but if we don't hurry, we'll miss all the action today. Things are going down—right now."

Despite his youthful looks, Don turned out to be ex-Coast Guard, and he was now a civilian alliance worker with a vague job description that included babysitting Glenn. He was also a big talker, and as they walked together, he told Glenn about the attack on Fenton and how the alliance had rallied afterwards. "The boss wants you to see what's happened here, and so we'll go through town and join a convoy with some other jeeps. We're heading to a flag-of-truce meeting with the feds at the old Fenton High School."

This has to be the plan Dell-X told them was in the works, Glenn thought as the two men walked, for reasons that made sense only to the military minds in charge, about a quarter of a mile to reach their jeep. And as soon as they were barely seated, their well-armed driver gunned the engine and tire spun off to the south along what Glenn supposed was once Fenton's main drag. Don talked as they rode, but Glenn only half paid attention to what he was saying; he was busy studying the town they were driving through. He could see that it had once been a very beautiful place, but recent times and circumstances had not been kind, and it now sagged, reality-whipped and declining.

Don had mentioned a recent federal attack, but Glenn decided that attack couldn't have caused what he was looking at now; this part of town must have fallen into decay a decade or more ago. But the scene changed as they moved along, with it looking more and more like a recent violent rampage had caused what they began seeing. Indeed, fires still smoldered in some of these once stately houses, and they all looked like they'd been vandalized and left open to the heavy hand of the weather and the curious, human or otherwise. And adding to that specter of doom before him were the remains of the once proud trees that had lined the road in the old days. Most had been cut back for fuel in recent years, and the few remaining survivors of those past assaults now stood sadly limp and fire-molested, all silently waiting for the next indignity that was to befall them.

"Won't be worth a plug-unie ..." Glenn, lost in his own thoughts about what he was seeing, just caught those words, and they interested him. But as he leaned forward to ask Don why he was talking about fake United Nations Inefficient Economy script, the sight of a squad of feds lined up across the road in front of them sidetracked him.

They had passed other motley groups of feds walking along the road as they drove, and he had worried about them at first, until it became clear that the feds didn't seem to care about them or what they were doing. However, this squad had an obvious purpose, having set up a barricade to block the way. Seeing that, Glenn sat up and looked quickly at his companions in the front seat. But they didn't seem to be concerned, and so he tried to relax, sitting back to watch as their driver downshifted, braking the jeep to a stop.

"Papers," a bored sergeant mumbled, holding out his hand as he stepped up to the passenger side. Seemingly not noticing their armed driver and casting only a glance at Glenn in the back seat, he barely looked at their travel document and then yawned and waved for his men to lift the barrier. Glenn was surprised, wondering how the man could complete his whole task without any sign of real interest in the jeep, the people in it, or its contents ... including the very obvious gun.

"Now, there's a man who loves his work," Don muttered as they pulled away.

"Yep, true love," Glenn added, laughing when he turned around to look back at the feds and saw that not one of them was watching them drive away. Shaking his head in a strong vote of no confidence, he turned to face forward again and was starting to settle back into his seat when he remembered Don's earlier words. So leaning forward again, he shouted up to the front seat, "What's not worth a unie? What'd you mean?"

"I meant our chances," Don replied, and looking around, he threw his arm over the back of his seat, eyeballing Glenn with an inquisitive half-grin on his face. "You haven't been listening to me at all, have you?"

"Sorry, I've been lost in my own thoughts," Glenn confessed, offering a thin apologetic smile, but before they could get into a discussion about Don's unies comment, a sudden, stark change of scenery jerked Glenn's mind away once again—and it was not because he was lost in thought; this time, it was because he was stunned. Shocked!

As they approached the railroad tracks, Glenn saw what was left of the town's business district, and the destruction was incredible. A war crime, a major war crime, had been committed here, if such a thing could still be acknowledged in these days of oft' promised, Change! What they had been driving through had been bad, but this! This was infinitely worse. All around him the core of the city lay flattened under piles upon piles of still smoking debris. Scattered and charred brick, twisted metal, broken glass, and splintered sooted wood lay strewn about in a hazy devil's study in black and gray.

A real-life tragic nightmare had been visited on Fenton and on its people, and the only ones who could have done it were the so-called friendlies. Although they no doubt had a lot of PAC running-dog help on the ground, only *they* had the jets and the bombs to deliver this horror—this death. So many must have died! It all took Glenn's breath away, and as they slowly drove through the debris, his heart ached at the reality of it all. How could they? What possible reason could they have had for something like this?

"Like I told you, just one bomb run." Don called back to him, speaking now through gritted teeth. "Just a practice run for Whigville. Caught us off-guard for sure. Never happened here before, and,"—his voice broke—"we just flat out didn't expect it … And, Glenn, they hurt us real bad, killed a lot of people, a lot of wonderful people."

"Bomb run … like the jet that flew over earlier? This is incredible." Glenn spoke without looking at Don; he couldn't take his eyes off of all the destruction around him. He'd been told two or three times that there had been an attack, but the reality of it didn't register before; it couldn't register, not until now, not until he could see it and smell it—and even taste it. He would never forget this atrocity, and he'd never forgive it.

"They bombed and strafed, and then the feds swarmed in to kill some more," Don muttered, "And when they pulled out of the area, they torched what was still standing."

"This is criminal," Glenn shouted up to Don, shaking his head. "How could they?

They didn't have to use jet planes against unarmed civilians. And why'd the feds tolerate something like this against their own people? Why would PAC?"

"Tolerate it?" Don signaled for the driver to stop and turned to face Glenn. "PAC begged for it. They bombed us as a warning to others, but now that they're getting some heat, they've switched tunes, saying that the Alliance set-up the whole thing. They want that to be the final word—with no questions asked or tolerated. Like I was sayin' earlier, our lives wouldn't be worth a plug-unie if we questioned their 'truth' in PAC-land."

"I'm sorry. I should have been listening. Of course it was Chinese air, it had to be. How could PAC think anyone would believe differently?" Sagging back into his seat as the jeep started forward again, Glenn clenched his teeth, overcome by the destruction around him. His eyes stung in the haze, and the smoke and smell of the burn so clawed at his nose and throat that he had trouble breathing. But it was his soul that suffered most. And as he continued to study it all, his mind turned to how easily he'd lulled himself into thinking of the friendlies as a benign presence. Just because they had helped him, he'd allowed himself to overlook the stark realities of the world around him, even putting the criminal murders on the ferry leaving

Arbortown out of his mind. Wasn't that a real atrocity done by the friendlies, by Chinese friendlies—just like here?

And how about that, oh so friendly, "friendly," Major Han? Who'd he think the major meant when he talked about using their power to control and dominate? He was talking about using it against any and all necessary targets, most certainly including us. Clenching his teeth and angrily squeezing his fists until the nails bit into his palms, he swore on the destruction that he saw all around him that he'd never allow himself to fall into such a naive trust trap again. There is no such thing as a "good" enemy or a "bad" enemy. An enemy is an enemy is an enemy, never benign, always the foe. Even though, he reminded himself of the Alliance Creed: "Their people are like our people, people who deserve freedom and the right to a life under a servant government that is subject to them."

But this! He shook his head. All it had taken were a few helpful gestures on their part to lull him into thinking that they just want what we want. Oh, maybe in a sense we are all the same thing at the core, but there are very big differences between us. The Chinese government has allowed itself to be used by PAC, yes, but only because it fit their plan to gain a total victory. But we, in America, have also allowed ourselves to be used by PAC, and for what? A bombed-out, smoking Fenton and the loss of our liberty across this once great land screams out the answer. From sea to shining sea, we are pulled down, our future warped and twisted, and we just let it happen. Our nation of free people under God, working to become fully *one people,* became instead, *one colony* of entitlement-mongering PAC serfs, a weak, divided, chaotic nation under foreign guns.

No focus on victory for us, not us, not now. After WWII, things got to be so good that we lost that focus, and from the sixties on, we favored comfort and ease over such old-fashioned things as honor and duty. And by the nineties, when it should have been obvious that PAC-like thinking was leading us to destruction, what'd we do? What a joke! By then we were so addicted to ease and entitlements that we openly threw our own kids' future into the fire to use as kindling to warm our own sorry backsides.

Smashing his fist into his palm, he felt even more determined now to find a way to serve, even more committed to a real victory for the alliance. Yes, it'll take a lot of time to get there, but we will win, and our fires will be freedom's fires, not like this. "I'll never let my guard drop again," he whispered to himself, "and our people should never allow a crime like this to happen again—ever!"

He looked up as their route abruptly changed. Their driver, working to pick his way around the remains of the bombed out main street bridge, had to ford a small stream. And as they pulled up the bank on the other side, three other jeeps joined them, merging to form a convoy that then swung off on a new road to the right. Heading toward their next meeting place, Glenn supposed.

As they moved along, Glenn noted that the scene leaving the city's bomb-out and destroyed center was a mirror image of what they had seen entering on the other side.

There were now "only" burned, not bombed-out buildings with some still smoldering.

The streets around them here were lined with many more feds, with even more guns being carried, and they were all walking in the same direction that Glenn's jeep was going. Curiously, like those earlier, they paid little attention to the three as they drove by, which led Glenn to wonder again why they were allowed to drive through here so freely—and with a weapon. Of course, they had a pass of some kind, but only one group had even asked to see it, and none of the clowns straggling along these sidewalks seemed to be interested in them at all, interested in their jeeps, perhaps, but not them.

The men they were now passing, and they all seemed to be men for some reason, were no doubt the same monsters who had laid-waste to what had once been a beautiful town, the same men who had helped kill who knows how many of its people, but they didn't look dangerous now. They looked ordinary, or at worst, they looked like nothing more than a sad collection of pathetic hang-about, street corner louts. Of course, he reminded himself that even in the old and better days, it had been louts like these who had robbed the weak and helpless and helped make America's inner cities dangerous and crime ridden. He shook his head. Crime was yet another self-destruc-

282

tive challenge that we'd failed to meet, choosing to merely politicize it and to use its victims as campaign fodder, instead of solving it, instead of actually helping those involved—victims *and* perpetrators. Both needed help, but it was bundled votes that counted, not them as fellow citizens or even people—fellow human beings with lives that needed to be nurtured.

We blew it bigtime, he thought, and sagging back once again with a deep sigh of frustration, he couldn't understand why. It was just like the conversation he'd had with the Chinese major back at the training center all over again. How'd the American people at the height of their power and wealth allow the impoverished areas in the countryside and in the cities to be the way they were? Why did we leave so many tragically adrift? And more to the point, how can we find a way to pay off the debt now owed to all of the children ... really, to all of our children? The answer has to be, We—*E pluribus unum*.

"We're here. You still with me or are you gone again?" Don looked around, grinning as he watched his voice bring his lost-in-thought companion back to the now.

Flashing an apologetic smile, Glenn looked up just as they swung left into a large field in front of yet another set of burned out buildings. It was the old high school, he guessed, but why were they here and what was about to happen? Then, in response to Don's question, he grinned self-consciously and leaned forward to reply.

"Sorry, this has all really gotten to me." He had to lean up close to Don's seat because of the increase in noise all around them. They were now part of a huge throng with what looked to be a couple hundred feds lined up across the field on the south side and, facing them from the north was a small company of about fifty blue clad ... what? "Whigvillians? Alliance-ateers? Blue Company regulars? What are we called anyway?" he unconsciously muttered out loud and was surprised when Don answered him.

"Patriots," Don shouted back. "We're called patriots, and Dell-X says that we're standing up against even bigger odds today than our forefathers faced in the American Revolution. But he believes that we've got something that'll help us now that the patriots didn't have back in those days. We've got what he calls the sure knowledge that such a thing as America can exist. We know it can exist because it did exist. We had it—once. And you know, Glenn, I believe we'll have it again."

"Yes, I agree. We *will* have it again. These punks are nothing more than a band of rampaging Lilliputians, and 'We will win' is more than a slogan, it's promise," Glenn replied. But he spoke softly now, seeing that his once cheerful companion had teared up.

"I believe that promise," Don whispered as their convoy eased to a stop. "We've got to win. You know, this is my city. They burned it, and they bombed it, and they killed my people for no other reason than to show us that they could. They could do all of this because our country, my country, didn't stand tall years ago. They could do this because PAC was willing to sign a pact with the devil-friendlies to use and to be used."

"I like that, a PAC pact, sort of like a contract with the dev ..." Glenn tried to add to his friend's thought, but a sudden roar from the crowd, mostly on the federal side, drowned him out. Turning quickly around, both he and Don were surprised to see a real life, just like the old glory days, spit and polished marching band, emerging from all the gloom and smoky haze around the still smoldering school buildings. After exploding in near perfect march-step out onto the field between the federals and the patriots, the band held forth, playing the great *Washington Post March* on all their flashy new instruments. It was like nothing seen in America for well over ten, maybe fifteen years.

And as he leaned forward in utter amazement, Glenn realized that this was the first time he'd ever seen or heard a real live marching band perform. This wasn't the squawking canned speaker music of Arbor U; this was the real thing. PAC was pulling out all the stops for this show, or whatever it was, and it all made him wonder even more about what was happening and why they were here. Apparently ... it was not to fight.

Leaving that thought still unresolved, he settled back in his seat to listen and to enjoy the sound and the feel of it all—despite the faint admonition of his better angels, this being a PAC event. The show lasted for about half an hour, and by the time it was done the number of feds on or around the field seemed to have almost doubled. And even more troubling, as Don pointed out in repeated whispers during the performance, was the fact that the patriots were not only outnumbered and surrounded, but as the music played, the federals had grouped themselves into military formations that looked almost professional. In fact, they looked like they were getting ready to make war.

"We're here under a flag of truce," Don muttered from behind his hand, "But I don't trust this lot; I don't trust what you call our Lilliputian friends at all. They don't look very *Lilli* right now."

"But very *putschian*, I'd say," Glenn replied, grimly wondering how they had a chance against such numbers and what the alliance was even doing here anyway. But he reminded himself that it was all part of a plan of some kind, and so as he settled back, he shouted up to the front seat, "Hey, when you don't have an option, you exercise it."

"What?" Don turned, looking curiously at him. "What does that mean?"

"I don't have a clue; we just put your heads down and move toward the sound of battle, I guess," Glenn replied, and leaning forward, he added, "Hey, it looks like we'll find out what our options are real soon. I see Alex, or I mean, Major Crosby, and he's got the other jeep riders in tow. My guess is that we'll get our orders right now."

As he reached them, Alex motioned the convoy groups to all come together into a small semi-circle facing away from the parade ground, and then, after a quick glance at his watch, he said, "OK, gang, here's the situation. As you know, we've been invited here by the feds under a flag of truce, but their troopers don't like it, and they *are* going to try to get us to break that truce, so they'll have an excuse to attack and overwhelm us."

"They'd better have their lunches with them, because it'll take a while." A woman's voice shouted from the back of the group, and all heads nodded in agreement.

"No, lieutenant!" Alex cut her off. "No. We're not here to fight that way; we're going to form up and stand our ground without fighting." A loud murmuring then spread through the group, and Alex only smiled at first, looking down and waiting patiently for their chipping to subside. But they had a schedule to keep, and when he felt that they'd had enough time, he held up a hand, and looking all around, he eyed each person, one by one, as he went on, "OK, all of you, you've had your turn. Now, if you let me—and you *will* let me," he paused, eyeing them, "—I'll tell you not only what will happen today, but how it will all end if we follow our orders and hold our ground in a disciplined way."

"We're way outnumbered," the lieutenant started to protest, but she backed off under Alex's impatient look and settled for just shaking her head and whispering, almost too low to be heard, "Just how are we gonna *peacefully* hold our ground against the kind of odds we've got here?"

"First, lieutenant, we will do just exactly what we're ordered to do," Alex replied, scowling at her before taking another quick glance at his watch. "We will form up in a solid military manner, and no matter what happens, we will not break ranks, nor will we make even the smallest move—body or mouth—without a proper command to do so.

"Second, they *will* try to intimidate us and force us to break ranks. We may even get some shoves, a punch or two, and even a lot of threats and verbal garbage, but we *will not* break ranks. None of us will Lone Ranger on the rest of us." As he spoke, he again looked around at each one in turn, and his eyes were sparking as he added. "We can leave here with a huge victory today, but only if things go as planned. If even one of you steps out of formation or if even one of you violates this order, chaos may ensue and cost us our victory. I know it'll be tough, but that's our plan, and you gotta trust us on this."

"Where do you want me?" Glenn asked. "I don't have my orders yet, but I'm on board to do whatever you say."

"You'll have the biggest job here," Alex replied, visibly relaxing as he turned to answer his old traveling companion's question. And laughing as he went on, he reached for Glenn's hand, squeezing it hard as he added, "Listen to me, my friend, I'm sending Little John over here to sit in that jeep with you, and it'll be your job to keep him from trying to find the jawbone of an ass so he can start slaying feds once they get in reach. He's not exactly a sit'n take it kind of guy. But Glenn, he's got to cool it this time, and you're the only one here who can keep him from blowing this whole thing wide open."

"You're saying this is all just a show?" another voice broke in. "Why? Why are we playing games here when we should be back there with our own people waging war on these thugs? They've come here and bombed us and killed us, and all we're doin' is watching their fancy PAC band and playing patty cake with them. I don't like it. And I'm not alone. We got hit hard, and we all want to hit back even harder!"

"No one likes it! But listen up, people, we're flat out not ready to win a fight right now, and this plan gives us time to get the supplies in place that we need to actually bloody their noses instead of settling for a mere symbolic gesture that leaves us with no gain and even more dead. You're going to have to trust me on this," Alex urged, and as he spoke, he offered a hand to both the woman who had questioned him earlier and the still grumbling man. The lieutenant accepted his handshake, but the man and some others in the group turned angrily away, still grousing and complaining. Glenn, watching it all, wondered how this group would hold together with a plan they didn't believe in.

"I don't know you," the man finally said, glaring back over his shoulder and still ignoring Alex's proffered hand. "But I can tell you this, major, I do know far too many of the good people who died here, and I know this town."

"Do you know the preacher?" Alex asked, and he carefully studied all their faces after he asked the question. Then, apparently liking what he saw, he added, "Well, this is his plan, and it'll work if we let it work ... if we *make* it work. It's all up to us."

"The preacher?" Several others mumbled, eyes flitting about. "Is he here?"

"I can't answer that question," Alex replied. "But this is his plan, and it's all been worked out by both sides over the last two days. Please believe me, this opportunity fell in our laps because bombing us was a stupid, hideous mistake on their part, and people who are important to them didn't like it. Because of that, we now have a shot at gaining a gift of time and postponing a battle we are woefully unready to fight. So work with us on this, and what could have been a defeat can become a victory." He smiled then as he looked around at all of them. These were good people; he knew it, and he trusted them.

"The preacher, all of us, are just asking for your trust," he went on. "We've got a lot in the works both here and across the country, and events are shaping up in our favor. We just need time for it to all fall in place, and as I said, striking back right now would be a horrible waste for us here, with too many good people dying for nothing more than a symbolic stand. So, instead of a loss like that, my friends, let's stand together, and we'll gain a victory here today—perhaps it'll seem like a strange victory, but it'll still be a real victory—if you see gaining the time we need and getting all the feds out of Fenton and leaving us fully in charge here again as a victory, as I hope you do."

With that, they broke up and the rest, being military, moved off to brief their troops and to get them into formation while a very disappointed Glenn returned to his jeep, as ordered. He felt like an idiot sitting there, the only one sitting in a row of empty jeeps, while the real warriors formed up in military units; this wasn't the big assignment he had expected; this was babysitting. Ten minutes later, as he sat slumped down in his seat still feeling sorry for himself, a large angry hulk slammed the back of passenger side front seat with his huge paw and plopped-down on the back seat next to him.

"Is this the way we're gonna to fight? Lincoln got rid of McClellan for using his troops to parade about instead of fighting." Little John was steamed and verbally off and running. "I'm not happy about this. I'm not happy about this at all. All this mumbo-jumbo about a big plan of some kind and a so-called gift of time!" He hit the seat again.

"Hey, I'm not happy about it either," Glenn replied in what he hoped sounded like a calming voice as he reached over to shake the other man's hand. John barely accepted the hand and so Glenn pressed his effort to calm him. "Come on, John, there's a bigger picture here. We have a plan that seems to have come to us all the way from the Alliance Round Table itself, and Alex said that it was the preacher who approved it. So we each need to do our part, whether we like it or not."

"And our part is to just sit here, no matter what happens, that's what Alex said. We've got to sit here and take whatever they dish out without givin' it back to 'em. He told me to do nothing even if they start cutting my hair and trimming my beard. That's stupid. You gotta be kidding me!"

"Orders are orders," Glenn replied, wondering about all the Sampson references from Alex; he didn't know the man was a Bible scholar. Smiling as he thought about that, he went on, eyeing John as he continued, "We do what we're told to do, no matter what they throw at us, and you just need to remember our little talk at the Two-Eyed Cyclops."

"I know, I know. I'm supposed to babysit you and not the other way around. I know that," Little John replied, but with a curious short laugh that was followed by a loud groan as he reached out and smacked the back of the seat in front of him, yet again. But then, after a side glance at Glenn, he grinned and added, "You know what? It doesn't make any sense. I need a haircut, I'll give him that, but I don't even have a stupid beard."

"I'm with you, old buddy." Glenn laughed, relaxing a bit. "I'm with you."

So smiling and now somewhat relaxed, both settled back to wait and to watch the two armies aligned across the field in front of them. One, numbered about three hundred by now, with most of them armed, and the other numbered only a few dozen, with only part of them armed with anything but a plan, a lot of faith, and steel resolve. Something big was about to happen that they didn't fully understand—didn't even make sense to many of them, but they were ready for it.

A few minutes later, two fighter jets roared overhead, and the band started playing again. But this time it played to welcome the two helicopters fluttering into view through the smoke, and as every-one watched, they circled down toward the parade ground and settled into the space between the two armies, kicking up an air gust of dirt, cinders, and debris that whipped over the waiting officials. Once the rotors came to a stop, the gust died down, and the two comrades leaned eagerly forward, keenly watching and waiting to see what would happen next.

"This is all a lot of garbage," Little John groused. "Alex told us that the music was from the director general's own marching band, so I'll bet one of those is her copter.

And those jets, they're probably the same ones that bombed us. They're all here for her."

"PAC director general," Glenn shrugged. "Big stuff. Bigger than the president."

"Oughta take her out right now," Little John replied. "She deserves to be dumped for all the evil she's done. Can you imagine how anyone like her sleeps at night?"

"No, I can't, but killing her wouldn't change anything in our favor," Glenn said, looking at his friend who seemed calm enough now, still mad, but more relaxed. Noting that, he relaxed himself as he added, "She's nothing more than a small cog in PAC's sick wheel of evil. She goes, someone else comes, nothing really changes."

"There she is now," Little John whispered, his eyes now full on the field.

Glenn, sitting up even straighter, watched as a head appeared in the copter's door, and he was surprised by the snappy salute the federal officer made as her leader was helped from the copter. Once she was on the field, he couldn't actually see her in the throng of people, even after standing to get a better view. Then, as the band replayed the PAC salute, a new flurry of activity began, and all attention turned back to the copter.

"It looks like the director's helping someone else off the copter, but I can't tell who," Little John called out as he also stood.

"I see a wheelchair there, but too many people to see who's in it," Glenn said.

They both sat back down then and waited for whatever was happening across the way to run its course. Something big had to be up to bring both the director and some hotshot guest here, and of course, the preacher was involved, although not out on the field. So this was a high level gala, but whether or not the Alliance would end up with more than it was giving up today was hard to know. Would they even be able to tell?

It took some twenty minutes to get the two dignitaries seated in a make-shift reviewing stand, and then the band moved to line up along the side the field, marching to *Semper Fidelis*, a tune that surprised Glenn even more than their first number. Leaning over to John, he shouted, "I'll bet Alex is steaming right now. Can you imagine the sheer gall of these people? Do you think they actually know what they're playing?"

"It'd be funny if he broke ranks and ran over there to stuff-snuff that band leader," Little John shouted back, grinning. "He's been worried about me and my temper—ha!"

Once the music ended, a new group straggled out into view, and recognizing them at once, Glenn quickly looked over at John and shifting in his seat shouted, "OK, Little John, you know these guys, and you know you gotta take it easy."

"Yeah, it's my old Brute Squad buddies," Little John grinned, his eyes narrowing as he spoke. "I know 'em well, and I've twisted those big noses before, more than once."

"Not this time," Glenn called back, reaching over to get a hand close to his buddy and shaking his head at John's pleased expression. Things might be ready to get a little hot here. Of course, he knew the Brute Squad was all male, all huge, and often used in Arbortown to put down riots, particularly between town and gown.

"These are the idiots who used to try to break up the singing at Hirve Park, and I had me a lot of fun knocking their heads together. They didn't even know I was a student, thought I was one of the townies." Little John laughed, causing Glenn to frown at the sparkle in his friend's eyes. "Yep, that was sure a lot of fun," the big guy added.

"OK," Glenn shouted. "Here they come. So, get ready, and remember our motto."

"What motto?"

"You got me, make one up," he called back, and then laughing, he added, "Oh, I forgot; you're a mute."

"Stuff it, don't remind me of that gig," Little John snapped back, scowling at Glenn. "But, whatever, this time's gonna be bad … probably worse than bad."

Federal troopers now began parading up and down the field, and the Brute Squad followed, but only for a short while. They soon moved away from their place at the rear of the main unit and headed directly toward the Whigville lines. It was worry time.

Glenn watched as the small alliance force stiffened in anticipation of the coming blows, but the squad angled off just as it reached them. And instead of crashing directly into their ranks, its members moved along close to the front of their formation, giving only an occasional shoulder bump against the Whig troopers whose ranks held for that first pass. But it wasn't over. Individuals now broke from the Brute Squad and began sliding in between the lines of the Whigville formation where they moved along roughly jostling, bumping, and stepping on toes, even as the band played on. From time to time, they paused to shout into the faces of certain troopers, those who looked like they might break. And then, moving roughly on, they repeated their obnoxious behaviors over and over again until, finally, it looked like they might be getting bored and ready to quit. It was then that they spotted Little John, and they moved in with big grins on their faces.

"What do we have here?" one of the squad moved up to Glenn's side of the jeep, but he was grinning over at Little John. "You sitting here with your daddy, little fella'?"

"Just move on," Glenn said, speaking through clenched teeth, and he tried to stay calm as he shifted to face the jeering oaf who was now being joined by several others.

They seemed to flock in from everywhere, and all began noisily sneering and jabbing at John—while pretty well ignoring Glenn. He, however, was keeping his eyes on John and flinching each time one of them ran a finger along the big man's face or poked at him. He can't handle this for long, Glenn thought, worried now, very worried.

"Look at the size of this boy's hand," one of them called out as a surprisingly compliant Little John allowed his hand to be lifted. "Look, watch the little fella slap his own face." There were two loud slaps, but still no reaction from Little John.

Glenn prepared to jump in if the slaps continued, but a big hand landed on his shoulder as he tensed to move, and he turned to find another squad member, blowing his foul breath and glaring directly at him. He started to shove the hand away, but held off, reminding himself that Little John was over there doing his part to keep his cool right now, but seeing Glenn get into a tangle with this guy might be all it would take to light his fuse. With that in mind, Glenn focused on his own self-control while still keeping a close eye on the game going on next to him. It all lasted for what seemed like an eternity, the squad members taking ever more painful liberties with John and a bit with him. But John sat quietly in his seat through it all, putting up with far more than Glenn endured.

"Well, I guess this little lad doesn't want to play with real men, probably afraid he'd get his little bottom kicked," one of the clowns sneered into John's face, and Glenn tensed, looking nervously toward his friend, but there still was no response from John.

Then, suddenly, it was over, and as the Brute Squad moved away, crashing back through the Alliance ranks as they left, a relieved Glenn sagged back with a sigh. "Those louts obviously had orders," he muttered. "They could hassle us, but not kill us."

"Probably, but it's not over 'till it's over," John replied in a surprisingly calm voice, and they both sat back to silently watch the frustrated creeps return to their spot behind the fed formation. The other federals then turned to line up for what was still to come, and the Brute Squad, moving off to the side, soon vanished.

A few moments later, a lone trumpet sounded, and the federal commander, with ten white-gloved feds at her side, marched to the middle of the field where they all turned to face toward the alliance team, marching out to join them.

A flurry of whispers then swept through the ranks on both sides of the field when the director general herself moved up to the front of the federal formation and turned there to wait for a lone person, rolling along behind her in an electric wheelchair. Once she was in place, the two moved across the field between the two formations to where the federal commander and Major Alexander Bullard Crosby both waited. Smiling at that, Glenn wondered if the director general found it insulting to meet Alex there; after all, only females could be officers these days in the PAC-marked federal forces units.

When the director's party reached them, the two commanders exchanged salutes, and then each turned to face and salute the director general. After which, she motioned for them to follow as she led them to the wheelchair where she introduced them both to the celebrity seated there. Glenn strained to see, but all he made out was that there seemed to be a woman in the chair, and it looked like she was taking Alex's hand and the hand of the federal commander and placing them together. For a moment, all three hands were touching, and then the two commanders stepped back, and after saluting each other again, they turned to move one to each side of the director general as she escorted the wheelchair occupant back off the field. It was only when they moved to return to their own positions that Glenn and others on his side of the field could see the face of the woman in the chair. It was the lady, herself, the grande dame of Chicago—of America!

He was amazed. The lady was the highest quotaed person in America, an icon for decades and the counselor—indeed, the maker—of a president. Somehow, to this day, as old as she was and despite all that had happened, she still remained a very popular woman in America. Very fascinated by it all, Glenn felt drawn to get out there and to be at least a small part of this history in the making, but he resisted that urge and settled for remaining a mere babysitting observer, as ordered. But now, sagging back into his seat, he shook his head in wonder. What was the preacher up to? How'd this all come to be?

The rest of the event was a blur. The dignitaries were whisked away in their copters, the band vanished, and the federals, all of them, saddled-up and moved off to the south. A bloodied and burned-out Fenton was left free for now, and the Whig forces, all alone on the field, formed up and moved away in a solid military manner, marching to an old favorite alliance tune, *Waltzing Matilda*. They were led as usual by two kilted pipers in tuneful memory of the long ago Grong Grong connection to alliance beginnings.

Thinking to himself that his day was now perfect, Glenn smiled through tears as he listened, recalling his own late parents' sacrifice in that isolated little town far out in the Australian countryside. But recovering quickly, he turned to Little John, laughed, and slapping his buddy on the back, congratulated him, "Good job, big guy. You had me worried. I thought you'd crack under the pressure, but you were magnificent."

"Me?" John looked over at him. "You're the one Alex and I were worried about."

"Why were you worried about me?" Glenn stared at him.

"You're the one that blew it at the Two-Eyed Cyclops, not me."

Realizing suddenly what had happened, Glenn didn't know whether to laugh or be angry. But he chose to join John, both laughing at Alex's plan to assign each of them to babysit the other one. "Well, anyway, no matter who the baby is and who's the sitter, it's clear now why your Brute Squad friends were so civilized," Glenn said.

"Yeah, they had the big gal, herself, watchin' 'em, and they followed the script," John said, still laughing. "They and everybody else knew that it was either do it her way, including that stupid holdin' hands thing, or they'd never see the light of another day—no excuses allowed. You can bet they hated it, and so did I. I wanted to bash 'em, real bad!

They were still laughing about it all when their driver returned to drive them to the next meeting place. And once they got inside there, they quickly forgot all about both the Brutes and who was doing the babysitting. They didn't care. The sight of the feast that was laid out for their victorious army was all they thought about, and they wasted no time plunging into it. Of course, Little John plunged into double portions.

Their very long day was now ending with a celebration of the strangest victory imaginable, but was it really a victory or just a brief time-out? Glenn hoped that it was a real victory and that Fenton would stay free. And deep down, he believed that it would all work out that way and that this gift of time would prove to be a glorious turning point in their total war to destroy PAC and to regain and even surpass America's past glory.

Sharing that thought in separate units now moving south with the federal forces, three of their seven angels silently echoed Glenn's joy and hope. And, of course, the other four, hearing about it later, would also lift a happy glass to what the alliance would come to call their, Reclaimed Initiative Victory.

"RIV it up!" would soon sweep the country and become a rallying call and a new battle cry from coast to coast, and that same night the Alliance began installing the much needed equipment that had just arrived, guaranteeing that enemy aircraft could no longer fly across Michigan's skies, without paying a too heavy price. At long last, the tide was turning toward a real and total victory for *E pluribus unum*.

CHAPTER TWENTY

The Things that will Destroy a People

Glenn awoke with a burst of energy Sunday morning, excited about yesterday for sure, but also because it was Sunday, and he was going to church in Whigville for the first time in his life. His trip was over—his new life was now beginning! Treasuring that thought, he looked around in the dim light for a token to set this moment in his mind forever. But he saw nothing inside, and so he eased himself out of bed and carefully barefooted his way to the windows, tripping over his boots along the way. Once there, he knelt down at a half open pane, raised it a bit more, and began searching through the faint light of the emerging dawn, hoping to spot just one thing among all of those vague forms out there to earmark this day for him. But after a few fruitless moments, he decided to just give up on the search and began easing himself to his feet. But wait! There *was* something out there that was summoning—not his eyes, but his ears.

Crouching again, he leaned against the screen, cocking his head to listen. Yes, there it was, the feint sound of laughing and talking on the other side of his building. "Of course! It will be *people,* not just a *thing* that marks my day," he whispered, and standing up once again, he turned with a broad smile on his face and rushed back toward his bed, tripping over his boots one more time on the way. He now had his token!

Savoring that thought, he washed and dressed quickly, and then, sucking in a deep thankful breath against the swelling in his chest, he stepped out the door into his new life.

"Ah, sleeping beauty. A bit late, but good to see you," Alex called from the porch floor, greeting Glenn with a raised cup of steaming black coffee, sloshing about in what looked to be an old military canteen holder. He was sitting by the stairs, leaning back against a post with one foot down a step and a big breakfast plate balanced on his knee.

Little John, sitting across the steps from Alex, was also propped-up against a post, balancing a much larger heap of chow in his big metal plate, but he didn't bother raising his cup. He was too busy eating. "Whoa, it doesn't look like the beauty sleep worked for you," he mumbled around a mouth full of hash and eggs. "Better give it a little more time—a month or more might do it. But no, frankly, I don't think there's much hope."

"You're right, this is as good as it gets." Glenn laughed, and looking over their food, he felt a sudden hunger pang despite last night's huge meal. So, rubbing his hands together in anticipation, he asked, "Where can a man find the chow line around here?"

"Not to worry," Alex replied. "No chow line for you, food's on its way even as you hunger. We heard you stumbling about in there after you finally got out the sack."

Laughing at the comment, Glenn plopped down on the steps between his two friends, and when his food arrived, he quickly joined them pushing down some corned beef hash, eggs, gravy, and biscuits, all hot and good. As they ate, Alex shared his take on yesterday's adventure, and Little John once again related in gory detail what he'd had in mind for the Brute Squaders who'd hassled him, if things had gone wrong. However, Glenn got the biggest laugh by admitting that, although it annoyed him that Alex had assigned Little John to babysit him; he had come very close to being the one to blow it.

Of course, their conversation inevitably turned to the lost Brighton Worthy with all three sharing their own feelings about him and agreeing that yesterday's gift of time triumph, confusing as they still found it to be, should be dedicated to him.

"You know, I'm gonna miss you two," Little John said, standing after they'd all finished eating. "But I'm tired of babysitting and ready to find some real action."

"Hey, you'll *create* the action wherever you go, not find it, and that's been a big part of our fun together," Glenn said, and grinning over at him, he added, "And now you guys have your orders, and you're all set. But me, I'm still hanging and waiting, and frankly, I'm tired of always being the odd man out."

"Well, odd man, yes, but you can relax about the *out* part," Alex replied, and nodding toward Little John, he stood and moved down the steps and out into the yard.

"You'll always be the odd man, Glenn, but the odd man in, not out." John laughed, and then he began collecting their dishes. Once he had them all in hand, he turned and quietly carried them away, leaving a confused Glenn staring after him.

Alex, laughing at John's comment, said, "I knew he'd get in a shot at you, but he's right about you being, in. There'll be a jeep coming by shortly to whisk you away to Whigville Centre." And noting Glenn's obvious confusion, he added, "We'll follow in a day or two, once things are settled here. John'll be joining a training command, and I'm set for a short senior officer gig. After that, I'll be off. I don't know where to."

"What else?"

"What'd you mean?" Alex looked at him, and then, toying with a smile, he went on, "Oh yes, you'll be on the road soon, and so you'll have to miss church today."

"Come on, Alex, you sent Little John away for some reason."

"Was it that obvious? I must be losing my touch." Alex laughed. "But you can relax, it's nothing sinister; John just isn't cleared to see who picks you up. It's silly, he'd never say anything, but we do what we're told to do in the corps—and in the alliance."

"Am I cleared to know who's picking me up?" Glenn asked, studying his friend.

"Sure, his name is Atticus Ingles. John overheard the name when I got the word, and so he had to go. Ingles, by the way, will be with the lady who's going to take charge of you after you get toured and debriefed a bit." Alex spoke in a matter-of-fact, no big deal manner that usually means it is a big deal, but Glenn didn't catch that obvious clue. He was too eager for Whigville. About ten quiet minutes later, they heard the sound of a vehicle coming, and as he stood to greet it, Glenn felt his heart rate spike in anticipation. This was it—Whigville time!

And then came another treat. As the jeep pulled up next to them, Glenn laughed at the sight of the man in the passenger seat and bounded down the stairs to greet him. "Dell-X! It's great to see you. I didn't expect to see you again so soon," he shouted, and seizing the older man's hand, he began pumping it rapidly, up and down.

"And good to see you, my friend, but take it easy; I'm an old guy, and as you say, it hasn't really been that long." Dell-X laughed as he spoke, but he was making a very real effort to slow down the handshake.

"I'm sorry. I just wasn't expecting to see you right now." Glenn replied, flashing an embarrassed smile as he looked over Dell-X's shoulder, hoping to see his contact. But there was only the driver in the jeep, probably the woman that Alex had mentioned. And so, frowning in confusion, first at Dell-X and then at Alex, Glenn added a tentative, "I thought I'd be meeting someone, that there'd be someone else here, my new contact."

"Someone else?" Dell-X cut in. "Well, the only, else, with me is one of my oldest friends, Lee Sharp. Lee is an alliance leader, and I believe Alex told you that she'll be your ramrod beginning today, so you've got a couple reasons to treat her right."

Lee smiled and waved at him from behind the wheel, but she didn't say anything, leaving the still confused Glenn to politely smile and nod in return before turning to look back at Dell-X again. The older man, still saying nothing, maintained the same wide-eyed innocent look that he'd assumed when he first spoke. That should have been yet another clue, but Glenn was still oblivious, and so Dell-X, giving up on his little joke, raised both hands in an *oh-well-what-can-you-do-this-guy's-clueless* sign. And turning back to Alex, now leaning against his old post on the porch and enjoying the show, the older man pointedly asked, "What's this youth going on about?"

"Can't even guess." Alex shrugged, shaking his head in pretended wonder.

"Well, Alex, you said something about … I mean, I was expecting …" Glenn started, but a laughing Dell-X waved his hands to stop him from going on.

And raising his voice to cut him off, Dell-X called out, "Oh, I know, I know. Alex said something about an Atticus Ingles." That stopped Glenn, and the older man, now grinning broadly, scratched his head, looking first at Alex and then back toward Glenn as he added, "Isn't that the name that almost got us hung back at the campground?"

"Campground? What're you talking about?" Glenn sputtered, looking from one man to the other as the truth slowly dawned on him. "Atticus Ingles, that's *your* name!"

"Yep, and now you know why I've kept it a secret all these years."

"It is quite a handle, but I wouldn't call Dell-X exactly neat and ordinary," Glenn shot back, and the other three all laughed with him.

Ten minutes later a very excited Glenn was packed with his gear into the backseat of the jeep, and Lee was bouncing both Dell-X and him north along Fenton Road. And as they rode along, Glenn looked all around, taking in this Whigville dream he had finally realized, and feeling very full of the moment. Those were real people out there, not clueless feds or campus lay-abouts, but real people doing real work on real farms. It all seemed so right to him that he whispered, in a voice louder than he realized, "Even the air seems brighter and fresher here!"

"This is Baldwin Road," Lee called back over her shoulder, smiling at the young man's enthusiasm as she slowed the jeep to a stop at the intersection. "We fought a big battle here four years ago. Threw together a pile of logs and junk culled from all over the place and named the results Fort Zigzag. We built it like a maze, and so it confused the feds when they got into it, with all its zigzagging towards that small lake there. The ones in the front could see that they were headed into water and tried to stop, but their buddies in the rear were under pressure from us, and they kept pushing them forward, forcing their own people on into the lake. What a circus!

"Of course, it was a bitter victory ... with a very high price—they killed five of our people during the fight. Sure, we captured about a thirty of them, but big deal, they were swapped-out, and who knows? They were probably part of that miserable fed-crew yesterday. They survived, but our heroes aren't here helping us." She swallowed hard, pausing just for a moment before adding, "They'll never fight by our side again."

They drove on in silence after Lee's comments, the farmland giving way briefly to homes along both sides of the road, all looking like they'd been empty for many years. Then, after turning right onto Grand Blanc Road, heading east, they passed a couple more working farms followed by more empty, sagging houses, and then blocks of vacant and decaying apartment buildings. An overgrown park slid by on the north, just before a long closed school and more houses, with most of them now seeming to be occupied. Great!

"We're in Grand Blanc," Lee called out. "And we've survived the collapse here better than many other places because we returned to our farming roots right away. The land you see all around us is being worked, and our people are very well fed."

"Getting gas for tractors is a problem, and so horses are in style again. It's sorta like the nineteenth century's come back around, and with all our land under cultivation, even the school district's athletic fields, we need those beautiful creatures," Dell-X added as they turned north onto Porter Road. "And at long last, the message seems to be getting through to most people. We're all doing well because we're focusing on getting our act together again, no hangdog, wait for a handout for us. We ain't gonna stay down long."

"I've ridden in a couple of horse-pulled wagons lately, but never been on one," Glenn said, and eyeing the animals with appreciation, he added, "But I wanta try it."

He continued to think about those horses and the reborn fields as they rode on in silence past more homes, most now occupied. And then it happened. After turning right on Gibson, they crossed Dort and came upon a sight that Glenn had never seen before: a real shopping center, all open, with real people shopping! Arbortown had been relatively prosperous, but its malls were in ruins, and the stores were either shutdown or part of the PAC collective, meaning all very dull, drab, and poorly stocked. But this place was a real old-fashioned mall, and it all looked to be open for business!

"This, my friend, is Whigville Centre, the American hub of the Whig Partisan Alliance," Dell-X announced, beaming with pride as he pointed out the stores, and Lee obliged by driving them in a circular route through the mall to give Glenn a sense of its size and activity. "There's a bookstore, a real one, with no Internet, we're back to books, and over there's a restaurant with more on the other side of the building. There's a big grocery store, and—we're here." They circled to a stop in front of what had once been a large retail business of some kind, but now looked to be an office complex.

"This is Alliance Central," Lee said, taking up the briefing as they dismounted.

"You'll be living here in the dorms we have for trainees and some instructors, and of course, we have the usual offices and training rooms. There aren't many cars these days, so the parking lot we're on is also our parade ground and drill field."

"Very impressive," Glenn said, looking appreciatively at the buildings and across the rolling surface of the old parking lot. Everything he saw seemed to be in good repair and well-used. "A parking lot plus a drill field—for the military, I guess."

"Better guess again, my friend." Dell-X laughed, and pointing to the east across Dixie Highway, he added, "The military trainees live and do most of their work over there. That's where Little John will be, but this'll be your baby, and you'll be sweatin' buckets, marching and working out, right here. Today is your last day of idle bliss."

"We, in the alliance, believe that Americans allowed themselves—pretty much the whole nation—to become spiritually, emotionally, mentally, *and* physically soft," Lee said, taking over the narrative as they walked toward the entrance across what Glenn, all too soon, would learn to call *the Grinder*. "Reclaiming America means convincing all the people to tackle their own softness problems head-on, first, and to then turn to help others do the same. We want Americans, themselves, to freely choose to work together toward a more disciplined future for all."

"That includes political, social, and cultural flab," Dell-X added as he stepped out ahead of them to get the door. "We didn't keep our politicians on a leash, and so they played us off against each other, and *from many, one* became *for my group, everything, for all others, nothing*. The failed beggar-the-future order we have now is where that kind of small thinking nonsense will always take a people. But beginning here and in hundreds of other places all around the world, liberty's torch is now being rekindled, and the fire it lights will bring the dream of *E pluribus unum* back to life again. And, Glenn, this time it will be everywhere. It'll be everywhere because it must be everywhere or the rot of *my kind over your kind* will continue to pollute the world, and sooner rather than later, it'll raise its ugly head and bring us down again."

Glenn was still thinking about those words as they moved past a squad of young security guards. He guessed they were all teenagers, but they wore freshly pressed, very sharp uniforms, like nothing he'd seen before on an American—on Chinese, yes, but not our gals and guys. And as they walked along, he noted that the workers all appeared to be in very good physical condition. He smiled; perhaps they'd be out there with him on the grinder. As for the clothes, he had been more casual than these people, but he liked what he now saw. Smiling at that thought, he nodded pleasantly at the group passing by them right then and reached out to slap hands, but Lee intercepted the move.

"They're on duty, Glenn," she admonished him. "No fraternizing while on-duty, their focus and our focus is on duty, not socializing. It's our new way, so get used to it. We have to move beyond the gaga era of perpetual adolescence that brought us down."

Laughing at her wording, he glanced over at her expecting to see a big grin, but he saw instead that she was very serious. That sobered him, and thinking about it as they walked along, he began studying the people working all around them more closely, and he saw something new. He saw young people of all colors, shapes, and sizes, and while they were all seriously on-duty, getting their jobs done, they also seemed to be in good spirits. It was so unlike the all chaos, all the time, at Arbor U, with its teeming—and controlling--minority of PAC-obsessed mouth-running, privilege-mongering, ego-nursing *victims*. Frowning, he thought regretfully about the lost dream of that old university and about the city of Arbortown, about its old beauty, its long wonderful history, and its lost present. It was all so sad; the place and city he loved were now reduced to being nothing more than just part of the vast spiritual landfill that was our national purpose gone wrong.

Still weighing these thoughts, he looked over to share with the other two just in time to see Dell-X wave to a man standing near a door at the back of the building. The man waved back and stood smiling at them as they approached. And then, after shaking hands, he led them inside to a not plush, but very clean and professional looking office where what their guide referred to as the Sunday mini-staff was bustling about.

In keeping with the customs of the times, neither the man who met them, nor the young woman he handed them off to give their names. Instead, she simply greeted them and, quickly taking charge, led them past several named or numbered doors to the back of the building and the only unmarked door. Stopping there, she leaned in close, listened, and then knocked, very gently. Getting no reply, she smiled reassuringly at the three and, opening the door, ushered them inside.

"It's Sunday, so he'll be in the chapel for a few more minutes, but please have a seat, and he'll be with you shortly." She spoke in a hushed tone, and before closing the door to leave them, she motioned toward the only furniture in the room: five tall, stark look-ing, straight backed wooden chairs lined up side by side along the wall to their left.

The other two sat down and started chatting at once about changes that had been made since Dell-X was last here and about old friends and colleagues, but Glenn was too curious about where he was and why he was here to just sit and wait. Besides, the room itself nagged at him. Those chairs, the dim light, and the gray painted walls with just that one large picture hanging across from him near the only window were all just too stark and depressing to be that way by accident. And besides, looking around at it all, he sensed that this strange room had something to do with his assignment. But, what?

Curious to see what was outside, he walked over towards the window to take a look, but a strange thing happened as he passed in front of the picture. He only glanced at it, but something about the two half poster-sized photographs positioned side by side in the same large frame stopped him.

One picture was of the Washington DC mall as it looked years ago with the then still open Capitol building standing proudly in the background. Obviously taken in the spring, it showed the trees and flowers in beautiful bloom, all radiating warmth and a sense of new beginnings, anchored by the touch of the old and enduring in that majestic building. He shook his head, smiling wistfully at that scene of what had once been a great national centerpiece. It was all mostly gone now, both the beauty and the hope it represented—as was that old building, for all practical purposes.

Sighing as he thought about that lost past, he allowed his eyes to shift away to the other photograph, and he was jolted as he looked at it. Taken a year or two ago in stark black and white, this picture presented the same view, but in a cold winter scene—and there was no sense of beauty or new beginnings here. Instead of the spring warmth and the impression of enduring seen in that first picture, this one seemed to be coldly shouting out, "All is lost. It's over. Endure if you can! Endure what you can!"

But it wasn't just the absence of color or the skiff of snow or the dark skies that caused the chill that ran up his spine as he looked at that sad scene. No, there was much more to it than just the bleakness of winter hanging over Washington D.C. This picture was not a mere seasonal statement. This picture was a judgment.

The once proud building that stood as a cornerstone to a great and growing nation in the first picture now sagged in dark and forbidding ruin in the second, like a toppled gravestone. And its foreground was littered with piles of kindling stripped from what was left of the stick-like trees that still lined the old mall behind rows of shaky stick huts and hole-ridden, sagging tents. Yet, there was something else. As gut-wrenching as that portrait of defeat was, even that was not enough to evoke the mood of evil-doom that Glenn felt, and as he struggled to control his breathing, he looked for a "why" answer.

Searching the picture, he looked for truth … and, yes, he found it. It wasn't just that this once great city now lay in ruins that clutched and held him; no, he was captured by the horror carved into his soul at the sight of the *people* there. Clothed in rags and bending faceless under tattered blankets, they stood over fires, stirring pots of uninviting rations for their even more tragic children—children huddling together to gain just a bit more warmth close to those illicit fires. And he realized that it was especially to the few visible faces of those children that his reluctant eyes were drawn—and held.

Their wide, soulful eyes seemed to be starring up and out of that picture, and they pointed directly out at the viewer like jabbing fingers of blame, silently calling down a judgment on each and every person alive now and on all of the past generations that had failed them—had failed these, their own children.

Shivering suddenly against the bone-grasping chill he felt on this hot August day, he inadvertently held his breath as he looked at this picture of horror undeserved. And then, breathing again, he swallowed to ease the burn in his throat, and blinking his eyes against threatening tears, he tried to turn away, to turn away from that picture, from those eyes, but he couldn't do it—not at first. No, it took all his strength to pry his own now fearful eyes away from those, oh-so-judging, other eyes. But … he finally did it.

He finally managed to overcome the wave of emotion that held him—and to look away. And as he stepped backwards, his knees feeling weak and his breathing labored, he forced himself to turn aside, hoping to get away to somewhere, anywhere else. But some mysterious force seemed to direct him, forcing him to turn back to those pictures, and this time his weary eyes traveled by their own volition to a quote below those tragic images, a quote he knew well because his mentor had insisted that he memorize it. It was from a speech that was made almost a hundred and a half years ago, during another very challenging time in our country, a speech made by President Teddy Roosevelt:

The things that will destroy America are prosper-
ity at any price, safety first instead of duty first,
a love of soft living and the get-rich-quick theory
of life. This Country will not be a permanently
good place for any of us to live unless we make
it a reasonably good place for all of us to live.

"Powerful stuff," whispered Dell-X. Now standing next to Glenn, he gestured around at the stark cold walls of the room and added, "This all actually says the same thing. We had a challenge to rise to, a people to lead through the wilderness, and we blew it, we blew it bigtime. That's what those kids in the picture are accusing us of, and Teddy's words speak today not only to and for Americans, but to and for all of the other once privileged nations—and to the world." As Glenn nodded in sad agreement, Dell-X pointed over to the room's lone window, just off to their right, and grimly pursing his lips, he added, "Out there, Glenn, just below the window, is our new mission statement. Take a look at it and tell me what you think."

"Out there?" Glenn replied in a hoarse, dry-throated whisper, and expecting to see an inspirational sculpture of some kind, he moved thankfully over to look out at it. But instead of the expected work of uplifting art, he saw that their window was just above the loading dock and that directly below them stood a half-full, dark, filthy dumpster-wagon, complete with mice and flies and stink. Confused at first, he peered down, studying it for a long minute, and then, running his tongue over his now dry-feeling lips, he mouthed a short prayer and then slowly nodding, whispered, "Yes, I see it. This filthy dumpster represents our *now* reality—what is, is. It speaks to where we are *now*, just like those two pictures do—and like all the 'night caller' kids we saw on the way to the Two-Eyed Cyclops did. They all say the same thing: there's work to do and we need to do it, *now*."

"Well put, Glenn," a new voice came from the now open door behind them, and Glenn turned around to see a tall, somewhat stooped, white-headed man with a close cut beard smiling over at him, and he was leaning on a very familiar looking walking stick.

Glenn's eyes locked on that stick. It looked just like his own, out in the jeep!

"You guessed it, they're twins, my version of Teddy R's *Big Stick*," the man said, holding up his own. "I heard how you got one of these, but I've come to need mine for walking these days a lot more than you need yours, a product of both our age difference and of my several tours over the years in a few PAC reeducation camps."

Dell-X was also surprised by the older man's quiet entry, but recovering quickly, he rushed over to greet and embrace his old friend. And then he turned and, gesturing toward Glenn, announced with a broad, proud smile, "Sir, it's my honor to present one of my newest friends, Glenn Alleyne Stanton. And, Glenn, I'd like to introduce you to one of my oldest friends. Please say hello to the Reverend Ian Pennington."

"The preacher?" Glenn had the words out before he realized how star-struck they made him sound, and he rushed to retrieve his error—but failed. "I mean, of course. Ah, yes sir, it's so good to see you, ah, to meet you … at last … sir …"

"Glenn, I've looked forward to meeting you for a long time. Please call me Ian."

The preacher spoke with a warm smile, and taking the young man's right hand in both of his, he studied his face with fatherly affection and then pulled him in for a hug. "You are the son of old and dear friends who suffered far more than I did in those camps, and I'm so glad to see you here. But come, let's all go up to my study to get better acquainted; it's a bit more comfortable up there. This room is my combination prayer closet and decompression chamber. I want my guests to use it to refocus on our mission when they come to visit me, but I use it too, coming here to pray when I find myself forgetting who I am and how little I did to help stop the fall of our great nation."

"Well, sir, I think you did a lot," Glenn started to protest, but he stopped when Ian shook his head and, holding up a somewhat trembling finger, pointed toward yet another framed piece behind him. Glenn had overlooked it before because it was on the same wall as their entry door but on the other side of it, away from the chairs positioned there.

The new picture contained a collage of what had to be photos of politicians, all with blurred faces. Some of the pictures were large and some were small, some in color and some in black and white, but they all caught their subjects in what looked to be their campaign poses with political slogans displayed around them like crisscrossing snakes, curling all about each picture in pink and purple and green. And beneath it all, so faint that it was almost not showing, was a reproduction of that stark black and white photo of Washington DC. And as Glenn studied it, he noted the bold lettered quote below the picture that revealed all anyone needed to know about today's challenge:

ALL WITHIN THE STATE, NOTHING OUTSIDE THE STATE, NOTHING AGAINST THE STATE. —Benito Mussolini

"That, Glenn, is the real *Power-at-the-Center* position that the so-called Peace, Accommodation, and Culture party represents," Ian said. "And like Nazis, Communists, and Benito, PAC believes that the state and the party are one, and more tragically, they agree with the devil himself in C. S. Lewis's *Screwtape Letters*: '[That] to us a human is primarily food; our aim is absorption of *its* will into ours.' Absorption is PAC's true aim.

"Such totalitarian beliefs are the real enemy that took the lives of your parents and of millions upon millions of others around the world in the past and of course, continue to do so today," continued Ian. "For us, today in America, those words describe not only PAC's position, but also where we as a people are now, after frittering away the gift left by the founders and passed on until it got to us. For the rest of the world, it represents the much darker life they now face because we—and they—went wobbly and fumbled away that gift of freedom." Ian spoke softly, and there was a hint of a deep sad shadow across his face as he turned to leave, gesturing for them to follow him.

"An awareness of this must shape our planning and doing as we go forward, Glenn. Our starting point is now, our starting place is right here," Lee whispered as they moved into the elevator with Ian. Moments later, the doors reopened onto the beautiful rooftop patio garden outside Ian's study, and a wide-eyed Glenn stepped out, silently looking all around. This was Whigville. His new beginning had begun.

"When my son-in-law was a young man, he once played with the notion that this earth of ours might be nothing more than God's feedlot for souls, as he called it." Ian spoke as he directed them across the garden to some comfortable, cushioned chairs in a gazebo that overlooked the parade ground. "According to that notion, what we do or don't do with our lives doesn't make any real difference. We're only here so our bodies can provide a nurturing vehicle to get us, as souls, on to our real purpose, which is to take soul-wing and fly off into eternity. Towards what? Some people think it's to do very important work, and I certainly hope that's right, but only God knows."

"So he thought we're sort of like Japanese Beetles," Glenn said, playing with the idea. "They start as grubs, hanging out in the soil, and then take wing and attack our trees. Eating to live to eat seems to be their only purpose for living. Is that all we are?"

Dell-X, who was filling coffee cups and passing out donuts, laughed at Glenn's example, but said nothing. He knew how important this meeting was to Ian.

"Yes, I see your point," Ian replied, also laughing. "He, at least, compared us to butterflies, but it's all stuff and nonsense either way. On the other hand, your example fits us better than his in one way. The single party statists, now controlling so much of the world, toiled hard in the political, social, and certainly the easily rolled over academic soil under various ism-guises for many decades before emerging openly to attack our social branches as true power-at-the-center types. But those branches were left weakened by the many flabby generations of Americans who inherited the gift of healthy, strong roots, but didn't have the grit to do the heavy lifting necessary to maintain a free and open society. And like your beetles, PAC feeds on those neglected branches, consuming the leaves of our present and future and gifting us with the present blight of PAC misrule. But don't despair, Glenn. If we're willing to finally do the heavy lifting and spraying and pruning that needs to be done, all this idiocy will be only a temporary nightmare."

"Sir, are we doing the heavy lifting we need to do when we work with the bad guys?" Glenn asked, thinking of his own walking stick as he nodded toward Ian's. "I got my stick from a very amiable Chinese officer whose people had just bombed Fenton.

I didn't know it at the time, but they had just killed and wounded a lot of good Americans in what was truly a criminal bombing run. Did he get the stick he gave me from you?"

"Yes, he did, and you're right to ask about it," Ian replied. "But consider this, within our values and reason, we must do what we have to do to win. We talked about human rights during our own revolution and—correctly, I believe—pulled ourselves away from a people we called tyrants who, ironically, were even then beginning to move themselves and the world toward an end to the widespread evil of the slavery that *we* still supported. In World War II, we—also correctly—allied ourselves with the Communists who, I believe, were worse than the Nazis, and then we had to turn to face off against that ally in a long and bitter Cold War. Right now, my own preference would be to work with India, because I think that country offers a more likely road back to real freedom for the world and for us. But as India has very little presence over here, our choices are PAC, Russia, or China. Russia is focusing on consolidating its position in Europe, and so they're more a nuisance than a threat to us. China is over-extended and will have to pull back soon to deal with serious internal and regional problems in Asia, but they're here right now, and they've helped us against our main enemy. PAC is that main enemy, and they're not going anywhere unless we defeat them. This nation cannot recover until we destroy PAC, root and branch. That means that we will sometimes work with China.

"And, Glenn, I believe yesterday's result shows that to be the right choice. I can't tell you the number, but many lives were saved by yesterday's agreement, and I can tell you that our victory gave us time to get ready to push back—hard. Now, once you finish training and get into the field, perhaps you'll help us find a better balance point. We'll be open to your ideas, but even then, we will continue to need to make tough tradeoffs."

"Sir, I drove through Fenton." Glenn continued with his point. "I saw what they did there, and everyone knows about the firing squads and prison camps in Detroit. I just don't understand how we can overlook all of that."

"I hear you, but I'm not sure you hear me," Ian replied, and standing, he walked slowly across to the rail overlooking the grinder. Turning around there, he faced them again, and leaning back against that rail, he took a sip of coffee and, peering over his cup, smiled at Glenn. "My young friend, I should have mentioned earlier that the friendlies who allowed that bombing run to happen and the PAC leaders who pushed for it are all paying for their mistake, which is the only reason we were able to negotiate yesterday's farce and buy ourselves the time I mentioned. Only days ago we were getting ready for an all-out battle with the feds that we had no chance to win. Today, we're sitting up here peacefully enjoying the warm sunshine. Tomorrow, new supplies that just came in, will allow us to counter whatever they throw at us, including jets. And Glenn, I believe that we're now on the verge of putting PAC off balance both here *and* across this great land.

"But that doesn't mean there won't be the same kind of evil attack again if PAC and the friendlies decide they want to do it, and we will surely be faced with decisions about making other compromises every step of the way going forward. Your mentor and I wrestled with this issue for years, but let me approach it this way. Blaise Pascal made the point of my position way back in the 1600s when he wrote of the sheer folly of the human condition. He offered the example of a river, which he said had his friends on one side, and on the other side there were people whom he'd be praised for killing—as I think he put it. His point was that we humans, foolishly feeling cut off from God, are endlessly preoccupied with defining ourselves as OK. We then group ourselves to face off against other not-OK groups: tribes, clans, nations, ethnic or religious groups— you name it.

"It's my belief that our people, Americans for sure, but also all other privileged peoples, are called in modern times to build bridges that will put an end to that kind of ancient tribalism and clan-ism. It divides us and holds us down. Think of Afghanistan or any of several countries in Africa or Asia right now, or think of one of my own ancestral homes, Scotland, many years ago. All failed to move beyond tribalism or clanism in time to stand as one against their enemies, and all paid the price for that.

"But I wander afield. Let's get back to us. By the mid-1960s, it looked like we had the job of becoming one with each other well started, but then we fell into the trap of the endless divisions and group power seeking of the late 1960s and beyond. It's our task now to undo that misstep and to honestly build and not just talk about building bridges to each other. We must take the Whig Partisan Alliance creed seriously: First, let's be honest with ourselves about our own shortcomings by holding ourselves up to the Two-Eyed Cyclops mind/soul test. And second, we must reach out past today's Hush-Now garbage to engage others as caring listeners; and finally, we have to commit ourselves to a no-exceptions *E pluribus unum*. That means that all of us must reach out from our own groups, whatever they are, to embrace others on the bridge and then to help those others do the same thing, passing it all forward in time and outward, all around us."

"What does all that mean in relation to your stick?" Glenn persisted, nervously pointing at it and swallowing hard as he added, "Sir, I'm not trying to pick a fight, I just want to understand. How can we work with people like the friendlies?"

"I hear you, Glenn, but there are no perfect allies. We're a bit like a drowning swimmer, grabbing any hand that reaches out to us. Right now, that's the Chinese, but it may be someone else on down the line. Our eye must stay on our mission," Ian replied.

"But let's be clear about this, Glenn. I'm not talking about vainly and haughtily running about apologizing for ourselves all over the place, and I'm certainly not talking about holding ourselves up to some self-indulgent perfect standard while accepting and blindly accommodating pure evil on the part of others. We've seen how that kind of PAC pathology works over the last many years. Pascal talked about that kind of self-insecurity, which I think, in the past, was seen mostly among elites who knew they didn't deserve what they had. But here, in our time, we've managed to make it a broad-based round-up corral for all the PAC toadies, endlessly chanting, *Down with Ustatesia; it's all bad—all but own narrow little, self-privileging, wonderful group.*"

"Why not just focus on ourselves?" Glenn asked, and recalling the major's words, he added, "Is it really our duty to run around the world, trying to save the democratic souls of others by helping them build and rebuild over and over again?"

"Wow, this conversation is wandering afield, a bit, but I'll answer your question. Yes, I think it's our God-given duty to help others, but by that, I mean that we, the people, should help others, not by forcing anything, but by modeling the character and the kinds of behaviors and attitudes that help people prosper. That means we have to get our own act together as a people and keep a harness on our politicians. But Teddy's words apply now, here in America, and they apply everywhere, unless we help make it reasonably good for most people everywhere, it won't be good for anyone for long. Rot spreads."

As he spoke, Ian returned to his chair, and glancing around as he sat down, he shook his head and laughed. "That blasted stick, I think I'll give up carving these things."

"No, sir, I didn't mean ..." Glenn started, but the preacher waved him off.

"It's OK, it's OK, we're good, Glenn." Ian laughed. "Our way forward calls for each and every one of us to show honest respect for all others, and that means—and this is crucial—holding not only ourselves accountable, but those others as well, beginning with those closest to us. Let's try to understand each other by *listening* to other opinions, not just pushing our own. Let's raise each other up instead of shouting each other down."

"I understand, sir. I've been well-schooled in our creed," Glenn said, and now embarrassed by his stick fixation, he tried to apologize, "I shouldn't have pushed ..."

"No, no, you had an itch and you felt safe to scratch it," Ian replied. "A huge problem for us since the late sixties has been the *hush-now* attitude that cuts off that kind of honesty. PAC's shutting-off others and penalizing them for questioning so-called settled science, or settled anything else, greased the skids for our fall from power. We need to be an open society that not only tolerates but encourages honest civil debate."

"And, Glenn, you're here because you were chosen. Do you know why?" Lee cut in to get them back on schedule. And after she spoke, she cleared her throat and turned in her seat to closely watch the young man's face as he answered.

"My parents died fighting PAC," he replied, lowering his eyes as he replied.

"That's only partially right," Ian said. "Your parents' sacrifice marked you for nurturing. They were both close friends, and I owe them a lot, but you had to earn your own way here, and you've done that. And let me add,"—he chuckled—"that you've also proven your mettle by challenging me on the stick thing, reminds me of your mother, no hush-now, shrinking violet, she. But now, it would be my honor to welcome you into the Blue Company, if you're ready—and willing to suffer through a little training that is."

"But you need to understand what that means," Dell-X stepped in. "There are some very good people among us who want to just withdraw from society and to focus on their own close-knit communities. But we, in the alliance, aren't called to that kind of service. A better example for us is the German theologian, Dietrich Bonheoffer. He gave his life trying to save his people from the Nazi horror of the 1930s and 40s, and he said that God wants us to be real human beings, not ghosts who shun the world. Our task now, like his was then, is to begin by reaching out to those closest to us, right here, and to work with them to rebuild the little 'help others' platoons that once shored up this great land."

"That's right, Glenn," Ian said. "Those platoons are our key to the future. We'll need to link with others to keep the bridge open for all. Otherwise, we become mere tribes caught up in the ancient game of my group over yours again—and we all lose."

"And Bonheoffer said something else that's key for us," Lee said, smiling and reaching over to squeeze Glenn's arm as she spoke. "He said that in all of human history the most significant hour we have is the present, and if we want to make this world better, we need to serve our own times, where we live and work. Is it OK for us to regret that we face what we face? Sure. But we are immobilized if we content ourselves with silly blame seeking and finger-pointing. That's a very big 'no.'"

"I agree with you," Glenn said. "The Founders handed off freedom's baton, and it's been every generation's job since then to take it, to run an honest race, and to pass it on to the next generation. But that baton slipped out of our hands a while back, and it's now rattling around on the ground, waiting for us to grab it up and to get back in the race again—not to stand around, self-grooming and pointing fingers at others, and not by elbowing potential allies aside in order to gain or preserve our own special little place."

"I like that dropped baton image. Let me build on that," Ian said. "The key for us all right now is to establish a new political and social rule for how we position our ... let's call it, our 'pivot foot.' Lately, we've been required to plant our hopes and dreams and sense of self and community foot on the special-privileges-for-favored-groups spot, as decreed by PAC. That has divided us and brought us down. The alliance calls for us to place our pivot foot squarely on the *E pluribus unum*-friendly rule of fairness-for-all spot—as free individuals and not as mere groupies seeking privilege or favor over others.

"We all should have stepped-up in the 90s to turn things around. Our economic and social plight was obvious to everyone by then, and both political parties talked about doing something—but they only talked, they didn't do. And the crazy rioting that swept the country during the *2018 Rising* should have ended by moving us to come together as one people, seeking solutions and not scapegoats. But instead, we fell short. By not stepping-up to slap a bridle on our above-us-in-the-clouds, self-grooming politicians and preening elites—or especially, *ourselves*—we accelerated our downward spiral.

"After those *Bash-the-Boomers* riots were over, we got what we didn't need. Yet another destructive round of mindless bellying up to the pig-trough of government handouts, all supported by empty political promises and a soon to be dead dollar—replaced now by unies and fed-script." Laughing, he added, "And, obviously, we also didn't need my pathetic *World Wide Hogarth Redux Plan*. What a stupid name and plan that was!"

"Benjamin told me about your plan. He said it should have worked," Glenn said.

"He didn't understand why our people, particularly in the Heartland, didn't embrace it."

"You know, W. E. B. DuBois urged a similar thing early in the twentieth century, Ian said. "He called for a *Talented Tenth* to take responsibility to be models for others. Before that, the churches led a major turnaround in England in the eighteenth century, but a new talented-tenth leader didn't step forward here, and our churches were too busy following either PAC or their own narrow interests to lead us out of the wilderness. But in fairness, the biggest part of the problem, I believe, was that we weren't willing to risk or tolerate honest debate. That left us all to twist alone in the PAC-directed social winds."

Smiling a sad smile, he looked around at the others as he added, "And honestly, I wasn't the right person for the job anyway. My silly effort flopped big-time, and I didn't handle that failure very well. I felt that I'd stepped out to do the Lord's work, and I sort of blamed God for not appreciating me enough to make it all happen. It ended up taking a lot of prayer—and my daughter and son-in-law—to get me back on my feet again."

"I'm glad they were there for you," Glenn said. "We need you."

"Let me add, Glenn, that Ian got on his feet again just in time to not only get back into the fight but to earn his way into the then brand new PAC reeducation camps," Dell-X said. "Each one of us faces that same possibility, but it's a price worth paying."

As he spoke, Dell-X stood, and looking around at the others, he grinned as he added, "We have our WWW hand sign and Ian just mentioned his pivot foot idea, but let me add one other such notion. The best way to give others a hand is like this (he held up both hands clasping his own forearms). By taking hold of their forearm and offering our own, we accomplish two things: First, we offer a hand-up, and second, we offer them a chance to grasp our forearm both to accept our help *and to help themselves.* One of our main harm-others-and-our-country failures in the past was the way we enabled free riders to smother themselves in our charity-without-expectations programs, thus short-changing themselves as well as their own neighbors. Glenn, the best way to show respect to others is by expecting them to be part of the team trying to help them. *That's* true compassion. Using others to feed our feel-good needs or to build PAC power condemns those others to a dead-end life. From now on, WE, working together, must be the new way."

With those words, Dell-X held up his cup in a toast, and the others, now also standing, raised their own cups, "This is to the Whig Partisan Alliance and the wonderful dream of *E pluribus unum.* May that dream come true for everyone, everywhere."

Lee shouted out, "Hear, hear! People have rallied to crawl out of holes deeper than this in the past, and we will do no less now. Each generation has within itself the ability to become a new 'greatest generation,' and that's our goal." Smiling around, she then added, "In a good book, written long ago, a father told his son that there's a lot of ugliness in the world and that while he wished he could keep it away from him, he knew that he couldn't. We face such ugliness today—and the challenge that goes with it."

"Pascal called it the human condition," Ian added, looking over to Glenn. "The church offers faith and duty to God and others as our rallying cry, and I can't improve on that. So, Glenn, welcome to the fight ... or I should say, welcome to the construction crew. We're going to build that bridge over Pascal's river, and as Dell-X just said, we're going to do all we can to help the traffic on it flow freely and fairly both ways for all of our people, everywhere—equally." *That* is the Whig Partisan Alliance way.

"That is the only way!" Glenn proclaimed.

"Of course, he means the word, only, in a strictly non-hush-now, let's openly talk about it kind of way," Dell-X quickly stepped in to add in response to Glenn's comment, and they all laughed.

EPILOGUE

One Journey Ends, Another Begins

That evening Lee drove Glenn about a mile north to a place called the JDJ where she parked in the lot of an old police station, now the WPA security HQ. And she waited for him in her jeep while he visited the beautiful Celebration of Life Garden located there.

It was an emotional time for him, and as he walked along one of the two winding, cinder paths running on each side of the low memorial wall that led through the garden, he carefully scanned the list of names engraved there, looking for two in particular.

But the beauty of the place soon captured him. That long wall was complemented on all sides by well-kept flowers and shrubs and by what Lee had called "*Living Life Now*" figures. These colorful plastic sculptures of downsized teenagers and sections of their old cars evoked the 1950s to 60s drive-in era, and they, along with all the natural beauty of the place, combined to boost the spirits of those who came here to honor citizens of Grand Blanc and Whigville whose names had been added to that wall because of their service to the community, the schools, and their country, in the military or as civilians.

The *JDJ* got its initials from an old drive-in that once stood on that spot, and Glenn had been told that there were many versions of the actual name. Some said the initials stood for *Johnson's Drive-In Jubilation* and others suggested *Jalopies-Dates-Joy*. But the official name of this delightful place was *Journey-Dream-Jubilate!*

For most people, however, it was simply the *Jube* or the *JDJ*, but Glenn didn't really care what it was called. He was there for the first time in his life to honor his parents whose names were engraved on that wall, and once he found them, he sat for a long time, just looking at their names and thinking about them, about those wonderful people that he had never really known. What would they think, he wondered, about all these scaled down, splash-of-color figures of teenagers and their vintage cars? Which figure would they choose as a favorite? Would they agree?

He imagined that his father would like the one showing a guy wearing jeans and a white T-shirt and socks, holding a root beer in one hand as he stood, leaning back with his arm around a girl in a long skirt, sitting with crossed ankles on a car fender. Did girls actually wear long skirts and white socks like that back then? His mother might prefer the one of two girls, also holding root beers, who were whispering to each other while they looked across the way at a young man who was leaning back with one foot propped-up against the wall of the drive-in building, trying to look nonchalant. Of course, Glenn couldn't really know which they'd like, but he enjoyed thinking about it. And it felt good being where he was sure they would want him to be.

He sighed, gently shaking his head as he thought about the bitter irony of it all. Just as the Chinese people, now less afraid of their own government, were seemingly on the verge of asserting their right to control their own destiny, the sad-sack, eager-to-be-taken-care-of American people were bending their own knees to near-total government control, thus giving themselves up to a pathetic and perverse PAC-Ustatesian version of the now fading rule-by-elite style.

He wished he could talk to his mother and dad about things like that. If only we had endured longer or China had progressed faster, it could have been tucked into a new coalition of free peoples along with Korea, Japan, India, and others in the Pacific. With all of them to support us, our own collapse might only have been a mere short stumble, impacting on fewer people, and causing less damage around the world.

He wondered what his parents would have said about that turn, but then, as the sun slowly lowered itself behind the trees, he bent his head for a short prayer. Standing afterwards, he waved over to Lee that he was on the way and as he started back along the path, he recalled her words about the potential that every generation had to become the next "Greatest Generation." That term, once used for the World War II generation, must now be owned by every generation, he thought. Only then can we can build on what people like his own parents, the preacher, and so many others around the world have already started.

With that thought and a sense of being one with all of those listed around him and with so many others, everywhere, who have stood up for freedom, firing him up, he smiled, and remembering the Roman salute he had given at the beginning of his trip, he lifted his fist to his chest in the same salute again. It was now his generation's task to retrieve that long ago dropped *E pluribus unum* baton *and* to carry it on into the future as an act of loving responsibility.

And as he walked along back to the jeep, his heart swelled, and although no tears came, it was a very husky voice that proudly proclaimed, "We will win."

ABOUT THE AUTHOR

*A*s a grandfather, w l jennings shudders, feeling guilty, when he looks at the long history of Americans, all of us, allowing our politicians to shrug off their responsibility to actually pay for all their too easy, vote-for-me promises. And he hangs his head in shame as he looks toward the now bleaker future that all of our kids and grandkids face. They deserve better from us.

During his lifetime, he has watched as this country came so close to the dream of Frederick Douglas in the nineteenth century that we would someday see a time when "we utterly repudiate all invidious distinctions, whether they be in our favor or against us, and only ask for a fair field, and no favor."

We came close, that is until we fell away in the late '60s and turned instead to a type of easily manipulated group against group favor seeking, thus allowing power to begin drifting away from being increasingly open to all the people toward a new future controlled by an all Power At the Center political and social elite way high up in the sky above the rest of us. Take a look at Fritz Lang's fantastic 1920s movie, *Metropolis,* to get a sense of the direction we're headed unless we, as one people, step up and proclaim a new march toward ...*E pluribus unum.*

CPSIA information can be obtained
at www.ICGtesting.com
Printed in the USA
BVHW030502091218
535136BV00001B/38/P